A SINISTER LOVE

SPENCER HIXON

www.spencerhixon.com

ISBN: 978-1-959544-15-9

FÆROS PUBLISHING
Austin, TX

This edition distributed through Ingram

Cover art by Graziel Joanna Tallongon

Interior art by Graziel Joanna Tallongon and David Hixon

FÆROS PUBLISHING is an imprint of Wootton Major Publishing, LLC

www.woottonmajorpublishing.com

To Dad, whose love will never be forgotten.

To my wife,
For her support
And her blood, sweat, and tears.
And my kids,
Because of whom
This book took me years.

Chapter 1 – Rotworm

"Don't you dare do it, Jeremy!" Scribble muttered at the mass market romance she huddled over while hiding under her desk. She turned the page so fast it almost tore, then covered her mouth to soften her gasp. "No! I can't believe you actually did it! Kim is too good for you."

"Subordinate #8281."

Scribble completely missed the robotic-sounding voice coming from just above her head. She bit her lip and turned to the next page. "Oh no! Kim! Don't kiss him!" When a book had its fangs in her, not much else registered.

"Subordinate #8281!!" The electronic voice sounded urgent, irate.

"What? Who? Ow!" In her rush to respond, Scribble stood up too quickly and rammed the stubby horns on her head into the underside of her desk. They got stuck... that is until she heard the voice again.

"If you do not answer me, #8281, I will have you flayed!"

The threat worked. It took a few tugs, but Scribble managed to break free and step out from under her desk. Her gray, swirling eyes opened wide at the sight of a computer sitting on top of it. She examined it with wonder—the sleek design, the corners twisted into little points, the logo of a serpent twisting around a partially eaten apple. The faint sound emanating from it reminded her of the agonized screams she often heard from the mortal souls she dealt with on a regular basis, only worse. On the monitor, a window displayed the dark silhouette of a distant figure.

"B-B-B-Belphegor! Sir!" Scribble said, straightening herself. Her barbed tail curled around her body, but when she tried to grab it and saw the book still in her hand, she let out a squeak and tossed the book under the desk.

"#8281. You're fired."

The words felt like piano wire around her neck. Her face, normally a pleasant shade of red, grew pale.

"Have your office cleared out by—"

"F-fired!?" Her voice cracked as she spoke. "B-but why? I've always been a good worker!"

"*You're too far behind!* Fifty million souls find their way to Purgatory every year, and you're in charge of monitoring them. Yet I find you slacking off with a book. A *human* book."

Scribble's pointed ears swiveled back at being caught. She wrung her tail in both hands. "It's my first break in a year. Sir."

"And your last. You don't have any more human contraband, do you?"

In the corner of the small office stood a cabinet full of all manner of knick-knacks. It held comics, dice, a collection of lights, playing cards, and even a rusty sword, but the books brought her the most joy. Just thinking about one of her coworkers opening it and discovering her stash made Scribble tremble. "N-n-no, sir."

"Hmm. Besides, the old methods are just too slow. A whole year of backlog has built up. Typing everything out by hand just won't do it. That's why I've decided to upgrade. This computer will be doing your job now. I doubt you were even aware it was installed." On cue, the computer opened a new window. A list of names appeared, each with a date of death and an empty bar labeled "processing." The bar for the first name was filled in a matter of seconds, then the name beneath moved up to replace it and its bar started filling. Scribble had to admit it; the computer did her job much faster than she ever could.

"I-I can learn! This job is all I know! I've worked here for thousands—"

"—*You are incapable of learning, imp!*" The distant silhouette moved closer until Scribble could see Belphegor in exquisite and stomach-churning detail. Numerous scars, lesions, pustules, and pockmarks marred his pale flesh. His emaciated limbs had wires in them, strung to some vast, dark machine filling most of the scene's background. The wires even penetrated the skin of his face. Whenever he moved, instead of using his muscles, the appropriate wire pulled on him. The voice box in his chest did all the talking for him so he didn't have to. Scribble couldn't imagine a better paragon of slothfulness. "You are a coward, and you have no ambition. It disgusts me."

She cowered and lowered her ears subserviently. "Wh-what's going to happen to me?"

"I don't care."

The window closed, leaving the imp alone in her office with the machine that had replaced her. She felt tears welling in her eyes, but tried to contain herself and straightened her posture. *Deep breaths, Scribble. That's it. I'll just gather my things.* She adjusted her blouse and pencil skirt before heading to the cabinet. Several large demons wearing security outfits appeared at the door just as she reached out to open it. She certainly did not need the guards to see her collection and add to her troubles, so she stepped back.

"On second thought, I do have a job for you." Belphegor's silhouette appeared in a little window on the computer's screen once more.

Scribble felt a twinge of hope and turned to the monitor. "Y-yes, sir?"

"Since you love humans so much, report to Rotworm on Level 1. From now on, you will be tempting a human."

"I'm going to be a Sinister? But I've never even *seen* a living human!"

Belphegor drew closer to the screen again, lips pulled into a disturbing smile. "Then you better prove me wrong and learn fast. But I'm not doing this to be nice. I want you to provide me a soul for my experiments. You're already on thin ice, 8281. I've had to cover for several of your mistakes. I have it on good authority that one of the souls in Purgatory has been *gaining* weight, not losing it! Imagine if the Order catches wind of this!"

"B-b-but sir, I haven't seen any evidence—"

"This debacle puts me in a precarious situation, so I suggest you avoid messing up again, or I'll be using *your* soul to tinker on."

The image on the screen changed to a new scene. A lanky demon lay strapped to a metal table, all manner of mechanical devices sticking out of him. His torn wings hung from hooks, his limbs appeared broken, and he cried out in agony.

"I'm nearly done with this one. You have until the computer finishes processing your backlog."

Any hope Scribble harbored disappeared. A number showed up on the computer screen, "15 minutes." She gasped in horror, but a moment later, it changed. "22.4 hours." "3.7 hours." "90,027 hours." It eventually settled near 1000. Belphegor's window closed and the security demons escorted her outside. As they guided her along, she stole glances at the windows passing by. Far below, millions of human souls suffered rehabilitation to prepare them for Heaven, each occupying their own small cubicle. From her vantage point, the myriad cubicles melted into a hauntingly beautiful Fibonacci Sequence of pain and redemption.

*　　*　　*

The gates of Hell stood before Scribble like the open maw of some dark and twisted leviathan. It dwarfed every soul that passed through it, but Scribble, in particular, keenly felt the insignificance of her three and a half feet. A hot breath from within flowed over her soft red skin as each step brought her closer to its sharp, ruthless fangs. But only when the two luminous guards moved to block her way did the imp cower in fear.

"State your business," one of them said in a melodic voice—a voice that did not seem to match the rest of the angel. Each wore golden armor and held a weapon of divine nature—a blade made of a dancing tongue of steel flame, a hoarfrost-covered spear that chilled the air and created its own descending fog. Their helmets completely covered their faces, but four eyes that looked like some ancient artist had painted them into existence floated in orbit around them in eternal vigilance.

"I-I-I'm Scribble. I was sent here... by B-Belphegor, my boss." The ensuing quiet egged her on. "He told me to report to... Rotworm?"

"The Order has not received word of a reassignment. No one has been reassigned from Purgatory in thousands of years." One of the floating eyes paused and examined Scribble, from her professional office clothing to her diminutive wings. She felt exposed as it darted around her, but soon, it returned to its place and the two angels stepped aside. "I sense no threat. Proceed."

Scribble quickly slipped past them. Immediately, the ambiance changed from that of a vast cavern filled with the sounds of pain to a busy hub filled with chatter. Long hallways stretched out from the center. Demons filled the place, some in business suits and some wearing nothing at all. They huddled in groups, stood in queues, or rushed about haphazardly. Signs and overhead screens directed the traffic and displayed tidbits of news or other information. Vendors lined the walls, selling various Infernal Devices and diabolical contraptions like spiked clubs and travel pillows. A painting of a rather severe-looking angel pointing at the observer overlooked it all from a mural high above with the words, "Report contraband. St. Michael is watching," printed beneath.

"It's like an airport!" Scribble said to herself.

"A wot?" The voice came from an overweight demon behind an "information" desk.

"An airport! I read about them in books! Oh, I hope I get to see my collection again." Despite the despondency in her voice, she gazed in awe at all the comings and goings around her.

"Books, eh? Ain't those, y'know... illicit-like?" the overweight demon asked with immediate interest and a menacing grin.

Scribble turned pale and looked between him and the mural of St. Michael behind him. She backed away but tripped and fell on her rear. Before she could get back on her feet, she felt a sudden tug as if an invisible rope pulled her back towards Purgatory.

The larger demon laughed. "Yer soul ain't weigh nothin'!"

In the back of her mind, Scribble vaguely remembered what she'd learned about soul weight long ago. She flapped her wings and, immediately, the tug stopped. "Ah... I never had to do this back home."

"Hmph. Must be one of 'em Purgat'ry types. Hardly demons, if ya ask me."

"We are too!" she protested. When she got to her feet, she found that all it took was a single flap every now and again to keep that pulling force at bay.

"No self-respectin' demon would let 'imself be seen there, I tell ya. Yer gonna need a soul stone if ya wanna go past Level 1, wot with yer tiny wings."

"Level 1?"

"Green, eh? This is Level 1. Gets ya where ya wanna be. Them's the tunnels to the other levels that way—Ministry o' 'ternal Torment over there—and Outgoing on the other side." He pointed a sausagelike finger at signs for each.

"Outgoing?"

"Yeah, Mor'al Realm mostly."

"Is that where I'll find Sinisters?" Scribble asked.

"Could be, could be." As he spoke, Scribble brightened and started moving towards the sign that had a picture of a globe on it. "Now, why the rush? Tell me more about them, ah, books o' yers." He glanced over at a few other large demons that began to approach her slowly. She noticed them just in time to keep them from completely surrounding her.

"Ah!" she squeaked. "Th-th-that's okay! I d-d-don't know what you're talking about. I better be... going... now..." As Scribble walked away, one of the other demons stepped in her path to block her. She stopped short and tried moving in another direction but to the same effect. Suddenly, her ears flattened and she began trembling in fear as she looked towards a new, imaginary assailant. "Wh-what do you want?!" she cried out.

The bluff worked. The nearest demon looked behind him to see who, or what, had chilled her so. That gave her the opening she needed. Scribble dashed between her would-be assailant's legs and ran as fast as her own legs could carry her down one of the hallways. By the time she came to a stop, she couldn't see any of the others.

When she caught her breath, Scribble realized she was lost. All along the walls, she saw doorways with labels on them in languages she'd never seen and could not even begin to read. She wandered from sector to sector, the signs changing languages until she found some that she recognized. "London" displayed over one doorway, "Paris" above another.

Nearby, a tall, moderately handsome demon with a long, bent nose and red skin took notice of her meandering. His greasy black hair was slicked back, exposing two small horns. The perfectly tailored and pressed suit he wore gave him a chic, cut look. Behind him sprouted a pair of strong, black wings covered in lizard-like scales. With one hand, he held a black briefcase; with the other, he held up a sign with the word "Doodle" scrawled across it. As Scribble moved closer, he smiled the kind of smile that could sell curtains to the homeless.

"Doodle?" he asked before she could get too far away.

"What? N-no, I'm sorry, you have the wrong person," Scribble said as she tried to move on. He followed her, easily keeping pace and looking her over.

"Short, dumpy, shy, lost... you fit the description. You're Doodle, all right." With the level of conviction in his voice, she almost believed him.

"Dumpy?" Her voice got quieter as she suddenly became self-conscious. "I'm not..."

"Oh, it's nothing a makeover or two can't fix." He smiled at her again, his deep red eyes looking into hers uncomfortably. She half-wanted to buy whatever he was selling just to get rid of him.

"My name isn't Doodle, it's Scribble, and I'm looking for—"

"Rotworm? At your service." He took her hand in a firm, confident grip and shook. "Doodle, Scribble... whatever. It's a terrible name. You should change it." He talked fast, making it hard for her to get a word in edgewise.

"You're Rotworm? Oh... I was told—"

"Yes, yes," he interrupted again. "Bel told me all about you. Come with me and we'll get you set up." Without pause, he began walking towards one of the portals. Scribble followed close behind him. "So, you don't have any experience with humans?" he asked as they walked.

"N-not really, sir." She thought better than to mention her books this time.

Rotworm "tsked" and shook his head at no one in particular. To Scribble, it felt like she had already failed at her new job. He turned a corner sharply and spoke without so much as a glance back at her. "The primary job of a Sinister, your job, is to *persuade* the human, your client, to add a little more weight to its soul."

"But don't their souls always get lighter?" Scribble asked as if making a meaningful contribution to the conversation. "They always end up in Heaven sooner or later."

"That's only in Purgatory, and that won't be the case for much longer if... here we are." Before Rotworm could explain himself, he stopped at a doorway that led to a long, curved tunnel. It had buzzing, fluorescent lights along either side and a beige and blue carpet with a simple block pattern that repeated frequently. Rotworm stepped behind the small, vacant desk next to the portal and put his briefcase on top of it. With a pair of mechanical clicks, the case swung open, obscuring him entirely from her view. "Before we visit Earth, there are some rules that you must know. Don't get me wrong, I couldn't care less if you break them. I am *required* to give them to you."

A hand shot out from behind the briefcase, holding a piece of paper for Scribble to take. On it, she saw a list of official regulations printed in gold ink that seemed to shift upon the page just beyond the word her eyes focused on. Even as she read it, Rotworm started speaking them aloud to her. "Rule number 1: Don't attack another Immortal. Angel or demon, it doesn't matter. The Order will find you. Rule number 2: You cannot kill a human or save a human's life. The Order will find you. Rule number 3: Do not reveal yourself to the humans. The Order will find you."

"But what if it happens by accident?" Scribble asked in a soft voice.

Rotworm lowered the lid of the briefcase far enough to peer down his nose at her. "Rule number 4: No accidents. Look, most of them won't believe it even if you *do* reveal yourself. Just... don't say or do anything stupid, like showing the way back here or possessing one of them. And take breaks... we shouldn't spend too much time there. It's not healthy." He waved his hand dismissively. "You can read the others. These are all just formal rules—you won't even be dealing with most of them."

Scribble already felt overwhelmed as she scanned through the rules once more. Her grey eyes suddenly turned to Rotworm when he shoved an accordion-like folder into her hands. It contained nearly half a foot of papers inside of it. *How did that fit in his briefcase?* she wondered.

"One more thing before I throw you to the wolves," Rotworm said as his smile twisted. The slight bend in his long nose made it appear more diabolical, lending him the look of someone about to enjoy watching two men fight to the death. "This is your client's dossier."

"What about a... a training period?" Scribble asked.

"That *was* your training period."

"Y-you mean..."

"Sink or swim, baby. I'm *required* to go with you on your first run, but don't expect me to do any of the hard work. Your client's name is Peter or Patrick or something like that." He nodded towards the dossier. "This is where you'll be keeping track of every decision it makes. I recommend you memorize everything; that'll help you tempt it better."

On the front, in stamped lettering, was the name 'Paul Taylor'. Scribble glanced inside. She found photographs, handwritten notes, typed pages, and endless post-its scattered throughout. The hodgepodge was a monument to inefficiency and disorganization. "Th-there's so much! What happened to his old Sinister?" she asked.

"Grimtooth? Oh, he didn't do a very good job. He was fired... into a pit. Of actual fire. Don't worry about him, worry about yourself. Because if you disappoint me, I'll have to hand you over to Bel in pieces, and he doesn't like it when bitsss go misssssssing," Rotworm said. Along with the new sibilance, a forked tongue slithered from his lips and his horns grew a little longer. He turned his briefcase so she could see inside it as he slowly lowered the lid. On top of some papers sat a collection of demon horns, each one unique. His eyes followed Scribble with a bestial quality, like a predator playing with its food. "Shall we get ssstarted?"

CHAPTER 2 – SINISTER

As Scribble stepped into the tunnel, the carpet and lighting moved unnaturally past her. It seemed that, with each step she took, she moved five steps deeper into the tunnel. She glanced behind her and could only just perceive the entranceway as it quickly disappeared into the resolution of reality.

"Don't fall behind," Rotworm said. He walked ahead of her towards a small source of light in the distance. In order to keep up with his long stride, Scribble broke into a run. The light source grew closer, larger, soon appearing as a door. Scribble became aware of a sound, rather like white noise, coming from the other side. She could see the words "Sir Burrah's Security" printed in reverse on the door's frosted glass.

"What's that sound?" she asked.

Rotworm rolled his eyes. "It's just rain. See?" He opened the door and walked through into a gray, nondescript alley. To Scribble, it was like discovering that unicorns were real. She stared wide-eyed at everything around her, from the simple dumpster covered in rust to the broken street lamp at the corner.

"Won't the files get wet?" she asked.

"Of course not." Rotworm stepped out into the downpour, arms spread, and turned in a circle. "See? Does it look like I'm getting wet? No. So, come on, I'm a busy ifrit."

Scribble winced as she stepped out into the rain, but it simply passed through her. "Oh." The pair started off towards the main road when Scribble noticed movement near the dumpster. A bum lay there under something that might have been a piece of cardboard in another life.

"Rotworm! There's a person there! He'll see us!" she said in hushed tones.

"That's not a person. It's a client. And no, it can't see us. Remember Rule 3? It'd be pretty obvious we're not from around here if they saw this," he said and pulled roughly on her tail, making her fall on her rear. "They don't see you or me, or even the door unless their attention is called to it."

Scribble stood up and rubbed her rear with her free hand. "Then why the strange name on it? Sir Burrah's?"

Rotworm grinned and put his hands in his pockets, rocking back onto his heels. "Cerberus. Like it? My idea. Helps us Immortals to know which ones are ours and which are... *theirs*. Of course, it guards itself. We haven't used any three-headed hellhounds in centuries." His moment of pride was cut short when they heard a buzz from his pants pocket. He pulled out a smartphone and glanced at it. "Crud, we're late. It's almost time!" Before he'd finished speaking, he had already left the alley.

"Time? For what?" Scribble asked and ran to catch up to him. The instant she stepped out of the alley, the daily hustle of city life surrounded her. Cars zipped past. People crowded the sidewalk under their umbrellas. The lights and sounds of the city overwhelmed her. The imp just stood there, trying to take it all in. "No screaming... it's nice."

"Come *on*, Dribble!" Rotworm pulled on her shoulder and dragged her down the sidewalk. She quickly realized two things—she could pass through people as easily as through the rain, and humans made up only about a third of the people she saw. Demons dressed in business attire and angels in white robes accompanied each human. Those humans that didn't have an Immortal walking alongside had them on their shoulders, only three or four inches tall.

A few blocks had passed by when Rotworm stopped suddenly in front of a small shop that stood at the end of a row of small shops. "Here we are," he said as he glanced down at his smartphone again. The shop's window proudly displayed *Othello's Books* in red and gold lettering. But the other storefronts, all part of an old, brick, two-story building, had no names on them, no wares in their windows. Neither did any of the stores in the neighboring building.

Scribble got the distinct impression that the little bookstore was out of place, just like her. But she didn't have long to take in the scene before Rotworm walked right through the wall, hammering home just how out of place she was. She held her breath, closed her eyes, and walked forward. When she opened them, she was inside the store. The muffled sound of the rain almost felt soothing. The faint scent of books captured her attention. Rows of shelves, all stocked with books, lay before her like the cubicle-filled halls of Purgatory. Books that didn't have a place on a shelf sat in piles on the floor. Magazines, eReaders, CDs, travel guides, comic books, maps, and even a few newspapers also called the store home. Next to the counter, she saw a bin with a sign above it, "We Buy Used Books," but unlike the rest of the store, that bin had no books in it.

Everything about the place fascinated Scribble. Books had been her window into the human world, but despite being on Earth, she still wanted to read them all. "I've never seen so many books..." she whispered in reverential awe. Before she had a chance to look at any of them, Rotworm pulled her deeper into the store and past several displays.

One display had a few games on it. When he passed it, a wicked smile crept over his face and he reached up to swipe one of the decks of playing cards. As he stuffed it in his pocket, he put his finger up to his lip with a "Shhh." Scribble suddenly realized how all those books in her collection had made it there. She decided to try it herself, but every time she reached to pick up an item, her hand passed through it instead.

"Takes practice," he whispered. He then waved her over to follow him and stepped past the counter into the room beyond. Scribble again closed her eyes before following him through the wall.

"There's a problem with the cash register, Ginger," said a deep male voice. Scribble gasped as a young man passed inches in front of her face without warning. She jumped back and tried to flee, but Rotworm grabbed onto her tail to keep her from bolting out of the room. When she looked back at the man, she noticed that he had dark skin—nearly black—and no hair on his head. A pair of glasses rested on his nose, giving him an intelligent, authoritarian look. Even the way he dressed stood out from others—a button-up shirt and pair of slacks instead of a t-shirt and jeans. He walked up to a paper-covered desk placed along the wall.

Next to him stood a girl who didn't look anything like what Scribble had seen yet. Her dark-brown, chin-length hair had long pink locks that fell on either side of her face like a frame. She wore a short top with corset-like lacing in the front, which exposed both her midriff and plenty of cleavage, as well as a short plaid skirt and knee-length leggings, all black with pink accents. The fishnet that covered her did nothing to obscure the artful tattoo of a thorny vine wrapped around her leg in a spiral. Dark eye shadow that had been skillfully applied finished the look. She held a clipboard in her lap, which she used to mark down inventory.

"What is it?" she replied without looking up.

"It's missing cash. About $200."

This got Ginger to look up at him. "Surely you don't think I took it, Paul."

Paul took off his glasses and pinched the bridge of his nose. "It was on your shift, and it's the second time it's happened."

"Are you accusing me of stealing?"

"That's our man," Rotworm whispered to Scribble as the argument continued. "It's time to get to work." He took Scribble's hand and placed it on Paul's shoulder. All at once, the world changed. Everything grew. In less than a second, the two of them stood atop Paul's left shoulder, just a few inches tall. The scene before them had slowed to a crawl. "Sinisters usually tempt like this, it's just easier."

"Easier?" Scribble parroted.

"No need to run to catch up for starters. Now, shush!"

Scribble watched with a bit of jealousy as Rotworm unfurled his large wings and floated a few inches away, looking past Paul's head to his right shoulder. She beat her own wings but only managed to make a pleasant breeze down her backside. Without being able to see what Rotworm looked for, she decided to take in her surroundings. The single, large room had a makeshift office in front, separated from the rest by tall filing cabinets. She noticed the desk held a computer not unlike the one that had replaced her, as well as a phone that had so many buttons that it required a manual to figure out how to use it. Beyond the filing cabinets, racks and shelving units full of random supplies reached near to the ceiling. Old signs, cleaning equipment, reams of paper, rolls of receipts, and even more books took up most of the space. But the back of the room only had a table, chair, and microwave. A piece of paper taped to the wall behind the microwave said, "Employee Lounge." A water heater filled up most of the furthest corner.

With time paused, it felt like they had been waiting for *something* to happen for an eternity. "What if I'm not here?" she asked. "Do I have to stay with him all the time?"

Rotworm scowled. "Eventually, you'll have a phone like mine. But... you're too new. Stick to the client like glue; maybe you'll learn something."

"But didn't you tell me I shouldn't stay on Earth too long?" Scribble looked a bit concerned as she tried her diminutive wings out again but could only get a hair's breadth off Paul's shoulder.

Rotworm rolled his eyes at her. "Not exactly *Night On Bald Mountain,* are you? Just take breaks once in a while," Rotworm retorted, his gaze returning to Paul's right shoulder. "It has to sleep, you know. You just gotta be there for the big decisions. If you're not stupid, you'll pick it up. Now, let's find out who this guy's Dexter is."

"His what?" Scribble asked, managing to float just behind Paul's head to see what Rotworm had been looking for so intently. The sound of chimes blowing in the wind rang out. Rotworm groaned when a robed figure appeared, aloft on golden wings just off to Paul's right.

"Boniface," Rotworm growled between clenched teeth.

As Scribble slowly fluttered a little higher, the figure became clearer. A warm, serene smile looked like it was an essential part of his face. Over his head shone a stereotypical golden halo. A gold, corded belt cinched his pure white robes around his waist. All around him, Scribble could sense a holiness that both attracted and repelled her.

"A Dexter, dear Sister, is God's advocate." He had a pleasant tenor that made him seem impossible to hate. Rotworm, however, had apparently found a way and looked like he could just manage to hold his seething rage at bay.

"Shut up, do-gooder!" Rotworm said curtly. "We don't need *your* help."

"But I live to serve, Brother," the angel replied amicably. "I am Boniface. I'm here to make sure Paul Taylor remains on the Right and True path to Grace." Scribble could *hear* him capitalizing the words. "Brother Rotworm and I have worked together many times in the past," he said, chuckling as one would when sitting down for tea to tell old jokes with old friends.

Scribble looked up at Rotworm, whose forked tongue danced menacingly in Boniface's direction. Scales appeared on his face. His eyebrows became mere ridges. His nose receded into serpentine nostrils. "And you always cheat!" he spat. "You know you couldn't win any sssouls if your God didn't pull cheap tricksss."

Boniface just smiled jovially at Rotworm—the armor of his demeanor not showing even the slightest chink or sign of wear. "Well then, Sister, shall we begin?" he asked, turning towards Scribble. She nodded.

"Oh, we'll show him, Ssscrabble," Rotworm said to her in his best attempt to be supportive. As he spoke, his face began returning to normal.

"I-it's Scribble..."

"Remember, your goal is to get it to sin. Because it's your first time, you should start off small. Work towards the bigger sins later."

Before she had a chance to come up with a strategy of temptation, a voice echoed in her mind—Paul's voice.

I've worked so hard for this store! How dare she do this... and twice! What am I supposed to do? Why do I even bother?

"Because it is the right thing to do. You know Ginger needs this job for college. She's always been a good friend," Boniface said. "Remember the parable of the debtors. You have been blessed with this store. You should forgive her debt."

Rotworm nudged Scribble in the side. "Use the dossier!" he whispered hoarsely. Scribble nodded and opened the folder, then began to flip through the pages, a few of them falling out.

"Um... but... what kind of friend would steal from you?" she asked. She struggled to find the information about the store's past that Boniface referred to, let alone anything of value in Paul's history.

We're barely staying afloat as it is. If this keeps up, we'll be in the red again. The store will be a failure. I'm a failure.

As he spoke, the air around Scribble grew colder. She looked up at Rotworm, who held an intense, focused expression. When she glanced at Boniface, the smile that seemed impenetrable now showed concern. "What's going on?" she whispered.

"The client seems to be a little... depressed," Rotworm said.

"Why is that a problem?"

"Oh, it's not a problem. Only, if it gets worse, you won't really be able to make it sin. Or do good. It'll affect all its actions and decisions." He gave a toothy grin to Scribble. "I don't envy you on this one."

Boniface spoke up. "You are not a failure, my child. Remember Bishop Myriel, and how he was an inspiration and role model to Jean Valjean. You can be the same." The air warmed slightly.

A light gleamed in Scribble's eyes. "Jean Val—that's Les Misérables! I've read that book! Let's see, uh... but when Javert arrested Valjean and his business closed, remember how it hurt all the workers? If the store closes, you'll both be unemployed. Oh, but he did use his money to help Cosette, didn't he?" Scribble felt quite a bit warmer as she kept talking. "I always wondered why he buried it so close to the—"

Rotworm smacked Scribble in the head. "Stop babbling and use the capital sins!" he said urgently.

Scribble pouted and rubbed the back of her head. It had been a while since she'd really thought about sins. Cradling the folder in one arm, she began to count out fingers and mouth the sins. *Greed, Lust, Envy, Gluttony, Sloth, Pride, Anger...* She didn't know how any of them would help.

Before she could figure out what to say, Boniface chimed in. "You *are* providing work for them, but isn't it more important to be their friend? Do not worry about the business—the Lord will provide. Make your rewards in Heaven." Rotworm hissed at the angel and his eloquence.

A thought occurred to Scribble. *How was he blessed with the business?* She resumed flipping through pages of dossier. "Um... oh, here's the store. Uh... it was left to him in his mother's will. Ah!" She turned to Paul's ear and spoke in a louder voice, trying to counter Boniface's confidence with her own, though not very well. "B-but at what price did you get the store? Can you just let it fail?"

Mom... what would you have done? How can I make you proud?

"What about your dad? Can he help?" Scribble asked as she flipped through the dossier to find more information, several more pages falling out. Without warning, the air turned searing hot. Rotworm smirked, staring at Boniface as rage bubbled to the surface of Paul's thoughts. The paused scene before them started to move again.

Paul clenched his fists and slammed them against the desk, making Ginger recoil. But just as suddenly as that anger had filled him, it faded. The air that had been an inferno froze in an instant. Paul opened his hands and leaned against the desk, his head slumping. "Just... go home, Ginger."

Ginger nodded and gathered her belongings, but instead of looking scared of Paul, she shared Boniface's expression of concern and worry. "Paul, I'm sorry. I promise I didn't..." she said, and heaved a sigh. "Have a good night," she said softly and left.

"What was that?" Scribble asked once Boniface had disappeared in another gentle chorus of chimes. With a flash, she and Rotworm grew to normal size, standing where they had been before the whole thing began.

"Depression. Sometimes it's like a mental disease. Most depressed humans aren't completely in control of their actions, and that just makes it harder to get them to actually sin." Rotworm glared at the spot where Boniface had been a moment before.

"What do you mean 'depressed'? And why did it get so hot?"

A long, annoyed sigh left Rotworm. He rolled his eyes and tilted his head towards the imp. "For Beelzebub's sake, what am I? Exposition? Look, I will NOT see that do-gooder, Boniface, win again! He's taken too many souls from me in the past." He straightened himself and drew closer to her, his expression one of determination... and hatred. Scribble whimpered and closed her eyes. Her body shook in spite of itself. She'd failed in front of her new boss and wished she could just curl up into a ball back in her office in Purgatory. Suddenly, Rotworm ripped the folder from her grasp and pushed something sleek, lightweight, hard, and cool into her hands.

"What's this?" she asked, opening her eyes. She held up a tablet computer with a large, clean, black screen that took up the entire front surface. The screen flashed red, then showed a stylized image of a serpent-wrapped apple. On the back, she found a small camera, no larger than the width of a pencil lead, and the word "iBad" printed next to the same logo as on the screen.

"It's a tool. Only senior Sinisters like myself get them. But you need it more than I do, don't you? Because you're going to use it to wipe that smug grin off that stupid angel's face."

"I am?"

"Yes. Just point the camera at the human you want to tempt, and it will do the rest. Dossier, recent sins, temptation strategies... you can even use it to research things like 'depression' and stay out of my hair."

Scribble watched as the screen displayed a simple desktop interface. She touched the icon in the shape of a camera, then pointed it at Paul's head. It clicked. A page appeared on the screen showing several useful tabs along the top like "Childhood" and "Fears." She selected the one labeled, "Basic Info." A photo of the cover sheet from Paul's paper dossier appeared.

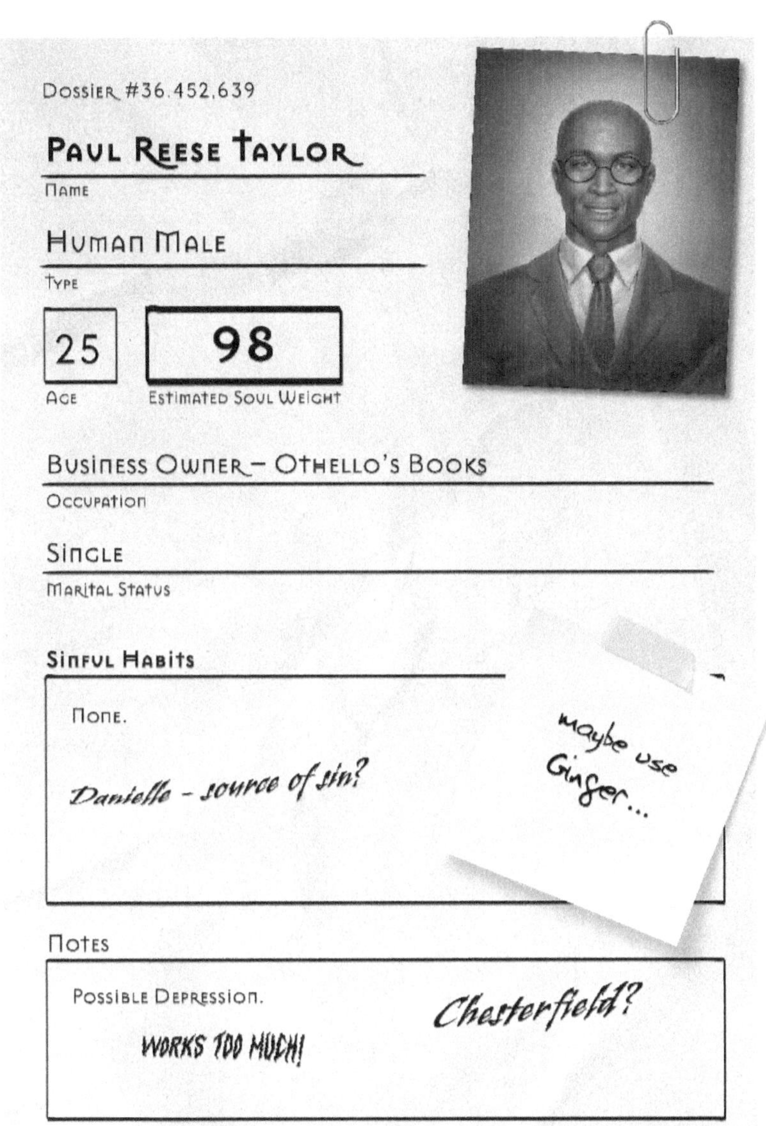

Rotworm peered over her shoulder for a moment, then drew in a quick breath between his sharp teeth. "Ninety-Eight? If this was a normal client, I'd say you're good, but even the three points you need to bring his soul to Hellweight will be hard to get on this guy before his depression gets the better of him." Rotworm rubbed at his sharp chin and grumbled. "I guess I should check up on you to make sure that no-good do-gooder goes down."

"You're leaving?"

"You didn't think I'd stick around, did you? You'll do fine, kid," he replied with a nod. "Or else." With that, Rotworm picked up his briefcase and winked at her before walking through the wall and out of the room.

CHAPTER 3 – SECRETS

Rotworm muttered to himself as he walked swiftly through the terminals on Level 1. Passersby gave him looks of recognition, but when they heard his growls, they would recoil and shuffle aside. A line leading to a particularly busy terminal split because the demons that saw him jostled each other to give him a wider berth. Within moments, fights broke out among them. Those that managed to escape cast relieved glances at his back. But when he turned down a corridor marked "Level 2," he bumped into an armored figure that didn't so much as flinch.

"Hey! What's—" Rotworm fell silent when he realized he had run into a four-armed angel who stood guard at the entrance. Painted eyes floated around her head. In one hand, she held an ebon spear as long as she was tall, and in another, a shield of the same material. It had the symbol of the Order— an eye like those that circled her—emblazoned across it. Only her mouth remained visible; a smooth helmet obscured the rest.

"What is your purpose, demon?"

"What's anyone's purpose? To live, laugh, loathe." The angel stepped closer. "I'm just trying to see my boss," Rotworm said. One of the angel's painted eyes looked over him for several seconds, then resumed its position.

"You have just come from Earth. I sense contraband." She grabbed Rotworm with her two free arms and pushed him face-first into the wall behind her. The shield pressed on his back while she frisked him, hands quickly going into pockets.

"Hey now, Angelface. How about a date first?" Rotworm protested, getting a disgusted groan in response. She turned him around and pulled out a deck of playing cards from his pocket.

"What is this?"

"It's nothing, just a little pastime, doll."

"Section 42, paragraph 7 of the Eternal Accord strictly forbids any Immortal from taking anything from Earth. Where's the rest of it? Or am I going to have to get rough?"

Rotworm swallowed hard but gave her a coy smile. "Hey, if that's how you like it, I'm willing to try." She pushed him back against the wall and sneered. "Okay, okay! I was going to return it, I swear! I just thought some of you hard-working angels might like a—what's that! A distraction!" He pointed behind her with a face of mock horror.

"I *do* have eyes in the back of my head," she reminded him flatly. Rotworm sighed and pulled out a stick of chewing gum and some batteries. She quickly took them and looked him over. "Go, before I change my mind and have you arrested." When she returned to her post, Rotworm straightened his suit and glared at her as he passed by into Level 2.

"Not my type anyway," he muttered just loud enough for her to hear.

The terminal-like corridors gave way to brick and stone, like the dark streets of some corrupt city. Far fewer demons could be seen on Level 2, offering a bit of privacy. These factors made it the perfect place to hash out a dirty deal or two. Rotworm passed through the section quickly, tuning out the screams of torment as he headed straight for the next level. But there, again, he found an angel standing guard. "Not another one..." Before he got too close, he quickly ducked into a dark alley and pulled out a smartphone from his suit, which appeared more solid than he was—more physical. The screen lit up. He punched in a few numbers and held it up to his ear.

"What?!" came an electronic voice from the device.

"Belphegor, sir, there's a problem."

"Oh, it's you, worm. What do you want?"

"There are angels everywhere, my Lord. I've already been searched once."

"That's not my concern. They're always suspicious. They probably just detected that glitch in the Purgatory system." The voice on the other end seemed preoccupied.

"I don't think that the prototype is safe. What would you like me to do with it?" He heard a disturbed grunt on the other end. A demon clad in sackcloth and dragging a club behind himself passed by the alley. Rotworm gave a guilty smile and turned to hide the phone from view.

"Stash it. Secrete it away as if your welfare depends on it because I assure you, worm, it does."

Rotworm bowed reflexively. "Yes, your Greatness."

"If they discover what's in that phone you're using, they might trace it back to me. And if that happens, I'll make you suffer ten-fold what I do."

"I assure you they'll never find it."

"And worm, if you try to disappear on me like your idiot sister, Firemange, *you* will be the next one on the receiving end of that thing."

Rotworm sneered wordlessly at the phone, but he failed to intimidate it. "Understood. Sir."

Belphegor's sigh sounded like static. "Any word on the human test subject?"

"Last I heard, she was still gaining soul weight, but we lost track of her somewhere in Purgatory."

"*Still* in Purgatory? Bah! It's that damnable human soul. It resists the added weight. If she hadn't died, this whole thing would have been much simpler. No one would have questioned a living human gaining soul weight! Why did I ever let you be the one to try it out on a human?"

"It was—" Rotworm began, then realized he'd been hung up on. "Bastard."

Scribble felt overwhelmed. For a full week, she either watched on Paul's shoulder or hovered nearby, yet she still hadn't learned much about him. The only social interaction he got was small talk, he didn't go anywhere other than work and home, and he spent what free time he did have in front of his computer, typing away. She tried reading about him in the iBad, but soon realized that everything in its databanks was just a digital copy of whatever disorganized notes Paul's previous Sinister had recorded in his paper dossier. Reading through them would be a waste of time. She had had to act as his Sinister and try to tempt him several times, but they all ended in disaster. The first time, Boniface "graciously" declined to say anything. Not only did she not succeed, but she ended up convincing Paul to donate to the local soup kitchen. The second time, he helped show a homeless kid where to find that soup kitchen. She did not see his depression return, but the choices he made had still moved his soul weight in the wrong direction. In addition, she still hadn't learned much about Earth, and kept discovering amazing new things—things that distracted or confused her at the worst times. When she saw the sun for the first time, Scribble thought the Order had come to arrest her for some crime she didn't even know she'd committed. And, as if all that wasn't enough, the threat of Rotworm's impending visit kept her on constant alert.

On the evening of the seventh day, Scribble took advantage of a lull in activity to begin organizing all the notes in her iBad.

"Frank, you can lock up alone tonight, right?" Paul asked a middle-aged man with a well-trimmed beard. Scribble had seen him working at the store before. "There's a play tonight my friends are in that I'd like to see."

"I'd love to," the man replied. "But I thought I told you that I was hoping to duck out a bit early tonight. Addison and I are going out for dinner. We already have a babysitter. In fact, Addison said she'll be here any minute," he said, looking out of the store window.

Scribble looked up from her tablet to see Frank and Paul looking out the window at a fancy German sports car that idled in front of the store. An attractive woman with bright red hair waved from the driver's seat. A small smile graced Scribble's features as she stood on Paul's shoulder and leaned into his ear.

"Isn't he lucky?" she whispered. "Beautiful, successful wife, well-behaved kid, a social life…"

The scene before her suddenly slowed down. She didn't realize that she could force him into a decision like that, but it felt good that she could.

Yeah, he is lucky. Everything I've ever wanted, while I can't even afford college or finish one screenplay.

"Screenplay?" Scribble thought aloud. She'd had no idea he was writing a screenplay. All the time he spent on his computer, she'd spent on her tablet.

Chimes announced the arrival of Boniface. He looked over the situation for just a moment, still smiling as warmly as ever. "You should be happy for him. But remember that you're lucky too. You have a great store, good friends, and the blessing of God."

"Sure, but Frank has a Porsche!" Scribble said, smirking a little. "You work hard, don't you deserve nice things like that?"

It would *be nice if things went my way for once. I work so hard and for so little. I could definitely use more money.*

"So far, so good," Scribble said to herself. The air around them had not turned cold yet.

"Money is not everything, my child. Remember the parable of the woman who gave her last copper coins and earned her reward in Heaven." Boniface never lost a beat.

Scribble scanned through pages on the tablet. "But you can't eat your rewards in Heaven. W-what about his wife? It's not fair that he gets a great girl like that while the only girl you've ever loved—" She couldn't find any information about what happened between him and his former girlfriend, Danielle. The files just stopped. "—is gone?" she ventured.

No, it's not fair. I'll never have someone. I don't have time for someone. I don't deserve someone.

The air chilled quickly and kept chilling until Scribble could see her breath. The smile faded from Boniface's visage into something serious. "Perhaps it's not fair. But what happened to Danielle was a tragedy. An accident. You can't be blamed for that. Think back on all the—"

It's my fault she ran off!

Scribble gasped and scanned faster. *Boniface knows what happened! Why is it missing from the files?* she thought. *I've got to stop this cold.* "Um, why don't you deserve someone? You're handsome, nice, a hard worker, a good person. Better than Mr. Darcy! I bet you could have anyone you wanted. Maybe it's time you started looking." A sudden warmth flowed from him and dispelled some of the cold air.

Boniface's eyebrow lifted curiously. "Clever." He opened his mouth to speak when Scribble cut him off excitedly.

"You work so hard, you deserve a break, and it sounds like they can just go out later. You even have a ticket. And maybe you'll meet someone there. You can even show her off later like Frank does."

"You should be thankful that a friend of yours has been so blessed and that you are able to provide even more happiness for him," Boniface said. "If you must, perhaps you can ask someone to take over tomorrow night."

The scene sped up, but the slight chill in the air didn't go away and she could still sense his thoughts.

"I'm sorry, Frank, but you'll need to call your babysitter. I won't get another chance to see this," Paul said. He grabbed his coat as he talked, and before Frank could get a word in edgewise, Paul walked out of the building with Scribble and Boniface still on his shoulders.

Scribble heard a small beep from the iBad. She watched as it showed Paul's soul weight tick up from 98 to 100. An alert appeared on the screen.

"New Sin: Envy."

"I... I did it!" she said brightly. But then Scribble felt something, not so much a presence as a lack of one. When she looked down, she saw a dark hole forming in Paul's chest like a pit of nothingness. Boniface saw it, too, and muttered a soft, "Oh dear."

Paul slumped against a wall out of view of the store, his cheeks wet. The air grew cold around Scribble. "What's that?" she asked.

"Despair. His depression is getting worse, and now it appears to be fueled by guilt."

"But at least I'm almost there. Just one more point!"

"There is much time yet for things to change. However, you *are* improving, Sister."

"How much time?" she asked with growing concern.

"No one knows when death will come. Decades likely."

"Decades?! But I don't have decades! If I don't make sure he's going to Hell in the next few weeks, I'll be thrown into a pit of fire or lose my horns for sure! Or worse!" She reached up and felt one of her horns ruefully.

"Those are quite severe punishments for someone who has only been on the job for a week," Boniface said.

"You have no idea," Scribble replied.

Paul pushed from the wall and began to walk again, but he did not head towards the theater. Instead, he went home to his apartment. For the first time, Scribble felt a pang of regret for something she had done.

"If I might make a suggestion, Sister," Boniface replied. "Before you were assigned as this young man's Sinister, I recall working with one named Grimtooth. Perhaps if you were to find him and ask for some assistance..."

Scribble looked over her opponent's face with suspicion. "Why would you help me?" she asked softly.

"I enjoy helping people—even if you *are* a demon. At the very least, you deserve to have an even playing field." He didn't show the slightest trace of mischief or misdirection in his disposition. "For a while now, there has been no joy in Paul. His depression has been steadily increasing. But you were able to lessen it, at least for a time. Perhaps if you are informed, we may be able to inspire him... bring him out of this situation before it gets worse." Scribble could not help but feel he kept something to himself and she didn't understand how Paul having joy would help her, but she had to admit that it sounded like a good suggestion.

"Maybe I will go and see him. But not for long!" Scribble kept her eyes fixed on the angel as she floated off Paul's shoulder and returned to normal size. *It's not like he'll make things any worse if I'm gone than if I'm here*, she thought and ran through the streets towards the alleyway she'd come through a week before.

*   *   *

Walls of flame surrounded Scribble as she gripped a small piece of paper with a handwritten note on it. She had no problem getting back into Hell, but finding Grimtooth proved to be more of a challenge. She had to wait for hours in long lines at the Ministry, surrounded by demons two or three times her size. The Ministry stored all the records of Hell, keeping tabs on the whereabouts, punishments, and jobs of every soul in Hell, including the demons. Asking for Grimtooth's information made her feel out of place, as if everyone there already knew about him, and she should too. Even the short, twisted-nosed demon that had helped her looked down at her, despite of the fact that she physically looked down at him. Now, she had to search the fifth level of Hell, following his vague and barely legible directions. After spending eons in Purgatory, her wings had to work hard to keep her at such a low level.

Fiery walls gave way to stone, then iron that looked as though it had been hewn using some massive, blunt axe. It narrowed into a tunnel before leading to a large, circular chamber lit by blue, dimly fluorescing globes. All around the floor wound wires and strips of metal, each one leading directly to the center. There, on a dais, Scribble saw a broken, demonic form hunched over. All the countless wires bound his arms, legs, and wings, penetrating the demon's thick, black hide. Scribble recalled Rotworm talking about a pit of fire. This did not look like a pit of fire.

23

"A-are you Grimtooth?" Scribble asked as she slowly stepped forward, driven by her own desire to not find herself in a similar situation.

The figure did not stir, but she could just make out a deep, calm, guttural voice coming from it.

"I-I'm sorry, I didn't h-hear you…" Scribble said, drawing even closer.

"JUST GET OUT!" the figure roared and looked up at her. The lights in the room flared, giving her a perfect view. He had large, square teeth, just like his jaw. Every inch of his body, even his bleeding eyes, had wires in it—wires which ran from him to the walls in taut lines. With every movement, they strained against his demonic flesh.

Fear gripped Scribble's mind as the demon watched her. She turned to run, but her foot caught on one of the wires and she tripped, tumbling to the floor. Grimtooth moaned briefly, but then began to chuckle at her misfortune.

Scribble closed her eyes for a moment and tried to calm herself down with deep breaths. She stood up and turned a sharp eye towards Grimtooth as if false confidence could make him forget about her blunder.

"I won't leave. Not until you help me," she said with only a hint of fear in her voice.

The demon turned his gaze back to the floor. "And why would I help you? What will you give me in return?"

Scribble hadn't considered that. She didn't have the power to get him released, and she certainly didn't have anything that Grimtooth might find useful. But at least he was talking to her. "Revenge." She said the first thing that popped into her head.

"Revenge? Revenge against who?" he asked. The lights in the room flickered a yellow hue with each movement he made.

"Revenge against the human, Paul Taylor. Isn't he the reason you're in here? I've been his Sinister for a week and I already hate him."

Grimtooth looked up at her with a smirk and pulled forward a little, the wires behind him tugging back. "So, you're my replacement? It's not the human I want revenge against," he growled. The lights shifted to a deep red and he jerked against his restraints.

Scribble jumped back and put a hand to her chest. Although he looked like he could tear her apart, he couldn't move more than a few inches in any direction. She imagined herself in the same situation and gripped one of the wires unconsciously.

The wires wound into cords as they got closer to Grimtooth. Each one piercing his flesh connected from several places in the wall or floor. When the lights flared, the flesh around the wires faded from black to gray for a moment. "You're providing power, aren't you?" she asked as curiosity got the better of her. "It's like a giant soul stone. I never knew they used this on demons."

The lighting became purple. Grimtooth looked away from her. "You bore me. Go away or I will eat you," he said, though his tone held no malice.

"I could always disconnect some of these wires for you," she offered. However, she showed no sign of stepping closer to the hulking demon.

"Are you an idiot *and* a fool? They're tied to my soul. If you managed to yank one out, you'd risk turning me into a grigori." Again, the lights shifted to red. "And *no one* wants that."

Nearly every strand of her being wanted to flee from his wicked gaze. One part of her, however, saw an opportunity. She tightened her hold on the wire to keep herself from running. As she did, it tugged sharply on his chest. "A lost soul? I've never seen one before," she said, hoping he wouldn't hear the bluff in her voice.

"You *are* mad," he said and sneered at her. Another tug. "Fine! Fine. What do you want to know?"

"I need to know how to tempt my new client."

Grimtooth laughed loudly. The entire chamber filled with an orange light. "That's it? That's all you want to know?"

Scribble felt unsure of herself. Was that really it? Did she dare ask about what had happened to his mother or girlfriend? Or was there something else she wasn't thinking about? She slowly nodded her head. "I think so. Does he at least have a weakness?"

"He is human, of course he has a weakness. He is nothing special. I had no problem making him sin."

"But I was told you were fired because—"

"*I was not fired!* I was ambushed. This? This is all *Belphegor's doing!*" He stood up to his full height for a moment, his impressive body dwarfing hers. The room blazed blood-red. Scribble felt the bottom of her stomach fall out and her legs began to lose all their strength as he towered over her. But the wires stood fast where they anchored in his flesh. After a few seconds, the light dimmed and he sank to the dais once more.

"W-w-why would they ambush you?" Scribble asked. She stepped back.

"It's because I saw—" She heard an electric buzz in the wires and he cut his sentence short. Scribble let go when he began squirming and reaching for his own flesh with open claws, though his arms remained bound so tightly that he could never quite reach himself. The wires drew out all the demon's strength. "Nnngg... Danielle..." he grunted before the electricity stopped. He hunched over once again, smoke rising from his skin, the lights a pale blue.

Once again, her curiosity piqued. "Danielle?" Scribble pressed, but she got no response. "Can't you tell me anything more?" She felt more lost now than before she came. "Please?" Still nothing. "If you're not going to talk, then I better get back before Rotworm sees I'm missing."

"Rotworm?" Grimtooth intoned. He chuckled softly. "You better watch yourself around that one." He continued his low laugh and ignored Scribble entirely until she finally left him to his misery.

Chapter 5 – Deal

The coffee cup in front of Scribble hadn't had any coffee in it for a while, but she liked to imagine steam still rising out of it. She'd found it abandoned on a small table in the corner of the bookstore and empathized with it. She didn't know what coffee—or anything else—tasted like, but it somehow made her brooding feel more justified. She had been watching Paul from a distance all day, never bothering to even try tempting him. It usually end badly anyway.

"How's it going?" came a voice from behind her. Scribble jerked and looked around, her eyes wide and alert. When she spied Rotworm's sleazy smile, she grew pale and shook lightly.

"I-it's just you..." she said, trying but failing to sound calm. "If you're going to fire me or hook me up to some machine, just get it over with." The demoness turned back to face Paul. She slumped forward and propped her head up with one hand but shut her eyes tightly in anticipation of what was to come.

Rotworm laughed. "I don't know what you're talking about. I'm just here to check up on my favorite Sinister, maybe lend a hand," he said and put his hand on her shoulder. Scribble jumped in fear and fell out of the chair, passing through the table on her way to the ground. It took her several tries to climb back up into the chair as she struggled to get a grip on the solid surfaces.

"Then what do you want?" she asked and settled back in her seat.

"I just want to see Boniface suffer, that's all." His smile faded as he spoke. "Why aren't you over there tempting Simon right now?"

"His name is Paul and he sucks. Besides, it wouldn't do any good. I'd just end up making things worse." The fear subsided and she slumped against the table, flicking her fingertip through the cup.

Rotworm leaned down closer to her ear. "Well, you aren't going to get *better* by just *sitting here!*"

"I went to see Grimtooth," she replied plainly. "I needed more help."

"*Grimtooth?* That suspicious shit was always following me around, trying to prove something." He paused for a moment in thought, then cast a wary eye at her. "What did he tell you?" His voice held a dangerously sharp edge.

"*Nothing!* I didn't learn a darn thing! Except that I'm a terrible Sinister. Even when Paul isn't feeling depressed, I can't tempt him. Look at that... that stupid angel always knows just what to say." She sat up straight, puffed out her face, put on a fake smile, and closed her eyes in imitation of the angel. "I'm Brother Boniface. I'm perfect! There's nothing I don't know. Don't forget that parable about the wounded monkey, child! Heaven rules!" She let out an exasperated sigh and slumped forward again. This time, as she flicked the cup, it moved slightly.

Rotworm smirked and picked the tablet computer up from the table where she'd left it. "It can't be *that* bad. Let's take a look." He pointed its camera at Paul and scanned him. "Ninety-Eight. Ninety-Eight?!" His previously calm expression changed to one of growing anger. "Did you get it to sin even once?"

"Once, but smiley over there undid it." At this point, Scribble had slipped out of the chair and was heading towards the door. *Maybe I can be some demon's footstool. That's a much less stressful job,* she thought to herself. Rotworm looked up from the iBad in time to catch her retreat and ran to her with his long stride. The moment he grabbed her arm, the door opened and a couple of kids walked into the store, passing through them.

Both Scribble and Rotworm watched as the kids wandered down an aisle. Something about them grabbed their attention—a similar feeling to the times just before Paul had to make a decision.

"C'mon. No one'll see," the shorter kid whispered to the taller one. They were both boys around the age of 12, and both wore large coats, awkward for the beginning of autumn.

"I don't know. It doesn't feel right," the taller one replied. His eyes shifted around the room to Paul and Ginger, who were busy talking near the cash register.

"Who's it going to hurt? Besides, they'll never know it's missing. It's just one. And it'll go for a Benjamin easy!"

"Are you sure? What if we get caught?"

"Then run. Oh, shit, they're coming this way. Quick!" The shorter boy pulled an eReader off a shelf and shoved it into the other's hands, then grabbed one for himself and put it under his coat—oversized security case and all. "Come on!"

The taller boy hesitated for a moment. An angel appeared on his shoulder, leaning into his ear and moving at high speed. But when the boy saw his friend walking to the door, then noticed Ginger working her way towards them, he bolted and the angel disappeared. The door swung open and the two shoplifters ran for freedom.

"What? What just happened?" Scribble asked.

"They shoplifted. What do you think happened?"

"But there wasn't even a Sinister or anything!"

"You've been here a week and you haven't seen humans tempting other humans before, Snapple?"

"They can *do* that?" Her mouth hung open in disbelief.

"Psh, of course! They do it all the time. Sometimes they do it just for the fun of it. If you're lucky, a human might even tempt itself." Rotworm let go of her arm and straightened his suit and tie. "Of course, *I* never needed them to."

"Then, why are we even here?"

"Well, they usually need a little... nudge in our direction. Those Dexters are always there, so why should we let them have all the fun? Plus, humans can be both bad and good influences on each other. It's safer to just do the work ourselves."

Scribble had stopped listening to him as an idea gradually formed in her mind. *An influence.* "I want a body."

Rotworm tilted his head. Even though she'd interrupted his ramblings, he didn't reprimand her. "I know it's a bit stubby, but you already have one."

"No, not THIS body. I want a human body!"

"That's a pretty tall order, Scratch," he said. "I mean, it's not like we can kill one. What do you want a body for anyway?"

Scribble waved her hands frantically, ignoring that he messed up her name yet again. "A living body! Something Paul—I mean something the *client* can see so that I can tempt him better!"

Rotworm was silent for a moment as he thought through what she was implying. "You can't possess a human without special permission. It's too dangerous."

She bit her lip and looked up at him with pleading eyes. "There must be *some* way." When she realized that her argument had not yet swayed him, she decided to change tactics. "Wouldn't it be great to see the look on Boniface's face when he loses to a tenderfoot like me?"

Rotworm's hand ran over his angular chin for a moment as he started to smile. "Well. There is *one* way..."

*　　　*　　　*

Scribble had never seen so much silk and satin in her life. It covered the walls, floor—even the ceiling. In the distance, she could hear soft moans and cries that made her just a little nervous. And excited. She had no idea there was a place in Hell that looked or sounded like this. "Where are you taking me?" she asked Rotworm.

"We're visiting a good friend of mine. We go way back." He just smiled to himself as he led her through the maze of tunnels, passing several definitely occupied rooms. The sounds coming from those rooms were a dangerous mixture of pain and pleasure, though mostly pain. Once in a while, she heard the familiar sound of a screaming human. This was decadence in every sense of the word and definitely part of Hell.

A black gate barred their path, a pair of angels with four painted, floating eyes standing on either side. Scribble instantly recognized the symbol of the Order. Both brandished several exotic weapons that seared the air around them with holy might. The ornate armor they wore was even larger and thicker than that of the angels guarding the gates of Hell. Scribble clutched the dark stone she had been wearing around her neck on a chain. Rotworm had told her that they needed to wear them during the visit, but he didn't tell her exactly why. The moment she put it on, however, she felt compelled toward these gates, as if the stone itself was pulling her.

Rotworm did not hesitate to walk up to the angels and pull out a small dark booklet from the inside pocket of his suit jacket. One of the painted eyes of the nearest angel darted in an arc around the angel's head and stared unblinking at Rotworm, then at Scribble, then down at the booklet. Just as the eye returned to its vigilant forward position, the angels both moved to the side to allow them to pass.

"What is the Order doing way down here?" Scribble whispered to Rotworm after they had passed between the angels.

Rotworm turned a curious gaze in her direction. "The Order guards all of the Princes of Hell. Surely you knew that."

"Princes!? We're going to see a Prince?!" Despite her mistrust, she followed closer to him. Beyond the wall, the lavish décor grew ever more opulent and depraved. What looked at first like a fur draped over a wall was, on closer inspection, a collection of scalps that had been artfully arranged. The screams of pain and pleasure grew more desperate, and a distant, echoing jabber joined them. Scribble gripped the black stone that hung around her neck even tighter.

"Hey! Careful with that thing! That soul stone was expensive. It was once Elizabeth Báthory." He got another patented Scribble blank stare. "The Blood Countess? Ba'al, learn your history, girl. Don't break it! With your soul weight, you'll go flying out of here like an angel in a brothel. Remember, this is Level 11. They don't get much heavier than this one."

She gazed in awe at the thing. It was smooth, and upon closer inspection, she found it wasn't black but a very deep red. If she looked at it long enough, she could just make out something moving beneath the nebulous façade.

Rotworm snapped his fingers to bring her back to reality. "Hey. Snap out of it. Stay close and don't speak."

The pair turned down a long, nondescript corridor that seemingly led nowhere. They approached a large door made of human flesh stretched over an array of random bones. Before it stood a large man who appeared human. His arms were thicker than Scribble's legs and he was nearly twice her height. A pair of sunglasses hid his eyes from view. The human was incredibly handsome, with details that could have been chiseled from stone by a master mason. Despite this, there was something slightly off—something that Scribble could not put her finger on.

"What do you want?" he asked without inflection or expression.

"And a good day to you, too, Incubus. We're here to see your master," Rotworm said proudly, even though he, too, was dwarfed by the size of the man.

"She is busy," he replied.

"Oh, I think she will make time for us. We have a proposition for her. One that she will not want to pass up."

Incubus stood silent for a moment, then nodded. "Follow me," he said and turned, pushing open the door with ease. Scribble wondered if she could even make it budge.

"Incubus?" she asked Rotworm quietly as they followed. "A sex demon? Where is this?"

Rotworm winked at her, "The lair of Asmodeus." Seeing the blank expression on Scribble's face, he continued, "THE Asmodeus. Prince of Lust. One of the Seven. What *do* you know about the Princes?"

"Um... well, I know Asmodeus is the Prince of Lust," she said with a sheepish smile. "Oh, and Belphegor is the Prince of Sloth!"

"That's right," he replied, nodding to her. "There's also Mammon—Prince of Avarice, Beelzebub—Prince of Vanity, Amon—Prince of Anger, Leviathan—Princess of Gluttony, and Lucifer—Prince of Pride. This is all basic stuff, Scruple. Didn't they teach you anything up there in Purgatory?"

"It's Scribble. But how will Asmodeus help us?" she asked.

"Ever wonder how sex demons tempt humans?" Rotworm replied with a wicked grin.

A look of surprise settled on Scribble's face. She walked silently the rest of the way, watching Incubus' back until they entered an ornate chamber, where he let them pass and remained at the entrance. Soft light emanated from the dome above, giving a warm, seductive tint to the rest of the room. In one corner, a large bed rose up from the floor. It was stone with a rough pillar for a headboard, which made the entire thing look as though it had been cut from a stalagmite. A table was set in the center of the room, covered in oysters, chocolates, and fruits. All along the walls, Scribble noticed an array of devices, most of them made of leather and bone—she could only guess at their purposes. On the far side of the room was a couch, and draped over it was a woman in a long, red dress. She had flowing locks of glossy red hair that fell over her bare shoulders. Her flesh was supple and had no blemishes. A well-placed slit in the dress left one long, luscious leg exposed. Scribble realized that both she and Incubus were different than the other demons; their bodies looked solid—*human*. And her human eyes were fixed on Rotworm's.

"Well, well. Look what the hellcat dragged in," she said in a voice equally as seductive as her figure.

"Asmodeus! You're looking as irresistible as always." He winked at her and gave a sly smile.

Scribble leaned in to whisper in Rotworm's ear but could not seem to tear her eyes away from the woman. "Aren't the Princes supposed to be male?"

"She's whatever she wants to be," Rotworm replied from the corner of his mouth, his eyes also glued to the woman's. "It has been too long since I saw this seductive form," he said to Asmodeus.

She laughed pleasantly. "Please, worm, you're the one who left my employ. You and I both know you only show up when there's something you want." She flicked her long hair out of her face with a slender finger, then turned her gaze on Scribble. "Who is this rather innocent specimen?" Asmodeus stood up and walked towards her with a provocative gait, her hips swinging in such a way that men would go to war over them. As she drew closer, however, her body changed. By the time she was close enough to touch Scribble, Asmodeus appeared as an attractive young man with long, blonde hair and blue eyes. "How do you like this form, my dear?" he said to Scribble as he gazed at her hungrily.

"This," Rotworm said, motioning to Scribble with his head, "is why I'm here. She would like a human body."

"Is this true?" Asmodeus asked Scribble directly. The imp merely nodded. "Well, I'm afraid I can't just give you one. They're difficult to make, and all of them are being used. You understand." He trailed a finger under Scribble's chin before turning away and walking back towards the couch. By the time Asmodeus reached it, she was once again in the body of a beautiful woman.

"Oh, we'll pay you," Rotworm stated. "I've been sa—"

"You cannot afford me," Asmodeus said with disinterest, not bothering to turn around. "I'll thank you not to waste any more of my time."

Scribble stepped forward as images of flames and wires flashed through her mind. "I'll do anything!"

With that, Asmodeus slowly turned. "Anything? Do you even know what you are offering?"

Scribble nodded again, this time, with more hesitation. Of course, she had no clue.

A smile crept across Asmodeus' face. "Then I think, perhaps, I can accommodate you after all." She looked to Incubus, who then departed from the room. "Come, sit. Scribble, was it?"

Scribble nervously approached the table in the center of the room and sat in one of the chairs. "Yes, how did you know?"

"I have very good ears," she replied. "Tell me, have you ever tasted an apple before?" Scribble shook her head as she eyed the food that was on display before her. Asmodeus sauntered to the other side and dragged a finger over a red apple. "I see. It's a shame really. We Immortals do not eat, so we have no need for taste. We do not breathe like humans do, so we barely have a sense of smell. Even our sense of touch is limited. For such fragile creatures, humans are certainly... interesting. It makes them so fun to play with." She picked the apple up and bit into it, letting the juices flow down her chin and onto her perfect breasts.

Before Rotworm or Scribble could respond, Incubus entered the room once more, wheeling a large, metal cart. On the cart stood an unconscious human woman, naked and held up by large braces that wrapped around her slender chest and legs. Her shoulder-length black hair contrasted gorgeously against her pale skin. She had the kind of face that could be both cute and alluring with the same glance.

"She's beautiful, isn't she?" Asmodeus asked as they watched Incubus place the cart near the bed, then retreat back to his place at the chamber entrance. "She's my magnum opus. I've been working on her for quite a while now, but the eyes could still use a little help. She'll need glasses. Other than that, she's perfect. Too perfect. Unlike my other succubus bodies, this one requires food. To get the feedback I wanted, I had to design her to bond fairly closely with the user's soul. Sadly, there haven't been any demons willing to try her out. Cowards, I suppose. I might be convinced to let you borrow her for a time, as a sort of test drive."

"She's... not real?" Scribble asked, looking over every detail of the woman. Asmodeus laughed.

"Oh, please. She's real enough."

"W-why would they be scared?"

"Bonding as closely as this body requires may have... side effects. And like any good machine, she takes maintenance. You can't simply leave her, or she might get damaged. And if *she* gets damaged, *you* get damaged," Asmodeus warned. "Not many demons are willing to risk staying on Earth for weeks at a time. It does... things to your mind."

"But I'm no succubus. I don't even know..." Scribble's voice faded.

Asmodeus leaned back and folded her arms under her bust. "True. You are rather green. I need to make sure you can handle the task. I assume you have a specific target in mind."

Rotworm stepped up and handed over the iBad. "His dossier."

The sultry woman took it and tapped her pinky against her teeth as a smile slowly stretched her lips thin. "Young, but not too young. A virgin, too. And this body would fit his type. Your awkwardness he might find cute. But his condition? Tsk, tsk, tsk. I think you'll find it hard to feed off his soul." She handed the tablet back to Rotworm.

"Feed?" Scribble asked. Asmodeus and Rotworm stared at her in disbelief.

"Is she for real?" Asmodeus asked.

Rotworm just nodded.

She continued, "Yes, feed. As in sex. A succubus feeds off the souls of her victims to keep her body in shape, but I doubt you'd be able to get him in any sort of compromising condition on a regular basis. And if he catches you having sex with another... well, let's not tempt fate. No, you'll need to power this body with your own soul."

Scribble bit her lip nervously. "That sounds dangerous. Can't a soul stone do it?"

"Out of the question!" she shouted suddenly. "I told you, she will bond with your soul. We don't want her bonding with some depraved *human* soul. Who knows what it will do? You'll just need to come back here once every few days or so to refresh."

"That doesn't sound too hard," Scribble said.

"Of course, I expect something from you." Asmodeus walked over to the body and ran her hand along its side. "Quid pro quo, Scribble. I want a soul."

"I-I can't! I've already promised his soul to Belphegor!"

Asmodeus' gaze turned hard for a moment, but softened as she looked over Scribble. "I have plenty of *human* souls. I want something different—unique. Perhaps yours? It won't be forever. Let's say I give you three months with this body and then I get three months in return. And if you damage any part of her, I guarantee you they will not be pleasant months. At least not for you. Still interested?" She flashed a hungry smile.

Scribble swallowed hard and stared into Asmodeus' eyes. After what seemed like a lifetime, she finally said, "Yes."

CHAPTER 6 – HUMANITY

The sky blushed as the tip of the sun peered over the horizon. Rotworm and Scribble kept watch, waiting until there was no one nearby before they let Incubus carry the body into the alleyway. It had been dressed in a knee-length skirt and button-up blouse with short sleeves. A pair of smart-looking glasses sat on the nose. Over one shoulder, Scribble had placed a small, rather chic purse that Asmodeus provided. Its hair was up in a bun, giving it a professional and slightly flirty look. Scribble was amazed that Asmodeus had such "modest" clothes. Incubus dropped the empty body roughly onto the ground next to the dumpster, which it hit with a loud clang.

"Careful!" hissed Rotworm sharply. "You're being too loud!" He stood at the end of the alley, looking back and forth to make sure there was no one coming. "Remember, Inky, you're in a human body. If anyone sees you doing this, we could all get in trouble. The last thing I need is the Order snooping around."

Scribble knelt beside the limp body for a moment, examining it. "What do I... do?" she asked no one in particular.

"You possess it," Incubus replied. "Just enter. It has no soul to resist you."

"Possess it? But isn't that dangerous? Rotworm, didn't you tell me—"

"It'll be fine!" Rotworm said over his shoulder. "If anyone suspects anything, just tell them you're from out of town or something. Humans are stupid. They'll believe anything. Now, hurry up!"

Scribble hesitated a moment longer, but she could feel the gazes of the other demons on her. If it hadn't been for the threat of being punished by Rotworm, she would have run under such peer pressure. She clenched her jaw tightly, then leaned forward against the body and passed into it with ease.

Cold. The air, the ground, the dumpster—all of it was cold. Scribble breathed in sharply, filling her lungs with the heady scent of garbage and dirt. As her gray eyes flew open, the warm light of the rising sun filled them. It shone down on the group from between the surrounding buildings.

"I... can... feel so much!" she said. She took in a long, deliberate breath. "What is that strange sensation?"

Incubus chuckled deeply, the kind of chuckle usually reserved for when children think they know better than you. "You have all the senses of a human now. I'm sure you've noticed how much stronger your sense of smell is."

"Smell..." she said and took in another breath with a smile. "I had no idea...

it could be so intense! And... I don't feel any pain!" In fact, the pain that she had lived with just by being in Hell had vanished like a constant pressure being lifted. When she took her third breath, however, her body started to reject the fetor of rotting garbage that sat just on the other side of the dumpster's metal wall. She doubled over.

Incubus took her by the hand, helping her stand and move away from the dumpster. The body had weight to it, it had muscles, it had a pulse. Scribble could feel it moving slightly even when she wasn't telling it to.

"Take a deeper breath before speaking, then breathe out slowly," he said. "But don't concentrate on your breathing too much. Let it just happen."

Scribble leaned against him and looked up at his face. He seemed much more handsome now for some reason. And he smelled how she'd always imagined a campfire would smell. To her, it was... *masculine*. However, she could still sense that something was off. He was too ideal, too perfect, but more than that, he had a feral aura about him. Just a glance would tell her he was no ordinary human. "Is this better?" she asked after taking a deep breath.

"A little. Be careful with this body, it is precious. It took my master a century to perfect it out of clay. She will be *very* displeased if you break it."

Rotworm turned and grinned, seeing Scribble in the human body. "It's about time! Let's get over there and see you make a fool out of Boniface!"

Scribble ignored him. Her attention was on her new body as she felt the brick wall, the soft warmth of Incubus, her cotton clothes. She practiced with her new sense of balance, using Incubus to help keep her steady. As the sun hit her skin, she smiled, feeling its warmth start to take away the bite of the cold. "So many new sensations..." she said, mostly to herself. Slowly, she let go of the man and stood up on her own, then took a few shaky steps before falling back against Incubus. Her muscles clenched as she tried again.

"We don't have time for this!" Rotworm complained, walking over to her.

"She cannot go out there like this. Give her a few minutes to adjust to the homunculus body," Incubus replied, getting some annoyed grumbles in return. It took a few minutes for her to begin walking, talking, and breathing like a normal human. The breathing part did tend to take care of itself, but she thought she'd never get the hang of walking *and* talking at the same time.

"Can we hurry it up?" Rotworm spat. He felt something in his pocket and his demeanor changed in an instant. "Oh, uh, here, you might as well have this," Rotworm said as he walked with her to the end of the alleyway. He handed her an iBad. It was different this time—smaller. The device easily fit in the palm of her hand or pocket like a smartphone would. "I figured you could still use the help. Because you're in a physical body, I was able to get you one that is also physical, so I better get it back in one piece!"

"Where did you get that?" Incubus asked, his eyes wide with desire.

"My boss, Inky Butt. Hey!" Rotworm tried to stop Incubus from taking the device from Scribble, but he was too late. Incubus turned it over and removed the back plating. A smooth, black disc was set inside looking rather like a large button cell battery.

"Soul stone? It's so light and different. And physical."

"Don't touch that!" Rotworm grabbed the iBad and put it back together. "Of course she has to use a soul stone, I just made it look like this to fool the humans. She can't power this thing on her own in *that* body. And if you even think about taking that stone, *I* will be the least of your troubles." He leaned threateningly towards Incubus, who tried to keep his ground. Although Incubus was taller and larger, Rotworm seemed to ooze power as they stared at each other. In the end, Incubus faltered under Rotworm's stare and diverted his own gaze silently. During the entire showdown, Scribble was blissfully inspecting her new fingers, completely unaware.

Rotworm handed the device back to her. It was extremely lightweight, as if made of dense air. Behind them, Incubus stepped through the door back to Hell without a word. Scribble swallowed hard, knowing she would have to learn how to be human on the job.

"If you need help, you can contact me. I have the other iBad. Now, come on, let's see what this new body of yours can do," Rotworm said, letting his forked tongue lap at the air in front of him. However, he stopped cold in his tracks when a buzz sounded from his pocket. Scribble was both curious and amused when his red skin paled slightly and he took out his pager with a shaking hand to read its message. "Damnation! I have more pressing business, so you'll be on your own. Make me proud." He rushed over to the door, turned at the last moment, and added, "I don't have an imp horn in my collection. Yet." Then he walked through. She was alone.

*　　*　　*

Scribble had read the phrase, "Like butterflies in your stomach," but she never understood what that meant until now. She decided it wasn't an entirely unpleasant sensation. What *was* strange was to have humans looking at her after spending so much time among them invisibly. The men noticed her more than the women. She stood near *Othello's Books*, trying to appear inconspicuous as she awkwardly scanned through the iBad for ideas. If knowledge truly was power, then the demonic smartphone should have taken over the world long ago. It had information on almost everything, and the way it was organized made it fast and easy to access. In fact, Scribble found herself searching through random files in awe and curiosity for several minutes when a bicyclist went by and nearly clipped her. She was used to passing through people, so when she saw him coming in her periphery, she thought nothing of it. But his "Excuse me!" and the sudden swerve of the bike to go around her snapped her back into reality. Scribble held the device close to her chest—a reflex to make sure it didn't get knocked from her hand, even though the danger had already passed. She backed up slowly, looking suddenly very frightened.

What if I scratch this body? Will Asmodeus come after me? She looked down at her new body, then smiled and started to inspect it more closely, turning her hips and looking down her long legs. It really was a perfect body with muscle tone and sharp reflexes, proportions she had always imagined for the heroines in the contraband human books she read, and as she turned in circles a few times to try to get a look at her back, she realized it had no wings— no wings or tail to get pulled on or caught in doors or crushed. Her worries of what might happen melted away. But the moment was short-lived, interrupted by a vibration in her hand. She looked down at the phone.

"Get to work, Simple!"

was displayed on the screen. She flustered and looked around. Sure, there were other demons there, but none of them paid her any attention. Still, she was convinced Rotworm had somehow been keeping an eye on her. That, or he knew her far too well already. Either way, she went back to searching the phone, but the volume of information was overwhelming. After a fruitless hunt, an idea struck her. She turned it around and pointed the camera at herself.

Name: Scribble
Type: Succubus
Age: Unknown
Estimated Soul Weight: 1
Occupation: Sinister

"I'm a succubus?" she asked out loud as a man standing at the nearby crosswalk raised his eyebrow at her. He took a few steps away and gave her a look that made even Scribble think that she must be crazy. She turned her back to the man and held the iBad closer with an awkward smile. Its screen had changed on its own to a page entitled "Seduction Suggestions for the Serious Succubus." To anyone else who might have seen that screen, it looked like the lovechild of a woman's magazine and a bad porn website. To Scribble, however, it read more like an owner's manual.

If you don't know where to start, try placing yourself in these situations:

Secretary. Older men often have affairs with their secretaries because they are young and available and their wives would never know. Be sure you know how to file papers so you can keep your position as long as possible.
Nightclub/Bar. Wherever the alcohol flows freely, you'll find young, desperate men with few inhibitions. Be sure you do not indulge in drink or drugs yourself as your homunculus body is not immune to their effects.
Internet. The Internet is for more than just porn. Casual hook-ups, cybersex, and adult dating sites are everywhere! Just don't get addicted to City of War Guilds.
Co-worker. Nothing says "sexy" more than sneaking into an abandoned room for a tryst. Don't worry about getting caught—you might even get the boss interested!
High School/College. Be it the naughty teacher or the class slut, sex is plentiful on campus! A mixture of curiosity, hormones, and peer pressure makes it almost impossible to resist. A word of warning, however: you will have plenty of competition from the actual human girls.

Scribble absently curled a lock of hair around her finger as she pored over the text. "Paul doesn't need a secretary," she said to the iBad as if it could hear her. "I'm not sure what a 'nightclub' is. And it's not like he's hiring..."

Then fate decided to play a joke. A "Help Wanted" sign appeared in the window right in front of her.

A grin spread across Scribble's face as she walked up to the front door of *Othello's Books*. Unfortunately, it was short-lived. With a ringing *BONG*, her now physical body smacked face-first into the door. She held her nose and reeled back as blood started to flow.

"Are you alright?" Paul asked as he came out of the shop in a hurry and rushed to her side

"I fink fo," she said.

"Here, let me take a look..." Paul leaned closer when she moved her hand and inspected the injury. "May I?" he asked. Scribble nodded, so Paul reached out and gently held her nose between thumb and forefinger. "Does that hurt?"

"A little."

"Doesn't look broken... come on in, we'll get you fixed up." Paul led her inside and walked between the shelves and piles of merchandise, brushed past

Ginger, and headed straight for the back room. "Here, have a seat," he said once the door closed behind them. He guided her to sit down on the desk and brought the desk's arm light closer. It lit up her face from above. He once again pulled her hand away, took off her glasses, and was staring at her nose. All the while, Scribble was looking into his deep, dark eyes. He was so close that she could see them clearly without the glasses. A blush spread instantly across her high cheekbones and she felt her heart beat faster and harder.

Is this body working right? It feels strange... Paul didn't seem to notice and began to rummage around on top of a cabinet for a first aid kit.

"Ha! Here it is!" He put it next to her on the desk and grabbed some cotton balls from it. Again, when he moved close to her, she began to blush. "It's just a little bleeder, nothing to worry about," he told her while pressing a cotton ball to her nose.

"I'm so embarrassed..."

Paul brought her hand up to the swab. "Hold it just like that," he said, then started putting the kit away. "Don't worry about it, I've seen it happen before." He nodded to the iBad still in her other hand. "It's not the first time technology caused someone to walk into the door. Those little things can get pretty distracting. So, what brings you to *Othello's*? I assume you knew there was a store here." He raised his eyebrow at her almost playfully. Almost.

"Yeah," Scribble said in a nasally voice. "I..." She stopped short and glanced down at the iBad. She didn't even have to search for help; it was already offering prompts in large lettering for her. "I saw the... sign in the window and... de-de-decided! to apply." Scribble glanced over to Paul and smiled innocently as she mentally pieced together the sentence she'd just read. "For work!" she added at the end, lowering the cotton from her nose.

"Really? I just put that sign up," he said. Something seemed to grab his attention—he stopped what he was doing and gazed into her eyes. No one had ever looked at her with such awe and interest before. Scribble held her bottom lip between her teeth as she felt tingles all over. Then she was caught in the trap herself, looking back into his dark, curious gaze.

Why can't I look away? Look somewhere else! You're being awkward! No matter how much she protested in her mind, it did little good. *Damn him for making this body act on its own!* Even those thoughts of objection eventually died down.

She had no concept of how much time had passed. Seconds? Hours? But the moment was shattered when the door flew open and Ginger stood in the doorway. "Paul, what's going on? Is she all right?"

He cleared his throat and looked away from Scribble. "She'll be okay," he said, but he couldn't hide the growing grin on his face. "Just a bloody nose."

"Oh. Well, good. It doesn't look like it's bleeding any longer." Ginger looked at the two of them with a suspicious air. The way she folded her arms beneath her bust made Scribble think that she was trying to emphasize just how bountiful her breasts were. Her deep V halterneck didn't hurt. Scribble looked down at her own chest and narrowed her eyes. *How can I compete with those? Couldn't Asmodeus have given me a little more in the chest department?*

"Oh, where are my manners? Ginger, this is Miss..."

"Scribble," she replied, then froze in sudden panic. She knew such a name was not at all common among humans, but she'd already said it. Her mind raced to try to find a solution. The backwards lettering of "Othello" stood out in the window behind Ginger and gave her an idea. "Desdemona Scribble." She smiled as genuinely as she could fake, hoping they would fall for it.

Paul considered the name for a moment. "Miss Scribble," he said.

"Oh, you can call me Dez."

"Dez," he corrected with a nod. "This is Ginger. Dez is looking for a job."

"That was quick." Ginger's eyes narrowed a little as she looked Scribble over. She might as well have been a warrior surveying a foe on the field of battle. "I don't trust her. Looked to me like she ran into the door on purpose."

This was nothing new—Scribble was used to people not trusting her. In Hell, people only did things for you if they got something in return. But nothing in her novels led her to think it was the same here on Earth. The good guys always acted nobly. As Ginger moved to Paul and held onto his arm, Scribble knew right away that this girl was not acting noble. She was trying to keep her away from him. Ginger was trying to stop her.

Paul put up a finger, then led Ginger several steps away and spoke in a lower tone, though not low enough to remain unheard. "That's a mean thing to say," he said. "You don't even know her!"

"She's probably trying to get pity points. Also, she smells like garbage, and I bet she just made up that name."

"I did not—" Scribble tried to say, but it was impossible for her to defend herself when Ginger just kept talking over her.

"Why do you even *want* to hire someone else? Is this about the missing money? I told you I had nothing to do with that."

Paul took off his glasses and pinched the bridge of his nose. "I haven't had a break in nearly a year, I have few friends outside of work, and I have no hobbies. All I do is work. I even work in my dreams. It's burning me out."

His words reminded Scribble of how she'd felt for ages. Even the reprieve her books offered did not give her the rest she really needed. For the first time in as long as she could remember, she felt empathy for another person.

"I need some more time for myself," he continued after a pause. "She'll just pick up a few shifts for now." A smile tugged at the corners of Scribble's mouth as he sounded more and more like he might take her on.

"But we can't afford it," Ginger countered.

"I can't afford *not* to hire someone. I've been so tired that I've started to make mistakes. I think a fresh face will help us all out." Paul turned to Scribble and walked back over to her. "I'm sorry about all that. So, Dez, have you ever worked retail before? Do you have a résumé?"

"Résumé?" Scribble asked. She was completely unfamiliar with the word. "O-of course, I have one... doesn't everybody?" She gave a smile that came off as either uncomfortable or crazy.

"I bet she's lying," Ginger said in singsong as she came up behind him. She seemed incapable of niceties or common courtesy. Even the denizens of Hell knew how to fake being polite.

"What is wrong with you today?" Paul asked under his breath.

Ginger's demeanor changed quickly, from outgoing and vicious to withdrawn and apologetic. "I'm sorry. I just don't want to see you get hurt again. Hiring someone is a big decision," she replied. As the two of them talked, Scribble looked up the word "rezumay" in the iBad. In an instant, it began loading a music video, opened a website about some sort of "influencer," and ordered something rather risqué from Japan. A folded piece of paper then stuck out of a small slit along the top of the device. It fell in Scribble's lap. She unfolded it, revealing a long list of imagined achievements and previous jobs, some of which actually sounded like things she'd done in Purgatory before.

"Is this what you need?" Scribble asked, interrupting the awkward conversation the other two were having. They looked at her, then down to her hand in concert. Paul took the paper and examined it.

"Hmmm... I see a lot of secretarial work: sorting, filing, things like that. It says here you've done some editing?" He glanced up to see the slightly worried expression on her face.

"Um, well, writing mostly."

"Yeah? What sort?"

Her voice got a bit softer. "Sometimes I'd write a story based on a book I've read." Scribble had never admitted this to anyone before and it made her nervous, even if he was just a human.

"Ah! Fanfic. No shame in that. So, Dez, why did you leave your last job?"

Scenes from her old office brought a small frown to Scribble's lips. "I was replaced," she said with a sigh. "By a computer program."

"An AI? That's terrible! Did you work there long?"

"It felt like an eternity." She'd spent almost all of her time working in the Purgatory control tower; how many human years had passed, she couldn't say. Probably thousands, but time had little meaning there.

The room was silent for a few moments. Eventually, Paul put her résumé on the desk. "Well, I can't let you just wander around the streets running into doors." He gave her another smile—the first real smile she'd ever seen from him. Not only did she find it handsome, but it seemed to brighten the whole room. It occupied all her thoughts so well that she barely heard the next words he spoke. "Can you be here early tomorrow for training?"

What broke Scribble out of her trance was the sound of Ginger letting out a frustrated groan. The girl muttered something and left the room.

"Yes! I can be here tomorrow!" Scribble said when it finally dawned on her that she got the job.

"Good! I'll see you first thing in the morning, then. And, watch where you walk with that thing from now on," he said. "I don't need some other store hiring you between now and then."

Chapter 7 – Lust

It didn't take long for Scribble to discover the pleasures of the palate. Once her stomach started to growl, the iBad recommended a host of places to eat and even provided her a fake credit card in the same manner as it had given her a résumé. She was soon alone in a booth at a restaurant bar, surrounded by enough food to feed several small villages, or one average American family. Although she hadn't finished any of the food, she had taken bites out of everything: Alaskan cod, tofu stir-fry, Salisbury steak, death-by-chocolate cake, chicken cacciatore, Waldorf salad, and yellowfin tuna. She still didn't know what a "Waldorf" was. Accompanying the impressive spread was a cadre of alcoholic beverages, despite the warning that she'd seen on the iBad. By midnight, she was quite drunk.

"You! Y-yeah... wass yur name? I wanna nudder of these lil... green drinks..." she said to the waiter passing by. He stopped.

"Ma'am, I think you've had enough. Do you have a designated driver?"

"Pppsshhh!" She was much louder than she realized. Suddenly, she narrowed her eyes and looked at the young waiter with grave severity. "Is there summ'n wrong with my body? Whenever I see 'im, I feel all... funny. Izzat normal?"

A blush bloomed on the waiter's face. "N-nothing wrong with it, ma'am! I... I'll be right back with your check."

Scribble let out an exasperated sigh. "What is WRONG with me?!" she said to no one in particular. The iBad buzzed and lit up on the table in front of her, offering a list of possibilities, but she just ignored it and slumped forward against the table.

"This is a dangerous stunt you're attempting, Sister."

Scribble looked up to see a blur sitting across from her. She lifted her head and straightened her glasses, turning the blur into the appearance of a full-sized Boniface. "Oh... 'ss you..."

"Yes, it is. I am simply concerned." He looked down at the smorgasbord on the table. "Your predecessor seems to have ended up in trouble, and I do not wish the same for you."

"My wha?" It took her a moment to work out the words. "Oh, Grimtooth! Say, you know everthin'. Wha'appened to him? Wha'd he do?"

Boniface shook his head. "I am afraid I do not know. He was there one day, and the next he was gone."

"Oh. Well… I'm ffffine. I don'need yur help."

"Perhaps, Sister, you should not indulge in so much drink. It can make humans sick." The angel's persistent smile turned to a look of genuine worry.

"Why d'you care?" Scribble asked, leaning back. "It's not like *I'm* a human."

"I suspect that body is more human than you might realize. I was not expecting them to offer you one with such… detail. Did you not find Grimtooth's advice helpful?"

The demoness waved her hand dismissively. "He din't help at all! An' this is hard! I just need an edge. Wait! Whadayu mean? You knew I'd ask fffor a body?" The waiter dropped off the check while Scribble talked. He moved quickly as if not wanting to spend time around a girl who talked to herself—drunk or not.

Boniface tilted his hand from side to side. "I had hoped you would. If you can help him get out of this depression, we both benefit. And I believe you can by being his friend. I saw how you connected with him on your very first day. And using my analogy against me? Very smart."

Scribble let out a sound like a breathy raspberry. "Rotworm stopped me."

"Do not sell yourself short, Sister. Connect with him. You know, I saw him smiling today. Was that your doing?"

Instead of answering, Scribble's face became confused. She burped, then looked surprised at herself and giggled.

"Just be careful that you do not get too close to him. Remember that we have a job to do. Once he has recovered, we can return to doing it. And, please take care of yourself and this body, Sister Scribble. It's risky to stay in it for too long." Boniface's smile returned as he stood and walked out of the restaurant through the nearest wall.

Scribble watched him disappear, then let out a loud sigh and put the credit card on the table. She picked up the iBad and ran her finger across the touchscreen. "Stup'd angel. Thinks he knows everthing! Hhhow's this body a risk?" she asked, directing the question to the smartphone itself. A few phrases appeared on the screen, but in her haze, the only thing Scribble saw was the clock in the upper corner. 1:15 am. "Oh no! I hafta get to work! I don' wanna be late!" Her stomach growled loudly and she curled her upper lip. "Ri' affer I figger out how this whol' bathroom thing works…"

*   *   *

When Scribble arrived at the shop, it was still closed. The street that was alive with commotion in the daylight had grown dormant. In the distance, she could hear a single car making its way to some dark location. Shivers passed through her short, lithe frame as she held her arms around her midsection, watching breath condense into an ethereal mist. She leaned against the wall and sank to the ground. Even after she had been waiting there for several hours, the haze of alcohol lingered on her mind.

The sky was still dark when the rattling of keys roused her. Paul was unlocking the front door.

"You're here!" Scribble said, rising to her feet like a pregnant giraffe before pushing away from the wall. Paul jumped in surprise. He looked toward her. Her hair had begun to fall out of the bun and hang in wisps over her face.

"Oh, Desdemona! It's you," he said with a relieved tone. "How long have you been waiting?"

"I don't know... I think I got here about 2 am?"

"What? That was four hours ago! Why have you been waiting that long? Didn't you sleep?"

Scribble walked up to him, shivering. "I... couldn't sleep. Plus, you said to be here first thing..." she explained in a soft, tired voice.

"Well, come on inside and warm up," he said and opened the door. As she nodded to him and walked into the dark bookstore, she heard the faint sound of chimes blowing in a breeze. She glanced at Paul, who quickly averted his gaze from her. Boniface sat on his shoulder and began to whisper into his ear.

Why can't I hear what they are saying? Why is he even here? she thought and peered at Boniface curiously. She tried even harder to listen to his thoughts while he turned on the lights in the store, but they were silent. And still, Boniface kept constantly whispering.

"So, the first thing you do when you open is turn on all the lights?" Scribble asked with feigned interest. She pointed the iBad's camera in Paul's direction but tried to make it look like she was taking notes. It sprang up with all of his stats, just like before, only, at the top of the screen was a new flashing bar. On it were the words,

Temptation: Lust – Fantasizing.

Scribble's swirling gray eyes nearly popped out of her head. *He's fantasizing about ME? I suppose this* is *the body of a succubus...*

"Yeah, but don't turn on the open sign yet," Paul said. "Are you sure you're all right? I mean, you've been out there in the cold all night."

Scribble stumbled, but managed to make it look like she'd tripped over one of the piles of books at her feet. "Oh, I'm fine! It wasn't that cold."

Paul raised his eyebrow at her with some doubt. "If you're sure," he said and waved her over to him. "Well then, come over to the cash register so I can show you how to use it. We only have the one. It's the one my mom used when she owned the store. It's old but still works fine." He stood behind the desk and put a key into the top of the register, turning the machine on.

"Family business?" she asked him as she scanned Paul's dossier on the iBad for anything that might help—his turn-ons, his fantasies, his type.

"You could say that. My mom left it to me."

Scribble remembered the frustration she'd been having in learning more about his past and decided that this might be a good chance. "I'm sorry to hear that. What happened to her?"

Paul clenched his jaw for a moment. "She had a heart attack. I've been running the store for about two years now. It's been a bit more work than I was expecting, though. To be honest, I wanted to write plays. I just haven't had the time to finish anything. I'm so exhausted at the end of the day."

"A playwright?" she asked. "Like Shakespeare?" She put the smartphone into her purse and walked over to him, trying to be slow and seductive. Unfortunately, seduction was something she had only ever read about—a theory more than anything else. She recalled the descriptions she'd read in bawdy romance novels and walked towards him with awkward, wide swings of her hips. Her arms folded under her small bust, propping it up just a little. As he looked up at her, she took off her glasses and put the end of the earpiece in the corner of her mouth. If she hadn't been sleep-deprived and fighting off the effects of alcohol, she might have been able to pull it off. Instead, she stumbled on the corner of a display she couldn't see well and steadied herself against the counter before putting the glasses back on.

"I'm hardly Shakespeare," he said, trying to hide a silly smile. "What are you doing?"

The fatigue and the last of the alcohol in her system did her in. With one unsure footstep, Scribble's leg wobbled and she fell, grabbing onto one of the nearby bookcases. She hit the floor with a series of loud THUMPS and a gasp.

"Woah! Are you okay? What happened?" Paul asked, coming out from behind the counter to rush to her side.

"Ow..." she replied, wincing. She'd landed on her rear with her legs somewhat spread.

"Are you hurt?" he asked. She blinked a few times and shook her head.

"Just my ass, I think..." Scribble took Paul's offered hand and stood, leaning against him a little. Her face started to flush again as his masculine scent filled her lungs.

"I'm sorry... let me get you some ibuprofen." Paul's voice displayed genuine concern. On his shoulder, Boniface was smiling and nodding.

"No, I think—"

The scene blurred. Scribble felt light-headed. Then everything went black.

*　　*　　*

When Scribble woke up, she was in a bed with clean sheets. They had a slightly musty smell as if they hadn't been used in some time. Next to her was a nightstand that held her purse and an alarm clock with a dark display. Behind the clock sat a dusty picture of a large black man whose arms were draped around the shoulders of a young woman with skin the color of rich clay. Both of them looked incredibly happy. Next to it was a picture that was unmistakably Paul, but as a teenager, dressed in a brightly-colored gown with a square hat on his head. Along all the walls were bookshelves filled with books that sat behind glass. They weren't just along the walls, Scribble realized. A few stood back-to-back in the middle of the room. A window on the other side of the room had only just begun letting in the bright, cool light of morning. As Scribble took in the scene, Paul walked in from another room.

"You're up!" he said in his deep, soothing voice, removing his glasses.

"What happened?" Scribble leaned up but stopped short. She clenched her eyes shut and held the bridge of her nose.

"Well, I thought you might have fainted, but you were snoring. Loudly. So, I brought you up here," Paul said.

"Here?"

"Yeah, this is the apartment above the shop. My family used to live here, but all I use it for now is storing these old books." Paul sat down on the bed next to her. "When was the last time you got any sleep?"

Scribble had never truly considered that the body might need to sleep. In fact, she wasn't even certain how to sleep. Usually, when Paul was asleep, she would take the time to read up on his dossier—what little good it did her. Now, she wouldn't get that extra time to study up on him. "Sleep?"

"Ah, that long, huh?"

"Why does my head hurt?" Scribble moaned rather than asked and ran a hand through her hair. The bun fell apart and her hair fell around her shoulders. Paul had been close to her, but when her breath hit him, he leaned back.

"Whew! From the smell of things, I'd say you have a hangover."

At first, Scribble didn't understand what that word meant, but then she recalled a description from a book that summed up her experience quite accurately. "'The light did him harm, but not as much as looking at things did; he resolved, having done it once, never to move his eyeballs again'." Scribble had started the quote, but Paul joined in before the end.

"*Lucky Jim*, by Kingsley Amis," he said. She would have smiled at him had smiling not also hurt. Paul looked at her with concern. "Where do you live? Is there someone who might be worried about you?" Scribble slowly shook her head. "No one?"

"I haven't been in town long…" she answered. She pulled the hair from her eyes and risked looking up at him. Like before, their eyes met. And like before, she felt that confusing flutter in her chest.

The moment of silence between them stretched. They were mesmerized, at least for a few seconds. When she remembered to breathe, it broke the spell. He cleared his throat and said, "I see. Well, no one's living here. You can stay until you find a place of your own, if you like."

"R-really? But you hardly know me," she protested.

"True, but I'd like to. And it's safer than wandering the streets and bars!"

Scribble felt her ears heat up as a blush formed. "Thank you," she said demurely. Paul gave her a sudden smile filled with warmth. She soon realized that they were looking at each other's lips. His arm was pressed against her side as he leaned closer to her, but the iBad interrupted them with a loud buzz and broke them out of their moment.

"I'll let you get some rest," Paul said while running a hand over his bald head. He fished his glasses out of his shirt pocket and put them on again. "We can start your training tomorrow. And I'll work at moving these books out for you."

Once he left, Scribble lunged for her purse and took out the diabolical phone, then sat up in bed. The screen showed Paul's file with his stats. In the "History" section, there was a flashing "!" icon. Beneath it, it said:

New sin! Lust: Fantasizing.

Scribble held her breath as she saw his estimated soul weight tick from 98 to 99. She smiled, but that faded when another alert popped up on the screen:

Warning! Act of Redemption: Generosity.

This time, the soul weight ticked right back to where it started. Scribble let out an exasperated grunt and fell back on the bed. "I hate that man."

*   *   *

It was past noon when she finally arose. The muffled sounds of conversations floated through the vents on the floor, but no one was around. For several minutes, she lay in bed, her hand on her chest, thinking about what had happened when Paul was close to her. It hadn't happened just once, and it only ever happened around him. She was convinced that it wasn't merely a coincidence.

"There has to be a way to get in touch with Rotworm," she said aloud to no one in particular. She bit her bottom lip as she thought about going through the door to Hell, but didn't know where in Hell he was. He could just as easily be on Earth. As she sat up, Scribble noticed the iBad from the corner of her eye, laying on the bedside table. Names and numbers flipped by on its screen until it stopped on one labeled "Scrapple." As if it had a mind of its own, the smartphone dialed the number.

"Who is this?" Rotworm answered. His angular face appeared on the screen of the iBad with a vaguely familiar background. Scribble dove for the phone and held it in front of her.

"It's me," she said in a hushed voice. She was pretty sure there were no humans around, but she couldn't be certain.

"Me who? Oh, you. Scrubbrush. What do you want? I'm busy."

"I-I just have some questions," Scribble replied. "I'm worried this body isn't working right."

"And what makes you think *I* would know anything about your body?" he asked impatiently.

A slightly wicked smirk formed on Scribble's lips as the image of Rotworm moved to a corner and Rotworm's dossier suddenly opened. "Well, according to this, you used to work for Asmodeus," she said. "Looks like you were an Incubus a few hundred years back. He-he! It says that you were caught trying to seduce an angel once!"

"What?! Sh-shut up! Stop reading that! So what if I used to work for her?"

Scribble was giggling at Rotworm's reaction. His nostrils flared and his forked tongue was starting to show. "Well, I would think you might know a thing or two about these bodies. But if you don't want to help me, maybe Boniface knows someth—"

"That do-gooder? He knows more about committing arson!" Rotworm protested.

"Oh? Are you suuure he can't help?"

Rotworm let out a frustrated sigh. "Fine, what is it you want to know? Just... make it quick."

Scribble grinned victoriously. "Well, I think I've figured out eating, but how often do I have to do it? And why did I fall asleep this morning?"

"Look, your body is essentially human. A succubus gets her energy from men. But I doubt you're going to be able to handle that, so you need to eat a few times a day. Oh, and sleep for about eight hours every night. If you don't, bad things can happen to that body. And trust me, you don't want to return a damaged body to Asmodeus. You haven't bruised it, have you?"

"N-no! But that means I need to find more food." She made a show of grumbling, but the truth was, she rather enjoyed the food she had last night. "Well, what about a hangover? Paul mentioned that I had one when he smelled me earlier. How do I get rid of it?"

Rotworm narrowed his eyes at her. "*Smelled* you? Huh. You may have some hope yet. But this isn't some college fraternity where you can go out drinking every night. Limit yourself to one drink a night at the most! Ugh, I can't *believe* I'm saying this. It's like you're a freshman."

Scribble nodded to the iBad. She'd read about college fraternities, and thought they sounded like fun, if it wasn't for the hangovers. "Okay..."

"Anything else?"

"Just one more thing. Uh, whenever I see Paul... er... the client... I start to feel... strange."

"How so?"

"My pulse races, my face gets hot, and I can't think straight. Is this normal?" Scribble twirled a lock of black hair through her fingers as she spoke.

"Hmmm... sounds to me like Earth-sickness," Rotworm replied.

"Earth-sickness?"

"Earth can do funny things to a demon who stays too long if you aren't used to it. And it takes an expert to inhabit one of those bodies for more than a day at a time without side effects, especially that one." Rotworm was about to say something else when she heard a noise in the background. The image went shaky like he was moving. "I gotta go."

"Wait! What am I supposed to do?" she pleaded.

"Gah! It's probably nothing. You just need an energy boost. Get a human to have sex with you and it'll pass." There was a pause as his expression changed to one of intense interest. "In fact, that could help the client get over its depression. If the client lusts after you, give it a taste. Make it care. And when you have to return the body, make the client think it's his fault things aren't working out. Who knows what sins it'll commit when it's angry?"

Scribble paused in mid-curl as she thought about what he was saying. It hardly registered when Rotworm hung up.

CHAPTER 8 – HELPER

By the time Scribble made it downstairs, the shop had been open for hours. She peeked out of the door that kept the stairs hidden from customers, reluctant to make an appearance. A loud *creak* from the door, however, announced her arrival, making every head in the small, stuffy store turn her way. All six of them. She recognized three—Frank, Ginger, and Paul.

Scribble flushed and ducked her head. The door continued its cry of alarm as she opened it the rest of the way before stepping into the room. All on its own, it closed behind her, the sound sending a shiver through her spine. When it finally clicked into place, she smiled awkwardly at the staring faces and gave a small wave.

"Look who finally showed up for work," Ginger said curtly before turning back to the books she was removing from shelves. Everyone except Paul followed her example and returned to what they had been doing.

Paul stepped out from behind the counter with calculator in hand and a pen nestled firmly behind his ear. "How are you feeling, Dez?" he asked as he walked up to her. A rather smug-looking Boniface sat on his shoulder. Then again, he always looked that way to Scribble.

"Much better. I hope it's all right that I borrowed some clothes." Scribble looked down at the simple V-neck shirt and shorts that she had found in the closet. They were uncomfortable and squeezed at Scribble's borrowed body in unusual places. From the way one of the male customers looked at her, however, it appeared to be having the desired effect.

"It's fine. I know you're new to the area and all, but what about all of your things? I'm sure we could keep them here while you look for your own place."

There was a momentary look of panic on Scribble's face. "My things? I... left them behind. I was trying to make a fresh start. Guess that wasn't too smart." She wasn't very good at lying, but Paul simply nodded in an understanding fashion.

"Well, you can use anything you find. There should be some clothes and things left over from when we lived there."

"Thank you," Scribble said. But as Paul turned to get back to his work, she blurted out, "I'd like to start now... if that's possible."

"You're sure you're feeling up to it?"

"Definitely! I want to be useful!" She was earnest about her desire, even though it came from her fear of letting her boss down.

Paul folded his arms in front of his chest and scrunched up his face in thought. "Well, there is *one* task I've been meaning to do. Your resumé said you've worked with filing systems before? And books?" Scribble nodded but worry worked its way into her thoughts. "Good! Come with me, then."

He walked past her to the door leading upstairs and opened it. He then motioned for her to follow and headed back up to the apartment over the store. Scribble still felt like the eyes of a thousand people watched her as she closed the door behind them, though, in reality, no one paid her any attention. Once she was upstairs, she felt better. Upstairs... alone... with Paul... and a bed. Something sparked in her memory—a romance novel she'd once read. In it, the boss took his secretary behind closed doors, and then the two of them couldn't keep their hands off each other. In private, no one would be able to hear their cries of passion. Scribble didn't really understand it all before, but now that she was in this body and subject to all its strange sensations, she started to get it. She watched Paul carefully, feeling herself getting warmer as she anticipated what was to come. After all, she'd never seen him call Ginger upstairs to be alone with him.

But Paul didn't head towards the room she'd slept in, the one with the bed. Bookshelves and cabinets crowded the main room of the apartment, just like the other room, so that they had to wind their way through them to get to a door on the far side. Scribble hadn't explored the apartment yet and curiosity began replacing her anticipation. He opened the door and the first thing she saw was another bed. *He really does want to be alone with me!* she thought. *Oh no, I don't know how to do this! I should have paid more attention to that "Shades of Gray" book.* However, it wasn't the bed he led her to but rather a desk with a laptop, small glue bottles, a box of wet wipes, and a set of small drawers on top. And next to it, on either side, stood more bookshelves.

"What do you think?" Paul smiled rather proudly, indicating the books that lined the walls of the second bedroom. One cabinet looked older than the others, the hinged glass front that protected its topmost shelf adorned with thin, wrought-iron leaves. Paul used one of the wet wipes to clean his hands, then opened the bookshelf and very gingerly pulled out a book.

That was when the vanilla scent of aging paper and leather bindings hit her like nothing she'd ever experienced in her admittedly short time on Earth. For a moment, she was transported to one of the ancient libraries of antiquity. She forgot all about her need to tempt Paul. "It's incredible," she whispered. The praise lit up Paul's face and he looked truly happy, at home. "Are these part of the store?"

"No. They were my mom's. She collected everything, from Hemmingway to Stephen King, Le Carre to Le Guin. They were being kept at my uncle's house. When she died, he was going to toss them, so I saved them and brought them up here. I know some of them are valuable, so I've been learning how to restore and repair them." As he spoke, he carried the book, a copy of *The Fellowship of the Ring*, over to the desk and lay it open to show off some of the repairs he'd made.

"How valuable are they?" Scribble asked.

"I don't know. That's why I'd like your help. I haven't priced them all. So far, the most expensive is a signed first-edition copy of *Carrie*—about $2000."

It took Scribble a moment to calculate how much that really meant. *That's like 300 Bloody Marys! The books downstairs are only one or two.* "Wow! But I don't understand... how am I going to price them?"

"Ah! Well, that's what the computer is for," he said and turned it on. In seconds, it displayed a website dedicated to rare books. "First, make sure your hands are clean and dry when handling any of the books. Then put in the title, author, publication date, and edition into this database. Oh, and the condition. It has a guide to help you with that."

Scribble pressed against him a little as he showed her where to find all the information needed, and how to record the price of each book in a ledger. Despite being so close to him, her fascination with the books kept tempting him off of her mind.

"What are you going to do with them?" she asked.

"I might sell them. We've been in the red for a while and I need money to renovate and advertise. It's not cheap."

"Sell them? But weren't these your mother's? They're part of your family!"

Paul paused for a moment. "I know. I don't want to. If they're worth enough, maybe I could use them as collateral for a loan." He looked introspective, the way he often did when the air around him would turn cold during a depression, but this time, she didn't feel any change in temperature.

"Well, I don't know what 'collateral' is, but if it means you get to keep them, let's focus on that! I'm sure it'll be enough. I mean, look at how many books you have!" She put her hand against his back and felt a rush go through her body. Paul was leaning back against her, his eyes closed. When he sighed, she remembered the bed just behind them and her legs felt weak.

"Thank you, Dez," he said in a soft voice.

"You can count on me, boss," she replied in an equally soft tone. He looked at her and she felt herself blushing. Never before had she felt the urge to *kiss* someone, but before she could act on that urge, he cleared his throat and looked away.

"You won't get distracted by all these enticing books, will you?" he asked with a boyish grin.

Scribble shook her head as the real world came back to her. "Not at all!"
"Good. Just come down if you need anything. Remember, no reading!"

*   *   *

The temptation to read the books pressed on Scribble's mind. Books had been her only solace when she worked in Purgatory; they were her window into the humans' world. She had managed to keep to her task without too much trouble for a while. But when she ran across an old, illustrated copy of *Pride & Prejudice* from 1899, the desire to fawn over Mr. Darcy overcame her and she was soon at the first chapter.

"It is a truth universally acknowledged, that a single man in possession of a good fortune must be in want of a wife," she read aloud.

"Oh, please. They only want a little action."

The voice was small, feminine, and came from the desk.
"What? Who said that?"

"Or a lot of action. Speaking of which, that boy of yours could use some."

Scribble pulled the chair out from the desk and started opening drawers. "Where are you?"

"I'm on the desk, right where you left me."

She closed the book but all she saw was her iBad, which had been beneath it. When she looked closer, however, she realized that the screen had gone black, all except for a small, cartoonish imp's head. The words

"It's about time!"

appeared just as the voice spoke them.
"You can talk?" Scribble asked.

"Sure sounds that way."

"Do you... have a name?"
The pointed ears on the phone flattened to the sides.

"I'm Surli."

Scribble smirked. "Is that your name or your attitude?"

"What do you think?"

"Why didn't Rotworm tell me you could talk?"

"Hell if I know. I'm just here to ridicule you and offer advice.

55

'Great' job tempting the human, by the way."

Next to Surli's head, two pairs of fingers appeared and gave little quotation motions at the word "great."

Scribble bit her lip.

"Stop doing that... acting all demure. It's unbecoming of a demon. Keep that up and you'll cut your lip open."

"Sorry!" Scribble picked up the book and put it back in its place on the shelf. "I've just never tried to be all tempting like this before. Maybe this was just a big mistake."

"Of course it was a mistake. But it doesn't have to be the end of the world. I just might know a few tricks that'll help."

A feeling of suspicion rose within Scribble. "You'll *help* me?" She walked back over to the desk and peered down at the device. "No one's ever helped me. At least not without demanding something in return."

"Oh, trust me, it's not because I want to. I *have* to. I was programmed that way. Who do you think pulled up Rotworm's files? You're a bookworm... haven't you read any steamy romance novels?"

Scribble smiled a little and nodded.

"I thought so. You're *that* type. So, use some of their tricks! Unbutton that blouse. Put on some make-up. Let down that hair."

"You think that will really work?"

"Of *course* it will work! Here, I've found a few more tips."

Surli moved to the side of the screen as a website opened up. At the top of the page was the title of a magazine Scribble had seen around the store, *Modern Sass.* Surli scrolled down the page with a cartoon finger, opening other pages until she came to an article, "15 Sexy Secrets to Drive Him Wild."

"I'm not sure about this. What if he doesn't like these sorts of things?" Scribble asked as she browsed the article.

"There's no harm in trying, is there? Tell you what, you finish your work here, and tonight, we'll start working on getting him interested in you. If he isn't all over you by the end of the week, we'll try something else. Deal?"

Scribble held the second knuckle of her finger between her teeth while she read. When she'd finished with the article, she nodded. "Deal."

*   *   *

The next day, Scribble woke up early. She had never put on make-up before and didn't want to get it wrong. Surli was propped up on the bathroom countertop giving directions on how to achieve different looks. Images of made-up faces flipped by on the screen. The pictures and directions were so fast and varied, Scribble was soon lost. The result was an excessive amount of blush, dark eyeliner, smoky eye shadow, and ruby-red lipstick.

She headed downstairs as soon as she heard the front door open. Paul was making his way to the register. Although he held a folded newspaper in front of his face, he managed to maneuver around piles of books and loose magazines as he read.

"Good morning!" Scribble said brightly, her hands clasped behind her to help her push her bust forward a little. Unlike the night before, she had made sure to leave two buttons of the blouse open, giving a tantalizing view of her cleavage. Her hair was up in a bun, held in place by a pencil. This was a trick, Surli insisted, that no bookworm boy could resist.

Paul resisted. "I didn't think you'd be up already. I was sort of on auto-pilot there. Good morning." He gave her an awkward smile and walked past her to the counter, putting down a bag he'd been holding in his other hand. "You look... different. Did you sleep well?"

"Oh, um, yes. I think so," she answered, though truth be told, she wasn't entirely sure how good she was at sleeping. It was not a skill used in the afterlife. Being unconscious for hours at a time was both disconcerting and, in its own way, pleasant.

"This morning, I realized that I don't have any food up there for you. If you could make a list of what you need, I'll pick it up for you. In the meantime, I've... what are you doing?"

Scribble was leaning against the counter, pushing her breasts together with her arms. When Paul's brow raised questioningly, she let out a soft, "Oh, yeah..." and reached up to pull the pencil from her hair. She tried to toss her hair gorgeously around, but without having much practice at it, she ended up with a face full of hair instead.

"Are you *sure* you got enough sleep?"

Scribble brushed most of the hair out of her face and nodded. "Sorry. I was just, uh, trying a new look."

"A new look, huh? Well, I wasn't used to your old look yet," he said. After a small pause, he ran his hand over his head and pushed the bag towards her. "Hungry?" When she opened it, the scent of cheese, eggs, and bagel brought her hunger to her attention.

57

"Famished," she said and presently forgot all about trying to be seductive. Instead, she pulled out the bagel sandwich and stuffed it into her mouth almost like she was trying to see how few bites she could eat it in.

Paul raised his eyebrow. "I can see that. Did you have anything to eat last night?"

Scribble looked up at him with puffed cheeks and shook her head. She swallowed hard. "Mmm, no, I forgot! I was so busy with the books and... stuff."

"Oh? How far did you get?" he asked, turning back to his paper. The slight smile that had appeared on his face seemed empty to Scribble, like the ones he would give when he didn't want others to know how he felt. It wasn't at all like the ones he'd given her the day before.

"I finished," Scribble said before taking another substantial bite.

"With the bookshelf?"

"No, with all of them."

"*All* of them?" Paul asked, some surprise in his voice.

"Um... yes?"

"I was expecting it to take you a week at least! Let me see." He went upstairs, leaving Scribble to eat in solitude for a moment. When he returned, he held the ledger and was flipping through its pages.

"That's amazing," he said. "You really *did* do it all. And this is really thorough, too. I'm impressed!" A genuine smile cracked through his glum demeanor. "Hmmm, the numbers aren't bad. It might just be enough." He glanced up at her while she took the last bite of her breakfast. "You've got egg on you," he said and pointed to his cheek.

Scribble reached for the opposite cheek, missing the egg.

"No, it's... it's here." Paul reached up and brushed the errant piece of egg away, causing a burst of color to spring in her cheeks.

"So... wh-what now?" Scribble asked nervously. All the lessons Surli had been teaching her about how to be forward and alluring just disappeared. But whatever she had been doing seemed to work. Paul began to loosen up and smile more.

"Well, I guess your training starts now. You'll be following Ginger or me around for the most part. She should be here soon. Don't be nervous! If you have any questions, one of us can help you. So, here's the register. This key turns it on. *Voila!* You won't have to worry too much about this until you start opening for us."

Scribble paid close attention to all Paul taught her, from how to make a sale to what to do if a customer returned a book. She took her training seriously. Before she knew it, it was closing time and Scribble spent the evening looking over a list of the store's inventory. The next morning Paul once again greeted her at the bottom of the stairs, but this time, he brought groceries up to the apartment before opening the store. Nearly an hour passed with just the two of them before the iBad in her pocket vibrated violently while Paul was showing her where to find the supplies in the back room. Scribble pulled the iBad out and saw Surli on the screen.

"What are you waiting for, the Second Coming?"

was printed next to the impish face. Surli looked put out.

"A text?" Paul asked.

"What? No. Yes." Scribble smiled and pushed the "off" button, despite the silent protests of Surli. "It's nothing."

"I don't have a problem with you using your phone during working hours, as long as there aren't any customers around and no work to do." Paul winked at her. "Which hopefully won't be very often. Say, have you seen that notepad you put those numbers in yesterday?"

Scribble returned the device to her pocket and shook her head. They searched around the desk together. Once again, they were alone. His hand gripped the desk while he leaned down to look under it. She couldn't get her eyes off it.

That's right, humans like to hold hands. They're always trying to do that in those books. Scribble leaned over the desk, making a pretense at reaching for papers on top of the filing cabinet. Her hand moved slowly along the desk towards his. After what she felt was a sufficiently long build-up, she let her hand slide over his.

Paul didn't react, at least not the way she thought he would. When he finished looking through the desk's drawers, he simply moved his hand away with an apologetic smile. Scribble let out a soft huff of exasperation. Determined, she put her hand back on his, where it belonged.

"What's all this?" Ginger asked as she came in through the door. Instantly, Scribble jerked her hand away and turned her back on them. She tried to look like she was too busy to notice where her hand had been and pulled on one of the filing cabinet drawers, but it was locked.

"Ginger! Good morning. We're just looking for that notepad Dez was using a couple nights ago. You know, the one with last month's figures in it."

Scribble pulled harder. The cabinet knocked loudly against another and she winced, not daring to look away from it.

"I thought you put it in the desk," Ginger suggested.

"I did too, but it's not there now. After I left, did you close or Frank?"

The more she pulled, the more disheveled Scribble's hair became. She strained against the cabinet, tried to twist the handle, hit it on the side, rocked it back and forth, but all she managed to do was make sure everyone's attention was on her. When she finally gave up and glanced over at the others, their mouths were agape. Ginger walked over to her and pressed on a small button next to the drawer's handle. It opened easily.

"Oh! A button. Of course. Th-thanks," Scribble said.

"Uh-huh…" Ginger replied.

Scribble brushed her hair out of her face and realized they were still staring. "Um… good morning," she said and rummaged through the files briefly. "It's not in here. You know… I think I remember everything I wrote. I could rewrite it for you."

"Really? You've got all sorts of hidden talents. That would be a huge help! Thank you, Dez," Paul said. "But I still need last month's figures. How about you go and help Ginger open in the front while I figure things out back here?"

*   *   *

Scribble watched Ginger's hair as it swung in time to the girl's perky gait. They headed to the front of the store but stopped among the shelves.

"Look, I don't know you, and I don't know what you were up to back there, but don't get any funny ideas about Paul. I've known him for years. He's a close friend of mine, and right now, he's vulnerable. The last thing I'm going to do is let him get hurt again, understood?"

Scribble stepped back. "U-understood. Vulnerable?"

Ginger waved her hand dismissively. "Forget about him; focus on your job. First, you need to flip the open sign. Then we need to deal with your hair."

Already feeling self-conscious that she was caught by Ginger and unable to make much headway with Paul, Scribble just did what Ginger told her without a word. In fact, she found it hard to get out of her slump the entire morning. She thought that working at a bookstore would be exciting. Books were contraband in Purgatory, stolen from Earth, so her selection had been rather limited. She was already surprised at just how many books the store had and looked forward to reading them all. But the excitement faded quickly when she discovered she wouldn't get the time to actually read any of them. Instead, she needed to take books off of shelves, put other books back on shelves, scan books with a funny-looking gun, and clean the bathroom. Although Paul had spent most of the morning on the phone, writing on a new notepad, or pacing back and forth as he crunched numbers on his calculator, there were a few brief moments where Scribble had a chance to talk to him without Ginger's penetrative stare. Ginger confused her. One moment, she gave vague threats, the next, she showed Scribble how to put in a ponytail.

That morning had the demon's mind so preoccupied that she was utterly incapable of doing more than smiling at him while playing with her own hair.

Just before lunch, Scribble realized that one of the few customers who walked in had been lingering in the Self-Help section for quite a while. He was a tall man in a black coat, but his back was turned the entire time, so she couldn't make out any further details.

"Can I help you with something?" she asked, trying to sound as chipper and upbeat as Ginger usually did.

The figure slowly turned. It was Incubus. He appeared more massive than she remembered—stronger, imposing, and with a stare that shot straight through to the core of her. "You are the one who will need help if you continue like this." With that, he walked out of the store, leaving Scribble feeling small and pale behind him.

Chapter 9 – Raven

Fear followed a step behind Scribble no matter what she did to try to shake it off. She withdrew herself more, following Ginger's orders in a subservient manner. Whenever she was in the aisles, she tried to keep her back to the wall so that Incubus couldn't sneak up on her if he decided to show up again.

Some time had passed since she'd been given instructions. Ginger was busy on her phone, and Paul was writing on his notepad. There were no customers, so Scribble moved to the Fantasy section and grabbed a book she'd had her eye on all day, *Tempter's Kiss*. She was immediately transported into the world of Talia, the young vampiress who was in love with her master's arch-nemesis, Drake. She got so into it that she had lost all track of time. Before she realized it, the sky outside had turned dark.

"Paul, I want to go out tonight. Can we go to *The Gray Raven*?" Ginger asked. It took Paul a moment to break out of his concentration and register what she asked him. He looked up at the clock hanging behind the counter.

"Oh, geez, it's later than I thought. We need to close up."

Ginger smiled and walked to the front of the store to flip the 'open' sign to 'closed.' "Yes, but, what about tonight? The *Raven*?"

Scribble peeked her head out from the aisles. She knew her grasp of human emotions was not very strong, so she watched them for a while, silently, to learn what she could. Ginger leaned against the counter, offering Paul a brilliant smile while he evaded her gaze and her question.

"How do you think Desdemona did?" he asked as he opened the cash register and began counting up the money.

Ginger puffed her lips into a playful pout and leaned forward on the counter. "She did fine. A bit awkward at times. So, can we go?"

As Ginger leaned over, it put her bust on display. Scribble's eyes widened as she remembered trying that same move on him just that morning. *She likes him?!* The thought made her feel sick to the stomach.

"I don't know... I was hoping to get home and have some time alone tonight," Paul said.

"You do that every night," Ginger retorted. "I can't even remember the last time I saw you at the *Raven*! Come on, please?"

Scribble saw the empty smile settle on his features and she suddenly remembered what she'd read in her free time about the symptoms of depression. 'Never going out' was at the top of the list. Both Rotworm and

Boniface told her how important it was to help him, plus the warning from Incubus remained fresh in her mind.

"Um, I'd like to go. With both of you. Maybe show me around some?" she said.

Paul looked up at her and his smile changed ever so slightly, but enough. He put down the notepad. "Well, I suppose we could show you," he conceded.

A short gasp of protest sounded from Ginger but she quickly swallowed it. Scribble was so excited, she was bouncing up and down on her toes. "Well then, let's go!"

*   *   *

The Gray Raven was an old bar, the kind where everything was made of iron or wood—not out of style or choice but because when it was built, options were limited. The aggregate sum of over a hundred years' worth of traditional cooking left an indelible scent on every surface. Despite its age, however, it had its share of modern conveniences. On one end of the large, mahogany bar sat a countertop arcade machine with a middle-aged man in front of it. A flat-screen TV hung in a corner showing a baseball game, but the classic rock that played over the speaker system drowned out the sound of the TV. The bartender—a pierced, toned, and heavily tattooed woman who was attractive despite, or perhaps because of, her gruff demeanor—used a computer screen to punch in orders. The mix of old and new seemed to draw a sizeable crowd. Only a few tables were empty. At the far end of the place, the pool tables were surrounded by people talking and laughing and having a good time. Scribble thought it was odd that none of them were actually playing pool.

"Hey, Paul! Long time no see. How's business?" the bartender asked as the trio approached the bar. Her simple black tank top had its share of stains.

"Yeah, sorry it's been a while, Naomi. You know how it is. Same old, same old. How about you?" Paul ran his hand over his smooth scalp and settled down on one of the bar stools. Ginger and Scribble joined him, one on either side.

Naomi leaned against the counter with a serious expression. "What does it look like? Slow as Hell, again. But it's always slow on Tuesday night. So, who's your friend?"

"This is Desdemona Scribble. She's new to the area. Just hired her. Dez, this is Naomi."

Scribble was distracted and confused. "This is a slow night?" she asked, looking around at all the patrons.

Naomi arched a thin eyebrow. "Yeah. Just you three, Bob," she said, pointing to the man at the arcade, "and that couple of tables over there. And me. What is that, ten? You feeling alright, hon?"

Scribble looked back at her and nodded. "Yeah, sorry. It's just been a long day."

"I think what she's trying to say," Ginger interjected, "is that we've had even fewer customers."

One of the other patrons walked just behind Scribble—and through one of the tables on her way to a group in the corner. It was then that Scribble realized she was the only one who could see most of them. Angels and demons were everywhere, unaccompanied by any human. Some of them had formed cliques that stuck together, but there were a few groups where both angels and demons talked with each other. Civilly. From what she could hear, they talked a lot about humans. At the door, she noticed a member of the Order—a six-armed angel dressed in full regalia, though she held three billy clubs rather than any traditional weapons. Despite her small stature, she was the most intimidating bouncer Scribble could think of.

"Imagine seeing *you* here, Sybil." Rotworm appeared from the crowd and sat down next to Scribble. His forked tongue slithered from his grin briefly.

"What is going on?" she whispered. She tried to keep up with the conversation that was going on between Naomi, Paul, and Ginger, but the din of supernatural conversations made it hard to hear what they were saying. Rotworm's proximity made it impossible. Scribble pulled out her iBad with an apologetic smile at the humans and put it up to her ear.

"Oh, this? *The Gray Raven* is a safe zone. More or less. I wouldn't pick a fight here if I were you." He nodded over to the bouncer at the door. "She has some mean left hooks and doesn't tolerate trouble. After all, we've been coming here to unwind for a century."

"There are safe zones?" she asked softly.

Rotworm smirked. "A few. We don't advertise them much."

"Has Boniface ever...?"

The laugh that came from Rotworm brought quite a bit of attention to them, but he didn't seem to mind. In fact, Scribble was sure he reveled in it. "*That* stick in the mud?"

Scribble quickly looked around with fear in her eyes. "Incubus?"

"No. I doubt he even knows about this place." He scooted closer to her and spoke in a softer, almost seductive voice. "So, how was it?"

"How was what?"

"The client!"

"Oh! I don't... we haven't... I'm working on it!"

His grin faded. "Working on it? You better work faster. Listen, that body of yours won't hold up forever. Without a practiced succubus in there, you've probably got a couple of weeks, a month tops! What's holding you back? You've got the looks!" He nudged her. It wasn't a simple push of a spirit against spirit; this had real, physical force behind it. She nearly fell out of the chair but managed to grab onto Paul to catch herself.

Paul looked at her with some worry. "Are you okay?"

"Yeah, just not used to these chairs," Scribble said. She pushed away from Paul, but in doing so, felt how strong and warm his body was. It felt good to touch and hold. After a moment, Ginger leaned back on her stool and peered over at her. That twisting, churning feeling in Scribble's gut told her she didn't *want* to let Ginger have him.

"That was it?" Rotworm growled under his breath. He glanced back at the bouncer as if to make sure she wasn't after him for practically shoving Scribble. "You saw Grimtooth. You know what will happen to you if you fail. Hell, if you take too long or injure that body, Asmodeus will get angry with you, and you couldn't imagine what she's like when she's angry. Really, I doubt you could imagine it... she's quite inventive. You better not let her find out that you've been wasting your time just flirting with the client."

"Incubus was there," she said as she got back into her chair and put the phone to her ear again.

"What?!" he spat. "Asmodeus must really prize that body if she's got him tailing you already. Hasn't it only been a couple of days?" Rotworm leaned back and adjusted his suit.

"Rotworm? What Hell-hole did you slink out of?"

It was a female voice with not a small amount of spite in it. He froze in place and cursed under his breath before turning around. "Sly... I can—"

"You bastard!" The slap across his face hushed the crowd into a tentative silence. Every Immortal eye turned and watched with keen interest, like they *wanted* some raucous scene for entertainment.

Scribble gasped and lowered her head, but looked out of the corner of her eye. Standing in a war stance before a hunched-over Rotworm, a shapely demoness fixed her scornful eyes on him. Some of her long, black hair had whipped around into her face. Even after she brushed it out of the way, strands of it remained, caught behind one of her slender, hooked horns. She wore a black dress that fit her form perfectly and ended around mid-thigh. "How *dare* you just leave me like that! And not a word since!"

All eyes turned to the bouncer. She already held a club at the ready and had made it halfway over to them when she stopped short and looked the offending demoness up and down, then Rotworm.

"Ugh. Have at him, honey," she offered, returning to her post.

"What? What did I ever do to you, Rosemary?" he called out, holding his hand to his cheek.

"It's Marigold, you dolt," the angel answered, but left his question unanswered.

Rotworm lowered his hand and opened his arms in a welcome invitation. "Slytongue, that was centuries ago," he sleazed, but paused and got lost in thought briefly before nodding. "*Centuries.*" When she failed to correct his name, Scribble wondered if he'd actually gotten it *right*.

Slytongue straightened herself and looked him over. The tension in the air grew as the crowd waited for the expected strike, but she just folded her arms and shifted her weight over one leg. "You're looking well." A chorus of disappointment came from the crowd and they returned to their various conversations.

"Why, thank you." Rotworm adjusted his suit a second time. "And you know why I left Asmodeus' employment. I doubt it was much of a surprise."

She gave a huff, but a smile cracked her lips. "I still say you were just avoiding me," she teased as she hugged him, trapping his arms awkwardly at his sides. Scenes of affection between demons happened so infrequently, Scribble couldn't remember the last time she'd seen one. A moment later, however, the affection faded and Scribble became the object of her distaste. "Who is she? She's not a succubus."

"Her?" Rotworm looked at Scribble like he'd forgotten she was even there. "Oh, she's no one important. I doubt she'll be around longer than—"

Slytongue gasped. "How did she get *that body?*" She glanced around before speaking more quietly. "*I've* been asking Asmodeus to let me use that body for *years!* How the Hell did *this* bitch get it?"

"I-I made a deal..." Scribble said into the smartphone, glancing at Paul, Naomi, and Ginger. Their chat kept them engrossed.

"You?" Rotworm said to Slytongue incredulously. "I can't imagine Asmodeus would let you within a thousand leagues of her most prized model—not after what you did last time." The succubus looked at him inquisitively. "Sicily. 1282."

She giggled. "Oh yeah, that was fun. I didn't expect all the killing, though. Has it really been *that* long?" When she looked back to Scribble, that mirth she showed Rotworm again disappeared. "Don't you dare get a scratch on that body. It's mine when you're done with it."

"I'm taking care of—"

"Ugh, you're not even feeding it right." Being constantly interrupted would have made Scribble upset if she hadn't felt so small, even smaller than when she was a normal imp. "Just give it to me. I'll get it the energy it needs, and you can go crawling back to Hell where you belong." She moved next to Scribble, a hand on her shoulder.

"I can't!" Scribble said and tried to lean away from her. A sense of panic began to color all her thoughts.

Laughter erupted from around the pool table. A purple demon with bent horns crouched low to the ground. Behind him, a group of demons sniggered and egged him on. Slowly, he snuck up behind a circle of angels and reached for one of their halos.

"Is he *trying* to get in trouble?" Rotworm asked.

A grin curled Slytongue's lips. "Yeah, lost a bet. Come on, I want to get a closer look." She pulled on Rotworm's hand, but when he didn't move, she let go and disappeared into the crowd without him.

The demon snatched the halo and ran to the other side of the pool table. It didn't even take a second for the angel to take notice and begin scanning the room for the culprit, who was acting nonchalant.

Rotworm turned and leaned over Scribble. "Do not fail me," he whispered menacingly. "Make Boniface suffer and stay on Asmodeus' good side because you don't want to see *my* bad side. Tick-tock, girl." He shoved her again before walking to the pool room.

"Dez?"

Scribble blinked and glanced up to see Paul and Naomi looking back at her expectantly. She hadn't kept up with their conversation at all. In fact, feigning interest was the last thing on her mind. Slytongue had frazzled her nerves completely. She felt lost and scared, and from the way Paul suddenly took an interest in her, she probably looked lost and scared as well. A raucous clamor from the pool tables caught her attention. Rotworm stood in the crowd, staring at her. When Paul put a hand on her shoulder, she stiffened, thinking Slytongue had returned to take the body from her. And in her growing anxiety, she thought for an instant that she saw Incubus sitting at one of the tables before turning his back on her. Muttering a soft apology, Scribble slipped from the stool and did what came so naturally to her when confronted.

She ran away.

CHAPTER 10 – NOT-A-DATE

The autumn breeze nipped lightly at Scribble's skin. There were no thoughts in her head other than the desire to escape. Hell was certainly not safe, Purgatory no longer had a place for her, and the apartment above the store was the first place people would expect her to go. So, instead, she walked aimlessly down the street, intent on getting lost.

"Dez! Where are you going? Wait up!" Paul called from behind her. She had only made it to the end of the block by the time he caught up to her.

A swell of emotions filled Scribble when she saw that he was alone. He'd left Ginger behind just to see if she was all right. No one had ever cared if she was all right in the past. The intensity of it hit her so hard, she lost her breath and tears welled in her eyes. She was crying. This was an entirely new experience for her. Reading about it did not do it justice. Though she wanted to pull away from him and hide, she instead ended up leaning against his strong chest, welcoming his presence.

Paul slowly put his hand on her back and began to rub. When the sobbing subsided, he said, "I'm sorry, Dez. I was so caught up in talking with everyone, I didn't realize we were ignoring you."

"It's not that. I'm just... scared."

"Of what? Was it your phone call?"

"I've just never been on my own like this before. I'm worried I'm going to fail. And I don't really have anyone I can turn to." She pulled back and sniffled, keeping her head down so that her black hair covered her eyes.

There was a moment of silence between them as Paul appeared to be scanning the ground. When he spoke, his voice was soft, shy. "Well, you can turn to me," he said. "I know we hardly know each other, but I'd like it if we could be friends. Maybe it's divine providence that brought you to the store."

"Divine? You believe in God?" she asked him.

"I'm not sure. I think there's just too much for everything to be a coincidence. There's got to be *something* more than this, right?"

Scribble smiled a little and nodded. "Probably."

"When I saw you needed help, it was like there was a little voice telling me I should help you."

She looked up at him with a dumbfounded expression. Boniface was nowhere around, but she was sure he was the one behind that voice. "I feel like such an idiot, trying to get your attention like I did."

Paul raised his dark eyebrow. "Oh, is that what you were doing? Trying to get my attention?" The tightness in his body slackened. "Well, tomorrow is Wednesday, our slowest day. So, we stay closed. How about you and me spend the day getting to know each other?"

"Like a date?" Scribble asked. Dates seemed to be a major deal when it came to romance novels and *Modern Sass* articles.

Paul let out a breath. "Not a date, more like a day out with a friend," he said, though Scribble felt he was trying to convince himself. Contrary to his words, his hand reached to hers and held it. "But promise me something. Be the Desdemona that ogled the books, not the one that ogled me." His touch was surprisingly intimate and familiar.

Scribble's heart beat a little faster. "You saw that, huh? Alright, deal."

When she squeezed his hand, he smiled shyly. "So, tomorrow around lunchtime? We'll do whatever you want. Coming back in to the bar?"

She shook her head. "I think I'll turn in, but thanks. Tomorrow!" The feeling of dread subsided on her walk back to the store. In its place shone that shy smile of his. Somehow, this not-a-date had changed everything.

*　　　*　　　*

Surli was not very good at coming up with potential outings, even though she'd had all night and most of the morning to think of one.

"How about a movie?"

Scribble's eyes crossed a little as the word plucked on a memory, but she couldn't recall it. "Movie?"

The sass in Surli's response turned up to 11.

"Mammon spare us. Seriously? Mo-vie. You know, like a play you can watch whenever you want."

"Oh. Oh! Like in those boxes I've seen humans use. TVs!"

"...Yes. Only, you can also watch them in a movie theater. Theaters can get dark, perfect for some fooling around. I've found five in your area..."

"I don't know... If we don't fool around, wouldn't we just be spending a bunch of time watching a screen indoors. No talking? No moving around? No, thanks," Scribble replied as she sorted through the clothes that hung in the closet. She held two shirts up in front of her and turned to Surli, who was propped up on the bed against the pillow.

Scribble looked down at her body. She was wearing only panties and a bra, a device she felt she was starting to master and wondered at times what diabolical mind had dreamed them up. Her skin was pale and flawless, her figure toned. She was sure she would look great in a bikini, but somehow, the thought of parading herself in front of a bunch of people made her nervous and self-conscious. It wasn't even technically *her* body, but with each passing day, she felt more and more attached to it.

She quickly pulled on the red shirt. "I don't feel comfortable doing that."

Sweat drops appeared on the iBad's screen next to the emoji of Surli's head, which displayed a panicked expression.

"I don't want something romantic! Or sexy, or flirty, or anything like that! I'm running out of time and... to be honest, I'm starting to have second thoughts about this whole job. I just want to forget about Incubus and Rotworm and everything and... have a good time. Maybe something will happen, maybe not. I can try to tempt him again tomorrow."

Surli's long ears lowered.

"So have I." Scribble let out a sigh and returned to the closet to pick out a pair of pants. "You wouldn't blame me if I ran away tomorrow instead, would you?" The bell above the shop door jingled and Scribble's eyes went wide. "He's here!" she said, rushing to put on the first pair of jeans she came across.

As she spoke, Surli's tone shifted from mock-matronly to suggestive.

"Thanks." Scribble stashed the iBad in her pocket and darted downstairs, nearly losing her glasses in the rush. Before opening the door at the bottom she paused, took several deep breaths, and tried to calm herself, but to no avail. The moment she opened the door, her stomach twisted with excitement.

Paul was standing in an aisle, a book in his hands. He hadn't noticed her yet, but was instead engrossed in what he was reading. Scribble tucked her hair behind an ear as she snuck closer to him. Her eyes fell to the book—it was *Tempter's Kiss*. It looked like he had read some way into it.

"You're a fast reader," Scribble said, walking up to him with a schoolgirl smile on her lips.

"What? Oh! This? N-no, I just found it on the floor. I... uh..." Paul paused before smiling in embarrassment. "Actually, I've read it before. I know it's a cheesy vampire romance, but it's one of my favorite cheesy vampire romances."

Scribble smirked and nudged him playfully in the side. "Really? What's your favorite part?"

"It's where Talia betrays Drake to get back on—"

"She does what?!" Scribble asked and pulled the book from his hands, quickly reading the open page. "Oh, Talia! You idiot!"

"Ah! You aren't there yet," Paul said. "Sorry."

She shook her head. "It's all right. I know they'll end up together in the end, anyway. It's how all these sorts of stories go."

"Not *all* of them," Paul replied.

Scribble smiled at him and put the book back on the shelf. "Well, it's how this one will end."

"Oh? You sound so sure of yourself," he teased. "You must read a lot."

"Mm-hmm. It's all I ever did, some days. Books let me see so many places I'd never get to visit for real."

One of Paul's eyebrows lifted. "Have you ever critiqued a book before? You know, pointed out the flaws and strong points?" She shook her head in response. "You'd probably be good at it. Maybe I'll have you critique my screenplay when it's done."

"So, you actually did write a screenplay? I'd love to look at it."

After a pregnant pause, he changed the subject. "Sorry I'm late, Dez. I was talking with Frank about the missing notepad and money. It's just a fiasco. He swears he hasn't seen either. Maybe I should install a camera. Frank says, 'Hi,' by the way."

Scribble nodded absently. That feeling Rotworm had called "lust" grew within her, but she was learning to ignore it. She had been so focused on ignoring it that she wasn't aware of how she was gazing at him. When he cleared his throat, however, she snapped out of it.

"Um, he'll be by later to move the bookshelves down to the storage room," Paul said. "But enough about work. This is your day in the city. Where do you want to go?"

Her swirling gray eyes lit up. "Everywhere!"

*   *   *

The afternoon sun was bright and warm on Scribble's skin as she walked through the park with Paul—a welcome relief from the progressively colder days. They'd already spent several hours at the mall, but it was so stuffy and enclosed that Scribble suggested they go outside. It reminded her too much of her previous job in Hell. The park, however, was nothing like the stagnant office she used to work in. They strolled down a path that meandered alongside a large pond.

"Thank you for taking me shopping, Paul! I hope people like the dress I bought," she said with a bright smile. Paul grinned and shifted the large paper bag from the department store to his other hand.

"As long as you like it, that's all that matters... you do like it, right?"

"I do! Someone should have told me how fun it is to go shopping! Thank you for the suggestion."

"Well, you *have* been borrowing my mom's old clothes. I thought you might want to find some new outfits while you wait for your things to arrive."

"Your mom's clothes?" she asked. She winced as she realized that the entire time she had been trying to seduce him, she'd been dressed like his mother. "I didn't realize! No wonder I was making you feel awkward."

Paul looked ahead along the pathway. "It's okay. If you want them, you can keep them. But it's about more than the clothes. I... had a girlfriend who died a year ago yesterday. I'm just not ready to move on, you know?" His voice caught a little as he spoke.

"Danielle?" Scribble asked.

"Yeah. How'd you know?"

"Oh. I think I saw the name in the apartment somewhere..."

Paul eyed her curiously. "Well, it was really hard on me." He clenched his jaw and became lost in thought.

Up ahead, Scribble saw a street vendor. "I've never had ice cream before," she said, desperate to break the growing tension.

"Hm? Never had ice cream? You're joking, right?" Scribble shook her head in response. "You had a deprived childhood."

"You have no idea," Scribble said off-handedly. They walked together to the vendor, a middle-aged man with a small paper hat, and began to order.

"I've got this," Paul said as he pulled out his wallet.

The iBad in Scribble's pocket vibrated. When she pulled it out, Surli's cartoon head was winking while she printed some words on the screen:

"If he pays, it's a date!"

"Um... are you sure? We don't want this to look like a date or anything, right?" She pulled the fake credit card out and gestured toward the vendor.

"It's your first taste of ice cream and you paid for everything at the mall. Besides, payday isn't until Friday," Paul reasoned. It seemed he was doing everything he could to make the outing feel more like a date than it was supposed to be.

"Thanks," she replied softly, putting the card back in place. The vendor leaned over into his freezer cart and emerged with a pair of pre-wrapped ice cream cones. As he and Paul dealt with payment, Scribble took hers and slowly unwrapped it. The ice cream was stiff and followed the same conical course that the cone beneath took, making it harder for Scribble to tell where one ended and the other began. She stuck out her tongue and touched it to the white, briefly. Then she let the taste roll around her mouth. Within seconds, she was making pleasurable moans and licking all around the cone. However, when she bit into it, the intense cold rushed through her teeth, filled her mouth, and moved from her palate up into her head.

"Mmff!" She winced and held her hand to her forehead. When she opened her eyes again, she noticed that both Paul and the vendor were staring at her. She hadn't been aware of the display she was giving them.

The vendor recovered first. "Ice cream headache? You should slow down!"

"'Ice cream headache?' Does it always do this?"

Paul stopped staring at her and shook his head. "Only if you eat it too quickly. Sure you're not from outer space or something?" he teased.

The headache started to subside. "I don't think so. Do they not have ice cream there, either?"

At first, Paul was dumbfounded, but then he began to laugh. To Scribble, it was a beautiful sound that made her forget all about Rotworm and Incubus and even the fact that this wasn't a date. She smiled and walked a little closer to him as they headed down the paved pathway once again.

The day slowly wore on, much to Scribble's satisfaction. That is, until they spied the indoor ice rink. It was far colder than Scribble had anticipated. As far as she was concerned, ice was something that belonged in drinks and nowhere else. Whatever human first decided to strap knives to their feet and try to walk on it must have been laughed out of their village. Even though Paul was holding both of her hands, and she was standing as still as she could manage in the middle of the rink, she felt they were already moving too fast.

"A-are you sure this is safe?" she asked. Her grip was so strong that her knuckles were white.

Paul chuckled. "I've been skating since I was five." He looked into her eyes with an almost mischievous grin and began to skate backwards, pulling her forward across the ice at a snail's pace. Her cries of protest echoed around the large building.

"Holy crap! You're going too fast! Don't move!" Despite her apprehension, the faster he pulled her along, the wider her smile became. There were even moments when she giggled. Thankfully, there were very few people at the skating rink that day, so they had most of the ice to themselves.

"You're doing great! Want to go faster?" Paul wrested one hand free and picked up speed. "Look up at me, not down at your feet. Good. Now, push off with one foot, then the other."

Scribble tried to do as she was told, but she hadn't figured out how to balance on one foot for the microsecond it took between push-off and glide, so instead, the foot she pushed off with just drifted further and further behind her until she was nearly doing the splits. She fell forward into Paul, who remained steady as a rock.

"When I said I wanted to try something exciting, I didn't mean deadly!" she said as he helped her get her feet under her again.

"I won't let you get hurt. It just takes practice."

"Easy to say... when you've been doing it... since you were five."

Paul started to skate backwards again, this time, more slowly. Scribble leaned into him, letting him bear a good deal of her weight. "I used to come every week. I even got my own pair of skates once, but I didn't get to use them much." His voice changed subtly, but Scribble wasn't sure what it meant.

"Why not?" she asked.

That empty look appeared on his face quickly, but this time, he didn't stop talking. "My parents separated a few days after I got them. I was 10 or 11. I didn't have much time to go skating after that because I had to take care of my mom. Mom eventually sold them. She didn't like things cluttering up the apartment. But that was a long time ago. Sorry, I didn't mean to bring up something so depressing. I don't usually talk about it much."

They slowed down and were soon leaning against the edge of the ice rink. Scribble wondered if every not-a-date between friends went this way, but she realized that she genuinely wanted to know more about him. "I don't mind," she said, adjusting her glasses. "I'd like to hear more about you."

"Well, what about you? What was your family like?"

"I don't have a family." She hadn't meant to tell the truth—it just came out.

"An orphan?"

Scribble nodded.

"So, that's why you wanted to make a fresh start. Don't you miss anyone back home?"

This caught Scribble by surprise. She thought back on her incalculable tenure in Purgatory, her various officemates. She couldn't say she *missed* any of them. But one name, one face, came back to her. "Val."

"Another orphan?"

She blinked in surprise at his question. "I said that out loud, huh? Yeah. We did everything together. But then we got in a big fight and I ran away."

"Don't you want to go back and apologize?"

Scribble shook her head lightly. "It's too late for that." Something tugged at her heart—a palpable sensation that she had never experienced before. The more she thought about Valerius, the more it filled her. It wasn't like the sadness she had felt earlier, but it wasn't exactly pleasant. "I… would like to see him again, though."

"You're crying," Paul said.

A tear fell down her cheek, and when she looked up at him, everything was blurry. She took off her glasses and wiped her face as a sad smile formed. "Sorry. I don't know why. Think we could head back to the apartment?"

"You don't want dinner first?"

Scribble shook her head. "I'm not really hungry anymore."

It had grown dark by the time they left the ice rink but Scribble had hardly noticed. She was too engrossed in their conversation to care. The two of them talked about every subject she could think of, from books to places they wanted to visit to terrible jokes to their goals and hobbies. She didn't want it to end. Even though the store looked foreboding without any lights on, their laughter scared away any frightening thoughts. Paul pulled the keys out of his pocket and approached the door.

"I like the talkative you!" Scribble said. "Thanks for walking me back. I had... what's wrong?"

Paul pushed against the door and it swung open. "It wasn't latched. Do you think Frank forgot to close it all the way when he was done?"

"I don't know." Scribble felt as if the bottom of her heart had given out. "Do you think someone broke in?"

"Nothing looks broken. Who would pick the lock in the middle of the day? Must've been Frank." Straightening himself up to his full height, he walked into the store. He flipped the switch. Artificial, cold light flooded the room. Scribble stayed in the doorway, a hand to her chest. She was too scared to actually enter. When she thought about it, she knew a demon didn't really have any reason to be frightened. Somehow, it didn't change how she felt.

Paul took a few steps inside and picked out a hardcover book from a shelf, brandishing it in both hands as if it could smite any possible intruder. "I'm calling the cops!" he yelled into the room in a booming voice, then fell silent. They both listened but only heard the moaning of the pipes in the walls.

"Is it safe?" Scribble asked.

"I think so." Paul walked through the aisles for a moment, scanning them. He checked the register, then disappeared into the back room for a few seconds, long enough to look around. When he came back out, he looked satisfied that nothing had been pilfered and waved for Scribble to enter.

She moved slowly. Fear was never far from her. Despite Paul having just checked, she looked around the corner of every aisle she passed.

"I'll need to bring this up with Frank." Paul sounded relieved as he walked with her to the door to the apartment. "I should get going."

The thought of him leaving her alone in that apartment made her skin crawl. "Don't! I mean, don't you... want to come up? At least make sure the apartment is safe?"

Paul raised an eyebrow at her and blushed a little, but her fear was genuine. Boniface appeared on his shoulder and began to whisper things into his ear. For once, Scribble was actually glad the angel was around.

"Alright. Just to make sure it's safe."

The apartment looked much larger with the bookshelves moved out. Scribble hadn't even noticed the kitchen before. She also discovered that the bookshelves had been hiding an old couch, a coffee table stained with dark rings, and an upright piano that would look more in place in an old Western than stuffed into the corner of a living room. Family pictures hung on the walls and sat on the top of the piano. Most of them featured Paul or his mother. And everything except the coffee table was covered in a years-old layer of dust.

Scribble stood frozen in the living room while Paul moved from room to room to make sure they were safe. "I'm sorry it was so crowded up here. It was the only place I could think of that had enough space for my mom's collection." Not all of the bookcases had been removed, but the ones that remained were in bedrooms Scribble didn't use.

"No, it's fine. I'm just grateful you took me in. You really didn't have to. I promise I won't be here long."

"Like I said, you're welcome to stay for as long as you need. Everything looks clear to me," Paul said as he emerged from the main bedroom.

She let out a relieved breath. "Thank you for checking." Once she found a place for the bags of clothes she'd bought, Scribble picked up one of the pictures on the piano. In it, a 20-something woman with caramel skin was laughing as Paul gave her a piggyback ride. "So, is this Danielle?" she asked.

"Hm?" He came up behind her and looked at the picture in her hands. "Yeah. That's her. That's Dani."

"She's pretty. And she looks happy."

Paul let out a sigh. "Yeah."

Scribble felt she was treading on dangerous ground, but curiosity got the better of her. "How did it happen?"

"I'd rather not talk about it." He headed towards the staircase. "You have my number if you need me, so I guess I should go."

She bit her lip. "Could you stay a little longer? We could talk more. I like talking with you. We don't have to talk about her."

Boniface furrowed his brow and leaned into Paul's ear, whispering furiously. In the end, Paul nodded. "I suppose I could stay a little longer."

"So, why'd you move out?" she asked.

Paul leaned against the piano. "Too many memories, not enough room. After my mom passed away, I couldn't take it. The books were the only reason I came up here. Not till I met you, at least."

Scribble nodded. "And what about your dad? What happened to him?"

Pain showed in Paul's face. She put her hand on his shoulder in concern. Before she could take the question back, though, he answered. "Last I heard, he moved across the country to be with a girl half his age. And he can stay there for all I care."

She didn't need to feel the air getting colder to know that Paul's depression was returning. *I'm pushing too hard! I've got to distract him!* she thought. "So... this is a piano, right? Does it still play?"

He looked down at the closed fallboard of the piano and slowly nodded. "I think so." The air warmed slightly when he sat down on the bench and cracked his knuckles. Paul lifted its lid to reveal the ivory and ebony that had been neglected for so long. Fingers pressed firmly into the keys, forming a powerful, confident chord. Then he tried a second chord, but several of the notes were off, resulting in a cacophony that made both of them screw up their faces.

"Is it *supposed* to sound like that?" Scribble asked.

"Uh, no. I guess it needs a bit of work. Let me try something..." Paul began playing a soft tune with a harmony that haunted the room. At times, he would hit an off-key or get a chord wrong, but despite these failures, Scribble listened intently, smiling.

"It's beautiful," she said. "I've never listened to music like this before."

"I'm making a mess of it. I haven't practiced. Mom always had me playing for her and her friends. At least it's not as out-of-tune as I thought it would be." Without needing further prompting, he continued as if the music pulled the words from him. "I miss her. The doctor said it was a heart attack. It was two years ago last week. This store was her passion. She poured herself into it. It's how she coped with my dad, I think." His fingers stopped, leaving one note hanging. "I just couldn't let it go under."

"She would be proud," Scribble offered.

"Thank you. Still, I don't know how much longer I can keep it afloat. We might be okay if Ginger wasn't taking money from the register. I'll have to talk to her about it, but I'm afraid I'll just scare her away. Or that she'll ignore me."

Scribble found a seat on the edge of the piano bench next to Paul. "You must like her a lot," she said. A new feeling rose up in her as the desire to have Paul to herself fought against the realization that Ginger already did.

"Well, yeah. She's been with me through a lot. Her family has always helped me and my mom. She's like a little sister to me."

Hope sprang in Scribble's heart, making it almost hurt with possibilities. "Little sister?"

"Yeah, I've known her for forever. We were in grade school together. She can get on your nerves at times, but she's a good person inside."

Scribble placed her pale hands on the piano keys. "Teach me?" she asked. Truth be told, she was hanging onto this feeling, this comfort that washed over her whenever she was near him.

Paul didn't try to move away. Instead, he took her right hand and positioned it over the keys. "That's middle C," he said. He played *Twinkle, Twinkle, Little Star* and then paused, waiting for her to repeat it.

She giggled as she messed up the simple tune. "It's harder than it looks," she said and pressed her foot against his. Paul breathed in deeply and closed his eyes.

"Don't give up just because it's hard. Keep trying and you'll get it," he told her. His voice was quieter, more intimate than before. "It's so easy to talk to you. I could get in trouble." Boniface looked between them and then slowly floated away as if to give them privacy. Meanwhile, Paul was leaning in closer and closer to Scribble, and all she could think about was how much she wanted to kiss him. She tilted her chin up to capture his lips with hers.

The music stopped suddenly. Paul leaned away from the near-kiss and put one hand in the air, index finger raised. He tilted his head.

"What?" Scribble listened. "Is there someone here?"

He stood up. "The pipes..." The entire time they'd been there, the pipes had been softly knocking and creaking behind the walls, but they had grown louder.

"Is that bad?" Scribble asked. Both of them jumped as a loud *POP* came from downstairs, followed by the sound of splashing water. They looked at each other with the same expression of worry and panic. "Where did you say Frank moved those books to?"

The realization hit hard and they both rushed downstairs as fast as they could. When they got to the back room, a puddle of steamy water greeted them, spreading underfoot. In the far corner stood the water boiler with a rupture in the top, sending a large spray of water right onto the bookshelves that had been moved from the apartment.

Chapter 12 – Missing

"I'll have to call the plumber in the morning," Paul said. He was sitting on the ground next to Scribble. Although the floor had been mopped and dried, a large fan was still on, angled to blow air out the open back door. Rows of towels covered with plastic and blank newsprint were spread out wherever there was room. On top were the books, some standing on end and slightly fanned, some laying flat. Paul and Scribble carefully thumbed through them, one by one, and inserted paper towels every few pages.

"I don't know if this is going to be enough," she said, looking at the paper towel roll. It was nearly empty.

"When we run out, we'll stand the rest of the books upright until I can get some more."

"Well, I hope that's soon." Scribble arched her back in an alluring display, but Paul didn't seem to notice. He was miles away, looking over the books yet to be treated. She had never tried to empathize with someone before, not like this. Though she didn't want him to slip into a full-fledged depression, it wasn't her job that made her want to comfort him. Scribble scooted closer to him and put her hand on his back, rubbing it. "It's going to be okay," she said.

Paul just leaned against her and shut his eyes tight. He sniffed. Tears wetted his cheeks. She'd never seen a man cry before and felt awkward and unsure about how to react, but he seemed content with what she was doing. Only the thrum of the fan could be heard. After a few minutes, he took off his glasses and rubbed at his cheeks and eyes, straightening himself.

"I'm sorry," he said. "I've just worked so hard for this place and now I don't know if I can salvage these or not. Even if I can, their value has dropped."

"Then we'll find another way," she said, but just then, the iBad in her pocket vibrated. When she pulled it out, Surli appeared on the screen, along with the words,

> "Somehow, what you're doing is working! He's vulnerable to sin right now. Make him angry. Tell him that was the worst date ever."

Scribble frowned and turned off the device. *How dare she try to get me to hurt him now. Who does she think she is?* But as she watched Paul, she knew that Surli was right. It was her duty to make him sin, even if it wasn't through seduction. She felt like her heart was being pulled in two directions at once.

"Just one step at a time," was all she could think to say.

"Thank you, Desdemona," he told her, placing his hand on her knee and squeezing. The tug on her heartstrings grew stronger and she leaned closer to him, but the distant sound of the bell above the front door cut the scene short.

"What time is it?" Paul asked, rubbing his eyes once more and putting on his glasses. They both got up and headed for the front.

Frank was there, facing the entrance. Although it was still dark outside, the prelude of dawn had begun to chase some of the darkness away.

"Frank! Is it opening time already?" Paul asked as he approached him.

The middle-aged man turned with a confused look on his face. "Paul? What are you doing here?"

He spied Scribble just behind Paul. She had one hand playing with her hair to try to smooth it out, but she knew she looked disheveled, tired, and a little sweaty. For some reason, she was suddenly self-conscious about how she appeared. Demons were not good at giving innocent smiles, but she tried as hard as she could.

When Frank eyed them judgingly, Paul caught on. "It's not what it looks like. We have a problem, Frank." He waved for him to follow. "When I got back from showing Dez around town, we found the front door wasn't latched, and then this happened..." He opened the door to the back.

Frank gasped. "Oh no! How?"

"The boiler burst and some of the pipes were leaking overhead. Think the plumber is open yet?" He pulled out his cell phone—a flip phone that was severely out-of-date.

Frank wandered around the drying volumes. "They usually have emergency services. It's a good thing we didn't move all the books down here." He squatted down to inspect one more closely. "What are you going to do?"

Paul leaned against the wall, looking exhausted. "I dunno. I was sort of banking on them for collateral. Dez did all that work and they were in good condition. You were here yesterday. Are you sure you locked up?"

"Positive. Though, this morning, I couldn't find the keys. I was planning on waking up Desdemona to let me in."

Paul frowned and pinched the bridge of his nose under his glasses. "Who was here with you?"

"Derek was helping me out."

"Ginger's brother?"

Frank nodded. "Surely you don't think this was done on purpose, do you?"

"I don't know what to think. I'm tired. And now I definitely can't use these for collateral."

"You could take out a second mortgage," Frank suggested promptly.

"You know I can't afford those payments." Paul tapped at his phone.

"Well, it's either that or sell. I hear Mr. Giacobbe is interested."

Paul huffed. "I'm not selling. You know that, too." As if dissatisfied with Frank's answers, he abruptly ended the conversation by putting the phone up to his ear. "Hi, is this White's Plumbing? I've got a situation."

Scribble felt awkward as she listened in on their conversation and walked back out to the main room. Although she was tired, sore, and still learning how to open the shop, she did her best and sat behind the register in case any customers did come in. A wave of drowsiness hit her. She braced herself against the wall and tried to keep alert, but the fatigue won.

The sound of the bell above the door woke her up. She jerked upright and said, reflexively, "W-welcome to *Othello's Books*. How can I help you?"

"Dez? Aren't you supposed to close tonight? Why are you here?" Ginger walked up to the counter, looking as perky and nubile as ever. She brought a finger up to her cheek. "You have some... drool... right there. Other side."

"What? Oh!" Scribble muttered an apology as she wiped her cheek and removed the hair that was stuck to it. "Sorry, Paul and I had a long night..."

Ginger froze on her way to the back at those words. Her already fair skin lost what pink hue it had. "What do you mean? What were you doing all night?" she asked with suspicion in her voice. Scribble was too tired to care.

"Oh, we were up all night together," she said, rubbing her eyes with both hands. Before Ginger had a chance to interject with something volatile, she continued, "The boiler burst and we were trying to save the books. He's back there now with Frank."

"What?!" Ginger rushed to the office door. Scribble, however, was relearning that sleep was something humans simply couldn't do without. When Ginger returned, Scribble was resting her head on her folded arms as she slumped against the counter. Ginger tapped her on the shoulder. "Frank is back there taking care of the books. He says Paul went home a while ago."

Scribble blinked sleepily. "He did? I'm sorry... I didn't—"

"It's ok, Dez. You should get some rest," Ginger said, putting a hand on Scribble's shoulder.

"Are you sure? I mean, I know I'm not supposed to work until tonight but now there's all of *that* to worry about."

Ginger smiled, which was something she'd never done towards Scribble before. "Yeah, I'm sure. Me and Frank will be just fine."

The bell above the door rang and the two girls straightened. "I do feel awful. I probably look it, too," Scribble said as she adjusted her shirt. "But I can't just let you handle the shop with Frank busy in the back."

Ginger would have none of it. "Hey. You. Are going. To bed." She pushed Scribble towards the apartment stairs. "Tell you what, tomorrow, you're on morning shift with me. I was going to go get my hair and nails done after. Maybe we can go together, but only if you get some sleep now."

Although reluctant, Scribble eventually caved in and headed to the stairs on her own. "Alright, alright. That sounds good. If you need any help…"

"I'll manage," Ginger replied.

Scribble nodded and walked up the stairs. The bags of clothes were still sitting on the coffee table, untouched. She walked right past them, ignored the bedtime routine she'd learned from Surli, and collapsed on the bed. In moments, she was fast asleep.

* * *

Sorry, Dez. Had to close up shop!
Paul can't come in tonight and there's
no one else to help you close.
—Frank

The sign was taped to the door at the bottom of the apartment stairs. Scribble knew she'd slept in a little, but it was still light out when she discovered the note. "I'm never going to actually get to work in the store, am I?" she said to herself. Having an apartment inside the shop meant that, at times, she felt like she was intruding. After all, there was the entire store available to her. Scribble realized that Paul had to be a very trusting person to allow her to stay there.

The thought of Paul brought with it a host of emotions she was still trying to understand. She paced up and down one of the aisles.

"Why does he make me feel like this? I should just focus on tempting him. Not on the books or his smile or… *grrr!*"

"If you're going to tempt him, maybe you need to learn more about him."

Scribble jumped at the muffled voice, not expecting anyone to respond to her soliloquy. When she realized it was just Surli, she rolled her eyes and pulled the iBad from her pocket.

"What do you know about it?" Scribble asked. "I know plenty about him." The image of Surli's disembodied head smirked at her.

"And yet you still don't know anything about Danielle."

Scribble snorted at the device. "I'll figure it out. I just need more time."

"You might not have time."

A picture of Incubus appeared on the screen.

"He seems impatient."

"Well, what am I supposed to do, ask Paul about his dead girlfriend? I don't even know where he is."

Surli winked.

"There are other ways to find out."

The screen changed to what looked like a website with the distinct logo of Belphegor on it. It was filled with hyperlinks and tiny print. Surli looked like she was concentrating, her eyes mere lines. Pages opened quickly behind her.

"What are you doing?" Scribble asked as she tried scanning over the flashing pages.

There was a cheerful *ding!* and Surli opened her eyes.

"Ready to search!"

Above her head was a small, blinking cursor in a search box.

"What is Danielle's full name?"

Scribble was intrigued. "Are you accessing the new Purgatory network? Um... Danielle Cooper," she said. Letters filled in the box.

"Middle name?"

Scribble drew a blank.

"Date of birth? Place of birth? Social Security Number? Birthmarks?!"

"Sorry, I don't know!"

Surli let out a cute grunt.

"You realize there are a million Danielle Coopers? Can't you give me something more to go with?"

After a moment, Scribble nodded. "She died around a year ago?"

Surli's emoji rolled its eyes.

"It might... Scanning... Ah, here we are. There are three Danielle Coopers who died around a year ago."

Scribble beamed. "Any in their late teens or early 20s?" she asked, getting a little more excited at the prospect that this might actually work.

"Just one! #10769283883, age 22, soul weight 12."

"Great! Can I see her file?"

After a brief look of concentration, Surli frowned and her ears drooped.

"Her file is restricted. I cannot access it."

Scribble hit a bookcase in frustration. "It's like a cover-up! No one will talk about this girl. There's no information." She leaned back against the bookshelf and looked up at the ceiling.

"You know, you could always go and visit her in person."

"I can?"

"Why not? With that soul weight, she should still be in Purgatory for a few more days before she ascends."

"I... I guess I'm not needed here for a while." Scribble chewed on her lower lip for a moment, then nodded. "Alright."

*　　　*　　　*

"It's smaller than I remember," Scribble said softly as she walked through Hell's Gate on her way to Purgatory. She kept her arms tight against herself. The imposing angels stood watch on either side, their painted gazes paying her no mind. Regardless, she somehow knew they were watching *her*.

"Aren't you normally an imp?"

Scribble was holding the iBad, trying to keep it hidden against her body.

"You'd have been half your size last time."

"I guess you're right," Scribble murmured.

When the path had become the carpeted office flooring that Scribble was used to, she felt a little more relaxed. There were very few demons here and the only sounds were of frustration, boredom, and torment. "You're *sure* she's here? Purgatory is huge! How are we going to find her?" she asked Surli.

"Sector 2, Section 38D, Cubicle 17929. It's easy to calculate when you know where and when she started. Easy for me. It's not like *you* could do it."

"Right. Thanks." Scribble picked up the pace, rushing along the hallways. In the distance, she could see the massive stalagmite tower she had once called home, reaching to the ceiling that arced high above. Even though everything seemed smaller to her, her new perspective only made the tower that much more overbearing. *Perhaps that's because it looks just as large as ever.* She looked away from it and broke into a full-out run.

Every few minutes, she would see a plaque on one of the walls telling her which sector and section she was in. By the time she made it to Sector 2, she

85

was no longer running, but had fallen back to a jog.

"It's... not as small... as I'd like it to be," she said as she doubled over, hands on her knees, to catch her breath. "Felt like... I was running... for hours..."

"Only one, slowpoke. She should be nearby."

Scribble nodded and hobbled along the corridors. Ahead of her, she could see Sector 1, the end of the cubicles, the end of the carpet. "I've never been so far Heavenward," she said softly. Curiosity got the better of her, and soon, she was standing at the carpet's edge. Beyond, the ground was stone. The ceiling that had been so distant before was sloping down towards her, meeting the ground a few minutes' walk away. She stared. "Is there light there? Are those the Pearly—"

"Don't get distracted, genius. Cubicle 17929."

Eventually, Scribble complied and walked back into Sector 2, looking around at all the cubicles. These were larger than the ones closer to Hell, often with doors, but surprisingly, there were fewer machines, fewer possessions. For souls this close to redemption, objects held less meaning. It was not long before she found 17929. With a deep breath, she walked up to the door.

"No, sir, it's not here." The male voice came from the other side. Scribble paused for a moment, then quietly turned the handle and peeked inside. Standing in the middle of the room was a tall, dark figure. His back was turned to her. "I don't know, Belphegor, sir. I've checked all the rooms I could. Both Sectors 1 and 2. This is a good sign, right?"

The figure turned and Scribble put a hand over her mouth to stifle a gasp. It was Rotworm. He had his own iBad up to his ear.

"It definitely hasn't ascended. No, sir. I have someone monitoring it, Master. Either the records were wrong or its soul is gaining weight. Yes, sir. I will double-check the records."

Rotworm closed his eyes in frustration and faced the door. Scribble panicked and pulled the door shut, making sure to keep it from latching. She was about to tip-toe away when she heard Rotworm's forced laugh. She stopped and listened again.

"Oh, no, you won't be implicated, sir. It's all arranged. When Cooper's soul reaches Hell, that incompetent imp you sent me will take all the blame."

Is he talking about me? Scribble thought as a sense of dread filled her. *What does he mean, "when" she reaches Hell?*

"They'll think it was an accounting error. By the time... yes, Great Prince. I'll make sure. I can't stay much longer; my soul is too heavy. I've been here for too long as it is. No, sir. I- I will. You just need to be more patient. Right away, sir." There was a pause, an electronic beep, and then a muttered, "Idiot."

The door handle turned. Scribble's blood froze with fear. She ran like never before, then ducked into another cubicle. Inside, a young man sat at a desk, filling out an endless supply of TPS reports, completely unaware of her presence. Outside, footsteps approached. They slowed down, then stopped in front of the door.

A million fears gripped at Scribble's mind. *Does he mean Danielle Cooper? What does he want with Danielle? Didn't Grimtooth say something about this? What is he going to do to me? I don't want to be connected to some machine for the rest of time!* Her heart was drumming so loudly in her ears that she almost couldn't hear anything else. She could swear that the door handle wiggled as if gripped from the other side. The iBad began to slip from her sweaty palms. She fumbled with it, managing just barely to keep it from hitting the ground.

"Damn thisss Purgatory," Rotworm said from the other side. "It tires out my wings." The footsteps continued on. Several minutes after they'd faded from her ears, Scribble finally ventured out, taking an even longer and more circuitous route back to Hell, back to Earth, back to her new home.

CHAPTER 13 – PLOTTING

"Another headache?" Frank asked as he peered over the top of the bookshelves to Scribble. She was leaning over the counter, her fingers digging into her forehead.

"Yeah, the third one this week," she replied and stood up straight. Ever since her jaunt to Purgatory, she'd been stressing out more about Rotworm and... whatever he had planned for her. Now that she was finally working normal hours, she spent all her free time trying to find more leads on both Rotworm and Danielle, but none of them panned out.

"Did you take a pill for it?" Frank asked.

She nodded. "A few minutes ago. Thanks for telling me about them. Paul gave me some once, but I'm still not used to taking medicine. Never really needed it before."

Frank nodded and looked back down at the shelf. "Well, it's probably just stress. We've all been stressed since the boiler. I've barely seen Paul since."

"Me neither. I hope he's okay. You... wouldn't happen to know where he hangs out, would you?" Frank gave her a coy glance. "I'm just worried! There's nothing going on between us!" she said with a slight blush.

"The lady doth protest too much, methinks." Frank laughed and came out from behind the shelf when the bell above the door chimed.

"Welcome—oh, hi, Ginger," Scribble said, glad she didn't have to adopt a smile. She was surprised to learn that a headache could make smiling painful.

Frank folded his arms over his chest. "I wasn't expecting you this early. I still have an hour before my shift is over."

Ginger headed straight to the office. "Well, this is the schedule he put me on for today," she said as she passed by him. "I thought he must have talked to you guys about it. He hasn't said a word to me."

"Us neither."

When Ginger came back out of the office she looked appraisingly at Scribble, who was squinting a little. Scribble's dark locks, hanging just past her shoulders, were unkempt and unruly. She had dark rings under her eyes.

"You look awful, Dez. Need another trip to the salon already?"

"Hm? Oh, no, I'm fine. I've just been so worried about things recently, you know, the books, Paul..." *Rotworm,* she added mentally.

Ginger nodded to her. "All the more reason to use make-up."

Scribble shook her head. "I tried that, remember? I looked awful."

"You're just not putting it on right. Didn't anyone ever teach you? Come over here…" She wasted no time in pulling out a compact from her pocket but stopped when the bell above the door rang out again.

Paul walked in with a radiant smile. He was wearing a button-up shirt but had the top button open and the sleeves rolled up to his elbows. "Good morning, everyone. I see you're all here," he said.

Scribble's cheeks darkened when she saw him and, once again, her pulse quickened. The joy on his face was almost enough to make her forget about her problems. Almost. It was the first time in a week that she'd laid eyes on him. "You look better," she said. *Is his depression gone?*

Ginger frowned as she watched Scribble's reaction. A little angel and demon appeared on her shoulders. She leaned in close and whispered, "Don't even think about it, girl. He's mine." With that she turned on a heel, walked up to Paul and gave him a hug. "Where have you been?" she asked. Scribble wondered how someone could go from friend to foe so quickly and effortlessly.

"All over. I've got some news." He motioned for Frank to join the girls at the counter. "So, for starters, thank you all for holding down the store while I was away. I appreciate it. Second, I got the money."

Frank smiled. "You did? Great! How?"

"I took your advice and got a second commercial mortgage on the property. It means I'll be paying a lot more money for a while to keep the store, but I think I've found a way to get us some more customers. It should turn things around." He strode around, pointing here and there as he spoke. "We'll need to remodel a little. No more piles of books. I want this place to be a hang-out spot. It needs to be inviting. A couch, some music. We'll also be getting an espresso maker and selling coffee. I've submitted the paperwork for the licensing. It's just a matter of time."

"Is that it?" Frank asked, doubt in his voice.

"Rebranding is only the first part. I have a plan."

Ginger smiled adoringly at Paul, making Scribble feel more and more like an outsider, like she didn't have a chance with him. She clenched her jaw and put her hand to her chest when she remembered her real job. *I have to tempt him, that's it. Nothing else,* she reminded herself. If Paul hadn't clapped his hands together in his excitement, she would have missed what he said next.

"I've hired a troupe of actors. Over the next few weeks, they're going to act out scenes from some of our favorite books in the middle of a crowded space. Not the whole scene, just enough to get people hooked. Then we'll hand out flyers. And someone will be recording the whole scene and posting it online. If we can go viral, there's no telling what will happen to *Othello's*." There was a moment of stunned silence. Paul turned to Frank. "What do you think?"

"That can't possibly cost enough for a whole mortgage. What are you going to do with the rest of the money?"

"Well, that new boiler took a chunk out of the account. First, I'd pay that back. Then I was thinking of shooting a commercial, getting a few ads out there. But I want to see if this actor thing works first. If I can get by without the ads, we could use the rest of the money on improvements."

Frank shrugged. "It *could* work. Worth a shot."

Paul turned to the others. "Ginger?" His smile faded a little.

"If you think it'll work, I'm behind you," she said.

When he looked at Scribble, the apprehension in his eyes was impossible to deny. But she smiled brightly at him all the same. "I love it! I think it's a great idea! When will it all start?"

Paul looked relieved. "Well, I'm planning on the grand re-opening in two weeks. While you're all passing out flyers, I'll be remodeling in here. The first event will happen on Saturday."

"*This* Saturday?" asked Frank. "That doesn't give us much time to prepare. What scene are they going to be playing?"

"A scene from *Les Mis*. It's not going to be word-for-word accurate, but something more modern. I'm going to have someone confront Jean Valjean in the mall. We still have a little time to work on others. Any suggestions?"

"How about *1984*?" Frank offered.

"Mmm... too hard and depressing."

Ginger chimed in. "*Interview with a Vampire*?"

"That's better! I'm sure we can find a good scene between Armand and Lestat, or maybe Louis and Santiago."

Scribble looked out of the window at the backwards lettering. "Why not something from *Othello*?"

Paul practically beamed. "Perfect. I'll get started right away!"

"Is that it?" Frank asked. "Do I need to stay, or can I call Addison to pick me up?"

Paul shook his head. "There's one more thing. I talked with the plumber about the water boiler. He said we were lucky it didn't explode or it could've caused some real damage. The safety valve was broken. He said it could have just been old, but he wasn't sure."

"What are you saying?" Ginger asked. "Do you think one of us did it? You know Dez has full ac—"

"She was with me when it happened," Paul said sternly. Ginger folded her arms over her chest in a pout. "When Dez and I got here that night, the door was unlocked. If it was done on purpose, it could have been anyone—even one of us. But I'm not pointing any fingers. Plus, I can't rule out Giacobbe. "

Ginger looked worried. "You mean the guy who owns the rest of the block? Why would he do that?"

"If I go under and have to sell, Mr. Giacobbe has 'right of first refusal'." After the confused looks he got, Paul continued. "It means I have to give him the option to buy it first, before it goes on the market. I can only sell it to someone else if he refuses. It was part of the contract my mom signed when she bought the store."

"If you think it was sabotage, why don't you call the police?" Ginger asked.

"I'd rather keep the police uninvolved. Remember the last time they came around? All I'm asking is that you three keep on the lookout for anything suspicious." Paul then turned to Scribble. "If you don't want to stay, I understand. I know it can be scary. Any luck finding a place of your own?"

Scribble shook her head. "Sorry, I'm still looking. I don't mind staying here for now. But I feel like I should be paying you for it."

Boniface appeared on Paul's shoulder. When he looked over at Scribble, his ever-present smile faded a little with concern. Then he whispered into Paul's ear at high speed.

"How about you help me write up these scenes? I could definitely use another pair of eyes. We'll consider that your payment for this month."

"Scenes? Why me?" Scribble asked.

Paul looked taken aback. "You listed editing as a skill on your résumé. And from what I can tell, you're probably the most well-read person here. I know it's not my screenplay, but I thought..."

Scribble had completely forgotten about critiquing his work and smiled nervously. "Are you sure? I mean, I've never done that before. Critiquing and editing are different."

"It's still more experience than I've got. I value your opinion. Your shift ends soon, right? We could go now." Paul was smiling at Scribble in a way that made her both lovesick and nervous. Ginger shot her a jealous glance.

"Why can't I help you? I've always wanted to try writing," she said.

Paul was caught in a conundrum and looked to Frank, who, with an off-hand wave, headed to the back. "You're on your own buddy. I'll be in the office calling home." He left Paul to navigate the waters of feminine wiles solo.

"Well, Ginger, uh, you could help by making the flyers for tomorrow."

"Flyers?! It's not the same thing!"

"Please?" he asked. His deep, dulcet voice seemed designed to work against her stubborn will.

After a moment, she grumbled and sagged her shoulders. "Fine. But I'm coming over as soon as I'm done." She flashed a death glare at Scribble, then turned her back to them with a pout.

"She'll be alright," Paul said softly to Scribble, who joined him as he headed to the front of the store.

"I hope so," she said. Without warning, the headache returned and the room spun. Scribble put her fingers to her temples.

"Everything okay?" Paul asked.

Scribble nodded. "Sorry, just a headache. I'm going to grab some medicine from the apartment. I'll be right back." She quickly headed upstairs, but the moment she was in the apartment, the dizziness got worse.

"Surli, what's wrong with me? Am I... sick?" she asked, pulling out the iBad.

Surli looked bored.

> "How should I know? You've gotta scan yourself with the camera first."

Scribble did as she was told, tapping her foot with impatience. The little figure on the screen concentrated for an eternity, then said,

> "Your body needs more energy."

"But I had lunch." She went to the medicine cabinet and pulled out a bottle of pain reliever.

> "Not *that* kind of energy. You're a succubus now, remember? The longer you go without feeding, the weaker your connection to the body will be. If you go too long, you'll have to leave it or..."

"Or what?" Scribble pressed.

> "Risk becoming grigori. A wanderer. The Order will be all over you."

Scribble sighed. "Is there any other way?"

> "No."

"With Ginger trying to get in the way, I don't have much hope of tempting Paul before I have to... leave."

"Are you all right?" Paul called up to her from the bottom of the stairs.

"Be right down!"

A sinister smile curled Surli's digital lips.

> "I could get her out of the way... with your permission."

Scribble put the iBad down on the coffee table and stuffed the bottle in a pocket. "You can? How?"

> "I have my ways."

"You're not going to hurt her, are you?"

"Not if you tell me I can't."

Anxious to rejoin Paul, Scribble nodded her agreement. "A-alright. Just... don't hurt her." She carefully walked down the stairs, leaving Surli behind.

Chapter 14 – Acting

The warm light of the sun cast its final gaze on the world as the iBad spontaneously sprang to life on the upstairs coffee table. Surli appeared on the screen, scrolling through the device's menus. She stopped on "phone". An instant later, *"Othello's Books"* was selected from an infinite list of contacts. As the phone app began to dial, Surli switched over to a custom AI chatbot she'd trained using recordings of Paul's conversations with Scribble.

Downstairs in the shop, the phone rang.

"Othello's Books. How may I help you?" came Ginger's bored voice.

 "Ginger? It's Paul!"

Surli sounded exactly like the man.

"Paul? Aren't you with Desdemona, 'writing' or something?" Ginger asked. A bit of the jealousy she had been trying to hide from him crept into her tone.

 "She stepped outside for some air. Listen, I'm sorry I blew you
 off earlier today. I hope I didn't hurt your feelings."

Ginger sounded surprised. "I... it's ok. I'm sorry if I came off as rude."

 "I guess we've all been under a lot of stress, huh?"

"Yeah. So, how's it coming along?"

 "Scribble is doing alright. I felt sorry for her, you know. She
 could use the time away from the store."

Surli's eyes went wide and animated sweat drops appeared when she realized she'd used Scribble's real name.

"'Scribble'? Since when do you call her by her last name? Are you going to start calling me 'Roderick'?"

Surli's panic-stricken image relaxed.

 "Well, she's not here right now, so does it matter? Or would
 you like me to call everyone by their last name, *Roderick*?"

Ginger giggled on the other line. "God, no. So, what's wrong, *Taylor*? Need that extra help?"

 "No. Ginger, there's something important I need to tell you."

"What is it?"

 "I can't tell you over the phone. But it's something I've been
 hiding for a long time."

"Don't leave me hanging!" Her voice was playful, but the rough edge to it betrayed a fear she tried to cover up.

> "Well, it's just... I know I've been spending a lot of time with Dez. But it's really made me realize how much I appreciate you."

"Appreciate?" The disappointment in her tone could cut cheese.

> "I don't mean it like that! Ginger, I... this is really hard to say."

The reply was hardly more than a whisper. "Paul, please, just say it. I need to know—"

Surli-not-Paul cut her off:

> "I love you! I've always loved you. I just never realized it until now."

"Y-you do?"

> "I know it's wrong. We've been friends for so long, and now I'm your boss. I just don't want to ruin anything or make things... awkward."

"I don't know what to say." Ginger paused. Surli worried that she had made a mistake. Then Ginger came back on the line. "I love you too," she said softly. "If it means being with you, I can quit if that makes it easier..."

> "No! I mean, I need you. At the store. We can just keep our love a secret."

"Have you been reading romance novels again? I don't think that'll work."

> "Tell you what, on Saturday, I'm having everyone hand out flyers, right? Well, I'll be at the store alone. Why not slip away and come see me when no one's watching?"

"...I think I can do that."

Surli made her voice sound deep and seductive.

> "And wear something naughty. Don't even let me know when you show up, just sneak in and show me what you're wearing."

There was another giggle. "What about tonight?"

> "No! Not tonight. Uh... this writing looks like it'll take a while and I don't want to be distracted."

"Mmm, that's true. So, how long—"

> "Oh, she's coming back. I have to go. I'll text you."

"Saturday, then," Ginger said in a saccharine-sweet voice.

"Saturday."

Surli hung up, looking rather proud of herself just before the iBad screen went blank.

*   *   *

To Scribble, the air in the mall was electric. Two days had passed since she worked with Paul on the scripts, and the thought of seeing their work acted out only added to the excitement she felt. She had been to the mall only once before, with Paul, but it hadn't been nearly as busy as on a weekend like today. Autumn had barely begun and there was already a hodgepodge of decorations everywhere, encompassing the entire holiday season into one commercial cacophony and drawing large seasonal crowds.

Despite the crowd, Scribble loved it. It was a different sort of crowd than she'd seen before. Children pulled their parents towards toy stores, teens roved in tightly bonded groups, elderly couples walked slowly hand in hand. There were people everywhere, and following each were Sinisters and Dexters.

"Everything is so *alive*," she said to Frank and Ginger. Her maelstrom eyes were like a child's seeing Santa Claus for the first time.

"Calm down there, Dez! We don't want to scare people away," Frank joked. He was holding his cell phone out, using its camera to scan the crowd. The trio had commandeered a small corner near the food court. Satchels filled with flyers hung at their sides.

"I wasn't there for the rehearsal," Ginger said. She was staring at her own phone as she texted away to someone. Scribble noticed that the skirt she wore was shorter than usual and the lacing along the front of her top was looser, showing off her full cleavage, but perhaps that was just the style. "Do either of you see the actors?"

"There wasn't a rehearsal. This seems all very seat-of-the-pants to me. I hope this isn't a mistake." Frank pointed suddenly, "There. I bet that's them."

The group Frank was pointing to split up, going into different stores. Ginger let out a sigh and tapped her foot impatiently. "I doubt it. Don't we need a permit for this sort of thing?"

Scribble nodded. "Yeah, Paul got permission for us to hand out the flyers. I don't know about the rest. Oh, I can't wait!" She bounced with excitement. "I really wish Paul could be here. Are you sure this is the right place?"

"This is it," Ginger said. "In front of the food court, like he told us."

"I don't think Paul wants to leave the store after he found more money missing from the register yesterday," Frank told them.

96

"STOP! Thief! You're under arrest!" The voice was strong and forceful, gathering an instant crowd of onlookers. It came from a jewelry store nearby. Scribble saw a rather muscular man being manhandled by someone in a blue uniform, but then someone stepped in front of her and the crowd thickened.

"Come on!" Frank whispered and grabbed her hand, pulling her around the crowd towards an empty area near the storefronts. He held the camera up in front of him, getting shots of the audience as he worked his way to the clearing. It was not the only phone being trained on the scene.

"I haven't done anything!" the large man said as he was forced up against the wall, face-first.

The uniformed man pushed his weight against him to prevent a struggle. He then reached into the thief's pocket and pulled out a diamond-studded necklace. It cast a rainbow of light over the crowd. A price tag was still attached. "Then what is this?" he asked. "You won't get away with it again, John! Once a thief, always a thief." In a flash, a pair of handcuffs came out.

"This man is innocent!" A well-dressed woman came out of the store with her hands up to placate the officer.

"And who are you, his accomplice?"

"I am the store owner," she replied. "This man has done no wrong!"

The officer raised the necklace aloft. "Then why did I find *this* on him?"

Turning to the crowd, the store owner raised her hands and spoke loudly, "Why, this was a gift! I saw this poor man and realized he needed the money more than I did." Then she turned towards the pair and pulled the thief away from the officer.

"Why are you doing this, ma'am?" the thief asked.

"Because I believe all men deserve a second chance. But before you go, you forgot the rest of your gift." She took off a pair of earrings and a ring, each of which looked like it had been coated in glue and rolled around in diamonds, then handed them to the thief.

"Do you know what you are doing, old woman?" the officer asked tersely.

"Of course. We all make poor choices from time to time. What matters is that we try to make them right."

The thief hugged the woman. "I promise you, I won't squander this. I will make my life better."

"We'll see about that," the officer sneered. "I'll be watching."

All three then addressed the crowd. The thief stepped forward. "We hope you've liked this short scene from *Les Misérables*. Want to find out how it ends? Come and visit *Othello's Books*, at the corner of 5th and Barley!"

As they bowed to the crowd's applause, Frank nudged Scribble. "That's our cue." They began handing out flyers advertising the store's grand re-opening.

Within five minutes, the crowd had dissipated. "So, you're friends of Paul's?" the fake officer asked them. He was a severe-looking black man with a well-trimmed goatee and angular face.

"Well, we work for him," Frank said, giving a playful grin. "Frank DeMills." They shook hands. "This is Desdemona Scribble."

Scribble smiled softly. "Hello."

"A pleasure to meet you. I'm Jack Chester. You know, our store owner here will be playing a Desdemona later." He waved his fellow thespian over, who had been busy chatting with an older gentleman—the store's real owner. "Hey, Abby, come here and meet a real-life Desdemona!"

The woman smiled fondly and held up a finger to the store owner, telling him she would be back in a moment. "A real Desdemona?" she asked as she approached. She was taller than Scribble, older in appearance, with platinum blonde hair tied back in a bun. Scribble figured she was in her 40s or 50s. "You're Paul's friend? I guess he would be our real Othello, huh, Jack?"

Frank laughed. "I don't know about that. But he can be a bit blind to what's going on around him at times, if you know what I mean."

All of them laughed, but Scribble had no clue what he meant.

"Where is Paul?" Abby asked.

"Oh, he had to stay with the store. He's setting up some new coffee machine and wanted to make certain the store was open in case anyone came in," Frank said.

"That's a bummer. He should at least try to see the second performance."

Scribble's eyes lit up. "There's going to be a second performance? Maybe I should head back and see if he wants to come. I'm sure I can watch the store for a few minutes!" She turned to Frank, begging with her eyes.

"I don't know... I doubt he wants to leave the store after yesterday."

"Pleeease? The worst he'll say is 'no', right? And I won't be gone long!"

Jack looked down at his watch. "Won't be for another hour."

With everyone looking to Frank for permission, he finally gave in with a sigh. "Fine. Just, make it quick. I'll hold the fort."

Scribble looked around. "Say, has anyone seen Ginger?"

*   *   *

Although the walk back to the store was not long, to Scribble, it felt like she was back in Purgatory. Something about Ginger weighed heavily in the back of her mind, but she couldn't figure out what it was exactly. That sensation of guilt returned to her, making her heart seem like it was turning in circles in her chest.

"Why do I have a bad feeling about this?" she spoke aloud.

The muffled response was coming from her pocket. She pulled the iBad out to see Surli grinning proudly.

"Surli? Did you have something to do with Ginger's disappearance? You promised me you wouldn't hurt her."

Surli's long ears drooped to the sides in protest.

When the store came into view, Surli added,

"What did you do?!" Scribble didn't wait for a response. Instead, she shoved Surli back into her pocket, ignoring the

that followed. She ran to the door and tried to open it, but it was locked. Cupping her hands around her face, she pressed to the glass and peered inside. She saw boxes, the espresso machine sitting on the counter, but no people. Then, in the corner of the room, she noticed movement. After a longer look, figures became discernible. Two figures.

They were sitting on a couch, which hadn't been there that morning. One leaned in close to the other. Its petite body slid into the lap of the first.

They kissed.

Scribble felt like a hand was gripped tightly around her heart. "No. No, no, no, no!" she chanted and pulled back from the glass, half-crazed with panic. She rummaged through her pockets again at a frenetic pace. The iBad slipped through her fingers and clattered on the ground. She pulled out the key to the store and tried to fit it to the lock. Her hand shook so much that the keys soon joined the iBad on the ground. Scribble turned away from the store, pressed her back up to the wall of the storefront, and sank down to the sidewalk.

For the second time in her borrowed life, tears ran down her cheeks. It ruined the make-up she'd worked so hard to apply, leaving dark streaks on her face. Scribble took off her glasses and drew up her knees, pressing her face to them. "W-why does it hurt so much?" she whispered.

Surli's small voice replied.

Scribble scoffed and picked the iBad back up. "What?!" she said as rage and dismay filled her. "How is this perfect?"

The entire world was nothing but a blur as Scribble raised the iBad over her head to throw it. "I wish I'd never met you!"

The digital imp cried out in alarm:

Scribble lowered the phone slowly. "How was it supposed to go?" she asked skeptically.

"Well, he didn't!" She slammed the iBad down on the pavement and sat in silence for a while. Even though the initial shock of seeing Paul and Ginger kiss had passed, a deep pain persisted in Scribble's core. The door opened with a light ring and Ginger stepped out, smiling widely and adjusting her top. She didn't notice Scribble as she headed back towards the mall. Scribble rubbed her eyes and cheeks before putting on her glasses. Without looking at the damage she caused, she put the iBad in her pocket before getting to her feet, but when she looked back at the store, she saw Paul still sitting on the couch, alone.

She stepped inside. Everything looked drastically different. There were no more piles on the floor. Some of the shelves had been removed entirely, replaced with cozy reading areas adorned with furniture that looked like they had come from a second-hand shop. And off to one side was the long couch Paul sat on.

"Paul?" Scribble asked in the strongest voice she could make, which wasn't very strong at all.

"D-Dez?!" Paul looked at her in a panic. "Oh, God, you saw that?"

"Not all of it," she replied. "Enough."

He looked disheveled, with his shirt uncharacteristically untucked. He had a guilty air about him. "I... Ginger just came in and practically jumped me. She told me she loved me. Said something about me calling her. Kissed me."

Scribble didn't want to hear it. Having it all confirmed only made the wire wrapped around her heart squeeze tighter. But she couldn't help herself. "What did you say?"

Paul looked away and covered his face with his hand.

"Please, Paul. You can tell me."

"I... kissed her back. Told her I loved her too." He leaned forward, elbows resting on his knees, hands folded as if in prayer, eyes downcast. "I shouldn't have done it. I just didn't want to hurt her."

"Why not? You both like each other."

He shook his head. "It's not that simple. We've been friends for years. I don't want to lose that."

It wasn't the answer she had been hoping for. Scribble sat down on the other end of the couch and brought her knees up with a hug. "I know what that's like. To lose a good friend, that is."

"Val?" Paul asked.

She nodded and sniffed as images of her friend flooded into her mind. "We were very close. Since I've come here, I've had so many second thoughts about how I treated him. I shouldn't have just run away like I did. But I can't go back and change things now. It's too late for... us."

Paul scooted a little closer. "Dez. I—" When Scribble drew herself in tighter, he stopped. "I don't want to lose you, either," he whispered. "Since I met you, I've felt happier, better. You're someone I can talk to about anything. Sometimes it's like you're reading my mind." He put his hand on her back. "You're important to me, Dez."

Tears started flowing again, so she buried her face against her knees to hide them. Her glasses pushed up to her forehead. "You're important to me, too," she whispered, then leaned into him.

Minutes passed. The moment Paul's hand began rubbing her back, Scribble straightened and got to her feet. "I'm, uh, happy for you two. Really. Don't mind me. I'm just thinking about Val," she lied. "I've got to get back before the next performance."

Paul nodded somberly. As she headed out, Scribble stumbled on something and put her glasses back in their proper place to see a small black and pink purse lying open at her feet. "It's Ginger's. I can get it to her," she said, though seeing Ginger was the last thing she wanted to do. But when she picked it up, a wad of cash slipped out of it, followed by a folded piece of paper.

Paul picked it up and groaned. "It's a page from my missing notepad."

Chapter 15 – Aftermath

"Are you telling me Ginger's *definitely* our thief?" Frank asked. It was dark out and the last of the customers had left, so he was louder than Scribble expected.

Paul, however, spoke in a quiet voice and acted defensively. "I don't know. Maybe. She left her purse behind and Dez tripped over it. That's how we found the money and the page."

"And it's the same amount as was missing yesterday?"

"Looks like it," Paul said. "But it could be a coincidence."

Frank threw his hands up in the air. "Why do you put up with her? She's robbing us blind. She's a liability!"

"Look, she's my best friend." Paul started counting the money in the register all over again for the fifth time that night. "And she wants to go steady with me. I can't just—"

"You're dating now?! How can you when she's robbing you?"

"It's complicated. I know she's saving up for college. If she really needs the money, I'm not going to keep it from her."

"She's going to put you out of business! And what about me?"

"Well, what about you, Frank? It's not like you need this job." Paul put the money down, focusing instead on his employee.

"Would you listen to yourself? You know Addison and I have separate finances!"

Scribble felt uncomfortable as she listened to her two friends argue. She wished she could be anywhere but there—even back in Hell would be better. But that wasn't an option, so, instead, she hid herself among the shelves and started to fiddle with her iBad. A small crack had appeared on the screen from when she hit it on the pavement. No matter what she did, the screen remained dark. "I'm sorry, Surli," she whispered. After a while, she gave up and grabbed *Tempter's Kiss* from the shelf, but the promise of raunchy romance wasn't enough to drown out the heated discussion nearby.

"I'm going to head upstairs," she said softly, but she doubted anyone heard her. Scribble kept her back to the wall as she worked her way over to the stairs, then darted up them quickly and shut the door at the top. Even up in her apartment, the argument drifted through the floorboards and vents.

"Don't you find the timing a little suspicious? And this has got to be killing Dez. I know you're both cra—"

There had to be a better way to drown it out, so the moment she got to her bedroom, she turned on the radio. That seemed to work. Then she started to fiddle with the iBad. She hit it, shook it, mashed at the "on" button, got angry at it, even negotiated with it, but nothing that seemed to work for humans had any effect. It was only after she took the soul stone out of the back and reinserted it that the device booted up.

"Oh thank Ba'al," she said out loud. But instead of the familiar display she was used to, the screen showed something more utilitarian. At the top of the screen were the words, "Basic Mode." Every icon looked the same, differentiated only by their titles, none of which made much sense to her. They all had names like, "Test_1," "WM5.4," and "StartUp_Protocol." A frown formed on her lips when she looked at the small crack in the upper right corner of the screen. She ran her finger across it, not realizing until the screen suddenly changed that she had activated an icon.

It briefly displayed an image of a phone before changing into a video feed. The room it showed was quite dark, but something began to move. She jolted on her bed and dropped the iBad onto the sheets when she saw the grotesque visage of Belphegor looking up at her.

"What is it, worm?" he asked in his electronic voice.

"I-I-I..." Scribble could only stutter.

"You're not Rotworm. Who are you? A human?! No. Whoever you are, I will have you strung up on hooks for disturbing me." Belphegor let out an unearthly growl, which did not come from his artificial voice box.

She grabbed for the phone but missed and sent it to the very edge of the bed. "Oh no!" she called out and lunged towards the device. The impact of her body on the mattress made the phone bounce off the edge. Just before it tumbled to the floor, Scribble managed to grab it. Reflexively, she turned it towards herself to see if it was okay, but the sight of Belphegor on the screen made her nearly drop it again. She put it on the bed and threw a pillow over it. Muffled curses in languages long forgotten by men came from under the pillow. The only thing that came to mind was jamming her hands beneath it and fiddling blindly with the phone until the cursing ceased. It worked. She let out a sigh of relief and cautiously lifted the pillow like the device would jump at her at any moment. When she turned a black screen towards herself, she slumped with relief on the bed and put the phone on the bedside table.

I never thought I'd say this, but I miss Surli.

*   *   *

Although the following day was marked by a heavy downpour, Scribble found it too bright in the store. A severe headache had been keeping her from worrying about Ginger, Paul, Belphegor, or anything else. To make things worse, she was on shift with Paul and everything was awkward between them. For the fifth time in two days, she headed for the medicine box in the back. When she returned to the front, Paul gave her a concerned glance. The only customer in the store was with him. She was a stout older woman in a floral dress; the distinct scent of ointment followed wherever she went.

"I thought it was real at first," she said. "Then the store owner talked to the crowd. It was very exciting! Whose idea was it?"

Paul had a blank expression. "I'm sorry, I didn't catch that?"

The woman frowned. "I asked, who thought of that play in the mall?"

"Oh, that was me. I wrote that one," Paul said.

"Well, it was very good. I saw it on the 6 o'clock news!"

"Thank you!"

"I was hoping to find a copy of it."

Again, he had that blank expression. "A copy?"

Scribble had thought ahead. Next to the register was a stack of *Les Mis*. She quickly grabbed one and walked over to them. "I have one right here," she said, smiling widely and squinting. "This one is on sale, only $5 today."

"Oh, that's lovely. Thank you, dear." The old woman rooted around in her purse and pulled out a few bills. "Will this be enough?"

Scribble nodded and took the money. "Yup! Can I get you anything else?"

"No, thank you. It is a lovely store. I've passed it so many times, I don't know why I didn't walk in earlier." Before she headed to the door, she patted Paul's arm. "Don't let her get away. You're such a handsome couple."

Paul and Scribble shared a knowing glance. The moment she was gone, a genuine smile formed on his cheeks. "Thank you."

"It's okay. I was hoping we would get a few people looking for that book."

When she winced, Paul raised his eyebrow. "Are you feeling all right?"

"Mmm-hmm. It's just another migraine. And I'm a bit tired. I just took some medicine for it, so I'm sure it'll go away soon. What about you? You've never blanked out like that before."

Paul nodded absently. "I didn't sleep." He stared at a spot on the floor and his voice went soft. The look was all too familiar.

"I'm worried about you, Paul. Have you considered that you might be depressed? Like really depressed?"

He shook his head. "I've just been down, that's all."

"No, it's more than that, Paul. You skip meals, don't go out, and now you're zoning out on customers."

It took him a moment to reply. "Maybe you're right. I'll try to see a doctor about it."

She had no idea whether a doctor could help with such a thing. "Good. And... I like to think you can talk to me about anything."

"I'll try, Dez. But I don't want to make you uncomfortable. I feel like I just stepped into *The Age of Innocence*."

Scribble didn't miss a beat. "Nonsense. I'm no Ellen Olenska. Besides, we're just friends. It's not uncomfortable."

Paul smirked and took her hand, getting an instant blush in response. "You're not a very good liar."

"I haven't had much practice." Scribble tried to stifle a yawn but couldn't keep it back. "Sorry. I don't know why I'm so tired."

"Well, why not try making a latte?" he asked.

She nodded. "You could probably use one, too. Do you think you could show me how to do it again?"

Neither of them moved. Scribble hadn't even been aware that they were still holding hands until her thumb was stroking the back of his. Despite the heartache from the day before, intense hope and longing sprung up. She wanted so desperately to invest in those emotions even though they were soon likely to crash.

Paul was the first to break out of their trance. "Yeah, come on," he said and led her over to the machine.

Scribble watched as he prepared it, which was little more than pushing the right buttons. As it poured into the cup, she nudged his side with her hip. "Snap out of it, Paul! This is a big moment for me. You know, I've—"

"Never had one before? I'm starting to sense a theme," he interrupted and slowly smiled. The last time she'd seen him smile like that was on their not-a-date. "My current theory is that you're secretly an Amish who ran away."

Scribble giggled. "I'll never tell," she said. How he made her feel like that so effortlessly befuddled her. Then again, all she had to do to stave off his depression was be herself, it seemed. When the machine finished, she picked the cup up and smelled it. The latte touched her lips and she licked off the foam. But Paul wasn't paying attention to her, rather some spot on the ground.

"I still can't believe I didn't realize she was in love with me."

"Me neither." She sipped her drink. "Maybe you need better glasses."

"What do you mean?" Paul asked.

"We all could see it, and I've only been here for a couple of weeks. Maybe you need better glasses."

Paul perked up a little. "Oh? What about your glasses?" he asked in playful banter. He put his hands on her hips.

Scribble felt an excited jolt run through her at the touch. *Maybe I really do still have a chance,* she thought. "Mine? What about them?"

"I bet you don't—"

The door opened and they both quieted down as they watched a man walk in. He was short but looked built. His thin nose was so pointed and straight that it could be used as a protractor. He wore a business suit that strained around his chest. The moment Paul saw him, he glowered.

"What... quaint changes you've made. Very hipster," the man said with a hint of an accent that Scribble couldn't place. He made wide gestures with his hands as he spoke as well, giving the impression that in order to properly gag the man, you'd also need a pair of handcuffs.

"What are you doing here, Giacobbe?"

"A little birdy told me that you were, uh, redecorating." Giacobbe didn't look at Paul, but instead, kept his gaze on the improvements Paul had been making. "I wanted to see what you've done. I take it your repairs went well."

"You're not welcome here, not after that stunt you pulled."

This was enough to make Giacobbe finally look at his accuser. "Stunt? What stunt?"

Paul narrowed his gaze. "Don't pretend to be innocent. I know the boiler didn't break on its own. You destroyed my private collection! And I bet you're behind the thieving, too."

Giacobbe walked up to Paul with a stern look on his face. "I would be careful with my words if I were you, Mr. Taylor. Such baseless accusations can land you in *very* hot water. Though I'd love to see you defending them in a courtroom." He nodded to Scribble, then turned and walked to the door. "I know when I'm not wanted. Of course, it doesn't really matter if you want me in this store or not. You're the last hold-out on the block, Mr. Taylor. One way or another, I will have this property. Eventually."

"Get. Out."

As the door shut behind Giacobbe, Paul leaned against it as if to make sure he was outside. The anger in his face faded to a blank mask.

Scribble put down the latte and stood next to him. "Paul?"

"I'm sorry you had to see that, Dez." He turned away but didn't move.

She put her hand on his large back and began to caress it. "I've never seen you talk that way to anyone before."

Paul's shoulders sagged. "He gets on my nerves. When my mom was alive, he used to come by just to harass her. Once he called the cops and told them I was robbing the place. He's an ass. If he can get my shop, he plans to tear it all down to build a strip mall. But he can't do it without damaging this building, too, so he has to wait until I sell."

"Is that what's got you so angry?"

Paul sighed and leaned against a bookshelf. "Not really." He was staring at nothing in particular when Boniface appeared on his shoulder but remained silent. Scribble could see the angel's breath as a depression came on. "It's my dad. He got in touch with me a couple of days ago. Said he's real sick, then told me he was sorry. Like I'd believe anything he says. Just thinking about what he did to my mom and me makes me furious. I guess seeing Mr. Giacobbe reminded me of it."

"What happened?" Scribble asked and joined him against the bookshelf. She knew it was dangerous to press him too hard, but she was feeling desperate for insight, any detail she could use next.

Paul was silent for a long while. He put his glasses down on the bookshelf and ran both hands over his face. When he finally did speak, his voice was wavery and weak. "Besides the constant affairs? He'd come home late, dead drunk, and hit Mom. Among other things. Even after they separated. She always put on a brave face, but I knew it was getting bad when she had to go to the hospital because of him."

Boniface floated off his shoulder and appeared full-sized next to Scribble. Words were insufficient, but the nod and hand patting her arm told her all that needed to be said before he backed away.

"He had a gun," Paul said just above a whisper. "I knew where he kept it, so I took it one night when Mom was in the hospital. I was just 14. I held it to his head as he slept."

Scribble gasped but didn't dare speak.

"I tried... It had no bullets in it. He must've kept them somewhere else. But I didn't know." He choked up and looked at the ceiling. "I've never told anyone."

The news stunned her for a moment. *Is that why his soul weight is so high?* The demoness took his hand in hers and squeezed it tightly. "It's hard being a human," she said, mostly to herself.

Paul let out a cathartic chuckle. "Tell me about it. Too bad we don't have much of a choice. I'd much rather be a vampire or something."

"Oh?" Scribble grinned slightly. "Well, what if *I'm* secretly a vampire? I could always bite you," she said and playfully snapped her jaws at him with a cute growl. As Paul smiled at her, however, she saw a face behind him that made her grow pale. Rotworm was standing right beside Paul, staring intently in disapproval at her.

"What's wrong?" Paul asked. "You look like you've seen a ghost."

In the space of a second, Scribble ran through every potential outcome, every excuse she could devise to explain to Rotworm what she was—and wasn't—doing. There was really only one choice; she would have to talk with him. And by the way he was glaring, it would have to be soon.

"I... uh... I just really need to use the ladies' room. Um... I might be a while," Scribble said and gave a fake smile as she held her stomach.

"Oh. Okay, take your time. We're not exactly bustling with customers. And, Dez, thank you for listening."

Just at that moment, the door opened and another customer came in. With a quick inhale, Paul straightened, rubbed his face, put on his glasses, and then forced a smile. Meanwhile, Scribble slipped away up the stairs to the apartment, and Rotworm followed close behind.

CHAPTER 16 – CONSPIRING

"What were you *thinking*, Riddle?!" Rotworm practically shouted. "Calling Belphegor himself? Do you know how much trouble you nearly got me in? He thought I had lost his precious prototype." He glared at her as she stood in the middle of the living room.

"I didn't mean to—"

"How did you even find his line? It was restricted! You were already on thin ice. One more slip-up like this…" he warned.

Scribble bit her lip and pulled the iBad out of her pocket. "It fell. It was an accident. I can't get it to work," she said, keeping her voice down. "Surli—"

"Surli? You found that old, broken thing? She *never* worked right. Let me see that." He grabbed the demonic device from her hands and started to mess with it. "You need to be more careful with this. I can take it away from you, you know. Let you do this job on your own. We'll see how long you'll last." The screen turned on.

A wave of jealousy hit her. She wished she could fix the iBad so easily, but she was mostly jealous that he was messing with the physical device without a physical body, and doing so with ease. "You're really good at that."

"Oh, great. Did you mess around with it in this mode?" he asked.

"No, I just pushed one button."

"Are you *sure*?" He looked up at her with a menacing stare.

"Y-yes, I'm sure!"

Rotworm's small, black horns began to grow from out of his slicked-back hair. His tongue slithered like a snake's. Even his skin darkened. "If you sssssso much as sssssssscratch this thing again, I will personally make sure you spend the rest of eternity in ssssearing agony."

Scribble felt mortal fear grip at her, but she didn't recoil like she used to. Something else grew within her—a hint of courage. When she found it, she clung to it. Somehow, this courage to stand up to Rotworm frightened her too, but in a different way. When he didn't get the expected reaction, Rotworm let out a "Bah!" and went back to the device.

After a minute of navigating menus, the iBad restarted. Scribble smiled when she heard the familiar sound of it booting up normally. Slowly, the horns and tongue receded back to their original forms as Rotworm relaxed.

"There. Don't ever do something like that again. But if you do, just bring it to *The Gray Raven*. Don't even try to turn it on or fix it." Rotworm put it down on the coffee table, letting her pick it up very carefully. "You need to take a break," he said suddenly.

"What?" She tried to get to the menu that turned Surli on, but was never really certain just how she had done it in the first place.

"You look tired. Got a headache?"

"How'd you know?"

"I've seen it before," he replied. "You're spending too much time in the homunculus body. You need to get out of it. Just stash it somewhere safe. Like in bed here. Take a day off."

"But there's so much work to do before the—"

"Work? Your *work* is to tempt that mortal scum. It is to make Boniface the Ever-Grinning suffer for me. It is to not get us both on Asmodeus' bad side." He let out a hot huff of air at her. "You thought *Grimtooth* had it bad."

Scribble clutched the iBad to her chest. "B-both of us?" she asked.

Rotworm went to the window to peek outside as if Incubus might be there, watching. "The only reason she gave you that body in the first place is because I gave her my word. We have a history."

"Look, I'm close. His depression is getting better. He's going to go see a doctor for it. And Surli said it should be easier to tempt him now that he's got a girlfriend. It's just a matter of time! I think he trusts me," she pleaded.

"Trusts you? And who would—" Rotworm looked over his shoulder at her and showed off his sharp teeth in a disturbingly wide grin. "Trusts you, huh? So, you're saying the client has real feelings for you?"

Scribble's cheeks darkened at the possibility. "I... I don't know..."

"Oh, I bet so. You're just its type, too—you're both bookworms! This is too good." He walked circles around her as he spoke, but she got the feeling he was mostly talking to himself. "Yes, if you manage to seduce it—*him*—he'll be a cheater. I bet I could recruit Ink-butt, too. He did seem to have his eye—"

"Wh-what? Recruit him for what?"

"For my plan, of course. You get that *human* to sleep with you. When his mate finds out about your tryst, she'll be sure to leave him. Then I'll arrange to have him catch you getting a little, uh, side action with Inky. He'll be alone *and* betrayed. It will tear his heart out. That should get his soul weight over 100 and keep it there with his depression. I can just see the look on that angel's face. This is going to be a good week."

Scribble felt her blood freeze with fear. "Week?"

"Yes, week," Rotworm returned in a factual manner. "Look, it's amazing you've had this body hold up so well for *this* long without taking power from men, the way a real succubus would. But a week is about all you've got left before real damage starts to show and *she* sends Inky."

Scribble stood in stunned silence as the reality of *one week* sank in.

"It's not like you've got much of a choice there, Griddle. Do it, or I'll redefine your concept of pain." He grabbed her arm with his hand, which had become a dark claw. Instead of it stopping at her flesh, it passed through and scratched at the soul beneath. Scribble let out a short cry before she managed to hold her hand over her mouth to muffle it. Rotworm just shook his head and stalked back down the stairs.

*   *   *

Many more hours of work passed before Scribble fell face-first onto her bed, arms spread out to her sides. "What an exhausting day..." she said into the pillow.

Something in her pocket vibrated. She reached down to pull out the iBad and brought it to her ear. "Hello?"

"It's about time you turned me back on!"

Surli's voice. Loudly.

"Surli! You're back!" Scribble rolled to her side to look at the screen. "I'm so glad you're not broken! I'm sorry I hit you on the ground. I tried turning you on but I couldn't remember how. Must have laid on you funny."

"So, what happened? Fill me in!"

"Ugh... now? I'm so tired. And I'm still a little angry at you." Scribble took off her glasses and put them on the nightstand. "I spent all day moving books and furniture with Paul."

"Oh? Did you—"

Scribble tried to ignore the glee in Surli's voice. "Nothing happened! Not after what you did."

"What *I* did? So what, my plan backfired. But Rotworm is right about getting him to sleep with you, so I guess it worked out!"

Scribble sighed into her pillow. "You heard that? Ugh. Now Paul feels all guilty about Ginger, and his dad called, and this Giacobbe guy got him riled up, and then Rotworm tells me I've only got a week left."

"Well, no time to rest then! We have a human to seduce and little time to do it in!"

The thought made Scribble's innards roll over. "I don't know. It seems... excessive. This could kill him. And, I don't want to do *anything* with Incubus."

Surli's impish image froze as Paul's dossier opened behind her and scrolled quickly by. Calculations then appeared on the screen.

"That is likely. Given the subject's family history and recent mental state, the proposed scenario results in self-harm in approximately 90% of probable outcomes."

She spoke in an informative tone, unlike any Scribble had heard before.

"However, if the subject is provided access to a firearm—"

"What?!" Scribble interrupted. "What do you mean? Are you still broken?" Surli's image became animated once more.

"Hm? I didn't say anything. So, now that you've got a deadline, what is *your* plan?"

Scribble raised her eyebrow. "But... just now you said something about self-harm." When a question mark appeared above Surli's animated head, Scribble just sighed. "My plan? I... I don't know. This is all new to me. To top it off, I think my body isn't working right..."

"What is wrong with it?"

"I keep blushing over Paul," she stated. "I can't stop thinking about him." Surli let out a playful laugh.

"Oh, that's just infatuation or lust."

"No, it's more than that. I worry about him. I want his business to succeed, I want him to get past losing his mom and Danielle. I want his dad to leave him alone. I want him to have a good relationship with someone. And I feel something strange. Guilt?" She turned over in bed and stared up at the ceiling. "I wish I could be his 'someone' and I don't know why," she admitted. "But I *do* know it'll never work. So, maybe Ginger really is his 'someone'."

A confused expression washed over Surli's image.

"This doesn't sound like any malfunction I've heard of."

"I thought I was sick, so I looked it up on the internet today. Some website Frank told me about. Either I have Scarlet Fever, or I'm in love."

"That is not possible. Your body can't contract diseases and no demon can love."

"I know! What's happening to me?"

"There must be another explanation. You have a week, right? I'm sure that once you start making some progress with Paul, things will sort themselves out. You're probably just getting cold feet. It is your first time, right?"

Scribble's cheeks flushed and she pulled the pillow out from under her head to cover her face with it.

Sitting up, Scribble shook her head and held the pillow in her lap. "No... I don't. I guess you're right. I have to try."

*   *   *

"To the remodel!" Frank said with a glass of hazy beer raised.

"To the re-opening!" Paul added. "Just two more days!"

Scribble had been thrilled when Paul invited her and Frank to go to *The Gray Raven* after a full day of lifting, sorting, and rearranging things in the store. Ginger had already gone home, so she figured it was a good chance to get Paul alone. Given how he'd been looking at her all day, she was sure it wouldn't be hard to get him away from Frank. But when they arrived, Ginger was already sitting in a corner booth, drink in hand. The pub was packed.

The four of them drank to the toast, but Scribble had her eye on Ginger. Despite the turn in weather, she wore a rather revealing black dress with a V-cut, which nearly went to her navel, and straps over her chest in the shape of a pentagon. It showed off enough skin to make even Scribble feel embarrassed. Surely it was for Paul. Around her neck, a red leather choker held a metal heart against her throat like she was trying to rub it in.

"It really looks great," Frank was saying. "Better than I expected. We should all be proud."

"I just hope I never have to move an electric fireplace again," Ginger groaned and rubbed at her shoulder.

But Scribble's attention wandered. Though the bar was much more crowded today, most of the patrons were avoiding walking through any tables. The classic rock had been exchanged for a baseball game, which showed on the large TV. There were still many angels and demons among them, including the six-armed bouncer standing guard. Rotworm was nowhere to be seen.

A roar erupted from the crowd and Scribble instinctively ducked her head. Frank laughed at the reaction.

"It's okay. The big game is on," he said, pointing to the TV. "Not much of a sports fan, huh?" Scribble just shook her head in answer. "If it's too crowded, we can go somewhere else."

"No, this is fine. I could use the distraction," she said, turning her attention back to the table. Paul's eyes were on her and she coyly smiled.

Ginger glanced between them. As if to cover his tracks, Paul leaned forward and said, "Don't tell me you've never seen baseball before."

"I've heard about it," Scribble replied. "Something about being as American as pumpkin pie?"

Frank laughed. "It's 'apple' pie."

She blinked in confusion. "But didn't they invent that in England?"

"Maybe so," Frank said with his beer to his lips. "But we perfected it."

"How can you not know about baseball?" Ginger chimed in.

Scribble felt self-conscious, and for the first time, was worried that her cover really would be blown. "I didn't watch much TV. I read a lot."

"That explains a few things," Ginger teased.

"I'm telling you, she used to be a Mennonite or Amish or something like that." Paul winked at her. "I'll be right back. Gotta use the restroom."

As he got up to leave, Frank took it upon himself to begin Scribble's education. "Well, it's not too hard to understand. See that diamond in the dirt? There are four bases, one for each corner..." He droned on, and before long, Ginger excused herself as well. Scribble bubbled over with jealousy and worry. She tried hard to contain it. The minutes ticked by.

"...If they hit the ball outside those two lines, it's called a 'foul ball' and counts as a strike—" Frank said, but stopped when she put her hand on his.

"Just a second, Frank, I need to take care of something real quick, okay?"

He nodded. "Well, I didn't think it was *that* boring," he said, but was already alone at the booth.

Scribble followed where Paul had gone—a hallway with the bathrooms on either side. Her heart sank. There, pushing his back against the wall, was Ginger. She was passionately kissing Paul, her hands wandering all over him. And Paul was holding her by the shoulders. Scribble squeaked and took a step back, fist against her chest. The sound roused them. Paul broke away from the kiss. When he saw Scribble standing there in shock, he looked away. Ginger, on the other hand, draped herself against him. One of the straps of her dress had slipped from her shoulder. "Well, if it isn't Miss Scribble," she said, rubbing Paul's chest and showing off how many buttons of his shirt she'd undone. "I told you he was mine." She playfully bit his ear, but Scribble just turned on her heels and walked steadily out the front door.

"Dammit! I can't believe I got so attached that I thought I had a chance!" she said as she walked down the sidewalk.

"What can I say, men are pigs."

It was Surli. Scribble sniffed as she pulled the iBad out of her pocket.

"He was opening up to me! I was opening up to him! I'm so foolish!"

Surli's digital ears drooped sympathetically.

"I know! But did you *see* how she looked at me? Why does she hate me?"

The electronic assistant warned.

Scribble hit her fist on the wall outside the *Raven* and shut her eyes tightly. "You're... absolutely right. I'll get him to sleep with me and then I can rub it in Ginger's face and watch *her* squirm."

"Desdemona?" Paul emerged from the bar and looked around.

Though Scribble's heart still leaped in her chest at his voice, she started getting angry—at him, at Ginger, at herself. "Paul?" she called and forced a smile, slipping the smartphone into her pocket. He ran up to her.

"Dez! I'm so sorry. I didn't—"

"What's there to be sorry for? She's your girlfriend and I just work for you."

Paul looked a little hurt. "You're more than just an employee. What she said was rude. And I know it had to hurt to see us."

"Why do you say that?"

"I thought that you and I... that we had a connection," he said softly. "Just because Ginger and I are together doesn't mean we should rub it in your face."

Numerous snide comebacks were fighting their way to Scribble's tongue, but she knew none of them would help her with her new goal. So, instead, she sighed and took his hands. "I appreciate that. I guess I really did hope we'd be something more."

Paul tightened his grip a little. "At least we can still be friends, right?" She nodded before pressing her forehead against his shoulder. When Boniface's chimes rang from his other shoulder, she briefly smirked. All those romance novels she'd read chock-full of seduction techniques, and yet her own instincts worked best. He let go of her hands and pulled her into an embrace.

Scribble had always liked his scent, but now there was an edge to it. She nuzzled into his shoulder more just to breathe it in. Though she wasn't hungry for food, her body was hungry nonetheless. It craved energy. It craved... *Paul*. Her face moved from his shoulder towards his neck. But before she could bring her lips there, he pulled back, breathing hard.

"Tomorrow," he said unsteadily. "The second play will be in the park tomorrow. Will you be there?"

Scribble let him have a manufactured but oh-so-charming smile.

"Of course."

Chapter 17 – Doubt

Scribble woke up feeling like her brain had been tied into a Gordian Knot. She, however, was prepared. Her hand blindly felt around the nightstand, knocking her alarm clock on the ground before finding her glasses. After fumbling to get them on, she grabbed the two pills she'd laid next to them. Already sitting on the ground was a cup of water; she had learned not to keep it on the nightstand so she couldn't knock it over. As soon as she downed the pills, she slipped out of bed onto her hands and knees and crawled to the bathroom. Fifteen minutes later, she emerged, looking more or less like a fully-functioning member of society, even though she still felt like crap. A quick breakfast didn't help. Food simply didn't satisfy her any longer.

Along with an aching head came a mild dizziness. Scribble had to use the handrails on either side of the stairs to keep steady. Once at the bottom, she paused, put a smile on her face, opened the door, and headed straight to the register. Frank walked out from the back and gave a start.

"Oh, Dez! I didn't think you'd be up yet. Good morning! Sleep well?"

"Frank? I thought you were scheduled for later," Scribble said. She put her hand up to her head.

"Well, after you ran out of the bathroom, I figured you weren't feeling too great and could use some help down here. So, how do you feel? Tired?"

Scribble swirled the word around her thoughts for a moment, testing its mouthfeel, its aroma. "Mmm… Yeah, we'll go with that. Tired. Or dying."

Frank sniggered. "Better not, at least not before the re-opening! You just need to take it easy. "

"I'm sure I'll be okay once the medicine starts working." She turned to the register while Frank gave her a worried look.

The bell above the door rang as Ginger stepped in. Her normally revealing attire had been traded for a modest pink sweater, pair of jeans, and red scarf. Scribble had never seen her in anything that didn't involve black or fishnet. Nor had she ever seen such a humble, demure expression on her face. All they got from her was a fleeting glance before she disappeared into the back room.

"What's wrong with her?" Scribble whispered. Frank just shrugged.

When she came back out, Ginger immediately got to work setting up the espresso machine. She all but ignored her coworkers. Not a sound did she make beyond mildly frustrated grunts whenever the machine didn't do what she wanted it to.

Scribble couldn't completely hide her smug smirk. *Maybe they had a fight. That'll make my work easier. She deserves it.* Whatever it was, she wanted to lord it over her, so she approached Ginger. "When you're—"

Ginger put up a hand and Scribble stopped. Once the *woosh! woosh!* of the machine started, she turned with a resigned huff of air. "Dez, about last night..." She started to say, before noticing Frank standing next to Scribble. "Oh! Frank!"

"Good morning," he said, apparently unaware of how much more awkward he had made things.

She nodded in reply, then looked at Scribble. "Say, didn't you ask me about applying mascara? Come on, let me show you."

Scribble was taken off-guard. She didn't recall any such conversation, though she did suddenly realize she hadn't put on any make-up that morning. Her fingers touched her lips and cheek. "Um... sure?" Ginger took her arm and led her towards the women's room. This wasn't going at all according to plan.

"Ah, well, I'll get back to it then," Frank said. "Trust me, you do *not* want me dealing with mascara. Last time, there were casualties!"

"If you say so, Frank," Ginger called back without turning her head.

Scribble figured Ginger just wanted to speak in private, so she was surprised when a make-up kit actually came out.

"I see you didn't take my advice from last time. You still don't have any of your own make-up, huh? Don't you have a compact? Emergency mascara? Back-up lipstick?"

Scribble shook her head. "It takes me forever to put on make-up," she said. "I don't wear it often."

"Well, you don't seem to need it most of the time. But it certainly can't hurt." She inspected Scribble's face closely and opened a compact. "It's not quite the right shade for you, but this should do in a pinch," she said and dabbed a small brush into the powder before applying it to Scribble's cheeks.

"I'm confused," she said. "Why did you really want me alone?"

The look of remorse returned to Ginger's face. "Dez, I wanted to... apologize. I'm so sorry about last night. How I acted, what I said... it was wrong. I wish I could say it was the booze, but I've not really been fair to you since we met. I tried to push you away without giving you a chance."

What? No, don't apologize! I'm supposed to hate you! Scribble screamed in her mind. What she said was, "Why are you telling me this?"

"Anyone can see you like him. And I think he likes you. I've been there. When he started dating Danielle, I felt like my world was over." She put the compact away and pulled out a lip pencil. "I remember I wouldn't have wished that on my worst enemy."

"Did he tell you to say this?"

"Shh, don't talk," Ginger pressed the pencil to Scribble's lips. "No. When he ran off after you, I got to thinking about it. You two have a special bond that he's never had with me. I was... jealous. You know, I hadn't seen him smile, really smile, since Danielle died. Not until you showed up."

"But he chose you," Scribble said. Her voice cracked a little. It took real effort to keep her emotions in check.

Next, Ginger began applying lipstick. "I'm not sure he did," she murmured. "Dez, maybe we can start over. I'd like to be friends. When you're ready."

Once Ginger was done, Scribble pressed her lips together and inspected herself in the mirror. Ginger fixed her own hair, so Scribble copied her. Female bonding, she was finding, had its own rules and ceremonies to follow. "But what if he had decided to be with me?" Scribble was hoping to hear how devastating it would be, but she was disappointed.

"Then I would've said that he deserves to be happy after the last two years."

"What? But wouldn't you be hurt?"

"Yeah, of course I would. But I'd have gotten over it eventually. If the right girl broke up with him, I'm not sure he would. Now, come on, Frank's probably getting himself in trouble."

*   *   *

Night and day. This was the change everyone saw in Ginger after her conversation with Scribble. She smiled more, opened up more, and even got along better with Scribble than she ever had.

For her part, Scribble *wanted* to hate her. It was hard to forget all the teasing at her expense. But this was a part of Ginger that she hadn't seen before. Perhaps it was the part that Paul liked about her.

"Why don't you open us up for the day, Ginny," Frank said.

"You know I hate it when people call me that," she replied and stuck her tongue out at him before walking to the front of the store to flip the sign around and set up the outside displays.

Frank wasted no time. He pulled Scribble aside and spoke softly. "What did you say to her?"

"Hm? Nothing much. It was just girl talk," she said.

"Well, you two should have more of it."

"Maybe. I still think she's hiding something, though. She's got to be."

Frank checked to see how Ginger was doing. "Why do you say that?"

"She's never this nice—not to me. Plus, she's being weird about Paul."

He nodded sagely and scratched at his ruddy beard. "Ah. *Him*. Well, don't tell anyone I told you, but I'm pretty certain Paul likes you," he said, then lowered his voice to a hoarse whisper. "And I think you like him."

A sunrise blush colored her cheeks. "You do?"

"Quite the conundrum. Ginger has to tread a very thin line between losing him by doing too much and not doing enough to keep him. But you know, I don't think you should give up just yet."

That new sensation, like being filled with both joy and worry, sprang up in Scribble's heart again. "Why do I feel such pain in my heart whenever I think about him?"

"Hmm. I guess you've never hoped for something so much it hurt."

She hadn't realized she'd asked her question out loud. "Hope? *Ugh!* Yes, that's why it hurts. Every time I feel it, it leads to disappointment and... and agony." She did her best to force it down. "When I saw them kissing, it *really* hurt. I *hate* hope!"

"Don't give up on hope! Maybe you two aren't meant to be. But hope keeps you looking forward. It keeps you moving. It keeps you alive."

This was the most honest, heartfelt conversation she'd ever had with Frank. Her mind took a while to process it all. But when Ginger walked past to grab a display from the back and bring it up front, her thoughts again drifted to that kiss and what her job really was. "What if Paul can't be trusted? I can't imagine how much it would hurt her if he and I..."

Frank nodded. "That's love for you. It's not just some silly emotion or nerves in your gut. It's sacrifice. It's risk. And like hope, it can hurt, too."

As he spoke, Scribble stared thoughtfully at the countertop. She examined her own emotions then lifted her swirling gray gaze to Frank. "Well, how do you know if you love someone?"

Frank let out a heavy sigh. "That is the million-dollar question, Dez. Many people go their whole lives never really knowing what love is, let alone if they are in love. Many others confuse lust or infatuation for love." He turned around and leaned back against the counter. "Are you religious? Do you believe in God and the afterlife and all that jazz?"

Scribble bit her lip, knowing that she was treading on ground dangerously close to the precipice. Under no circumstances could she give him proof of the hereafter. She spoke slowly, for fear of walking on a verbal landmine. "I don't know. I mean, there... might be a God. W-what do you think?"

"Me? I don't really know, either. Even if there is an afterlife, I wouldn't know which one to believe in," he said, much to Scribble's confusion. "But if there is such a place as Heaven and Hell, would you go to Hell if it meant saving someone else? I mean, if you knew someone you cared for was going to

Hell, would you take their place just to give them a second chance?" He turned and looked directly into Scribble's ever-changing eyes. "Would you die for someone? Would you live for someone? When you can answer these questions, you'll know if you're in love."

Ginger tapped him on the shoulder. They both turned to her, then turned to see what she was staring at. Customers. A couple dozen of them were filing into the store. Scribble had never seen half as many in the store at one time.

"Guys, I think we're going to be busy."

*   *   *

Despite the rush of customers, Scribble's focus kept slipping. She spent most of the time at the new espresso machine but had to remake drinks several times because of her daydreaming. Her mind kept running through the questions Frank had presented to her. She thought about Paul, and what it really meant to *love*. Doubts about her plan began taking root.

When Paul arrived after lunch, he was surprised to see how many people there were. He put down a thick stack of fliers as he reached the counter.

"Sorry I'm late. My printer ran out of ink and I had to get these done at a print shop." No one acknowledged him, so he stepped behind the counter. "Where did all these people come from?" he asked Scribble.

She jumped in surprise when she heard his voice. "Oh, Paul! It's you! Um, they were here when we opened. Apparently, someone 'posted it online'. I guess this play thing is working," she said. She briefly smiled before she remembered that she was angry at him.

"Well, we can't all go to the performance in the park. not with this many customers. And there's no way I'm closing now. Frank, I know you're not on the schedule, but would you man the store for me? And, Ginger, I need you to help him."

"Of course," Frank said. "Though I'm expecting overtime for this." Scribble couldn't tell if he was joking or being serious.

Ginger, on the other hand, had kept her head down the moment Paul walked in. The confidence she'd been displaying after their girl talk was gone. "Yeah. If you like. Or would you rather give Dez the experience?" she asked without looking at him even once.

"I'm sorry, but I need people who can handle this many customers, and it's too many for Frank alone."

She nodded slowly. "You're right. I'll stay. You're not mad at me, are you?" Her voice receded to a whisper at the end. She moved closer to him.

120

"I'm not mad…" Paul whispered back so the others wouldn't hear, but Scribble had *very* sharp hearing. "We'll talk about it tonight."

"Go on then. We've got things covered here." She finally looked at him and smiled. "You don't want to miss it."

Scribble picked up the fliers they were going to hand out and followed Paul out the door. She'd seen the two at odds before, but this felt different. Though she told herself Ginger was just getting what she deserved, she couldn't help but feel concerned for her new… *friend?*

Is that what she is?

*　　　*　　　*

Although colder weather had come in, the park was no less popular. Since the last time Scribble was there, the changing leaves had almost entirely fallen, making it impossible to walk around without crunching them underfoot. She and Paul both wore scarves and sweaters they'd grabbed from his apartment on the way, though the sweater she wore didn't quite fit. It was still too cold to spend a lot of time in the shade, which was exactly where they found the folding table set up for them.

"Are we going to have to carry that table back?" Scribble asked as she put the pile of fliers down on it.

Paul brought over a rock to act as a paperweight. "It's not heavy. I could make you carry it, but you're too short. You'd trip over it," he said, giving her a smirk. No sign of the tension in the store could be found in him.

Scribble punched his arm gently. "Am not! Would not!"

"How's my favorite bookworm?!" Paul was pulled into a bear hug from behind. When he was finally released, he turned and saw Jack Chester. He wasn't dressed like a policeman this time, but wore an "army" t-shirt over a long-sleeved undershirt. Standing next to him was a radiant young woman in her early 20s with long, bleached blonde hair wearing a light blue dress.

"Jack! I was wondering when you'd show up!"

"We've been here a while, man. Let me tell you, we practiced this scene at the subway a few nights ago and it was a real hit."

"You already ran it? Well, that might explain the customers we've been getting all day," Paul said.

Jack gave a huge grin, showing off as many teeth as he could. "Well, that's a good sign, ain't it?"

Scribble waved to him. "It's good to see you again, Jack. And who is this?" she asked as she turned to the young woman.

Jack looked at her in disbelief. The woman smiled and took her hand. "It's Abby Field. Remember, from the mall?"

Scribble was shocked. "*You're* Abby? But you look so much younger!"

Abby laughed. "Well, yes, I'm sure I do. It's all thanks to theater magic," she said. "And a wig."

Scribble's cheeks practically glowed with embarrassment. "Oh," was all she could think to say. In an attempt to save her pride, she changed the subject. "Aren't you cold in that?"

"Freezing!" Abby tugged on Jack's arm. "You ready, my *darling* husband, Othello?" she said flirtatiously.

Jack nodded and batted his eyes at Abby. "Whenever you are, Desdemona, my beautiful wife," he joked.

The pair walked away from the table, Abby still clinging to Jack's arm. The way they walked, chatted, even looked at each other made Scribble believe that they really were in love. It was only when a young man they had passed pulled Jack aside and into a clearing that she remembered they were actors.

"OTHELLO! You monster! What did you do to my love, Desdemona?" the young man shouted. Some people turned to pay attention to what was going on, others tried to avert their eyes and walk by a little bit faster. A kid with a cell phone walked in front of Scribble, filming the whole thing.

"I've done nothing, Roger, to your love!" the makeshift Othello shouted back. "I have taken *my* love, Desdemona, to be my wife!"

Scribble didn't want to miss any of this mini-play unfolding, even if she'd helped write it out. Plays were not something she ever had a chance to see in Purgatory. But when "Othello" declared "Desdemona" to be his wife, in spite of what was expected of them, Scribble found herself watching Paul instead. His lips were moving along with the players'. And, like Roger, she would soon be losing the person she cared about.

Roger rushed on Othello to attack. Another young man got between them and pulled him away.

"Do not provoke him, Roger! He is a general, remember."

Roger nodded and stroked his chin. "Yes, Iago, who knows what strings he pulled to trick Desdemona?"

Othello raised his voice in dramatic fashion. "I have not tricked her, Roger. All I did was tell her why I earned my promotion and medals." At this point, people who had tried to rush past began to get the idea that this was no ordinary fight and had slowed down to see what was going on.

"She was mine to wed!" Roger shouted and beat his chest.

Abby, as *Othello's* Desdemona, put her hand on Roger's shoulder to calm him. It worked, but she didn't linger with him and instead went to Othello's side. "You think me so weak-willed that I would let a simple trick fool me?" she said to Roger. "I made my decision to elope with Othello because I love *him*, not you. He is not a monster, he is my husband. *He* did not pay someone to try to woo me. You and your pimp, Iago, should just leave us alone. Now."

Roger turned to Iago with a growl. "How will I claim Desdemona now if she is already married?" he said loud enough for all to hear. Despite this, Othello and Desdemona feigned ignorance and continued down the path.

"Don't worry, friend," Iago said. "I happen to have some strings to pull myself. I promise you, he will pay for this treachery. They both will."

Jack and Abby returned to the clearing. "If you enjoyed this short scene inspired by Othello, tell your friends. We are the Chesterfield Players and we'll be at the grand unveiling of the newly renovated *Othello's Books* tomorrow morning at the corner of 5th and Barley."

Abby spoke up. "And if you didn't enjoy it, show up anyway! They'll have coffee and free Wi-Fi!"

There was a brief applause. Paul and Scribble took some fliers and began to hand them out. The afternoon passed by in a similar fashion. They talked, handed out fliers, and watched the play. The second time, there was almost no applause, but the third time, as the sun was going down, people had gathered as if expecting it.

By the time they had packed up the table and remaining fliers, the moon had risen above the skyline, partially clothed in a wisp of cloud. As they walked along the silvery streets back to the store, there was surprisingly little talking between them, but they nevertheless had a long conversation. Every slight glance in the other's direction, each awkward smile that was born when their hands brushed, the way she walked closer to him whenever a lonely car drove past—these were the words they spoke.

When they got to the store, it was dark and had already been closed up. Scribble leaned against the door frame with the remaining fliers in her arms. Although Boniface had appeared on Paul's shoulder, she was so focused on Paul that she hardly noticed him. His eyes shone in reflected moonlight, contrasting against his dark skin. When he leaned in closer to her, she had to tilt her head up to keep looking at him.

"Paul, I—" she said, but the words drifted from her mind. Instead, she pushed up on her toes and let out a muffled moan as their lips met in her first kiss. She was surprised at herself, but the pleasure and joy of kissing soon made everything around them fade away. He tasted like nothing she'd ever experienced. His lips were warm and soft in a way that made her feel light-headed. The papers fluttered to the ground as she melted. They were quickly followed by the folding table. Paul had a moment of hesitation, but then cupped her cheek and played with her hair. She let him take the lead as if they were sharing a romantic dance across the ballroom floor. As quickly as it had started, the kiss ended, leaving the two of them dumbstruck and out of breath.

Scribble's hands drifted around his waist while she gazed into his eyes. When she noticed Boniface, she was reminded of why she was there... what she was supposed to do. A kiss alone would not be enough.

"S-sorry, I shouldn't have. I don't know what came over me..." she said and let go of him to lean down and pick up the papers that had fallen. Paul cleared his throat and nodded. He opened the shop up for them and brought in the table. Her nerves threatened to ruin everything—her revenge, her mission, even her one chance to be with him.

"I'll see you tomorrow, Desdemona," he said. But before he reached the door, she grabbed at his hand and he turned back to her.

"Paul, would you like to..." She couldn't finish the sentence, but she didn't need to. This time, it was Paul who pulled her into a kiss. Their bodies pressed firmly together. His hands moved up and down along her back and she copied the movement with her own. The instant the kiss ended, another took its place, just as passionate as the one she'd seen Ginger give him. Scribble broke the kiss at the thought but kept her nose against his.

"If this is so wrong, why does it feel so right?" she whispered. Paul had no response. "Come upstairs?"

"Dez... I can't. We shouldn't," he said.

"Please?" Her voice grew husky as her body's hunger became ravenous.

"I'm supposed to go and see Ginger..." he said and let go of her. It sounded more like he was trying to convince himself than to stop her.

Their eyes met and Scribble tried to memorize what his looked like. She could press on, seduce him further. There wasn't a doubt in her mind that he would give in. When she took his hands, he didn't let go. When she planted a kiss on the side of his neck, he groaned and tilted his head as if to offer more of it to her. But she resisted. The part of her that knew what would happen prevailed and she turned her head aside and stepped back from him.

"I don't want to see you hurt. I'm not worth it," she said and bit her lip.

"Not worth it? You're beautiful, kind, funny, concerned for others, smart, and I think it's cute the way you bite your lip. Just like that!" Paul said.

She shook her head. "I'm not who you think I am, Paul. We don't really know each other that well." He tried to protest, but Scribble stopped him with a hand to his chest and a gentle push. "I'm sure Ginger is waiting for you."

Paul's figure sagged and he nodded. "Yeah," he said. They bid each other goodnight and he walked slowly out of the store and down the street, head hanging low. It was the hardest thing Scribble had ever done.

                    *   *   *

"Well, Squiggle, it appears you've proven me wrong. You do seem to know what you're doing."

Scribble turned around to see Rotworm standing directly behind her with an iBad in his hand. "R-Rotworm! How long—"

"I've been watching you all day, and I must say, I'm impressed. Bringing him out of his depression, keeping his soul weight at 100 without any help—you just might have what it takes. But you can do better." His mouth twisted into a sharp, sinister smile. The suave, almost playful Rotworm was gone.

Her whole being swirled with conflicting emotions. Scribble shook her head and tried walked past him.

He grabbed her arm with an unshakable grip. "Are you sure about this? Letting him walk now? Incubus is going to be here tomorrow. Maybe you won't need to bed the client to win, but I like to be certain. Right, Surli?"

From Scribble's pocket, Surli spoke in that weird digital monotone:

> "Without prior intercourse, the client is only 30% likely to achieve total despair."

Scribble put her hand on her pocket in an attempt to shut her up. "You're not helping, Surli."

"I can't force you," Rotworm said. "But you are out of time. The homunculus body will be returned tomorrow, one way or another. The only question is, what will I be doing with you once I wrench you out of it? Reward? Or punishment?" Again, he showed her his wicked grin. It was the only detail of his face that she could clearly see.

He let go of her and stood perfectly still as she retreated silently to the apartment stairs.

Chapter 18 – Fear

It was just like any other day, except that the constant fear of seeing Incubus or Rotworm kept Scribble looking over her shoulder every few minutes. She and Paul worked the store alone. This was the last day they would have together and Paul didn't even know it. He was also acting as if they hadn't just shared an intimate kiss the night before. It was probably for the best—customers waited everywhere Scribble turned. She couldn't help but feel lost and despondent each time one distracted her from her real goal. All she wanted was to spend as much time with Paul as she could before the end.

Coffee. Mocha. Latte. Coffee. The customer orders were endless, at least until she reached under the counter for a new bag of coffee grounds and found the counter bare. She held up a finger and walked to the back room on the hunt for more coffee. Before she found any, however, she turned to see Paul standing right next to her.

"Scribble," he said in a deep voice and grabbed her hand.

A tremble took hold in her body. No matter how much she wanted to pull away from him, to keep her distance emotionally and physically, her muscles simply wouldn't react. He drew closer, his lips a heartbeat away from hers. It was no use. Scribble wanted it as much as he did, and in a moment, they were locked in another kiss. Her eyes drifted closed as she held onto his cold body.

Cold? she thought and opened her eyes again. She wasn't holding Paul any longer... but Incubus. She let out a gasp as he pinned her against the desk with his body. Just then, the door opened and Paul walked in.

"Dez, what's going on?" he asked, his voice breaking. Scribble reached out for him, but it was too late. Wires snapped up from the ground into her hand and arm, striking through her skin. They pulled sharply, tearing her soul from the body. Slytongue appeared from nowhere, giving her a little goodbye wave before taking the body. Scribble fell through an opened door in the ground and into a giant chasm of fire beneath. Floating at the door was Rotworm and his wicked smile. The last thing she heard was the door slamming shut.

*   *   *

Scribble sat up in bed, panting and damp with sweat. Her body was still unharmed, she was still in the apartment, and it was still dark. She reached for the bedside table, found her glasses, and put them on. "Surli, you awake? What time is it?"

"Of course I'm awake. Computer programs don't sleep! It's 10:43 p.m."

"Ugh… what just happened? I was kissing Paul, then I was being dragged into Hell. It felt so real. Was that a… dream?"

"Impossible. No Immortal has ever dreamed before. Of course, they don't usually sleep, either."

Scribble nodded, putting her hand to her head. "Well, this body is a prototype. Maybe it's a result of being in here too long." She sat up in bed and noticed the two pills and glass of water she'd put out near the nightstand, then quickly took them. As she downed the second pill, a thump downstairs made her blood freeze. "What was that?" she whispered.

"It sounded like the back door opening,"

Surli replied at her normal volume. Quickly, Scribble grabbed the iBad and frantically mashed at the "volume down" button.

"Quiet!" she breathed. When she was satisfied the iBad was on silent, she slipped it into the pocket of her shorts and gingerly got out of bed. To her, every step sounded like a drum beat. She snuck across the room and grabbed a rather large, framed picture, clutching it to herself as if it would defend her. Another thump came from downstairs, followed by the sound of something being dragged across the floor. Scribble paused for a moment, grabbed a bigger picture, then crept down the stairs. She held the picture up with one hand and pushed open the door at the bottom.

Everything was ominous at night. In Scribble's imagination, each shadow hid a burglar, rapist, murderer, or worse. Was Incubus early? She wanted to be brave, to confront the intruder or at least find out who it was. But she was petrified, frozen in place with a single 11x14 frame to keep her safe.

THUD.

The sound came from the back room. Scribble jumped. Her mind raced with the possibilities. *This is ridiculous. There's nothing to be afraid of. I've been in Hell. Oh! What if there's two of them?! Maybe I could just lock the bedroom door…*

Before she had a chance to retreat back upstairs, she heard the sound of the back door closing, then footsteps walking quickly along the wet ground in the alley. She ran to the window and placed her back against the wall beside it. When the footsteps passed by, she glanced outside. A dark figure in the rain moved towards a car that sat idling nearby. Scribble snuck to the front windows and tried to hide by a display case to get a better view. Through the light rain, she saw the figure pass in front of the car's headlights. It was a woman, short, attractive, and with long, red hair. She got into the passenger seat and the car started off. When it passed under a streetlight, Scribble could make out a rather portly man with a moustache in the driver's seat.

"Is that Giacobbe and... Addison?" she asked out loud. As soon as she spoke, she smelled something out of place. Burning. With a sudden burst of speed, she ran to the back room, throwing her body against the door.

Some of the bookshelves that had been filled with Paul's collection were knocked over. More books had been piled on top of them, along with the file cabinet. A crackling fire rose from the mass of words and wood pulp, licking at the ceiling. Smoke was already filling the room just above Scribble's head. She dropped the picture.

"Oh no! What do I do? What do I do?" Her eyes darted around the room for an answer. The mop in the corner. Within seconds, she'd emptied the contents of the bucket it had been sitting in onto the fire, then rushed to the bathroom to get more water. The bucket wasn't even half full when she brought it back and poured it on top. It made no difference. The fire reached the ceiling and crawled along it. Suddenly, an alarm went off and water flooded out of the sprinkler system. Scribble watched the fire struggle against the flood, but smoke filled the room and obscured everything. She began to cough and ran out the front door into the rain. Sirens could already be heard in the distance.

*   *   *

It was just before midnight by the time Paul arrived. Scribble stood shivering under a fireman's heavy coat, wearing only a t-shirt and shorts beneath it. Although the rain had stopped, it had brought with it colder temperatures, but the firemen and police officers working around them didn't seem to mind. They erected police tape and barriers around the storefront and part of the street. Paul tried to get past them. "I got here as fast as I could. What happened?" he called towards Scribble.

One of the officers put her hand up and approached Paul. "I'm sorry, sir. This is a crime scene."

"Crime scene?! Let me through, I'm the owner! Hey! Don't push me, this is my property!"

"Back *off*, sir!"

Paul went still when he saw the officer's hand hover over her pistol. He slowly put his hands behind his head, staring with poorly hidden disdain.

Scribble quickly ducked under the tape and went to his side. "Paul, you're here!" She pulled him away from the officer and leaned against him. Her presence alone seemed to diffuse the situation. The officer kept her eye on them, but her body relaxed.

"Dez, are you alright? I couldn't understand you on the phone, but it sounded bad. What happened?" he insisted.

"I'm so sorry. I didn't know what to do when I saw the fire."

Paul gripped her shoulders and stared at her, terror painting his face dark. "What fire?" He didn't wait for an answer. He let her go and moved towards the store, but her hand held firm on his wrist and kept him from going far. He looked back at her with an expression that changed from angry to hurt.

"Don't. You shouldn't see it like this."

"It's that bad?"

Scribble nodded. "The sprinklers put the fire out before the firemen even got here, but the water got on everything."

The scent of burnt paper caught them on the night's breath. From the outside, the store looked untouched. But with that scent came a sense of dreaded, unexpected finality.

"Someone moving things around woke me up and I came downstairs," Scribble said softly. "I saw a red-headed woman getting into a car with someone who looked like Mr. Giacobbe. Then I smelled the fire."

"Could it be Addison? Frank's wife? I don't know what to do." His hand slipped from hers and he leaned his head against the building nearby. "What do I do, Dez?"

She put her hand on his back carefully. "I don't know."

"I mean, insurance will cover most of this. I'm sure it will. Right? But what about the rest? And what about the re-opening? It was supposed to happen tomorrow. And the customers? How am I going to make ends meet in the meantime? I still have to pay off that loan." He let out a deep sigh as she rubbed his back reassuringly. "I don't know what I would do if it wasn't for you, Desdemona. These past few weeks, you've really helped me out."

Scribble's heart sank. "Paul, I have something important to tell you."

"Are you the owner?" interrupted a gravelly voice. A police officer had approached them, a man with pepper hair and small glasses. Paul nodded. "I was told you were trying to get into the building. Sir, I'd like to get some basic information from you so we can get in touch with you later. I understand it's late and don't want to take up too much of your time."

Paul began to speak with the officer, sharing any information he could while Scribble held his arm. Something rustled in the street behind her, but all she saw was a homeless man sitting on the sidewalk at the end of the block. Something about him kept her attention, however. The man stood up—a tall silhouette. He moved towards them, but his body remained still like a man coasting and not walking. After a moment, the figure moved right through a fire hydrant. Scribble tensed in terror as she recognized Rotworm's predatory gaze fixed on her. He stopped beside her and leaned in close.

"Just one more mistake, Scribble," he said. His tone was calm, even soft, though the way he said her name—the first time he'd ever gotten it right—made it sound like an insult. "I will bury you ssssso deep that even the Great Deceiver himself will look down on you and use you as a toilet." Then he simply stood back and watched them from a short distance.

When the officer walked away, Scribble remained silent, withdrawn. She didn't even notice that she and Paul were alone together. "Dez? Did you say something? Hey, are you okay?"

She tightened her grip around his arm. "I don't have anywhere to stay. Can I come over to your place?"

CHAPTER 19 – LOVE

Neither of them said a word during the walk back to his apartment. Even though she had been in this body for some time, she still had trouble navigating her emotions. Usually, they weren't this strong—or this conflicting. It didn't matter how bad the news was, how hard an evening they had been having, she was still craving Paul, fantasizing about him. What was worse, she knew just where those fantasies would lead, especially if Rotworm had his way. Incubus. Self-harm. Hell.

"Here we are," Paul said. They stood in front of an unremarkable apartment complex. His voice broke her from her introspection.

"What? Oh," she said absently.

"How are you holding up?" he asked.

"Meh. Just a lot on my mind."

Paul let out a sigh. "Mine, too." He led her to his apartment on the first floor, number 108, and brought her in. It wasn't the first time she'd been in his apartment, but she'd never really looked around it before. Almost everything looked older than he was—probably older than the apartment building. Yet, it was all in remarkable condition. She remembered it being a mess the first time she'd been there. Now it looked like he had been cleaning up. Books sat on shelving units all around the place. A small TV in the corner of the family room faced a couch that had obviously been stolen from the 1970s. Down a small hallway, Scribble noticed an open door revealing a room filled with stacks of water-damaged tomes—the same ones she'd spent hours cataloguing. *At least some of them got out of there,* she thought with relief. Overall, the entire place looked more like an odd museum or unkempt library than a home. Unlike the apartment above the store, this one lacked something, and it took Scribble a moment before she realized what. Pictures. Not a single picture hung on a wall or adorned a table.

"So, this is the family room," Paul told her. "I'll take the couch tonight. I'll show you the bed where you'll sleep."

"That couch? No, you can't sleep on that thing. It looks like it might try to eat you." Scribble sat down on it and poked at a lump in the cushion. "Well, maybe not. I think it just ate."

A smirk tried to work its way onto Paul's face, but it didn't last long. "It's fine. I don't mind."

Scribble knew what had to be done. They were alone now, but she couldn't bring herself to take that final step. She glanced at the clock on the wall. It was just after 1:00 am. Although the first signs of fatigue could be felt, neither of them made any move to head to bed. "So... what are we gonna do?" Scribble asked, patting the seat next to her as she curled against the arm of the couch.

Paul pinched the bridge of his nose. "I don't know. Call the insurance company in the morning? I'd rather not think about it. Um... can I get you something to drink?" he asked and headed into the adjoining kitchen.

"Maybe some water." A chime came from her pocket. She jolted a little and pulled out the iBad. On the screen, Surli pointed a floating hand towards a link on a webpage.

"Who's texting you this late?" Paul asked from the other room.

"Hm? Oh, it's just an old friend from back home." Scribble lowered her voice to a whisper. "What is it? Why are you disturbing us?"

       "Just check the link!"

Appeared on the screen. At least this time, Surli had the forethought to remain on mute. When Scribble tapped the link, court records appeared.

"What is this?" Scribble whispered. "You're trying to be helpful? On your own? Are you sure you aren't broken?" Surli stuck out her tongue.

"It's not Val, is it?" Paul walked back into the family room and put a glass of water on the low coffee table for Scribble, then sat down beside her.

"Val?" She didn't look up from the screen. "Um... no. I told you, I haven't seen him in, like, five thousand years. Maybe six."

"Did you like him?" Paul asked. He didn't get an answer; Scribble just kept staring at her iBad. "What's so important over there?"

Scribble turned the screen so that he could see it, too. It showed a marriage document between Addison Giacobbe and Franklin DeMills.

"Why are you... wait, Addison *Giacobbe?* Frank is Giacobbe's son-in-law?"

"Looks like it," she replied, slipping the iBad back into her pocket.

Paul ran his hand over his bare head. "He could have been taking the money, too. Oh, God, I've been blaming Ginger this entire time! He must have planted it on her." He leaned forward and hung his face in his hands. Several minutes passed between them in silence. Scribble rubbed his back nervously. Suddenly, he drew in a deep breath and sat back, drying his wet cheeks with the back of his hand. "How am I going to get through this?"

Scribble leaned back against him and rested her head on his shoulder. Eventually, she said, "Take it one day at a time. You can't give up." She realized she was not helping herself but didn't care.

"Do you think she'll ever forgive me?"

She nodded. "I think so. She still cares for you."

"I pretty much accused her of embezzlement. I've got to talk to her in the morning. God, my mom would be furious with me."

"I bet your mom would have forgiven you, too. If you'd asked." Scribble bit her lip. "Is it hard to forgive someone who wronged you?"

"Sometimes," Paul replied. "You aren't trying to tell me something, are you? You're pretty much the only reason I've been able to keep it together." At first, he had a serious look in his eye, but then a small smile cracked through.

Scribble nudged him in the side. "What about your dad?"

"What about him? I don't think he wants to be forgiven. I doubt he even thinks he's done anything wrong."

"Well, would you forgive him if he did ask?"

Paul breathed in deeply, then let the air out like a smoker enjoying a long drag. "I dunno. That's a hard one." He rubbed at his cheek again. "My best memories are of me and my mom in the shop, my worst are of him, or the two of them fighting." He stared off into space as he continued. "The shop is really all we ever had. I gave up all *my* dreams to keep it going. What would my mom think? Have I been doing the right thing?" He shut his eyes tightly and let the tears fall. Scribble stroked his arm until he calmed down. "Sorry. It's just a lot to take in. So, what about you? What are your best memories?" He seemed eager to take the attention off of his past.

"Mine? Well, to be honest, my favorite memory is of you. Everything else was... well, Hell." She smiled a little as Paul shifted in his seat to face her more.

"Me? What about home? Don't you remember your parents?"

Scribble shook her head. "No. But if I live to be a million years old, I don't think I will ever forget you, or my first kiss." She brought her pale hand to his cheek and brushed away some of the tears.

"A million years? That's a long time." He pressed his cheek into her hand and smiled. "But not long enough." When he opened his eyes, she had her face inches from his. He gazed into her swirling, gray eyes with an almost desperate need for closeness. "Your eyes, they're—"

He never got the chance to finish. Scribble pulled him into a powerful kiss, muffling anything else he had to say into a moan. Their bodies squeezed together awkwardly before she slid into his lap, legs on either side of him. She peppered his lips with more kisses. His large, strong hands quickly ran up her soft form and pulled off her shirt. Soon, they were skin to skin, discovering new sensations and emotions as their bodies pushed and pulled and brushed together. Scribble gasped, feeling him bare beneath her. They lost themselves to their passion.

NO! Images of Ginger walking in on them filled her thoughts. She saw the heartbreak and pain, and for the first time, truly understood how devastating such a betrayal would be. Thoughts of Paul hurting himself quickly replaced the others. Then he was dragged into Hell by barbed wire and chains, branded and burned and bit by an army of tiny demons. They tore him open, tortured him, and then processed him into a soul stone to power some device with his eternal torment.

Scribble pushed away from him hard and landed on the far side of the couch. There were no wires, no chains, no demons. He was whole and unharmed, save for the expression of confusion and pain he gave her. Those injured eyes never strayed from her as she hastily got dressed.

"What's wrong? Too fast?" he asked. His normally strong voice wavered.

"I-I can't..." she said. Tears spilled. "It's not right. I'm not..."

"Not right? What do you mean? Is it because of Ginger?" Paul got up.

Scribble threw his clothes at him, making sure not to look right at him. "Not just her! I can't... I can't be here right now." She was pacing around the room, her dark, tangled locks tossing all about.

Paul pulled his clothes on quickly. "Dez, Ginger and I broke up tonight."

"What!? But why? Was it the money? You know she didn't take it!"

"It's not about the money. She told me she won't date someone who already belongs to somebody else."

"She—*what*—!?"

"Besides, we both realized that it's you I want to be with. I can't do this behind her back."

She hit her hands against her head. "Ahh! But we can't be together!"

"What are you saying?" he asked quietly.

"I love you!" she blurted out, hands tearing through her hair. "Oh, God, I love you! But... I can't! I shouldn't be able to! I'm a—"

"I don't understand. How is that bad? And what's stopping you?" He followed her as she threw open the front door of his apartment and started walking down the street lit only by the slice of moon that showed behind the clouds. The haze of breath that condensed around them blurred their silhouettes. "You're a what, Dez?"

"I'm nothing. Just forget about me! I can't have you, can't be with you!" She stopped walking and looked back at him, but his dark outline was almost impossible to see with the forgotten Boniface sitting on his shoulder emitting a bright, white light. Rivulets of tears flowed freely down Scribble's cheeks, silvery streaks reflecting the heavens. From her pocket came a buzz. Scribble rolled her eyes. "Damn it, Surli. Now is NOT the time," she said, but the iBad buzzed again, harder than before. She pulled it out and saw the most worried look Surli had ever given her. On the screen was an alert and a news article.

Paul balled his hands into fists. "What, you don't have time for me, but you can text your friend again?" He turned to the wall of his apartment and kicked it in frustration. "Shit, Dez. Talk to me! What did I do? Don't be like Dani. Don't run off and leave me behind."

"Dani?" Scribble echoed in a whisper while she continued to read the article. "Danielle Lee Cooper?" she asked, her voice tinged with worry.

The strange question broke him out of his anger. He pushed away from the wall and tried to get a better look at the screen. "Yeah. How'd you know her middle name?"

All the blood rushed out of Scribble's face. "Danielle Lee Cooper, born in Hartford, Connecticut?"

Paul furrowed his eyebrow. "How did you know all that? What are you looking at?"

She ignored him while she read the article through one more time.

PURGATORY SOUL GOES TO HELL

Purgatory – Late last night, the soul of Danielle Cooper descended from the redeeming fields of Purgatory and entered into the gates of Hades. "This has never happened before," said Izrathel (Throne) of the Order. "In all the years we have been guarding the gates of Hell, no human soul has ever come to it from Purgatory." The soul was found to have a weight of 101, just above the limit permitted to enter Purgatory.

Purgatory is the only part of Hell where human souls lose soul weight until they have redeemed their sins. Without the wings of an Immortal, human souls will eventually drift to the appropriate place for their soul weight. Questions have been raised as to whether or not this means that there is a problem in Purgatory.

The Order has noted that there has been a recent change in the way Purgatory is being run. They are investigating the possibility of corruption within management. The management, however, points their fingers at the demon they claim is responsible for registering her—Scribble (Imp, 4th type). "Infernal Devices never fail and never err," stated a memo from the office of Belphegor, Prince of Sloth and inventor of the machine that took over for Scribble after her reassignment. "We are searching for [Scribble] to determine whether or not this was simply an error or a malicious act of revenge at losing her position," the memo said.

Danielle Lee Cooper, born in Hartford, Connecticut, died last
December. Due to a backlog, her soul was registered just a
few weeks ago.

Scribble screwed her eyebrows together. "I think I might be in trouble."

Chapter 20 – Ambition

This is starting to look like Heaven, Rotworm thought as the fourth set of angels clad in thick armor looked over the small booklet he held. The long, torch-lit corridor that led to Level 10 was familiar to him, but he had never seen the Order posting guards past the level's gates before. The angels stepped aside and let him pass between them to the massive, heavy-set doors. Two ever-staring eyes of living paint watched him lay into the doors with his shoulder until they gave way with a loud, rusty creak.

He strained his eyes to see deeper into the abyssal cavern. It seemed darker, deader than usual. "Master?" he called out but got no response. Cautious step after cautious step, he made his way deeper into the chamber. *CLANG! Clang. clang...* The sound ricocheted around the room, making clear to the darkness that the intruder had hit his head on something large and metallic. "Ow!" Rotworm ducked and held onto his head with one hand while feeling for the object with the other.

"Who's come to disturb me?" came an electronic facsimile of a voice from overhead. Rotworm looked up just as lights started to switch on with a series of loud pops, starting at the far end of the room and moving closer. The room was a huge factory with random conveyor belts, pulleys, cords, and skeletal columns of metal all connected haphazardly. Rotworm had hit his head on a low-hanging conveyor belt. Just beyond it, he could see a dark shape suspended far above the ground in tattered rags.

"Oh. It's you, worm. Did you harm my machine with that thick head of yours?" The form changed shape and seemed to grow a pair of emaciated arms. Legs then fell from it and dangled freely beneath the figure. Thin, dark wires hung from a large matrix of convoluted machinery that made up most of the ceiling and were attached to each digit, each joint of the creature. These metal strings manipulated the body like a marionette being controlled by some invisible master. It moved closer, into the light, so that Rotworm could see how pale it was, almost like rice paper. A round belly tainted and warped with unknown maladies hung over the ragged loin cloth that hid what little shame it had. A small, round speaker, which looked roughly grafted into his chest, did all his speaking for him. Only the muscles that controlled his eyes ever moved.

"Great Lord, your machine is unharmed. I did not see it in the dark," Rotworm replied, falling to one knee and bowing his head in submission.

"You wouldn't have seen it, would you? I like it dark. Takes less energy." Belphegor's body lowered to the conveyor belt so he could look it over. The belt carried an endless line of soul stones, each one secured with clamps to prevent it from floating away. The belt descended from a hole in the wall near the ceiling. Once in a while, a scream or moan of pain echoed down from the hole. Belphegor's voice overshadowed them. "I'm busy with my battery. What do you want?"

"Sire, there's news. The subject we have been searching for has just been seen entering Hell."

Belphegor stopped inspecting the machine and looked down at Rotworm. "You're sure about this? If you're wasting my time, I'll make you wish you never oozed out of whatever creature you spawned from."

"I am sure. Danielle Cooper, client number 10769283883. I even paid it a visit. It's the right soul, all right. Even looks the same as when I shot it."

Although the demon Prince only slightly changed his expression, Rotworm recognized when the Lord of Sloth smiled. "Do you know what this means, worm? This means the weapon works. It works better than I expected." His rotting body swayed as the wires and machinery pulled him away from the conveyor belt and towards a monitor attached to the wall. "Even after death, it continues to add weight to the human's soul."

"Adding weight? That's possible?" Rotworm asked as he slowly rose to his feet. "How?" Of course, he already knew the answer. Rotworm was nothing if not a master of pandering.

Belphegor hunched over the screen as the box spoke for him. "I'm sure you're familiar with human diseases." Rotworm nodded. "Most involve microscopic invaders. But sometimes, the body turns against itself. Cancer, for example. A few cells start growing uncontrollably and spread throughout the body until they kill it. The weapon I had you use on that human girl gave her a cancer of the soul. Much like the effect of a sinful habit, it slowly grows and grows. If she does not treat it, it should consume her completely."

"Treat it, sir?"

"It would take a true miracle."

A look of awe settled on Rotworm's face. "It's ingenious! Imagine what this will do for Sinisters. Just one shot and the job is done..."

Belphegor laughed in his emotionless, metallic voice. "You think too small, worm. Do you still have the prototype?"

Rotworm nodded. "I have it stored someplace safe on Earth, Sire."

"You'll need to use it once more. The human was just a guinea pig. Now you must test it on an Immortal. I need to see if it can affect a soul that can't change its weight. Angel, demon... I care not."

"But the Order... I was lucky getting away with attacking a human. Surely if I attack an Immortal, it will attract their attention."

Belphegor looked away from the monitor and moved closer to Rotworm in a threatening manner. "I can try it on you, if you prefer," he said. The mounds of flesh where his eyebrows might once have been strained in an attempt to lower. "But you've been loyal. And useful. I'd prefer to keep you. Besides, your soul is already so heavy, it would difficult to know if it worked. Don't worry about the Order. The device should act much faster against an Immortal than a human. When I see that it works, I will free you from the angels. Just don't let anyone get in your way like that Grimtooth last time."

"I will not fail you," Rotworm said, bowing at the waist. "Oh, Great One, I know it is but a trifling matter, but earlier you had mentioned a promotion..."

Wires pulled Belphegor back towards the monitor. "What of it?" he asked as he returned to his work. The conveyor belt suddenly sprang to life, bringing more soul stones into the room.

"If I am successful, surely I could take on more responsibilities."

"Fine. I'll give you the promotion you desire when you return. Is there anything else?"

"Just one thing, master. I can choose any Immortal to test it on?"

"Yes."

A wicked, broken smile distorted Rotworm's features. "Then I know the perfect subject."

*   *   *

"What do you mean, you might be in trouble?" Paul asked as Scribble started to pace along the walkway. "And what does that have to do with Dani?"

Her eyes hadn't left the iBad since she'd read the article. "I-I can't tell you. It's too dangerous."

"Dangerous? Did you see something? Is someone after you? Is it that Val guy you had a fight with?"

She shook her head before turning away from him to speak in a softer voice to the iBad she held up to her mouth. "Surli, call Rotworm." Scribble tossed her head to the side so she could bring the device to her ear.

"Rotworm? What is that, a nickname? Is he why you stopped? Why won't you talk to me?" Escalating worry tinged the questions that poured from him.

"It's not like that. I just... I can't tell you! I wish I could. I shouldn't even be here. Look, I have to go." Scribble turned away from him and rubbed at the tears collecting in her eyes. She knew she had to get out of there and away

139

from him, so she began running from the apartment complex and down a dormant street. She didn't look back to see whether or not Paul followed after.

The iBad continued to ring in her ear without an answer. Ahead, light shone from a small screen. A figure walked into her path, shrouded in shadow. It held the screen out as if showing it off to the girl. Scribble halted and held the iBad to her chest, but a moment later, she realized that her name, her real name, was displayed on the caller ID screen the figure held out.

"Rotworm! You found me! Uh, I mean, you're here! I was just calling to see where you were." She very slowly took a step back. He didn't respond but instead slipped his iBad back into his pocket. His snakelike stare bore a hole into her false confidence. "I... I guess you heard they're looking for me. Look, it wasn't my fault! I don't even know if I was the one who registered that soul," she said, holding her hand out defensively and taking another step back. He took three closer.

"Is there someone there, Dez?" Paul called out, a good deal behind her. Rotworm glanced over at him and smiled, his tongue tasting the air before his gaze shifted back to her.

Scribble's eyes widened. "Oh, *him*. I can explain. There's still time. I'm just playing hard to—"

She swallowed the rest of her sentence. Rotworm rushed forward with unholy speed. By the time she realized he had moved, it was too late. He gripped her arms tightly. She struggled against him. His fingers grew into long, hard claws, which dug past the flesh and into her soul. The business suit he normally wore had become a scaly armored hide, steaming in the night. Dark wings spread out twice as long as he was tall and seemed to draw all the darkest shadows around into them. Despite putting her full strength into fighting against him, he never lost control of the situation. With one claw, he grabbed the small iBad out of her hand, then tossed her to the ground. It took only a moment of messing with the device before the top of it split down the middle and snapped open, revealing a mechanical ring that sparked with energy. He pointed it directly at her.

Fear made Scribble's body seize up. She just stared at the demon as the device drew more and more power into it. "P-please don't hurt me..." she pleaded in a soft voice.

A chuckle rose out of Rotworm. "If you insisssssst," he hissed, then shifted aim at Paul, who was rushing towards them.

"Dez?! Are you alright? What happened? Is someone there?" he called out, unaware of the danger. Scribble remained glued in place, giving Rotworm the luxury of aiming before pressing his thumb against the touchscreen. A beam shot out of the iBad with a scream that could freeze blood. It looked like a dark rip had temporarily been cut in the fabric of reality. Light and geometry from nearby bled into it until the tear closed itself a second later. Only after Scribble saw the weapon activate did she move again, reaching up to Paul in a futile attempt to rescue him. But the beam had missed him, striking just above his right shoulder instead. In a flurry of feathers and light, Boniface fell from his perch there and landed, full-sized, on his back in the street.

The angel remained motionless on the ground as a broken cackle erupted from Rotworm. "You sssssstupid angel! Sssssee who is the victor now!" He ran over to the angel and kicked him gleefully.

Scribble watched the scene unfolding in horror and quickly tried to get to her feet. Paul took her hand and pulled her up.

"What happened? It looked like you were struggling with someone, but there's no one else here," he said.

Scribble just shook her head. "Why did you *do* that?" she asked Rotworm, while pressing her face against Paul's shoulder.

"Do what?" Paul replied.

Suddenly, the resounding, clarion timbre of a massive bell sounded overhead. A golden shaft of light broke through a narrow slice of the sky and bathed the entire scene in warmth. Rotworm ignored it and continued to laugh and kick at Boniface, who had finally begun to stir.

Several angels clad in smart white uniforms adorned with gold trim appeared and grabbed the demon's shoulders, pulling him away. Emblazoned on their clothes was the symbol of the Order. Pain mingled with diabolic pleasure in Rotworm's laugh while wisps of black smoke began rising from the sites where their gloved hands held him. The iBad he had used to attack the angel—Scribble's iBad—fell to the ground with a clatter.

Near Boniface, a bright flash of light faded into the form of another angel. This one stood taller than the others and wore light armor. Golden cloth wound tightly over her eyes. The angel kept her auburn hair woven into a tight braid. Four mighty, white wings sprouted from her back, with each feather protected in a translucent shell of golden weave. Her most striking feature, however, was the large and ornate wheel of brass that revolved on several invisible axes around her head. It had carvings of eyes all along its edge. Unlike other members of the Order, she wielded no obvious weapon, but every quick, bird-like motion conveyed a threat inherent to her nature. She leaned down and took Boniface by the hand, helping him get to his feet.

"Are you harmed?" she asked in a voice like singing glass.

"Blessed Sister Raguel!" he replied gruffly. "Why are you here?"

"I have been called to deal with your attacker," she stated. "There has been disturbing news from Purgatory, and the Order is taking every precaution."

She walked towards Rotworm with awkward and sudden movements as if foreign to the very idea of walking. Scribble felt that Raguel stared at her as she passed by. She paused for just a moment near the couple and cocked her head slightly before continuing towards the struggling Rotworm.

At first, Rotworm ignored the approaching angel. He did not struggle with the two who held his arms. He laughed, at least until Raguel gripped his chin in her hand. Then, he screamed. His scales receded, his wings grew heavy and limp, and a pale color returned to him. Although he looked like a businessman in a professional suit once again, anyone who saw him got the distinct impression that he was little more than a worm in a businessman suit.

"I've won," he said. It was a plea, rather than a statement.

"Sinister Rotworm the Ambitious, you are guilty of violating the Treaty of Separation, Article 2, Section 9. You shall be incarcerated in the 11th Level of the 5th Circle until your trial, at which point your sentence shall be determined." As she spoke, she grabbed his arms one at a time and brought them together in front of him. In another adroit motion, she took a piece of her armor off of her waist and placed it around his wrists. It latched shut with a click just as a long chain fell from it. The end of the golden chain disappeared under the ground and pulled Rotworm's arms down so that his back hunched over from the weight. He struggled to lift his wings and found that chains fell from them, too. Gradually, the demon sank into the ground until Raguel reached down and took hold of the chain hanging from his arms. The nearly deafening sound of a bell echoed once more throughout the street and the warm light, the Order, and Rotworm, all neatly vanished.

CHAPTER 21 – PRIDE

"Are you okay?" Paul asked as Scribble pulled away from his tall, dark form. "What happened? I thought I saw someone." A few steps from him, a human-sized Boniface struggled upright and stumbled closer.

Scribble looked between the two but said nothing. Something shining on the ground nearby caught her eye. She leaned over and picked up the iBad, but the crack on the screen had grown large and jagged. Surli's face hovered just below an image of a big, red button, but she did not smile, did not move.

"What did he do to you? How long have you held this secret?" After a moment, Paul's broken image reflected on the screen. She remembered that Incubus would soon be after her. A list of things she needed to do before he arrived formed in her mind, including staying away from Paul. Conveniently, saying goodbye was not included.

"I tripped. I need to get back... home," she said flatly while trying to suppress all of her new human emotions.

"You didn't trip. It may be dark, but I saw that much. What's going on? And why are you pushing me away?" When she answered with an averted gaze, Paul raised his voice. "Who the Hell are you, really?"

"I'm no one. Just forget about me!" Tears mirrored smaller, imperfect versions of an imperfect world as they fell from her cheeks. She turned, her dark hair covering her pale face, and walked away from him.

"I can't!" Paul called out, following her as she rounded a corner that led down an alley. "I can't forget you, Desdemona Scribble. Ever! If something is wrong, I want to help. Please don't walk away!"

"Well, this must be embarrassing, Sister," Boniface said, his angelic voice the last thing Scribble expected to hear. The hint of sarcasm in his words sent a shiver through her manufactured body. She stopped dead in her tracks and looked back over her shoulder at Paul and his Dexter. Boniface had his hand on Paul's right shoulder and continued to wear that friendly smile... only, this time, it seemed a little *too* friendly. Scribble wiped the tears from her cheeks and watched Paul's actions unexpectedly slowing, his breath soon suspended in the air like a cloud. The world stood still once more—a feat that she had not seen the angel perform since she had taken the human body.

"Why did you slow down time?" she asked softly.

"Here you have taken the liberty of procuring a body in spite of my warnings. I encourage him to trust in you. I give you privacy. You had every advantage. And now you cannot savor your victory. Now that things go wrong, you have nowhere to turn." His hand tensed into a fist. "I put my faith in you because I thought you were different."

"What do you want, Boniface? You've won."

He narrowed his gaze at her. "I have spent a lifetime trying to keep this man on the path of righteousness, and in one night, you lead him astray. Even if he did not perform the act, he meant to in his heart. He meant to in his apartment and back at the store. I have not won, not yet. But I will."

"Are you feeling okay? What did Rotworm do to you?"

"I feel fine, Sister. Better than fine. I can see clearly for the first time. I see even the thoughts you conceal. You think you're better than me, don't you?"

"No, I don't."

"Don't deny it."

"No, I don't!" the demoness insisted.

Boniface glared at her, an expression that twisted his nearly perfect visage. "You dare to unravel this intricate tapestry I have woven in his soul, and yet you say you aren't better than me? That you would stoop so low to get to him is nothing less than pitiful. Now you're making him sin by actually throwing yourself at him?!"

"I didn't mean to! I mean, I did, but now I don't—"

"You're just a tenderfoot. A child. I bet I can do your job even better than you can, and without using your... assets." Before she could respond, he leaned in close to Paul's ear and spoke in a low voice. Scribble watched the layers of amiability peel away from the angel, revealing a harsh, competitive, cold-hearted disdain. "She doesn't want you, just like Dani didn't want you. No one wants you."

Time woke up once again, leaving Scribble to deal with the machinations of Boniface head-on. Pain hinted at the corners of Paul's face as the angel's voice slithered on.

"Why do you hate me?" he asked, his voice cracking.

"Paul? Of course I don't hate you. I-I love you! Maybe too much..." she said as she looked down, bangs covering her face.

"Then tell me what's wrong? What is going on?"

Boniface smiled wickedly. Scribble noticed the outline of cuffs slowly trace over his wrists in thin, pale lights. Trailing an inch or so behind the light, the outline filled in with color and texture. Then gravity took hold and began to weigh the angel's hands down ever so slightly. At the same time, several of the feathers in his wings fluttered to the ground.

"She's hiding something from you. She doesn't *trust* you." Boniface spoke just loud enough for her to hear.

Scribble held her arms around her midsection. "I can't tell you," she said. "I wish I could."

"Do you think I wouldn't understand? That I wouldn't like you anymore?" Paul's voice started to rise. "Why won't you tell me how you know Dani?"

"It's forbidden!"

Paul threw his arms wide in exasperation. "Forbidden?! By whom?!"

The angel's face darkened and his halo faded away. More feathers fell from his drooping wings. "Maybe she knows how Dani died. Maybe she was there. Maybe she *did* it." The lights that brought the cuffs into existence began to snake their way towards the ground in intricate, interlacing patterns. Thick, dark, woven chains with rough edges descended behind them.

Scribble's mouth opened, but the look of anguish on Paul's face struck her momentarily dumb. She could tell that he fought against the ideas being implanted by Boniface. "Don't listen to him," she pleaded under her breath.

Paul's brow furrowed and he shook his head. "What?" he asked, but it seemed that he didn't direct his words to her, but to Boniface.

She walked closer to him. "Paul, please, just trust me," she said, reaching out to hold Paul's fist.

Boniface tilted his ear towards Paul, listening to his thoughts. "You hardly know her, how can you trust her? Love? Ha! This is not love, it is *lust*! If you want her so badly, then just take her right here," he said, the timbre of his voice growing dull. His eyes never left Scribble. She winced when a deep growl sounded from Boniface. "Yes. There is no one around. She wouldn't dare tell on you, either. You're her landlord, boss, only friend. Take her! Take her now!" he exclaimed, his voice rising to a crescendo as he stepped away from Paul. The chains that continued to grow from his wrists clattered like bones and made his arms hang straight at his sides. Paul grew still.

"You're all lost causes!" Boniface roared. "I've been doing this for over a thousand years! How dare you, 'Sister!' You little whelp!" He mustered his strength and lunged at Scribble, hands sinking just beneath her fake flesh and taking hold of her soul.

*   *   *

Rotworm grumbled as the guards standing on either side of him jostled him. The group of angels moved quickly through the levels of Hell. They passed scenes of extreme decadence, groups of demons laying around like lumps of flesh stuck to the ground, feasts where ravenous monstrosities consumed fistfuls of human souls at a time. All of them ignored and were ignored by the swiftly moving cadre as if they were mere specters appearing in the corner of perception.

It didn't take long before the group stepped through a gate hewn into the rock that surrounded them. Rotworm could make out the number "11" roughly painted beside it. The only other beings in sight were a pair of angelic guards posted at the gate, plus a few others stationed at regular intervals along the corridor beyond. Each stood at the mouth of a hallway that branched off of the main passage. Raguel and her angels led Rotworm down one of these hallways. They kept him on a tight leash, especially when the walls narrowed down until they had to travel single-file. The ceiling sloped downwards. Rotworm's horns scraped against it, forcing him to lean over. When they pulled him along by the lead around his neck, he realized that none of the angels had this height problem. They seemed to change size with the tunnels.

The torches that lined the walls grew further and further apart before disappearing altogether. After the light vanished behind them, Rotworm felt and heard periodic changes in air pressure, passageways that they had passed or turned down in the dark. More and more empty spaces and missed tunnels rushed past them. They made sharp, chaotic turns. The angels expertly navigated through a labyrinth with no light and little sound.

Finally, after a long, twisting hallway, Rotworm could see a faint glow just around the corner, illuminating the featureless walls around him. The light grew in intensity faster than his eyes could adjust to it and left him squinting as his captors pulled him into a room. They drew his arms and wings apart and held them tight by the golden chains hanging from them. After a moment, a shadow fell over his face and he forced his eyes open. The blurred figure of Raguel stood before him, her ever-alert wheel of an eye fixed in one place, staring at him. She let out a huff of disappointment.

"Rotworm the Ambitious, you have been delivered to the 11th Level of the 5th Circle—"

"You told me already, Ragweed," he replied in defiance. The archangel gave pause. "All these years and not even a hug. Hmph. Do what you will. I won't be here that long, anyway."

Raguel remained unflustered and composed. "Your trial will not occur for several months. I suggest you acquaint yourself with your new surroundings."

Rotworm chortled and pulled forward against his bindings with a sly smirk, feeling the chains squeezing around him. "We'll see about that," he said. He could make out that the chain connecting his wrists hung over a large metal frame that seemed to grow from the almost crystalline, smooth walls of the cavern. He was essentially in an open cage. The metal itself shone brightly, even painfully, washing out any shadows and details. The other angels worked at connecting his legs and wings to the frame while Raguel watched with her body bent in an alien pose.

"No soul has ever escaped from one of my bindings, and the only way in or out of this tangled maze is a secret closely guarded. Of course, if you ask nicely, I may recommend your trial be moved up. I am willing to afford that much kindness to an old friend, Eritheius."

"Friend? Pshh... after what you did? And with no word for millennia?"

Raguel cocked her head to the side curiously. "I merely defended my superior," she said. Rotworm couldn't be sure, but he thought her voice shook for just a moment.

"And betrayed someone you cared about!"

The wheel that floated around Raguel's head turned about on its axis, pointing the eye to each other angel in turn. "Please give me a moment alone with the accused," she said. The others obediently left the room. She grabbed the wheel and removed it from around her head, letting it rest on the ground beside her. "Eritheius, will you accept my kindness as recompense for any wrong I caused you? Shall I expedite your trial?" she asked as she leaned in close, her voice hushed.

"Oh, yes, please. Move my trial up," he said mockingly. "Why not give ol' Raphey a big kiss for me while you're at it?"

Raguel frowned. "I hoped time would dull the experiences of the past."

"For me or for you? Cause let me tell you, 'Sister', I can show you experiences you won't want dulled." He winked flirtatiously at her.

The archangel paused. "Something is amiss. You are acting too cocky, even for you. What is it you know that I do not? What are you trying to distr—"

Without warning, Rotworm leaned closer, straining against his bindings, and kissed her on the lips. That distraction certainly seemed to work. Even after the kiss, she looked stunned and brought her fingers to her lips.

"It's 'Rotworm' now." Before the angel had time to recover, he nodded to someone behind her. "Don't mind us, Gabe. Just rehashing old times."

Raguel scowled at the demon and turned sharply aside. "What do you want, Gabriel?" She picked up the wheel and returned it to its regular orbit.

From the shadow of the entranceway emerged a tall, large-winged, androgynous figure who moved with preternatural grace. The purest snow of startling white kicked up around him and cloaked him, forming those wings. Gabriel dropped to one knee and lowered his head so that his white hair fell loose and covered his face.

"Sister Raguel. The situation on Earth has... evolved."

She glared at her prisoner. "What did you do?"

✳ ✳ ✳

Scribble reeled as Boniface dug his thin fingers into her neck. Although he was incorporeal, the pain was very real. She could feel it, not in the borrowed flesh, but in her soul—he wanted to rip her out.

"*His soul is mine!*" Boniface shouted. The weight of the growing chains pulled them to the ground with him on top of her, using both hands to strangle and claw at her.

"S-stop it! I can't—"

Time slowly returned, yet Paul remained frozen in place. He stared down at her as she gripped at invisible hands that clasped around her throat. "Dez?" Instead of leaning down to help her, however, he took a step back.

"*You bitch!*" the angel repeated over and over. He focused so intently on harming her that he didn't notice when the chains on his wrists began to pull tight, when his half-feathered wings fell from his back and lay on the ground beside them, or when the sound of a bell accompanied a searing holy light that descended from above.

Scribble's eyes widened in terror and she pushed up on Boniface with all her strength. He fell on his back and she quickly scrambled away from him. The invectives Boniface spat at her no angel had a right to know. Though he struggled, heavy chains anchored him to the spot.

"Dez?!"

Above them, four members of the Order descended, wearing the same sharp uniforms the others had worn. The moment their feet touched the solid ground, two of them moved upon Scribble and held her by the arms, but all four of them paused in disbelief at the words erupting from Boniface. His robe twisted and began to flow like a flame. Upon his face formed several deep scars that became deeper and blacker with each passing second. As he writhed against the chains, his skin cracked. Scribble pulled out of the grasp of the angels and soon realized that she was not their target; they were focused on Boniface. But in the next moment, all heads turned to Paul.

"Desdemona! What's going on? Who are all these people?"

Chapter 22 – Jailbreak

It had taken Rotworm less time than he would've thought to dislocate his left hand, and more pain than he expected to tear through the spectral ligaments, nerves, and muscles to remove it. He ended up with a stump that bled dark, thick ropes of his own essence onto the otherwise spotless, white floor. The golden chain hung from his freed right wrist. On the end of it, Rotworm's left hand hung, curled into a lifeless claw. His wings remained tightly bound to the metal structure. The angels had left in such a hurry that none of them remembered to confiscate his iBad beforehand. Now his demonic blood obfuscated part of the screen as he hunched over it on the ground. Its small screen flickered to life, displaying the shadowed struts and beams of Belphegor's dark prison.

"Master Belphegor?" he said in a rough, stressed voice. He only heard silence, but he could just make out a dark silhouette within the shadows. "Sir!"

"What is it? I'm busy, worm."

"It's done. I've been... detained."

"And?" the tinny voice on the iBad asked. It sounded even less alive, more electronic than before.

"The experiment was a successssss." Rotworm winced and his features became distinctly snakelike as he held his left arm against his body tightly. "I attacked the angel—"

"Boniface, yes, I know. You're now obsolete." The figure on the screen became clearer as several of the skeletal struts shifted out of the way with loud, metal screams. The matrix of scars that marred his body made it easy to see why he used a machine to move around.

"Ssssir, your prototype. I know where it is and will fetch it. I know how much you hate having to—"

"I have no need for it." Belphegor swung closer to the screen when a light source from behind the camera illuminated the room. The diseased demon had a new weapon suspended next to him. It resembled a rifle made entirely of human bones, sinews, and flesh. A fused spinal column formed the barrel, and for a muzzle, it had a blackened, open-mouthed skull—some flesh still clinging to it—captured in an eternal, silent wail. "Did you not understand the definition of 'prototype'?"

In the background, Rotworm could hear the faint voice of an angel, one of the guards to his lair, commanding Belphegor to surrender the weapon. A moment later, a dark beam that made the geometry around it bleed together shot from the weapon's maw, accompanied by a tortured cry. It was aimed off-screen. Rotworm could not see the angel, but he could hear the rapid descent of chains. Within seconds, the light from the guard faded.

Rotworm knew now that he had underestimated the Prince of Sloth. His voice, though still pained, became filled with false humility and groveling. "My Lord, if you free me, I will join you in your fight, even bring otherssss to free you."

The rusty moan of metal scraping against metal drowned out Belphegor's digital chuckle. "You cannot help me. I will be free in a few seconds, and no demon can follow where I am going." At that moment, a pair of ragged white wings came into view via a mechanical pincer. Belphegor winced slightly as large, knurled pitons grafted the wings directly into his crooked spine with a quick thrust. A sickly gray faded the wings and they instantly began to curl and rot on his back, yet they remained functional enough to flap.

"The Pearl Gatessss? But your soul is too heavy! You'll need my help!" Rotworm pleaded with him as he dropped to his knees and his body twisted to keep the pressure off his still-bound wings.

"The Gates and beyond."

"But how? No demon has ever reached the Gatessss..." If there's anything Rotworm had learned about dealing with his own kind, it was this: goad any demon on enough, and it will delight in revealing its own deviousness.

"These wings will help," Belphegor said. Another source of angelic light exposed his figure, now suspended in the center of the room. All the large beams and tracks that enabled his movement had shifted, pulled away from the walls. Again, he aimed the weapon at the intruder—another member of the Order. In seconds, a set of chains dragged the angel to the far wall, towards the deeper levels of Hell. The ones that had bound Boniface could not compare for speed. As the chains pinned the angel, its brilliant wings grew dull and fell to the ground. Belphegor then sent a large strut to strike the angel and knock it out into the hallway so the chains could carry it away.

Metal beams moved to surround Belphegor, attaching themselves to him by digging thin rods into his perverted flesh. The wires that had previously been manipulating him about still tugged at his skin, but now he used them to control the beams instead. Within a few breaths, the entire structure morphed into a dark, iron spider with myriad legs. The angel's stolen wings lay along the construct's back. They turned black and withered. In the center, wires and rods formed a shell that covered everything but Belphegor's head. A mass of soul stones sat behind him in the spider's abdomen, fused to the structure like a swollen sac. Cords fanned out of it, drawing power from the soul stone battery. The spider's unearthly movements both mesmerized and frightened Rotworm. Where the spinnerets would be sat the weapon.

"I should thank you for testing the prototype on that human girl, Danielle Cooper. I did not know if it would work or just destroy the user." As he spoke, more members of the Order rushed into the room. Belphegor swiftly disposed of them, each with a shot from the weapon and a swift strike from one of the spider's powerful limbs. Their wings soon joined the others on the back of the spider, displayed like broken trophies.

"Even with the power in these stones, it would be impossible to get through the Gates. I required angels' wings. You had to test the device on the human first—after all, my target is human. And since my target is also spirit, you had to test it on an Immortal. But once you attacked an angel with it, I knew you would be taken and they would eventually trace it to me. I must act fast." It seemed that his newfound freedom had turned him much more talkative than Rotworm ever recalled. Belphegor's machine pulled the camera away from its perch and moved with terrifying speed towards the long, narrow passageways that led out of his cell. "I will not make Leviathan's mistake. She let herself be caught. The Order forced her to eat herself for her crimes. I don't want to know what my punishment would be if they stop *my* plan. But with these stones powering their wings and my weapon, Heaven's Gates and all the angels beyond should prove no obstacle to me."

Rotworm tugged at his wings. "SSSsssssssir… let me go with you…"

"You would only slow me down." Belphegor moved the camera closer so that Rotworm could see his reprehensible face clearly. Rotworm fleetingly recalled that humans need seventeen muscles to smile as, somehow, Belphegor managed to pull together a similar and much more disturbing expression using far fewer. "Consider this your 'promotion'. Goodbye, Rotworm. You've been entertaining."

CHAPTER 23 – EXODUS

Scribble and the angels stayed as still as statues as they watched Paul back away from them. His eyes remained stuck between confusion and horror. He quickly looked from one ethereal being to another in apparent disbelief.

"Where did you come from? What are you?" Paul continued to move away from them until his heel caught on the curb and he toppled backwards.

"I was called?" Raguel's voice interrupted the scene as she appeared in a momentary impression of brilliance. She looked down at Boniface, who lay balled up on the ground with smoldering robes. The heavy chains that had pulled him down rattled and moved towards one end of the street. One of the other angels raised a sword that danced and crackled like electricity, pointing it at Paul who scrambled to his feet.

"This human can see us," the angel said.

Raguel never took her attention from Boniface. "He has likely been too close to us, exposed to our affairs for too long. We will have to take him. How did this happen?"

Scribble pulled away from the group and brandished the iBad in front of her. "Stay back or I'll make you like him!" she warned and nodded towards Boniface. She aimed the iBad at any of the angels that moved, despite barely understanding how the thing worked.

"You do not know what you are doing, imp," Raguel said and slowly stepped closer. "I don't know what happened here, but if you put the device down, I'm sure we can work with you to reach an acceptable outcome for all."

The words fell on deaf ears. Scribble inched closer to Paul and glanced quickly in his direction. "Are you alright?" she asked in a hoarse whisper, but Paul gave no response. "I'm sorry you got mixed up in this, but I can't let them take you away. Not now."

"Put down the device and let us help," Raguel continued, now in front of the other angels. "The human has seen too much. His memory must be altered while there is still time. You know this. The Mystery must be preserved."

"What? No! You can't do that!" Scribble turned towards Paul and grabbed his hand. "Run!" she cried. She pulled him towards a narrow alleyway before taking off. He followed behind her without a word. The pair darted along side streets and down alleys. In the distance, they could hear Raguel shouting orders. She had trained the members of the Order well. It took only seconds before Paul and Scribble were dodging hastily thrust weapons and turning away from flashes of holy light. Here, a hand grabbed at his shirt. There, a glint off a diamond sword crossed her face as the blade narrowly missed her.

In the lower parts of the city, a dense fog had closed in and enveloped the pursuit. The few people who were up and about appeared as wraiths—dark figures aimlessly wandering the haze. Each time a car passed by, the headlights washed out the entire scene, leaving the pedestrians blinded for a moment. Buildings built of bricks instead of wood and siding stood close together. The pursuing angels got further and further behind the couple. Scribble stopped dead in her tracks and looked around at the hazy scene.

"Quickly," she said in a breathy voice. She threw her back against a brick wall and tried to catch her breath. The last time she had seen the wide alley with its somewhat out-of-place door, only Surli had accompanied her. Now she prepared herself to break one of the cardinal rules.

"What... is going on?" Paul asked, doubling over and panting. "They're trying to... kill us! Who... are you?"

"You wouldn't believe me."

"Did they have swords? Who has swords!?" Several moments passed as their pulses slowed. Neither dared to speak, but rather listened for the sounds of their pursuers. "I think they're gone," Paul eventually said, but Scribble shook her head and put her finger to her lips.

"They're near. I'm sure of it," she whispered. "We should get going."

"No. Not until you tell me what is going on. Who are they? Why are they after us? And where the Hell did they come from? Are they aliens?"

Scribble smiled and shook her head. "Not aliens, and definitely not from Hell." She pushed away from the wall and walked to the door opposite. Across the frosted glass were the words "Sir Burrah's Security" in block print.

"Then where did they come from?"

Scribble looked over her shoulder, her swirling gray eyes fixed on his. "It's a long story... come with me and I'll tell you. They can't follow us in here."

"Come with you? Where?"

They both heard the nearby sound of metal scraping metal, rather like an unsheathing sword.

"There's no time!" she said and offered her hand. "Please... trust me."

At first, he only looked at her hand discerningly. Slowly, he reached for it.

"Halt!" The cry came from a young yet assertive voice. They both looked to the corner of the alley, where one of the armor-clad angels had discovered them. Its silvery wings splayed behind it in full span, reaching across the passageway with the tips disappearing in the walls on either side. It held a sword with a golden hilt and a blade that could only be seen from the distortion it caused in the light passing through it. The angel moved towards them with a quickness that frightened Paul. Scribble cried out. She reached for the door. It opened just as the angel's grip found Paul's arm and pulled him from the demoness. But Scribble would have none of it and grabbed at Paul with both arms. All three of them fell into the doorway when she threw her weight backwards into it.

*   *   *

The long hallway looked like a blur. When they were all inside, the door slammed shut behind them with a reverberant echo, leaving the trio struggling through the strange repeating pattern of carpet and wallpaper. Although the angel gained the upper hand several times, Paul seemed to grow stronger the farther down the hall they got. He managed to push the angel off and run for Scribble, who dashed to the door at the far end of the hallway as quickly as possible. The angel nimbly rolled into a sprint after them, but the closer it got to the far door, the more it strained to move. Its feet skidded along the ground back the way they'd come. Despite frantic flapping of silver wings, the angel could not overcome the force of its own soul weight rejecting Hell. After several more attempts, it gave them a stern look before launching back towards the entrance.

When Paul caught up to Scribble, she was resting against the far door, her hand on her chest in worry.

"He didn't hurt you, did he?" she asked.

"I'm... I'm fine, Dez," he panted.

Scribble slowly pressed herself against him. Silent tears soaked into his shirt. She wrapped her arms around him and squeezed. Paul hesitated for a moment, but eventually returned the embrace. "What... just happened? I'm ready... for those answers now," he said between breaths.

It took Scribble a while to reply to him. "They are people who wanted to take you away from me. I told you they wouldn't follow us here." A sense of guilt kept her eyes down.

"Why not? And why did he have a sword? At least, I think it was a sword. It was all a bit rushed."

"A sword? You're just exhausted..." she said automatically, then sniffled and wiped her cheeks.

He might be unsure about whether their assailant had a sword, but no one could overlook the distorted movement of space in that corridor.

"Maybe. But I don't think being more awake would make this look like a normal office building."

154

"Um... it's not. This is a... a safe place." She bit her lip and pulled away from him.

"What's keeping those guys out of this safe place? Who were they, anyway? They were sort of blurry at first. Were those..." Paul took off his glasses and pinched the bridge of his nose. "Maybe I'm asleep and this is all a dream."

Scribble tried to think up an excuse that would work, but nothing came to mind. So, she took his hands and looked at him with pleading eyes. "Do you believe in the afterlife?"

"What? Um, yeah, of course. I don't like to think about it much."

"I... found this door. It leads to Hell."

Paul chuckled. "What, fire and brimstone and all that?"

Scribble nodded, then shook her head. "It doesn't look like that, really."

"And those guys couldn't follow us because...?"

"They're angels."

"Angels," he said flatly.

"Yes, angels."

"And they're after me because...?"

"Because you shouldn't be able to see them, so they want to erase your memory, and me with it."

"Why you?" Paul asked.

Scribble bit her lip and looked down at the floor.

Paul rubbed at his temples. "Okay, fine. If you don't want to tell me the truth, I can't make you. First, my store burns up. Then you're running out on me. Next thing I know, you're being attacked by a shadow and I'm getting chased through the streets by... goodness knows what. And now you're telling me this is the doorway to Hell? This is by far the strangest night I've ever had."

"I know it sounds crazy," Scribble said. "But it's true. I didn't know where else to go."

"Then this isn't a dream, it's a nightmare."

Scribble's voice softened. "I hope I'm not a nightmare."

When Paul put his glasses back on, he didn't look at her with the affection she'd hoped to draw from him, but rather like he was trying to figure her out. "Come to think of it, you've been there every time something strange happened. The pipes, the fire, Ginger... why is that?"

"I-I suppose it might be because I'm..." The last two words didn't want to come out; she'd been spending so much time trying to hide her true nature that revealing it was difficult. But after a moment, she finally confessed, "I'm a demon. Your demon. I was supposed to tempt you, so I became a succubus."

Scribble winced, expecting him to either laugh or push her away, but he did neither. He spoke softly but steadily, with purpose. "A sex demon?"

Scribble nodded. "Well, not really. I borrowed the body of one because I wasn't good at tempting you without it."

"Just how long have you been tempting me, Dez?" Every muscle in him grew tense.

"Only a few months before we met. And my name isn't Desdemona. It's Scribble. Just Scribble."

"Did you set the fire or burst the boiler?"

"No," she replied.

"Did you trick Ginger into coming on to me?"

"I... might have accidentally."

"Accidentally?"

"My helper did it."

"You have a helper?" Paul closed his eyes in thought. "I can't believe I'm asking this. If I wasn't so tired, I'd probably think I've gone insane. You said you *were* supposed to tempt me? Aren't you now?"

"I've had a change of heart."

"Is that why you were running out on me?"

Scribble folded her arms across her belly and grabbed her elbows. "Not entirely. The plan was to have you cheat on Ginger with me, then catch me cheating on you... but I don't want to. To cheat on you. To hurt you. To hurt Ginger. I don't want to tempt you anymore."

"So... everything was fake?"

"No! Most of it was real. The way I feel is, at least. Every time I see you, I get nervous and my heart beats faster. I think about you all the time when you aren't there. A demon is not supposed to be able to fall in love. I'm not used to any of this, but it feels real to me."

It took a while for Paul to speak again. "You're not joking, are you? You really believe all this. So, if this is the door to Hell, why are you taking me here again? How do I know this isn't a trick just to get me into Hell?"

She looked up at him with a guilt-ridden smile. "You've started to see us Immortals when you're not supposed to. It's probably my fault for spending so much time with you," Scribble confessed. "Those angels want to erase your memory, erase *me* from your memory. Since they normally can't get into Hell, it was the only place I could think of where you'd be... safe. Until I figured something out."

"Safe? In Hell?" he asked with a look of disbelief.

"Yeah, well, maybe not at first. But I know a few places you can hide while I talk to them. If you want to go back, I won't stop you."

"What will you do if I go back?"

Scribble's features paled as she thought about the possible future. "I'll have to hide from... everyone. The angels will arrest me or at least punish me for telling you all this, my boss will have me tortured for the rest of time, and I won't be able to see you again."

"Supposing I go with you..."

A hint of hope sparked in Scribble. "You'll have to stay near me and do what I say. Don't talk to anyone. I'll have to take you into Purgatory. And if I manage to convince them to keep your memories, you can't tell anyone what you see."

"I promise I won't tell anyone," he said, his voice less serious than before, "Unless they ask politely." Then, more soberly, "I doubt they'd believe me anyway. I'm not sure I do, yet."

Scribble recalled one of the first things Rotworm had told her, that most of the time, humans wouldn't even believe her if she told them about the afterlife. She wondered how Paul would fare when he saw it.

Paul continued. "If you go to talk to them, couldn't they just arrest you anyway? Why risk it just to save my memories?"

She pressed herself against him again, her face on his chest. This time, he didn't hesitate to hold her. "I don't want you to forget me, to forget that you're... special to me. I know it's selfish. You have Ginger, after all."

Paul buried his face in her hair and smiled. He held her like that for a long time. "I don't think it's selfish to want someone to remember you love them. But you forget, I broke up with her."

Scribble sighed against him. "I'm sorry. I'm sure she'll make you happier than I can. Maybe it's not too late."

"What possessed you to trick her into kissing me in the first place?" he asked with a smirk and leaned back.

"You were *supposed* to reject her! You said she was like a sister to you!" She gave a light punch to his arm.

He just smiled. "But what if I want to be with you? You've made me feel alive again, like myself again. I don't think I've ever felt as nervous and excited as you make me!"

"We can't be together. I have to return this body. And I doubt anyone would be okay with a demon dating a human."

"There's no way to know until you try. I'm putting my faith in you. I don't want to lose our time together. I don't want to forget the woman I love."

Blushing was nothing new for Scribble, but never before had it been this intense. She threw her arms around his neck and kissed him fiercely, fully aware that it may be her last kiss. Paul held onto the kiss for as long as possible as well. But all good things must pass.

After they recovered from the kiss, he smirked at her. "So 'Scribble'?

Really? You didn't work very hard on your last name. And why 'Desdemona'?"

She looked up at him with a small, guilty smile. "I saw the name of the bookstore and it was all I could think of."

"Ah! So, that makes me your Othello? You know, I'm going to have to be honest. It'll be weird calling you 'Scribble'."

"I don't mind being your Desdemona."

Paul grinned, looking more relaxed than he had all night. "Emphasis on the *'demona'* part?" Then he turned the handle and opened the door to the first level of Hell.

*   *   *

The terminal lay in ruins. Stone and patches of darkness showed through cracks in the walls. Wires hung loose from the ceiling and sent a shower of sparks to the ground in fits and spurts. Most of the lights didn't work, giving a feeling of being closed in upon. Very few demons remained, though once in a while, a small imp or hellhound would scurry past. Scribble stepped into the rubble, taking Paul's hand and gripping it tightly.

"What happened in here? It looks like there was an earthqua..." Paul fell silent as a red-skinned creature zipped past and disappeared around a corner.

"I don't know," Scribble said softly. She led him to a large sign that flickered to life now and then, the word "Directory" marked on the side. Its massive map shifted about every time her eyes moved, blowing up with great detail wherever she focused. Paul blinked several times and looked away, disoriented and confused.

"It's this way." Scribble guided him away from it and down the long, large corridor that led towards the Gates. "I have to avoid the tower," she said to herself. "Oh, and sneak you past those angels at the gate. I'll hide you in a cubicle." As she walked, a long, dingy piece of ethereal fabric caught on her foot. She picked it up and then looked over at Paul. "This might work. Then again, it might go right through you."

It only took a moment to drape the fabric over him and make it look like a cloak so only his feet and hands could be seen. Scribble looked pleased that the makeshift disguise did not fall through him.

"So far, so good. But it smells like something died in here," Paul said, wrinkling his nose in disgust.

"Sorry. Bathing isn't common around here. It's just until I get you safe."

"Then lead on!"

They walked a bit faster. Cracks soon appeared in the tiles and followed alongside them. They widened and joined up with other tunnel ruptures until only a few intact tiles remained in the midst of the rubble.

"Who are you? What are you still doing here?" came a thin, nasally voice from nearby. An equally thin and nasally demon, wearing office attire covered in dust and small glasses that sat balanced on his up-twisted nose, hobbled into their path from a hallway. Under one arm he carried a disheveled pile of ancient papers. Above them, a sign swung loosely, advertising the Hall of Records. Paul stared at him in amazement and fascination, much like one would stare at a disfigured man. Beside him, Scribble looked at the demon as if she recognized him.

"What happened?" Paul peered at the demon's horns and bent nose.

"I tripped," he replied, brushing some of the dust off his clothes.

Scribble chimed in before Paul could continue. "You... I know you. You helped me earlier."

"Could be. I 'help' a lot of people. Why haven't you fled?" He held onto his spectacles and peered through them at the couple. "I believe all sex demons have been recalled."

"We're on our way, don't worry," she said in a tone of familiarity. "But, what exactly happened in here?"

The demon straightened himself and looked around like the walls might have ears. "Been a little too interested in your 'assignments' to catch the news? Belphegor happened here, if you must know. He's loose and on a rampage. And you should leave before he happens to you, too."

"Belphegor? My old boss, the..." Scribble looked over her shoulder at Paul, who was still staring, then leaned in and whispered, "The Prince of Sloth?"

"Do you know any other? He... tore through here on the way... to the gates. Look, is something wrong?" he asked, pushing past Scribble. Paul reeled back when the demon approached him.

"What? N-no! Nothing!"

"Then why are you staring at me? It's like you've never seen—"

Scribble came up behind him and smacked Paul on the head, giving a nervous laugh. "I told you not to stare at males," she said, pulling Paul away with her. "Remember, that's *my* job."

The demon gaped at the pair of them, then shook his head. "If you two get caught, I'm not doing the paperwork," he said and limped away with his files.

"You *have* to be more careful," Scribble sighed when the demon had left. She led Paul to one of the more stable-looking walls. "Do you believe me now?"

He stared now at nothing in particular. "Holy shit, that means there *is* an afterlife, and God, and... and everything! And I'm in *Hell!?*" He swayed, hand on his head.

"Woah, steady there! Breathe, Paul!" She put her arm around him to help support him. "I know it's a lot to take in all at once."

"No kidding." He put his hands on his knees and lowered his head. "My girlfriend is an actual demon."

That sentence made Scribble feel a lot better than it should have. "Are you good?" she asked after a moment. "We have to keep moving. I've got to get you to Purgatory where you'll be safe." She lowered her voice and her gaze. "Or... maybe we should go back."

Paul stood upright again and shook his head. "No. If what you're saying is true, then those angels will make me forget you." He pressed his forehead against hers gently. "I'd rather go through Hell."

Scribble's worried frown turned into a gentle smile, but only for a moment. "We'll be heading towards my home. My real home. Or at least it used to be." She put her hand on his cheek. "Stay close. If we find Belphegor, just run."

"I don't understand. If he's a Prince, how can he be 'loose'?"

"It's just a title. He's a prisoner here. We all are. But he's dangerous."

The reality of their situation settled in. They hugged spontaneously like each had thought of it at the same time. He made her feel safe just by holding her—a sensation Scribble had never experienced before.

"I'm just a normal guy. This is all so much bigger than me. I just want to wake up and have my store back. And have you. At least we'll get through this together, right?"

Scribble wanted desperately to tell him "yes." But in the back of her mind, she knew she would have to let him go at some point. She pressed herself even tighter against him and held firm to his warm, strong body.

"Paul? Where have you been? And who is that slut?"

He looked up in horror at the caramel-skinned girl standing in front of him. She stood about the same height as Scribble but had a much more athletic build. Her clothes had been torn and bloodied. Her hair would have been shoulder-length if it hadn't been for the knots and mats of grime. On her wrists hung heavy, dark chains that wound down the hallway into the distance. They periodically tightened and tugged at her. Although he seemed to take no notice of it, Scribble realized she could see hints of light passing straight through her from behind, like with all human souls. Paul moved away from Scribble and clenched his hands into tight fists. "Dani?"

CHAPTER 24 – DUES

"Of course it's me! Paul, where have you been? It's been terrible here!" Danielle stumbled along the craggy ground towards him and threw her body against him. The moment she made contact, she erupted in tears that left trails on her dirty face. Without warning, she slapped him.

Paul's face only showed horror, too stunned by what he was seeing to even react to the slap.

"It can't be..." he breathed.

Danielle pulled away with a scowl. "Oh? And why not? Did you want to find someone else? Is *she* my replacement?"

"What? No! I mean, we thought you were dead. We all did. Wait... we buried you. You really are—"

"You must have buried the wrong girl. Didn't you even look for me?"

"Of course we did. I didn't think—"

"You never think, Paul." Danielle eyed Scribble like she was inspecting some rotten piece of meat. "I'm better looking than she is. I've certainly got more where it counts," she said as a malicious smile snuck into her scowl. "Come on, who is she?"

Scribble shook her head and backed up, but the wall they'd been hiding behind stopped her. "I'm no one..."

"Damn right you are."

"Don't say that to her," Paul said. He reached for her but she suddenly doubled over in a chilling scream.

"No! You're not real! You're just another trick, another monster!" She withdrew from them and looked behind her, ducking, holding herself, eyes searching for some unseen horror.

Paul recoiled at the scream. "What is wrong?" he asked. Though he almost seemed afraid of her, he reached out and put his hand on her arm, testing to see if she was real.

Initially, she jerked away from him. But after searching his face, she relaxed and let him touch her. "They're after me. They're everywhere," she said in a tremulous voice.

"No, I mean... you've changed. You would never say these things."

"Paul!" She stepped back from him. "First, you abandon me, and now you insult me? What is wrong with *you*?" She tugged at her clothes, arms, and hair. "Don't I look the same? Don't I sound the same? Or are you just trying to... to break up with me? For that bitch?! Paul, I waited for you! I've been so alone! Why didn't you find me?"

"You... you can't be *here*! This can't be real!" Paul looked desperately back and forth between Danielle and Scribble as if one would provide an answer.

Danielle's demeanor shifted. "Would anyone else know about the little scar on your side that you got when we were kids?" She leaned her soft body against him and looked down at his chest. Her hands roamed over him seductively—an effect that was ruined by the cold chains that hung from her wrists and rattled with each movement. He let out a gasp and grabbed her wrist but didn't move it away once he had. Instead, he held it over his heart as tears began flowing down his cheeks.

"Remember?" she cooed. "You were trying to take off those skates and fell off the bench into that open locker. Or there was that time you made me brownies but mixed up the salt and sugar." She laughed for a moment and looked up into his eyes wantonly. "When you kissed me in the movie theater. You were so nervous—"

"—I nearly threw up," he whispered. "Why here?" He looked at Scribble with pain in his eyes. "She shouldn't be here, Dez! She was a good person!"

"Dez, huh? She doesn't look like she'd make much of a lover." Danielle gave his rear a playful smack. He reacted quickly, pulling her arms off of him and holding her wrists so she couldn't touch him.

"Dani! I'm not playing around!" His voice cracked as he battled the tears in his eyes. "Who are you, really? And how dare you make fun of Danielle! You may look like her, but you act *nothing* like her!"

The girl struggled until she broke free from his grasp. "Maybe I'm not the Dani you knew anymore! I've been alone, running and hiding for ages! I see monsters everwhere, Paul. And these... these chains! They pull at me constantly. Not just my arms," she shouted, hitting her see-through head. "But *me*. They pull at my mind! Besides, why should I act like the Dani you knew? The Dani you rejected? The last time I saw you, do you remember? That date in the park? You said you didn't want commitment, that you had to focus on the store. You put that pile of bricks before me."

Scribble could see Paul's heart breaking before her. "Of course I remember. You were so upset, you ran off," he said. "I tried to follow you."

Dani's eyes glazed over. "Yeah, I ran. It was dark, I was crying. I heard a scream, such a terrible scream, and turned to see." She looked down at her hands. "I fell. Into that ravine. Oh, God, it was so far. I died, didn't I?"

Paul steadied himself against the wall. "We couldn't find you for days." He looked at Scribble as anger and sorrow fought over him. "Why? Why is she here? Did you know this whole time? And why is she chained? Answer me!"

The more he pressed, the further along the wall Scribble moved from them. But before she had a chance to answer him, Danielle stepped between them. "Don't take it out on her. I'm the one who ran off. Wait, if you're here, does that mean you...?"

"He's alive. I brought him here," Scribble managed to get out.

Danielle snapped at her. "How *dare* you bring him to a place like this!" As quickly as she spat vinegar at Scribble, she offered honey to Paul. "Take me back with you. There must be a way!"

"Danielle, I don't think I can. But maybe I can help you here? I can remind you of who you were. This place, it's changed you. This isn't the Dani I love."

Scribble winced as she heard those words. *He still loves her?* she thought to herself. It felt like the bottom of her heart had given out.

The words had an effect on Danielle as well. She recoiled and looked down, her disheveled nest of hair covering her face. "Even after all this time?"

The sudden realization of what he had said was impossible to miss on Paul's face. "What? I..."

Danielle fell to her knees with a loud clattering noise from the chains splaying about her. "H-how can you still love me? I hate what I've become. I'm a terrible person now. You don't even know me."

"I never stopped loving you," Paul said as he knelt beside her. "I took part of you with me, to keep you alive. Remember when Chris stole your car and totaled it? You forgave him when no one else would. And because of that second chance, he got a job to pay you back, turned his life around. I'll never forget that. This whole time, I have been trying to live up to you."

Danielle was sobbing as she beat her balled-up fist against the broken floor tiles. "For so long I've wandered this place, I've felt this hatred building in me. I wanted to hate you! To hurt you! To have you and leave you! But now you give me *this*?"

"If you need to hurt me, then I won't stop you," Paul said.

Danielle stared at him with malice in her red-rimmed eyes. She shot her hands at his neck, closing them around his throat. They tightened and the chains that hung from her wrists started to pull taut as they stretched down the hallway. But a moment later, she loosened her grip and slid her arms around his neck. She rested her head on his shoulder.

"Forgive me," she said softly. "I was so angry that night, and I haven't been able to let go of it. I'm so, so sorry." She raised her voice to Scribble but kept her head on Paul. "And I'm sorry for what I called you. I'm sure you don't deserve it."

"It's-I've been called worse things," she replied with a little more confidence than before.

Danielle pulled away from Paul, sniffling and laughing lightly. "It's funny, this has been weighing on me for so long, I feel so free." As she rubbed at her face, a gentle light appeared at the edges of the chains. It slowly consumed the chains, making them thinner and lighter until they hung limp on the ground once again.

"Those chains look like... Boniface's..." Scribble whispered to herself. She watched the light fade away, leaving the chains half as thick as they had been.

"You've changed, too," Danielle said with a radiant smile, like the ones she had in the pictures Scribble had seen. "The old Paul wasn't so passionate. You never got riled up."

Paul glanced up at Scribble with a smile. "I've had some help."

When she looked at Scribble again, it was devoid of malice and jealousy, though there was longing in it. "Please take good care of him."

Scribble had to take off her glasses to wipe away a tear that threatened to run down her cheek. "I will," she said.

"How will you care for him without a body?" The voice came from behind her, deep and distinctly masculine. Scribble spun just as Incubus rounded the corner and stood before her, chest to face.

"Wh-what are you doing here?" she asked as she looked up to see his eyes. Her voice quaked. "Th-there's still lots of time..."

Paul jumped to his feet and took a sudden step towards the intruder, but stopped when Scribble put her hand back. "Who are you?" he asked.

Incubus inspected Paul and took off his dark sunglasses, letting them simply drop to the ground. There didn't seem to be anything remarkable about his dark eyes. But, the longer Paul looked into those eyes, the more he shrank into himself like Incubus had won dominance over him. When he looked down at Scribble, she felt a strange desire, a terrible lust building in her. In their situation, however, it was quickly replaced by terror.

"You haven't been taking care of the body. Asmodeus wants her back," he said. "Now."

"I'm not done using it." Scribble backed along the wall, looking for a way out, but found none.

"Yes, you are. Return it now, or I will take it, and you, by force."

Scribble gasped for breath under his heavy stare. He took a step closer to her, almost pinning her to the wall when she cried out, "No! You wouldn't dare damage this body!"

The demon slammed his hand against her shoulder and squeezed until she yelled. "Any damage will be blamed on you," he warned. "You're sure you want to make Asmodeus even angrier?"

With a wince, Scribble squeaked out, "A-alright! It's yours!"

Incubus smiled, if such a cold expression could be called a smile, and stepped back from her expectantly. She looked over at Paul and Danielle. Her forehead wrinkled with worry. Incubus cleared his throat. *Focus*, she thought. She had possessed the body, but no one ever told her how to un-possess it.

"Well?" Incubus asked impatiently.

She'd spent so much time in that human body that it was difficult to separate it from her spirit, but as she imagined her soul passing through the physical flesh that surrounded it, eventually, it did fall limp and lifeless to the ground. Only Scribble the demoness remained standing there. Incubus picked up the body and hefted it over his shoulder. Scribble glanced at Paul, worried he would be repulsed, but he just stared back. When the demoness looked over herself, she gasped. She was no longer the short, slightly feminine imp she'd been for untold thousands of years. After her time on Earth, she now stood tall and shapely, almost human had it not been for her small wings and the stubs that she called horns peeking out from her hair. Even her hair was longer, dark against her now gray skin—no longer red. The slight point in her ears made them passably human. Instead of the skirt and blouse that she had grown so used to in Purgatory, she still wore the shorts and large t-shirt that she'd been wearing a moment before. Looking over her shoulder, she wiggled her rear—no tail. "What happened to me? I look different."

Incubus chortled. "Interesting side effect. Asmodeus will be pleased with your new look. She likes her playthings to be pretty." His nightmare gaze trained on Paul and Danielle. "On second thought, you brought a more alluring treat with you."

"Leave her alone!" she said quickly. "I'm the one in the bargain!"

"I think you'll find she never specified that *you* were the soul owed. Besides, not her. She is tainted." Incubus walked up to Paul with his long stride, towering over the smaller man and grabbed at his arm.

"What?! No! He… he's not even dead!" she said and frantically ran to them.

"Precisely. She's never had a living human. I wonder how long he'll last." The demon cracked an evil smile and dragged Paul with him down the hallway despite his struggling. Scribble and Danielle grabbed at Incubus. It provided enough of a distraction for Paul to pick up a piece of broken tile and smash it into the demon's face. He roared in pain and tossed Paul aside, holding his nose. Blood poured out from under his hand. Incubus shrugged the girls off and let the body slump lifelessly to the ground. Something animalistic shone in his eyes. He got on all fours and bounded towards Paul like a beast, but another piece of tile hit him in the face and blinded him just long enough for the man to escape. Paul leaped down the trail of destruction, brushing past the sign labeled "Gate."

Incubus shook the daze off and galloped after him, followed by Scribble and Danielle. Before long, Paul scrabbled over a pile of stones where the gate to Hell had once been. Incubus flung himself at the stones, but his hands and feet slipped backwards. No matter how hard he tried, he could not overcome the weight of his soul pulling him back towards Hell.

Scribble passed him and tried to follow after Paul into Purgatory, but Incubus grabbed her shoulder again. "You'll have to do," he said menacingly and lifted her off the ground by the shoulder using just one arm. She screamed in pain and fluttered her wings desperately.

"No! Let me go! Aaagh!" Powerful fingers dug into her and clamped down, making her cries of anguish become terrifying grunts. With a rough tug, Incubus pulled her back down to the ground and started to drag her away. A length of dark chain suddenly wrapped around his neck. He stopped and dropped Scribble so he could pull at the chain in an attempt to keep his own body from being damaged further.

"Run! Go now!" Danielle cried as she hung from the demon's back. She gripped the chain with all her might but it began to glow again. Somehow, the girl managed to pull Incubus to the ground before Scribble scrambled to her feet.

The demoness gripped her shoulder and whimpered, crawling up the pile of rubble. She heard a shrill cry behind her and glanced back to see the chains that had been around Danielle's wrists had disappeared completely, leaving her on her rear with Incubus barreling towards Scribble.

"You will not escape," he said and reached up to grab at her hair.

Pain blinded her, but she never stopped, not even when he pulled out a fistful of her hair. Somehow, she managed to clamber her way over the pile of slippery detritus. She expected to find guards at the other end, but before her lay only the vast chamber of Purgatory and the trail of destruction that Belphegor had torn through it—she couldn't see a single other soul.

Scribble didn't dare look back or slow down, but ran until she no longer heard her pursuer behind her. The scenery changed from bare, broken stone to drab, gray halls. She looked around.

Paul had vanished. Danielle had never arrived. She fell to her knees, alone.

CHAPTER 25 – ROSE

Time passed differently in Purgatory than elsewhere. Souls who had moved beyond Purgatory looked back on their time as a blink of an eye, if they could remember it at all. But for those still stuck there, the hope of reaching Heaven made each second unbearable. For Scribble, the worry of losing Paul forever made her dread letting another moment pass without finding him.

"How did I let this happen?" she muttered to herself. "I've lost my body. I've lost the iBad. Asmodeus is after me. If they don't get to me, I'll probably end up like Grimtooth—hooked to some machine for the rest of time to power it. And now Paul is gone, lost in Purgatory... I hope he's still here in Purgatory and hasn't been caught." She instantly picked up her pace, vaguely hoping it would silence her thoughts.

The trail of rubble she found herself traveling passed through crisscrossing halls and pathways. Cubicles on either side of her, normally filled with tortured human souls, were oddly silent. Only the occasional distant sob broke the stillness. Scribble decided to leave the path and began calling out Paul's name as she wandered aimlessly along empty halls, but never heard a reply. "If I were Paul, where would I go?"

Something caught her eye.

In the center of Purgatory stood a tower that stretched from the ground to the ceiling thousands of feet above, impossible to miss. It looked like a massive stalactite that had grown to meet a rising stalagmite. Other spires rose throughout the abyssal cavern, some reaching the ceiling, some bent or twisted, some so distant they faded into the background, but none had the magnificence of the central pillar. That one was well-known to her; it had been her home for millennia. Now, it seemed cold and unwelcoming. Despite this, Scribble soon realized that she had been getting closer. It was familiar, it was a good landmark, it was tall.

Maybe if I get higher up, I can see where Paul is. She knew the task would be nearly impossible, but searching on foot would undoubtedly yield less fruit. Only hope, the thing she once despised, kept her despair at bay. The tower loomed over her. It felt like she'd been walking for hours, maybe even days, but she had no way of telling how much time really passed while in that place. The nearer she got to the tower, the longer she felt it would take to reach.

Soon, the cubicles gave way to a massive trail of rubble that looked the same as the one she'd left... only, here, it cut directly through cubicle walls, leaving ruination behind. She stepped out onto the path cautiously and peered down it towards the far side of Purgatory, where it met Heaven in the distance. Something in the debris ahead stirred.

Without hesitation, Scribble ran for the movement. "Paul!? Is that you?" She would have picked her way to him had it not been for the sound of crunching rock behind her.

"You didn't think you'd be safe in here, did you?" Incubus said.

Scribble cowered instinctively. "H-how did you get here?" she asked as she turned around. Incubus stalked towards her with a dreadful gait, dragging behind him the body that she had grown so used to. It was dirty, damaged, even bleeding, but he didn't seem to notice or care.

"I just followed your scent," he replied without breaking his stride.

"But, your soul! You're too heavy!" With each step he took, she would take a step back, but his stride proved considerably longer.

Incubus smirked as his dark gaze bore down on her. Without a body, however, she did not feel the lust that she had before, only the fear. "That girl you were with helped me," he said. "I had her *processed*." She hadn't notice it before, but a small soul stone bounced away at his belt, crudely tied to it with a bit of thread. Unlike the soul stones she'd seen before, this one wasn't black, but was, in fact, a brilliant white.

"Y-you didn't!"

"I did. She's so light. I wonder how close to Heaven I could go…"

Loosened by her attempt to flee, the rubble beneath Scribble gave way and she fell to the ground. Incubus dropped the body and leaned over her, slamming his fist into the debris next to her head. "You *are* coming with me to my master. But first, you and I are going to have a bit of… fun together." His huge body pressed down on her, the weight of his homunculus flesh easily pinning her demonic form to the ground. Scribble cried out, despite knowing that no rescue would come. It made Incubus laugh. "Keep that up… I like it when they struggle."

"Remove yourself from the lady." The voice held a noble, yet masculine quality. Between Incubus and that voice, Scribble could hear opposite ends of the spectrum of masculinity—one harsh and deep, the other smooth and melodious. And familiar. *Val?*

"And what are you gonna do ab—"

An armored foot hit him squarely in the face, throwing him from her. He left behind a trail of blood. "I do not repeat myself," the owner of the foot said. Scribble quickly crawled away from the demon and knelt behind her savior. Dust covered him completely, making him gray like her.

"Damn you! I'll rip you apart!" Incubus yelled. He rose up taller than ever.

Between Paul's strikes and that foot, his bloodied nose now sat crooked and broken on his face. The sudden lunge towards the intruder would have caught Scribble completely off-guard, but his motions proved clumsy compared to those of his opponent. His large hand grasped only shadow. A moment later, that armored foot hit him again, this time, in the chest, and nearly knocked him over. The fight continued like that. Incubus would attack while the stranger deftly dodged and struck him with a foot or fist. Scribble's savior toyed with Incubus, but the demon only realized it after his eighth time on the ground with his knuckles crushed beneath the heavy foot.

"Leave now or I will banish you." The stranger unfurled a pair of feathery wings and shook off some of the dust. The wings shone white, the same as his long white robe. Beneath it peeked out a set of armor with brown and gold highlights. The angel pulled out a sword whose blade had been snapped a hand's span from the hilt. Regardless of this impressive display, the demon snarled at him and refused to move.

Scribble brushed herself off and walked over to them. She felt like she drew strength and courage from the angel, even though he might turn on her at any moment. However, she saw no sign of aggression towards her, only curiosity as she squatted down next to Incubus.

"This doesn't belong to you," she said in hushed tones and reached for the soul stone that he had tied to his belt. However, before she got to it, his free hand shot to hers and gripped tightly, sending a jolt of pain through her and melting away that sense of courage and security that the angel had given her.

"Take it and I will have you as its replacement," he growled as he pulled her hand away.

Fear took hold of Scribble. She wanted to run, to escape, but his strong grip kept her in place. Most people know not to back an animal into a corner or it may attack out of desperation. Scribble's fear turned to desperation. It helped her see her opportunity. With her other hand, she grabbed the stone and tore it free.

"Give that back!" he snapped and tried to grab at her, but the loss of the soul stone's negative weight had an immediate effect. Incubus slipped away—pulled by the weight of his own soul—towards Hell, while Scribble fell back onto her rear from the sudden pull in the opposite direction. He howled and reached for anything he could get his hands on, but could find no purchase. An intangible wind had swept him and everything he touched up. His grip on the succubus body he'd brought with him pulled it, too, along the rocky path towards Hell.

Scribble couldn't help but smile as she watched Incubus disappear into the distance. She held up Danielle's soul stone and peered at it in the dull light.

"I'm sorry. I'll fix this," she whispered before putting it into her pocket. Then she noticed a small, metallic rectangle laying on the ground before her. I looked out of place in Purgatory, mostly because it was physical—material. She crawled over to it and dug it out, expecting her ethereal hands to pass through the physical object, but they didn't. "Surli!" she cried when she recognized the iBad. The screen lit up with the familiar logo. It had scratches and dents all over it. The fact that the thing worked at all surprised her. Incubus probably didn't even know he had dragged it all the way from Hell in the pocket of her previous body.

Before she could see if Surli was all right, Scribble realized that the angel still stood behind her, sword drawn. She got up, turned towards him, and smiled innocently, holding the iBad behind her to keep it out of view until she could find a chance to slip it unseen into her pocket. The angel had shaken off the dust that covered him, letting her inspect his robes and armor more easily. Little details, such as the intricately-wrought gold trim that ran along every piece of scale, awed her. His helmet, which had a bronze cross in the center of the faceplate, had suffered severe damage. When he took it off and cast it aside, Scribble marveled at how rugged his youthful face appeared. He had sandy, short hair and eyes the color of the cross on his helm.

"Th-thank you."

"'Twas my duty," he said with a nod.

"You... don't want to attack me, too?" she asked.

"I see no reason to attack you. Why? Should I?"

"No, no! Not at all! But, I *am* a demon. Don't you attack demons?"

The angel grinned and looked down at his broken sword. "Only when I need to. After all, we were once kin. But you do not look or act like any demon I've ever seen," he said as he examined her. Although she no longer possessed a physical body, that gaze sent her heart racing. "Are you unharmed?"

Scribble nodded to him. "I think so. Just a few scratches."

"I'm glad I was able to stop that Seducer Class in time," he said. "Though I'm not entirely certain what you did that sent him away." He brought his attention to his blade once more, turning it in his hand to catch the light. "This'll never do." The angel sighed and sheathed the sword fragment carefully before wandering around the area, eyes focused on the ground.

"What do you mean, I don't look like a demon?" Scribble looked down at herself curiously. She realized that her form appeared more human than demonic now, and she didn't seem to be reverting back to her old self.

"Just that," he replied and leaned over to pick up a metallic sliver, which he inspected thoroughly before slipping it into his scabbard. "Indeed, you seem familiar. Although I can't think why I would have met a human still in

Purgatory. Perhaps you're related to someone I know."

"You look familiar, too. But I truly am a demon. I'm an imp, Fourth Type," Scribble insisted, then bit her lip. *Trying to prove to an angel that you're a demon is probably not the best idea!*

"Truly?" The angel picked up a few more pieces of shattered sword and collected them in his scabbard as well before walking up to Scribble and looking into her swirling gray eyes. "You are far too tall for an imp," he said after a moment and smiled before resuming his search.

Her darkening cheeks betrayed how easily he could make her flustered. She looked up at the looming tower then back to him, torn between the stranger and her duty. "What are you doing here? I've never seen an angel in Purgatory who wasn't part of the Order."

He let out a long breath and squatted down to inspect some piece of metal. "You're right, I'm not in the Order. So, I suppose now you have."

Scribble let out a cute little huff of frustration at his answer. "But that doesn't explain why you are here!"

"No, it doesn't. But why are any of us here?" He chuckled as she tossed down a chunk of wall and stamped her foot. "I chose to serve God, you didn't. I became an angel, a Power, and entered the Lord's Army."

"A Power?" Scribble asked in a calmer tone.

The angel stood up and looked at her in doubt. "Are you sure you're a demon? Every Immortal knows about the Nine Choirs."

"I... didn't get out much. I just worked, all the time. Filing paperwork on incoming souls. Up there," she said, pointing at the tower.

"I see. Well, all the angels are part of the Great Choir. The Choir is separated into nine. Powers are one of the nine." He smirked at her as she impatiently motioned for him to continue. "Each choir has a job to do. Some do God's work, some govern the mortal world, and some mete out justice here in the Afterlife. As a Power, I keep the peace. If you want to know more, I recommend you ask one of the seven Archangels—they're God's 'go-to guys'. Then again, if you truly are a demon... you might not enjoy the experience."

"So, the Lord's army, huh? Are you still trying to stop Belphegor, or have you already done it?"

He looked at her, then down at the path of destruction, then back at her. "Right now, I am picking up pieces of my sword," he said. "We are indeed endeavoring to thwart the Prince of Sloth. I was in a squadron to intercept him, but before I was able to engage, he shattered this stalactite, which buried me and broke my sword. I must have been out for quite a few minutes."

As he spoke, a dark and twisted chain, much like the ones that had formed on Boniface and Danielle, appeared stretched horizontally between them. A fast-moving anchor led it as it rushed towards the Gate of Hell. They both heard a scraping sound and tormented screams. More chains appeared with more voices of anguish getting closer. The angel sprang to action instantly, attacking the chains with his shattered sword, but it had no effect. They could now see figures clawing at the ground and speeding towards them fast—all of them armored angels with missing wings. Just as the chains dragged them past the pair, Scribble and her new friend charged towards one of the angels and grabbed her.

"Sergeant! What happened? Was it the aggressor? How far did he get?" Scribble's savior asked.

The bound angel struggled against the sudden force as it pulled hard on her limbs. She let out a wail of despair, which Scribble later realized were words. "Don't try to fight the Prince! We cannot win! We've already lost."

No matter how hard the two pulled at the angel, they had no hope of holding onto her for long. She pulled them both to the ground before slipping out of their grasp and whisking off into the distance.

"What did she mean?" Scribble asked.

"I must hurry before it is too late!"

As he rose to his feet once more, Scribble grabbed at him. "Didn't you hear her? It's already too late. Maybe you should just run away."

He looked back at her with anger. "I am sworn to hunt this foe and I will do just that, even if it destroys me." He shook off her hand and strode up the path. "I never asked you to interfere."

"Don't go, please! We should hide... or make a plan. Stop! Valerius!"

The angel halted in his tracks. "How did you know my name?"

By now, Scribble had moved to a sitting position. She hid her face behind her hair and closed her eyes. "You always loved to tease me. And you were always so ready to just jump into things."

"Melani," he whispered, getting a nod in response.

"It's Scribble, now. We all had our names changed after the Fall."

Valerius returned to her and offered his hand. "Then come with me, Scribble. We shall go together."

She sniffed. "Why would you want me? I can't fight."

"I do not have time to argue. We can talk on the way."

"But Belphegor is up there. What if he finds us?"

"Then we will fight him sooner. I have never fought a Prince before. I was buried under this rubble before I had the chance." Valerius' eyes lit up suddenly. "You must know more about him than I do. You can help me!"

"But... just you? Where's the rest of God's army?"

"They... well, they have all been called to the fight. So I guess we are it, for now. Until the reinforcements arrive. But no need to worry; I will protect you. Trust me."

"I... I can't!" she protested.

"Can't or won't?"

"There's something else I need to do!"

Valerius' anger returned quickly. "Still running from your problems! Your appearance is different, but you haven't changed. 'A rose by any other name,' Melani!" He turned away from her, broken sword in hand, and marched towards battle. "I will make my stand, with or without you!"

Those words brought Scribble back thousands of years.

Chapter 26 – Fall

"Val! There you are! Wait for me!" Melani said as she jostled her way through the crowded Great Square to Valerius' side. Her arms clutched a thick book to her chest. Like all the other Immortals in Limbo, they had very few features—no halos, no horns, no tails. In fact, they had just enough unique details to differentiate one from another if you knew what you were looking for. Most wore rather baggy robes, which didn't help.

"Hurry up or you'll miss it!" Valerius warned. The square was teeming with Immortals, their incorporeal bodies spilling out of the massive area and into the streets of Limbo. In the center of the square, a dais rose above the crowd, high enough for everyone to see. An empty throne of gnarled wood and stone sat there. On one side stood a tall, proud figure adorned in shining armor, blonde locks spilling out from under his helmet. The sword he had planted in front of him appeared to be made of pure, white light, as did his wings. On the other side of the throne sat another Immortal at a table with a quill. Quill and Immortal alike crackled with lightning. The wings folded against his back appeared to be on fire, but a closer inspection revealed them to *be* fire.

"I can hardly see the stage," Melani said as she finally made it to Valerius, but had to rise up on tiptoes and sway from side to side to see over the crowd.

"How was combat practice?" he asked, keeping his focus on the stage.

"Ugh. Awful. I'm much better with arrows than a sword, and that's not saying much."

"Is that so? Mayhaps you just need a better sparring partner," he teased, nudging her in the side.

"Remind me again why we need to learn how to fight?"

"You remember, the rumored Rebellion. Just an excuse to keep us busy if you ask me. I doubt there's—"

"Is that Lucifer Light-Bearer?" she interrupted, pointing at the dais.

"Indeed. If God's right-hand man is here, it must be serious."

"I don't know the other one, the one at the desk. He looks so strange."

Val smirked and nudged her again. "You really spend too much time in the library. He's Metatron, the new official Scribe."

"He wasn't here at the last summoning, was he?" she asked, only getting a shrug in return. "Wait, is that his purified form? I thought we were only going to get that when we're allowed into Heaven."

Val shrugged as a clarion call rang out over the crowd and the din quieted.

Melani hopped up and down to try to see the dais better, but to little effect. She glimpsed Lucifer with his hand raised over the crowd.

"My fellow Great Ones," he said. "All praise to the Almighty." Lucifer's charismatic voice commanded attention. The throng erupted in cheers. "In these times of turmoil and whispered rebellion, we find ourselves being tested daily. Yes, word of insurrection has reached even *my* ears. Many of us complained when the Lord announced the creation of mortal Man. There has been fear, anger, and even envy spreading throughout our strong people. Some feel betrayed that they are still waiting for Heaven. But I say, we should embrace these mortals, allow them to serve God through serving us. Or, if it is His plan, the mortals shall be tested and may reside with us as equals. This is not a time for fear or envy, but for joy."

The speech continued, but Melani began to tune it out. She searched the ground for anything to stand on, but in the middle of the massive crowd, it was impossible to see more than a few feet in any direction. When no platform could be found, she glanced down at the thick book she held. With a sigh of resignation, she put the book flat on the ground and stood on it. A smile lit up her face as she could finally see Lucifer addressing the crowd.

"The Lord has called us together on this Holy Day to share another important announcement," Lucifer continued. "I am confident that this news will answer all of our questions and alleviate our misgivings. Let us now join in prayer and hearken to the Most Holy Word in our hearts." At that, the crowd knelt. Melani suddenly found herself well above everyone else and stood out until Val took her hand and pulled her down.

"Shhh! Do you remember your prayer song?" Valerius whispered aloud.

Lucifer lifted his honeyed voice in a single, exquisite note. The crowd gradually joined in, each singing and ending a single unique note at the proper time. What started out almost cacophonous quickly developed into one perfect song. Melani had never heard it all together before and listened in stunned silence. She could not imagine anything more beautiful. The wave of notes radiated out from the dais and soon approached the pair.

"Focus," Valerius whispered, holding her hand. "Pray."

Melani nodded and closed her eyes. As she concentrated on the song, a single note—her note—tugged at her mind. The urge to sing it grew stronger until, finally, it was too much and she and Valerius joined their voices to the crowd's. A warmth filled her and she squeezed his hand as the prayer song passed them. If even one voice had been left out, it would have stolen something from the song.

When the last tone echoed through the square and dissipated, a new voice rose. "I am pleased with your praise." The words did not come from a living being, but rather from the wind as it passed through the knots and gnarls of the throne that sat on the dais.

"My Lord, we are honored to serve you," Lucifer rose to his feet.

"Then what lies beneath your sweet words?" the voice returned.

"My Lord, there is nothing. I have been busy trying to root out the whispers against you and they weigh on my mind."

"Then you will rejoice and serve the mortals that I have created."

Melani gasped and turned to Valerius. "When did God make mortals?"

"A few days ago. Shh!"

When Melani looked back at the stage, Lucifer faced the empty throne. "The mortals, my Lord? But they are weak and flawed. They are easily led astray!" He looked out at the crowd, but to Melani, it seemed as if he looked at her directly. "You all heard about what the serpent did in The Garden of Eden. How can we serve a people that will turn from you so easily?"

"This is precisely why you must serve mankind. Help them to hear my Word, feel my Love, see my Hope."

A sense of unease filled Melani. She looked out at the kneeling crowd and noticed that not everyone was still kneeling. Several stood in bands here and there, staring intently at the scene.

Lucifer turned back to the throne and genuflected solemnly, his sword erect in front of him. "If that is your wish, my Lord."

"Because of my love for Adam, we have decided to send his descendants our Greatest Gift," the bodiless voice announced.

Lucifer scowled briefly and clenched his hands tight around the grip and pommel of his sword. "Your Greatest Gift? I was told I was your greatest."

"You are indeed my greatest creation, Light-Bearer. But my very Son shall become Man and open to men the Gates of Heaven. I will raise up the lowly and they shall stand by my side."

"And what will become of us once Heaven is full of men? What of me, who has no equal?" Lucifer asked. As the scene unfolded, the dread in Melani grew.

"Those who serve mankind serve me, and they will be my angels and reside alongside us in Heaven as mankind's aides. Those who refuse will cast themselves out into the darkness," God said.

There was a mixed reaction in the crowd. Some began to cheer and sing hallelujahs. Others murmured complaints.

Melani pulled at Valerius. "I'm scared, Val. Something's wrong."

Valerius nodded slowly. "I think you're right." He pulled open his baggy robes, momentarily revealing a pair of blades strapped to his sides. He reached for one with a slow, deliberate motion.

Lucifer rose to his feet again, not letting go of the sword whose tip was still planted in the dais. "You made us strong, yet you want us to serve the weak?"

"I made you strong *because* I want you to serve the weak," God replied.

It was then that Melani noticed a figure in the crowd moving towards the dais. It started out as nondescript as the others, except for the long, thin blade in its hands. The closer it got, however, the more the figure seemed to change. It grew larger, more masculine, and its robe began to burn as if on fire but without flames. What struck her the most, however, was how quickly and quietly it moved. Lucifer never even noticed until it was too late.

A cry rang out from the crowd as the figure jumped to the stage behind Lucifer and plunged the length of his sword through Lucifer's heart. He never had a chance to defend himself. His limbs fell lifeless to his sides. The figure placed a foot on his back and kicked him off the sword, tossing him to the side.

"You talk too much," it growled.

"Satan the Accuser!" Metatron shouted, getting to his own feet.

Satan grinned and swung his sword at Metatron but missed, and instead, lobbed off a large chunk of the throne. He looked down to see Lucifer holding onto his leg, keeping him at bay.

Chaos erupted in the square. Melani fell off her book, pushed by bodies hurrying every which way. Some began to draw weapons. Others tried to get to loved ones. Melani was swept away, her hand torn from Valerius'.

"Mel! Where are you?" he called out.

"Help me, Val! I can't get back up!"

"I am coming!" Valerius tried to reach for her, but the crowd pulled the two apart. He pushed against the bodies around him and drew his twin blades, which seemed to sing in crystalline voices. The Immortals around him drew back, creating a small bubble of calm in a sea of panic. Then he charged towards Melani, kicking Immortals away from her to keep the trampling feet at bay. Valerius knelt beside his friend but held his swords spread out to deter others. It did not take long, however, for the crowd to thin, despite the vast numbers. Melani clung to him while she sat up.

"Are we safe?" she asked him.

"For now." Valerius looked around at the emptying square, noting that the few who remained looked ready for a fight. None of them, however, approached the pair.

"It's good that you're always practicing with those things," Melani said, managing a smile.

"Indeed it is. But we cannot stay here. Look!"

When she looked back up at the dais, the scene terrified her. Satan had grown into a beast with massive horns as he attacked Metatron relentlessly. The Scribe wielded a spear made of lightning to deflect the blows. Lucifer's own red essence—his blood—covered him as he knelt motionless with chin on chest. The white of his robe faded into gray and the feathers fell from his wings, leaving them skeletal. Suddenly, he screamed, not in his own voice, but with two voices—one golden and the other harsh. As Satan knocked the spear out of Metatron's hand, a new ally who had already begun to grow horns pinned the angel to the desk.

Lucifer quietly stood. A single swing of his claw-like hand sent Satan into the crowd. That same claw then plunged into the back of the other one's neck and pulled him away from Metatron as easily as if he were picking a flower. The red color left him and flowed down Lucifer's arm. After a few seconds, the nameless Immortal stopped moving. His form withered and then, with a simple flash of light, disappeared completely.

Melani screamed. Other Immortals took notice. They all brandished weapons and, like Satan, their bodies had changed, each one a new and personalized form. Three of them gathered in front of the dais.

"We have to go help. Metatron is in trouble!" Valerius said, but when he stepped forward, a tug on his robe stopped him.

"Th-there are too many of them..." Melani whimpered.

He stopped and looked over his shoulder at her. "Nonsense. Once others see us come to his aid, they will join in."

The words did little to move her. "Metatron is surrounded. And what did Lucifer just do to the one with horns?"

Valerius frowned. "I don't know. Lucifer is a *grigori* now, I believe. I've only heard of such things happening once before. If we go now, I'm sure we can help him turn back."

Melani shook her head. "I don't have a weapon."

No sooner had she said this than she found herself precariously catching one of Valerius' swords, sheath and all. "Now you do. Come! Make haste!" He stepped forward, and as he did, his robe began to change. A gold trim appeared along the edge of it and Melani could see flashes of armor beneath.

She backed up, clutching the sword to her breast like it was her lifeline.

"Mel? Come on. We... where are you going?" Valerius came to a halt, trapped between friend and duty. He looked torn inside. But when Metatron let out a cry of pain, a look of resolve settled into Valerius' features. "I will make my stand, with or without you!" he said. He turned his back to her, raised his sword defiantly, and marched towards the fight. The last time Melani saw him, he was charging at the assailants, severely outnumbered and outclassed. She, however, did the only thing she could think of—the thing that seemed to come so naturally to her. She ran.

CHAPTER 27 – CUBICLES

Valerius had always been so brave around her, so strong, so willing to act despite the odds. Scribble watched his white figure retreating, still caught in her memories. When she snapped back into reality, a heavy burden pulled at her heart, heavier than any she'd had to shoulder before. Her frame hunched and her wings fell lifeless against her back as she sank to her knees.

Am I really like that? Do I always just run away? She recalled the times she simply gave in and took on extra work because she didn't want a confrontation. Then, when work overwhelmed her, she would just read one of her books and escape into the realm of human imagination for hours on end. And when she realized that she couldn't be with Paul...

"No!" Her voice rang in the still air of Purgatory, drowning out the distant moans of human redemption. "I... I'm not that person anymore! I am not a coward!" She had her fists balled so tightly that her gray knuckles turned white. She struck them against the rocky ground and stood up.

One foot in front of the other, Scribble forced herself to move forward. However, she didn't head along the path of destruction that led to Heaven, the path Valerius had chosen. To her own surprise, her feet carried her to the large tower that rose in the center of the cavern. She never felt smaller than when she looked up at it from the door at the base. Somewhere, up where the stalagmite and stalactite met, a computer running on the power of damned souls did her old job a million times faster and better than she ever could.

The tower door was nothing special. It looked like any of the other office doors around her, only built straight into the side of a scabrous rock column. Only its black, bold typeface sign set it apart from the others:

ADMINISTRATION ONLY

Scribble looked at it with trepidation. A lump worked its way into her throat. Despite her fears at what lay inside, she gathered the courage to push it open and step through.

Most of Purgatory looked, to the casual observer, like a large office building. Flimsy, mobile walls covered in drab gray fabric separated workspaces. Behind those walls, people performed mundane tasks for lengthy stretches of time. Papers were filed, lost, copied in triplicate, faxed, and revised so many times that the poor souls who wrote the things could no longer recognize their own handiwork. Most of the tormented moans occurred when a computer froze moments before the user tried to hit the "save" button. If someone wanted to find more traditional methods of torture, they had to head for the outskirts.

The only real difference between the inside of the tower and the rest of Purgatory was that the tower truly *was* an office building.

The door opened slowly to an atrium of black marble splashed with quartz crystals. The ceiling rose to some 30 feet above her head, making the entryway feel vast—vast and mostly empty. Faintly, she could hear the same familiar eight bars of Elevator Music repeated over and over *ad infinitum*. A security desk, little more than a cubicle with a service bar, sat off to one side. Scribble did not remember the desk; then again, she'd been among the humans for some time. It was, fortunately, unmanned. She walked past it, keeping an eye on her own ethereal figure as it displayed briefly on the security monitor, and headed quietly and quickly to the elevators. Before she got to them, she took an abrupt left turn and opened the door to the stairwell. No one tried using the elevators anymore—they'd never worked.

The stairs themselves felt smaller than she remembered, but she found that her new, larger body also weighed more. By the time Scribble reached the 10th floor, marked "Inventory" over the door, she had to cling to the handrail for support. She paused to catch her breath and pull her disheveled hair back into place. But before she moved on, the door opened to a four-foot-tall green imp with crustacean claws and a permanent scowl.

"Watch it!" he barked without even looking up at her. He seemed more interested in picking at something on his bulbous chin than in seeing the person he almost bowled over.

"Sorry, Crabstool," Scribble said to her old colleague.

Crabstool dismissed her with a wave of a claw and hopped, his small wings helping him to float down the stairwell at a painfully slow speed.

Scribble stepped through the open door and smiled half-heartedly at the two, distinctly female, blue imps sitting across from each other in the entranceway. They wore matching pencil skirts and blouses and both kept their hair long so that it nearly covered their pointed ears. They had been gossiping across the way with each other about one thing or another continuously, likely since Scribble last saw them. The moment they noticed her, both imps fell silent and stared in apparent confusion. One of them had a nameplate that said "Secretary", while the other's said "Assistant."

"Chitter. Chatter," Scribble called them by name without looking at either. She never could keep the two straight, anyway. They remained dumbfounded as they watched the stranger walk confidently past them, never giving them any opportunity to question or doubt her.

Keep your eyes forward. Don't talk to anyone, Scribble thought as she walked past cubicles, offices, and conference rooms. Most of the demons she passed by took no notice of her, and those that did quickly averted their eyes. Anyone walking with that kind of determination had to be important, at least that's what Scribble hoped they thought. She smiled lightly when she saw the familiar clutter of her old cubicle just a few yards away, but knew that *his* office was coming into view as well. With every passing moment, she could see more of the contents of her cubicle. In the corner, her cabinet fairly bulged with her collection of books and scrolls that she'd been able to gather over the centuries. Pinned pictures and drawings of scenes from Earth adorned the inside of the cabinet door, where no one could see them unless she opened the combination lock. Ledgers, notebooks, and pens all sat on her desk next to that diabolical computer, which ominously moaned away, flashing name after name on the screen. A quick glance towards the other end of the room revealed a door marked HOGMAUL. It remained, thankfully, shut.

"Scribble? Is that you? Wow, you've changed." The unwelcome voice came from behind her and made the demoness roll her eyes.

So close! she thought and turned, forcing a convivial smile. "Bramble, you're here. How could I ever forget about you?" Despite her smile and pleasant tone, she backed up towards her cubicle, catching it in the edge of her vision whenever possible.

Bramble was a very lank demon of brown skin that had the texture of bark. Scribble always thought that his body looked like it had been stretched on a rack, leaving him knobby, awkward, and thin. He had developed a permanent hunch due to his height, which still made her feel small. "You were gone a long time, yes?" he said as he drew closer to her. The concept of personal space had always been foreign to him. And his breath reeked.

"I received a new assignment."

"But you're back now, yes?"

"Not really... I'm only here to get something I left behind."

"Oh, it's all still there. Exactly as you left it, yes. I made *sure* of that," he said. In seconds, he had backed her into the wall just outside her old cubicle.

Scribble clenched her teeth behind her smile and slunk along the wall towards her desk. "Did you? How nice of you..." she said as his face moved close enough that she could bite him.

"Oh, yes. Even that machine is still running just like when you left." He pointed a wooden finger at the computer just as Scribble reached the edge of the wall.

"Thank you, Bramble. You're very helpful. I have to go in here now. Alone. And you should... go back to your desk." She quickly slipped into her old cubicle and breathed a sigh of relief when Bramble sluggishly returned to his. He kept watching her, though, so she sat down in front of the computer and typed aimlessly away with a fake smile. The names on the screen quickly scrolled upwards. She tried to peer out the window at the ground far below, hoping for a glimpse of Paul, but soon realized she was too far up to make out such details. When the names stopped scrolling, the computer made a loud beep. She glanced back at Bramble, but he was out of sight. With a sigh of relief, she leaned back in her chair. But before Scribble had a chance to look around, one of the names displayed on the screen caught her attention:

John Granger	58	#10769283882	Initial Wgt: 15
Danielle Cooper	25	#10769283883	Initial Wgt: 12
Cho Yun	75	#10769283884	Initial Wgt: 48
Naomi Hideyaki	17	#10769283885	Initial Wgt: 33
Arthur Stone	83	#10769283886	Initial Wgt: 10
Rudolf Heinrich	70	#10769283887	Initial Wgt: 26

"Danielle Cooper?" she whispered and leaned close to the monitor, tapping her finger on her teeth. A few clicks and keystrokes later and she had Danielle's file open.

Danielle Cooper
Age: 25
Soul #: 10769283883
 Initial Wgt: 12
Current Wgt: -ERROR-
Est. Departure: -ERROR-
Cause of death: Loss of blood due to fall.

If the computer has her file, then I wasn't the one responsible for putting her in the system. Scribble let out a surprised chirp, then covered her mouth and looked over at Bramble's cubicle. She still couldn't see him. *Her soul weight has increased! No wonder she didn't go to Heaven. It's just like… like those angels that flew past us… like Boniface!* She pulled the iBad out of her pocket and stared at it. "What the Hell is this thing?" She didn't dare check on Surli. The last thing she needed to do was bring any more attention to herself.

Scribble gingerly put it back in her pocket and went to the cabinet to open it. What she remembered as being neat, tidy stacks was, in reality, a haphazard pile of books and scrolls. It filled most of the cabinet and had everything from Shakespeare to Dr. Seuss in its varied tomes. She took books off the pile, one by one, and set them aside. But as the pile got shorter, so did her patience. Soon, she grabbed them by handfuls, then armfuls, and tossed them about. Behind the pile, slumped into the corner, she found what she wanted—a rod wrapped in ancient cloth. When she touched it, the fabric disintegrated under her fingers, revealing an old, rusted length of metal that had once, in some distant past life, been a sword. It was over four feet long and, as Scribble gripped the hilt, she realized that she hadn't been able to carry it so easily since she became an imp.

"Weren't you reassigned?" Scribble gasped and turned, keeping her hands, and the sword, behind her. The squeaky voice belonged to a short, fat demon with pink skin and a flat nose. His business suit strained to contain him. He looked like an attempt to draw a pig if the artist had only ever read a description of one in the dictionary. Bramble stood in stark contrast next to him, sporting a sycophant's smile.

"I got the boss," Bramble said. "I knew he'd want to see you again, yes?"

"Hogmaul! I didn't see you there! I was just about to leave..." Scribble said.

Hogmaul grinned and stepped closer. "No need to rush, Scribble. It's been ages! We should catch up." He reached up to put a grubby hand on her shoulder, making her shift slightly to keep the sword out of view. "I know. We'll have an office party!"

"Great idea, yes," Bramble replied.

"Isn't it the best idea? I'm such a good boss." Hogmaul puffed out his chest.

"The best boss."

Scribble shook her head and stepped back. "Oh, there's really no need. I'll just be going..."

"Stay! I'll tell you about how I won... say, what is that behind your back?"

Bramble leaned down towards Hogmaul's pointed ear. "I bet it's one of her forbidden things, yes? Should I call for security?"

"Don't you dare!" Scribble demanded in a voice that surprised even her. She swung the blade around and pointed it at them, gleaming edges peeking out from the rust and catching the light. The pair backed away, shocked. Bramble spun around and tripped over his spindly legs, landing in a mess of limbs on the floor. Scribble slowly moved past them into the hallway, keeping the sword aimed at them the entire time. As soon as she had a clear path, she ran, holding the weapon close.

A pair of hefty demons in ill-fitting guard uniforms already waited for her at the entrance. She skidded to a halt between Chitter and Chatter, who had resumed their incessant prattle. "That's her!" they said in unison to the guards and immediately returned to their not-so-private conversation.

The guards nodded to each other and pulled out long, dark billy clubs that vibrated, making a sound not unlike moaning. With a flick of the wrist, the clubs screeched in agony. Energy flickered over their smooth surfaces.

Scribble flashed the sword in front of her to ward off the approaching guards. The first swung at her and hit only the blade. Sparks and rust scattered every which way. The second attacked. Scribble clumsily countered in another shower of red and white. With each attack, her movements became more confident and fluid, but the two guards kept pressing hard. Scribble blocked a powerful blow, which pushed her back against Chatter's cubicle. The next landed squarely on her right shoulder with a loud CRACK. Intense pain shot through her entire body and all of her muscles tensed. As she fell to one knee, the guards chuckled maliciously.

"Drop it, or we'll make you wish you could die," one of them said while the other smacked the club into his own hand. He immediately grunted in pain and shook his head.

Scribble held onto her shoulder and gripped the sword tightly. "I have to take it... to *Val*..." Her bangs did not hide the look of resolve she shot the guards. She used the sword to help her get back to her feet.

"I was hopin' you'd resist," the first guard said and swung the club hard at her head. She held the sword up to block, but the weapons never clashed. All the remaining rust had fallen at once from the blade and it radiated a searing bright light. The naked glory of the angelic instrument made all the demons recoil and hiss, hiding their faces from it as if ashamed. Scribble was the only one in the room unaffected.

She ran past the guards and flew down the stairwell in a controlled plummet. Crabstool, who had finally made it to the bottom of the stairs, launched into a series of vituperations when Scribble barreled past him. She ignored him and headed straight for the door. In the marble entryway, nearly a dozen guards had assembled, each larger and meaner-looking than the last. They all turned when they heard the door open and sneered at the girl clutching the blade to herself. Weapons were drawn, but as soon as she held hers out in front of her, the guards groaned in pain and backed away to hide from it. Scribble walked slowly towards the exit, keeping the sword between her and them. They moved out of her way and had all but disappeared from sight when she backed out of the door marked "Exit."

The sharp pain in her shoulder lingered. Had the weapon struck her elsewhere, she might have been able to ignore it, but the club had come down directly where Incubus had dug in his fingers. It felt like a blazing fire burned under her skin, crackling at her bones. Through most of her existence, she'd only had to cope with the dull ache of Purgatory—she never realized that ethereal bodies could feel such intense agony. Then again, she had changed in her time on Earth.

Scribble's thoughts drifted to Paul. She began to fear how Paul's earthly body would handle such pain if he ran into one of those hellfire weapons. For the first time since she left Limbo, Scribble said a prayer.

"I know it's been a long time... a *really* long time, and maybe you won't listen to someone like me, but please let me find Paul. Please let him be okay. That's all that really matters."

She limped quickly towards the faint light of Heaven that illuminated one end of the massive cavern. The prayer still clung to her lips when a prone silhouette appeared just beyond the rubble path. Light pooled around the figure, but Scribble couldn't make out any details or features until she was nearly upon him.

"Paul! Thank God!"

CHAPTER 28 – REUNION

A bare landscape lay beyond the cubicles. Scribble stood at the carpet's edge, looking out over the rocky ground that stretched to the cavern wall. The path of destruction that Scribble had been following all but ended, replaced by a trail of small impacts and craters all around. Winding cracks snaked around them, casting long, dark shadows in the Heavenly light that surged from the end of Purgatory. The light poured over a hill and flowed along the ground like water. It would ebb and eddy around some of the larger fissures and rocks, as well as around the dark figure of Paul. Scribble clutched the sword more tightly and ran to him.

"Paul! I can't believe I found you! Are you okay? Are you hurt?" she asked and fell to his side. But the moment she got there, she saw a hole in Paul's chest—not a wound, but the same hole that would appear when he grew depressed. It covered about the size of a coin and seemed to draw light into it. She pressed her hand against his chest, fingers running over the hole, but she could not feel it.

"Is that from your soul?" she whispered to herself.

Suddenly, Paul jerked awake and recoiled from her. Terror twisted his face. "Get away!" he cried, trying to crawl on his back.

"Paul, it's me—Scribble! Dez!" she said.

He hesitated. His eyes stopped darting around looking for an escape, and instead, focused on her. "Oh my God, it *is* you," he said. "I didn't recognize you!" But their reunion did not bring with it joyful smiles as Scribble had hoped. Paul got to a sitting position and hung his head in his hands, hiding his tears from her, though many dripped down his chin to the ground below.

She moved up next to him and gingerly placed her hand on his back. He pulled away from her.

"Are you okay?" she asked softly.

"I will be," he said, heaving a sigh. "I wasn't prepared for all of this. I'm tired. And I hate this place."

Scribble nodded in agreement. "Me too."

"Did you know? About Dani?" he asked.

"No. Not until tonight." Once again, she moved beside him and put her hand on his back, but this time, he didn't recoil.

"How did you escape?"

"I had a little help. Well, a lot of help. But what happened to you?"

"Once I got away from him, I tried to find you, but some kind of... dog thing found me and chased me. The more I headed in this direction, the further behind it got. I just kept running until I couldn't go any further."

Scribble nodded. "You're getting very close to Heaven way up here. Whatever it was that chased you probably couldn't get any closer." She looked back at the cubicles and then up towards the source of the light that pooled around them. "Its soul was too heavy. And without my wings to help you, yours is probably too heavy to go on, too."

"Heavy?"

Scribble explained in a matter-of-fact voice, "The greater the sins, the heavier the soul, the deeper into Hell you fall. Human souls are less affected but, eventually, can't defy their weight. Immortals can, up to a point."

"That reminds me. That Incubus guy was saying something about owing him a soul. What did he mean?"

Guilt and remorse showed on her face. "That was the deal, Paul. His boss gave me that body. Without it, you couldn't even see me. In exchange, she was going to get to have her way with a soul for three months. I thought it would be mine. Yours, I owed to Belphegor." She cringed, waiting for Paul to get upset. Instead, he just nodded slowly.

"Over my dead body," he deadpanned.

"That was the idea." No amount of explaining made Paul look any more comfortable, so she took his hand in hers and tried a new approach. "You know, I used to be only three feet tall. Tail. No curves. Red skin. I have a feeling that I wouldn't have been your type. At the very least, it would have been a lot harder to kiss you," she teased.

He only cracked a brief smile. "I can see you now. Why is that?"

"I don't know. Perhaps I spent too much time around you, or something happened in the street last night when I was attacked. We did get rather... close. Intimate. Maybe that's all it took."

Paul leaned against her and squeezed her hand back firmly. "It should have been you I kissed that day, not Ginger."

She lay her head on his shoulder and breathed in his scent. It still had a calming, intoxicating effect on her. "I was meant to kiss you on our not-a-date. Turns out, I'm pretty terrible at seduction."

Paul chuckled. "So, now that I can see them, why do those angels want to erase my memory?"

Scribble did everything she could to suppress the thought of having to part with him. "It's forbidden to let humans know about the afterlife. Something about preserving the Mystery, so actions aren't tainted by mixed motives and mortals can have free will."

With each distracted word, her lips moved closer to his neck.

"Where did you get a sword?"

The randomness of the question broke her out of her trance. "Hm? Oh! The sword! It belongs to an old friend I ran into while looking for you. I was keeping it in my old office." She pointed up at the craggy column rising in the distance. "I'm lucky they never found it in there. But I have to bring it to him."

"Val?" After getting a delayed nod in response, he released a slow breath. "Why was Dani *here?* She couldn't have deserved to go to Hell."

"No. And, she didn't. She was assigned to Purgatory and she should have been in Heaven by now. I think this has something to do with it." When she presented the iBad to him, he took it and turned it over a few times.

"Your phone?"

"It's not really a phone," she said as he handed it back to her. "It was made to look like one. It's actually my assistant... and I think it's a weapon. I saw another demon use it on a... a friend. He grew chains just like Dani's and then attacked me. He's the one you saw last night."

"Why do you have it?"

"I don't know. Rotworm, my supervisor, gave it to me. He's probably the one who used it on Dani. Maybe he was testing it? I guess that would explain Grimtooth. If he saw that, he could have gotten Rotworm in trouble..." The longer she spoke, the more she addressed her words to herself.

Paul looked at her bemused. "So this weapon, it drags souls into Hell?"

"I suppose it does. Like a weight might pull someone underwater."

There was a moment of silence as Paul stared at the iBad. "I saw Dani's chains getting smaller. Think she's going to be okay?"

Scribble whimpered. "I don't know. Incubus processed her." She put the device away and pulled out Danielle's white soul stone.

"What's this?"

"This is Dani. Or it's her soul stone at least. We use them for powering things. I grabbed it off Incubus."

"It?! You mean this is all that's left of her? Can't she be turned back?" Paul's voice began to waver as he spoke.

Scribble shook her head. "I don't know. I don't think it's ever been done before."

He reached out for it, palms open and turned upwards. Scribble just held it closer to herself. "Please?" he asked. Slowly, carefully, she placed the stone in his hands. "This can't be happening, can it?" But as he held it, his hands gripped tighter and tighter and he clenched his jaw. "How did you let this happen to her?!" he asked.

"Me? I didn't mean for it to," Scribble said.

"Well, that doesn't make it better! Look at her! You should've been there to help her instead of running away again! *I* should have been there! I... I don't want to see you right now. I don't want to see you at all!"

Those words gripped around Scribble's heart like a closing fist. The pain stretched up into her neck and down to her belly until it filled her. It hurt worse than anything she'd ever felt in Hell. But Paul immediately looked remorseful. Before he could say anything more, he suddenly fell against her as if being pulled by an invisible rope. The soul stone dropped from his grip. He slid past her until he slammed against one of the cubicle walls. Thinking quickly, Scribble tossed the sword into the path of the stone as it rolled Heavenward, then ran to grab Paul with both hands. Her small wings beat furiously, but it wasn't enough to stop him from being pulled to the edge of the wall.

"Paul! Your soul is getting heavier!" she yelled amid sobs.

"What do you mean?!" He had to grip the edge of the wall to keep himself from getting pulled down the long corridor beyond.

"You're sinning!" Scribble replied and held onto his arm, one foot braced against the wall.

"But I'm not doing anything!"

"Please, Paul! I don't want to lose you, not again!"

Paul's feet dangled sideways as he struggled to keep ahold of the wall. He looked down at the long, straight path that led back to Hell. However, when he looked back up at her and saw the tears streaming down her face, he found strength enough to pull himself closer, arms bent. "I didn't mean it," he said. The force lessened. "You've been a big help. You're smart and funny and... I don't want to lose you, either. I'm just angry!" The more he talked, the weaker the pull against him became. "I know it's not really your fault. I just wanted someone else to blame this all on. I'm sorry."

Scribble smiled through the tears. "I am, too. About everything. I should have told you the truth earlier. I know I can't make everything right, but I promise I'll do whatever it takes to save Dani's soul. Then, if you still don't want to see me..."

The pair fell to the ground and slowly got to their feet. Paul's gaze landed everywhere but on Scribble herself.

"I'm not running away any longer. But I need to hide you before I get this sword to Valerius. Then, we'll see."

"No, take me with you," Paul said suddenly. He pressed his forehead to hers and brushed her cheeks dry with his thumb. "I might be able to help."

"I don't know. My wings let me 'carry' you as long as you're near me. But I'm weak. If you sin again, you might get too heavy for me."

Paul raised his eyebrow. "So, what does my soul weigh now?"

"I'm not supposed to tell you, but..." She stepped back and rubbed the remaining tears off her gray cheeks, "I guess I've already broken so many rules, another won't hurt." The iBad only took a moment to boot up, despite the crack on the screen. She quickly scanned him. "It looks like you're... 25! That's a huge improvement, but it's just an estimate."

"And what does that mean?"

"I think it means that if you die now, you'll end up in Heaven. Eventually. You'll spend some time here first, though."

"Can I see it?" When she handed the smartphone to him, he pointed its camera at her. "Definitely not a normal phone. It says yours is... it's blank."

"It really must be broken, then. My soul weight is 1. Always has been. Always will be."

"Well, assuming mine is accurate, is 25 too much for you to handle?" Scribble shook her head. "Then let's go get that sword to Val. Where is he?"

A finger pointed towards the luminescent gateway in the distance. "He's likely fighting Belphegor right now. Val's always been foolhardy. He'd do it alone and unarmed if he had to."

Paul hesitated. "You must care for him a lot to bring him a sword while he's fighting some powerful demon."

"I do. I just never realized how much until now." She began to walk and he followed without a word. A few feet away, Dani's soul stone pressed up against the blade of the sword. When they picked them up, Paul felt himself pulled in the direction they were going—towards Heaven. The rocky ground swelled into a small hill. Light flowed around it and swirled about their feet. When they waded through the light and crested the hill, the wall of Purgatory came into full view. A massive arch of simple design had been hewn into it, spilling the liquid light from within. The longer they stared at the light, the more colors they could make out, not all of which be found on Earth. Together, they had a pearlescent effect. Along the smoothly sloping landscape in front of them, they could make out a multitude of dark islands in the light, several of them the disembodied wings of angels. Near the archway sat a much larger shadow. Scribble broke into a run, flapping her wings to help move her along more swiftly. The sounds of battle gradually became apparent—metal scraping metal, the agonizing screams of the soulweight weapon, rocky ground crunching underfoot.

Paul trembled with fear when the weapon went off. "I've heard that scream before... the night Dani died." But instead of letting his fear get the better of him, he redoubled his efforts. They didn't stop running until they were twenty yards from the fighting.

Before them, an angel clad in white robes and golden armor was locked in combat with a gargantuan scorpion made out of dark, twisted metal. Several dozen pair of angels' wings, tainted with corruption, were pressed along its thick body like scales. At the front, between the mandible-like pincers, sat Belphegor, his bent and crippled body wriggling in sick joy. Behind him lay rows of soul stones, hundreds of them, collected over centuries, all providing the machine power. The tail of the scorpion looked like a human spine with a blackened skull at the end. There was no question that the monstrosity had been the cause of all the destruction.

"Val!" Scribble cried loudly, holding the sword out in front of her. The light from the sword shone even more resplendent than the liquid light that surrounded them. Belphegor took instant notice, wincing in annoyance. His foe welcomed the distraction and launched himself towards the scorpion's pincer. In a feat of acrobatics, Valerius bounded off the pincer towards Belphegor himself. The demon cried out in pain as the angel's broken sword sliced through metal and carved a deep gash along his pock-marked face. But before the angel could recover, the scorpion's tail darted forward and knocked him to the ground. A giant pincer flailed and struck, sending Valerius skidding bodily towards Scribble.

She saw her opportunity and broke into a full sprint. "Val! Your sword! I still have it!" She was just a few feet away from her friend when Belphegor spun with unnatural speed.

"Oh no you don't!" The metal scorpion lifted its tail and the skull on the end opened its mouth. It let out a wail like a soul being torn in two. A dark beam came from it, ripping through the light directly towards Scribble. She let out a stunned gasp. Something knocked her to the ground. Her skin tingled as the deadly shot narrowly missed her. When the attack was over, the scream of pain continued in Paul's voice. Terror seized her when she realized what happened. She dropped the sword and crawled to his side.

The iBad lay in two pieces in front of him. The once-narrow crack now branched across the entire screen. Its black soul stone battery rested between the iBad's halves, rolling lightly against one of them but not getting past. And around Paul's wrists, large cuffs of metal and light began forming.

Belphegor's metallic creation barreled towards the sword as it fell from Scribble's grip. He left a series of impact craters behind as his machine's pointed legs stamped into the ground. One of his dangerous pincers reached out for the sword, but in a flash of gold and white, Valerius appeared, keeping the pincer at bay with his broken blade.

"Take him from here, now!" he commanded.

Scribble scrambled to her feet and grabbed Paul's arms. She had only managed to drag him a few yards before Belphegor noticed. With one pincer against Valerius, he used the other to reach out for her. But Valerius used the distraction to grab the sword that lay at his feet. A sharp *CLANG* rang out when he threw his old sword at the Demon Prince's face. Belphegor had no choice but to give his full attention to the armor-clad angel.

"Move!" Valerius called and pressed the attack. Belphegor backed up and spat at the angel, but managed to match him blow for blow.

Spurred on by the imminent danger, Scribble summoned the strength to pull Paul away from the skirmish. From the safer distance, she watched the combatants disappear into the liquid light they kicked up around themselves. She then turned her focus to Paul, who stared, not at her, but through her. His hand reached up and gripped her shoulder tightly, causing her to wince in pain. When she pulled it away, she noticed a single point of light tracing the outline of a chain link extending from the cuff on his wrist. And there, on his chest, that hole spread wider with every moment.

"Paul? Can you hear me? I'm so sorry! You've got to fight this!"

Paul's expression didn't waver or even register that she was there.

The liquid light reflected in Scribble's tears like falling stars, tumbling to Paul's body. No matter how she struggled to get the cuff off of him, it wouldn't budge. The chain grew longer. The force pulling him towards Hell slowly built up. She wrapped her arms around him to hold him tighter. "I'm not letting you go!" she sobbed.

A loud crack took her attention away from Paul. The luminous cloud around Belphegor and Valerius settled. Belphegor had managed to dislodge a large stalactite and brought it down hard against Valerius, knocking the angel prone. The demon then threw it against him. The rock landed over his stomach, pinning him to the ground with its great mass. Belphegor let out a cold, electronic chuckle and pushed down against the stone, adding the weight of his scorpion-like machine to it until a deathly groan left the angel.

Scribble forced her eyes shut. She wanted to get up to help her friend but knew that she would only end up like him, or worse. When she opened her eyes again, she gazed down at Paul. He needed her, too. And she realized that she *could* help him. Belphegor, Rotworm, Valerius, Heaven, Hell... it all faded away. There was only Paul. Scribble leaned down and held him close. Heavenly light covered them beneath its bright surface. She'd only possessed a body once before, but she had been in that empty shell for so long that the act seemed like second nature to her. Time slowed down. Forehead pressed to forehead, then her ethereal body sank into his.

Possessing a body without a soul in it was very different than possessing one that was already occupied. At first, darkness concealed everything, but Scribble *felt* a presence. When she could finally see, she found herself alone on a cold, empty road covered in mist. But when she looked closer, she could see a dark silhouette in the haze.

"Paul!" she called and ran towards it, but the closer she got, the thicker the mist closed in around her. It formed a barrier that prevented her from getting closer than a few feet from him, so she had to keep her distance. She called his name again, but he didn't respond. He didn't even look at her.

His figure turned and walked in the opposite direction. The hole she'd seen on his chest, she could now see as a black mass, visible even on his back. She followed as closely as she could manage. Shades appeared along the sides of the adumbral road, standing perfectly still. After a moment, one appeared in the middle. As Paul grew nearer, details formed.

"Where are you running?" came Ginger's voice. A shock of dyed hair fell into a ponytail behind the figure. Tanned skin appeared, then eyes, then lips. In seconds, it was her doppelgänger.

"I don't know. I just have to keep going," Paul replied.

"Why? If you don't know where you are going, why not just stop?" Ginger's shade asked.

Paul hesitated. "I just have a feeling. Something is driving me forward."

"Don't you want to stay with me? We've been friends for years. We know each other. And we could know each other better," Ginger said with a smile somewhere between hopeful and seductive. "Stay here with me. That road is too long and hard for you. It's not worth it. But stay here and we can go back to how things were, how they should have been." She walked up to him and ran her hand over her corset top alluringly, then pulled the lacing loose. The corset fell, leaving Ginger in fishnet stockings and black bra. Scribble bit her lip and tried to move closer, but that invisible wall pushed back just as strong.

"No, Ginger, we can't," Paul said.

She gave him a pained expression. "But I love you, Paul."

"Ginger, we broke up. Remember?" He stepped past her.

"With a 10-minute conversation? No explanation, no chance to win you back?" She grabbed his arm and stopped him. "I know why. It's Dez, isn't it? You'd throw our years away over a fling?"

"I'm not throwing our friendship away."

Ginger's face twisted in a scowl. "Coward. You only agreed to go out with me because you're too much of a wimp to say no. You pushed away Dani when she asked if you wanted to get married. You couldn't even finish off your father after all those years of abuse. Have you slept with Desdemona yet, or are you too chickenshit to make a move?" In the last sentence, another voice joined in. Danielle stepped up beside Ginger.

"What? No. It's not like that..." he said.

"Is that why you asked me to wait? You were scared?" Dani asked. "You wouldn't sleep with me until you were 'ready'. I waited years for you to be ready. Did I not mean anything to you?"

Before he could answer, Ginger spoke up. "You can never be with Dez, Paul. You're from two different worlds. She won't be there when you go back. And neither will we."

Scribble clenched her jaw, feeling a weight tug at her heart. "I want to be there for you, Paul," she said, but still got no response from him.

"You both mean so much to me," Paul said. He turned to Danielle and reached out for her. "Please forgive me." The moment he touched her, she and Ginger dissipated into a cloud. Paul's hand tightened to a fist and moved to his heart. The hole instantly doubled in size, taking up half his chest. His body slumped as if a heavy burden had been placed on him, but he walked on.

Scribble followed in silence, feeling like an interloper, an eavesdropper. Here and there, the shades would reveal a person, likely from Paul's past, shouting disparaging remarks as he walked by. The shapes of buildings emerged on either side of them. One appeared directly in front of them. But before any details became visible, another figure stepped into their path from the murk. It was a black man, older, with a silvering beard and a stained, threadbare shirt. Paul stopped dead in his tracks.

"Dad?"

Scribble gasped. Paul had not talked about his dad much, and what he did say had never been flattering.

"Yeah," the man replied with a slight smile. "It's me."

"What are you doing here?" Paul asked. "I... I thought you never wanted to see me again."

"Why would I wanna see someone who tried to kill me? Oh, think I din't know? That I was asleep?" His dad's scratchy laugh grated on Scribble's nerves.

"Wh-what do you want with me?" Paul's face filled with horror.

"Oh, don't worry. I ain't here to hurt ya. To be honest, I din't think you had the balls to do it, son."

"Don't you call me that. I grew up without you in my life and it can stay that way. Mom worked so hard to keep things together because of you."

The older man let out a raucous laugh. "Is that what ya think? All them nights she stayed out late? Man! She was the village bicycle! That store'd've gone belly-up otherwise."

Scribble could feel Paul's shock. "Mom would *never* do that! You lying—"

"I ain't even the one that put her in the hospital! I mean, I was hard on her, sure, harder than I oughta been. I ain't no saint or nothin'. But she got around. And she bled me. Cost th' earth."

Paul clenched his hands into tight fists like he was about to coldcock the man. "You hurt her. You hurt *me*."

"And I shouldn't've. But I din't even know if you was mine. Guess ya know why I was gone so much now. I'm bettin' that you've been in the red since she died, am I right?"

Scribble couldn't tell if Paul's tears came from anger or pain or sorrow. He hid his face with the back of his forearm. "I'm turning it around."

"Pshh! Good luck with that. Tell ya what, though. I ain't the richest man, but I've been doin' pretty okay. When yer back home, come see me. Take a paternity test. If I really am yer dad, I'll put ya back on the will."

"I don't want to be on your will." Paul rubbed at his face and fixed his glasses in place, which now had smudges all over them.

"Ya sure? It's enough that you'll never hafta work again. Easy street. Write that play. Make them kids. Just think about it."

A light shone behind Scribble. She and Paul both turned to look. What had been an empty road before was now replaced by his apartment. The door stood open for him, the computer hummed, and his screenplay waited.

Paul looked forward. The haze that surrounded the building ahead of him grew denser. He pushed away from his father. "You don't know me," he said defiantly. "I've put too much into the store! If it fails, it won't be because I didn't try hard enough! And I don't need or want your money to do that!"

As he turned and walked away from the old man, his father said, "That's right. Work yerself to death. Give up on those stupid dreams, on a family. Who needs those anyway? They just let you down. The store'll be enough for you."

A wind kicked up and blew some of the miasma around the building away. It carried with it the distinct scent of fire and ash. *Othello's Books* appeared, its walls blackened, the windows broken, the books inside burned away.

"What's left of it, at least." He put his hand on Paul's shoulder. Paul sagged under the weight of it, as if his father's hand was made of lead. With a cruel chuckle, the old man vanished into smoke, but that weight remained, and the hole grew.

Paul pressed on towards the store with Scribble in tow. He had to labor through every action he made. Almost no sounds penetrated the mist, not even the sound of their footfalls. The bell on the front door let out a single muffled clang when it opened.

Scribble tried to follow Paul inside, but when the door shut in front of her, she could not open it, no matter how hard she tried. She moved to the broken window and watched. Ash stirred up all around Paul in a shroud. It covered the walls, the burnt shelves, the floor, the ceiling. But in one corner, a flash of color and lilting laughter drew their attention.

The color spread until it became the image of Frank sitting in a plush, red chair that belonged in a Victorian living room. His wife, Addison, leaned over him, wearing a seductive red dress that showed off her natural curves. Outside, his Porsche glinted in bright light that seemed to shine only on Frank and his things.

"Paul! Good to see you! You've met my wife, Addison," Frank said, nodding to the woman that hung off of him. She giggled and leaned in, kissing Frank on the ear. For a moment, she wasn't Addison any longer, but Desdemona, with her lips on Frank. The moment passed and Addison leaned against him once more. Paul clenched his jaw and stepped back.

"What are you doing, Frank? What is it you want?"

"Me? I don't want anything. I already have good looks, friends, a good woman, and enough money for my great-grandkids to retire at birth. But it's not about what I want. It's about what you want. Everyone knows you've always wanted a car like mine. You envy how I can just make friends without even trying. And I've seen how you look at my wife. Face it, I don't want anything. You do."

Frank stood up. Although he wasn't as tall as Paul, he made his boss appear small.

Scribble shouted, "Don't let him get to you, too, Paul!" but it didn't have any effect.

"Maybe I do," Paul said. "But I'm working towards it. I'll rebuild, business will boom, and I'll be able to afford—"

"Have you not yet realized why I work for you? Stocking bookshelves isn't exactly fun." Frank put his hand on a nearby shelf. It fell into a massive cloud of dust. "How many people had access that day *and* knew there were valuable books just sitting there? Who do you think put that money in Ginger's purse? I was planning on 'discovering' it but your little scene with Dez solved that for me." As he advanced, Paul stepped back. Another bookshelf turned to dust. "And even if the place didn't burn completely down, the clean-up and investigation will keep you closed for weeks."

"Why would you—"

"I'm saying that I can have anything I want without having to work at it. I'm saying that I will have *Othello's Books*, and you can't stop me." Frank's face twisted and soon became Giacobbe's. "I will gut the store and turn the building into my personal parking garage."

Paul backed up towards the stairs as more of the store fell apart around him. He tried to climb them backwards, but when his foot pushed down on the first step, it gave way. The walls groaned as cracks ran swiftly along them. They fell in on the store, kicking up a thick blanket of suffocating dust.

Scribble coughed and waved the dust out of her face. When the air finally cleared, Frank had disappeared and Paul was just a dusty, dark mass on the ground. The hole in his body took up most of his chest. The building had been reduced to ruins. Scribble tried to rush towards him, but after a few steps, the mist kept them separated once more.

In the center of the ruins, the dust gathered together into the form of a middle-aged woman. She had chains falling from her wrists and ankles, connected to a very small, black disk. No matter how much she tried, she never managed to move that stone.

"Mom!" Paul turned his face away from her. "Are you here to kick me while I'm down, too?"

His mother shook her head. "No. I'm here to tell you to get out of here." He responded with a confused expression. "Not this place... this place doesn't exist. It's only in your mind. Don't you remember? You were brought into Hell... into the Afterlife. Try to remember!"

Paul stared off into space, clueless. "I don't—"

"You ran into Dani... Desdemona betrayed you... you were shot by a demon..." She glanced for a moment over at Scribble.

"Paul! I'm sorry for what I did!" Scribble shouted. "Please, remember that." The glance turned into a venomous glare.

His face slowly lit with recognition. "Yes... I remember now. But, what is all this? How did I get here?"

"We're in your mind," his mother said.

"Then, this is all just my imagination?"

"The others are, in a sense, but they are real enough. As for me, I am not like the others. I'm not part of your imagination. I am truly real."

Doubt covered his face. "If you're real, then how do you know all this? You're dead. And you've never even met Dez..."

"There are ways to watch over you, even from Hell," she replied.

"What?! What do you mean, 'even from Hell'?" Tears began to well up in Paul's eyes. "I... I always thought... always hoped that you were in Heaven."

"Hope is a dangerous thing, Paul. When you find out the truth, it leaves only despair and anguish in its place. Don't trust in hope. Yes, I am in Hell. That's what happens when you live like I did. When you die like I did."

Scribble pressed forward against the mist. It gave a little, encouraging her to push even harder.

Paul looked up into his mother's eyes, blinking hard to focus through the tears. "The doctor said it was a heart attack."

"I'm sure that's what overdosing did to me," his mother replied. "The doctor was probably just trying to spare your feelings."

"You're lying! I can't believe you're in Hell. Aren't you supposed to be tortured there? You don't even look like you're in pain."

"Oh Paul, if you only knew. Everything is pain. This... body of dust you made for me, it is quite lovely, but it is what your mind has made, nothing more. I'm being allowed to share my thoughts with you. After so much time of pure suffering, you learn how to hide it."

"Then... I'll get you out! Come with me! I'll steal you. They'll never notice!"

His mother shook her head with the kind of smile that only comes from experience. "And how will you do that? No matter where I go, Hell follows. You cannot save me at all. I made my decisions in life, and this is the result."

Paul rubbed at his eyes with the back of his hand. "What decisions? Is that why Dad left us? Did you really cheat on him?"

"Oh, oh yes. I did cheat on that waste of air. As surely as Danielle would have cheated on you. But that wasn't the only decision I made that brought me here. Most of us are here, you know. Your grandparents, your uncle, even the priest that baptized you. We all have our dirty secrets, our affairs, our hatred for each other."

Paul clenched his eyes shut and shook his head. "No, that's not true! That's not fair! We loved each other!"

"Really?" his mother asked. "Do you remember that day no one picked you up from school and you waited there for three hours? That was because your grandfather was too busy getting drunk to remember. And the Christmas when you didn't get anything you asked for? Your grandmother and I spent the money on ourselves. Does that sound like love?"

"What? But you always showed me love!"

"Guilt! You were the constant reminder of all that I had done wrong. I felt guilty, so I pampered you, hoping it would make me feel better. It didn't. That store? I left it to you in the red as punishment for being what you are: a good-for-nothing bastard!"

Scribble had been silently throwing herself against the mist, but when she heard what Paul's mother said, she stopped, stunned.

Paul sank to his knees, unsettling the dust all around him. "This isn't like you. I'm... not like you," he said, mostly to himself.

"No? And what was going through your mind when you told Dani you weren't ready to marry her? Were you thinking of her, or were you using the store as an excuse to keep your options open? Or maybe you just didn't want to grow up, just like your father never did." She walked right up to him, her motherly smile twisted into a wicked smirk. The tears Paul had denied, had struggled to keep at bay, quickly flooded his cheeks. "Oh, hit a nerve, did I? You know, she was a very *good* girl. Not only did God take her away from you... but now she's here in Hell, too, despite her *good deeds*. And your new beau, Scribble? She's *from* this place. Give up and go home, Paul. Because, like me, you can never... save... them." She reached her hand up and pressed it against the hole in Paul's chest.

With a heart-rending cry, Paul pushed at his mother, but he could not push her away. Her hand plunged into the hole and she tore at its edges until the entire outline was cracked and spreading fast, threatening to overtake his body in a matter of moments. Finally, he struck at her, but she fell apart into a thick vapor that drifted to the ground. Everything, including Paul, faded into gray. The only part of her that remained was the small, smooth disk that she had been anchored to. Paul slumped over, unmoving, unthinking, uncaring.

Chapter 30 – Hope

Scribble came back to her senses and pushed forward again. To her surprise, the mist provided no resistance. She ran to Paul and fell to her knees next to him.

"Paul!"

"Go away," he muttered without moving.

Scribble narrowed her gaze. "No, I'm here to help you break free of this!"

"You can't break free from the truth. Go away."

"The truth? That wasn't the truth. It was spite. The truth is—"

"Sure it wasn't. You're just here to hurt me like the others. I don't want to hear it." He turned, facing away from her.

"Well, too bad! You're going to hear it." She stood and tried to force him to his feet but only managed to get him to kneel.

"You. You brought me here. It's your fault all this happened."

"Come on, Paul. Stand up! Look, I just want to help you."

"That's a lie. You just want to make me sin, don't you? If I don't do anything, then you'll fail."

"Paul, that's not true. That soulweight weapon is making your soul heavier. If you despair, it's all over!" He just shrugged. "Don't you *want* to go home?"

"What's the point? There's nothing for me there. Ginger hates me, I have no friends, the shop is destroyed, the business is going under, and everyone I've ever loved is still dead and in Hell."

"Not everyone," Scribble whispered and pulled his arm over her shoulders to help him stand. "Together, we'll rebuild it, all of it."

"How? You're not even a human. What do you know?"

Scribble grunted under his weight but pulled him to his feet even though she didn't know where she was going. "We have to keep moving forward, Paul. Please. This isn't like you."

"I don't even know who my real dad is," he said. "He's probably here in Hell, too. Maybe I'll meet him."

Scribble sighed. "Paul... do you remember when I walked into the door and you just hired me on the spot? You let me stay in the store's apartment rent-free because I had no money. You took me shopping, you took me out on the best day I've ever had, and then you wanted me to help you write that play because you were so excited to share it with me. *That* is who you are. The way your eyes sparkle when you talk about a book or hear a certain song—that is who you are. When your books got damaged, that didn't stop you. Giacobbe's threats didn't stop you. Your depression didn't stop you. And this fire isn't going to stop you. You've always been so strong, so determined. *That is who you are.* Please, just keep it up a little more and then you can rest." Her wings beat powerfully behind her as she tried to guide him towards the dark, unexplored road that led on from the ruins of the bookstore.

Paul's arm slipped from around her shoulders and he dropped to his knees. His mother's stone fell from his hand and clacked on the ground in front of him. He stared at it.

"Paul! I don't know how long we have. Please... I need you to be safe. I... I just need you, Paul." She sank down beside him, taking his hands. "It doesn't matter if the store goes under or if you never meet your real father. I'll be there, no matter what it takes. I'll help you start up a new store, one that we can run together. We'll repair your mom's books, sell video games and books and terrible coffee. And we'll make new friends, tons of them! Even if we don't, it won't matter because we'll have each other. You can show me old movies and we'll snuggle on the couch. We can fight about what temperature to set the thermostat and then make up later. I want to go to sleep with you and wake up to you."

There was no change in his expression. Her head pressed against his shoulder and her arms slipped around him. "Fine. If you're staying here, then so am I."

"Why?" He hesitated, but slowly, his arms moved around her as well.

"Because I've lived in Hell, and it didn't hurt half as much as losing you."

"I'm nothing special."

"You are to me! Once, you made a homeless man smile by buying him lunch. I watched you sneak a book that a customer's kid was looking at into their bag. At first, I thought I hated you for making someone happy even though you couldn't really afford it. Then I thought I was jealous. But I admired you for it. Then you did so much for me, gave me what I needed, trusted me. You made me happy, even though our time together has been brief. And I hope..."

Scribble fell silent as Paul tightened his grip on her. "Hope," he repeated. "What is there to hope for? I have no hope left."

His words stunned her. "Oh, Paul, you can't give up on hope! I almost did. But it was the only thing this terrible place didn't take from me. I always hoped that I would see Earth. That kept me going for more years than I can remember. When I got there, I hoped that I would do a good job as your Sinister. And now, I hope that I can stay with you, that I can..."

"Can what?" Paul asked. There was a pleading edge to his voice.

"That I can make you as happy as you made me."

Paul smiled and let out a quivering breath. He leaned into her more. "How?"

"I don't know... but I'll find a way."

The hug was completely unexpected. Paul buried his face into her hair as he held her. "Maybe I do have something to hope for after all."

Scribble felt a part of herself that had been dormant for untold centuries suddenly rouse. Her soul poured out in words muffled against his shoulder, the only clear word being "love".

Paul held her tighter as the dusty ruins fell away.

*   *   *

The great cavern of Purgatory surrounded them once again. A powerful yell nearby demanded their attention. Scribble and Paul looked towards the sound just in time to see Belphegor pull a wing off Valerius and stick it in the mass of black feathers that covered the sides of his mechanical monster. The wing's resplendent white and gold drained away, leaving it dark and defiled like all the others. He turned away from the scene and moved straight for the archway, through which all the light flowed. There, Belphegor spread his ill-gotten wings, which shivered along the scorpion's back before flapping in unison. Scribble caught a glimpse of the large mass of soul stones, wired and welded into the monster, just beneath the wings. A chorus of moans sounded as they sent power to the machine. Its shape warped into something insectile. With a loud clamor, the demon and his creation jumped through the archway and disappeared.

Even after Belphegor was gone, some of the moaning remained. It came from Valerius.

"Val!" Scribble sobbed as she left Paul's side and ran to her friend. The angel futilely pushed at the piece of stalactite that pinned him. Scribble threw her body into it, but the rock didn't budge. When Paul approached, she knelt by Valerius' side and stroked his hair. "It'll be okay, we'll get this off you. You'll be fine," she said. A pool of bright red light spread out from around the angel. "Paul, please, help me!" Scribble begged.

Paul hesitated at the sight of the angel, but only for a moment. When he saw Scribble's pleading eyes, he reached down and grabbed the narrow end of the stalactite. Gradually, it lifted. Valerius slipped out from under it and sat up. His holy essence freely bled from the wound in his belly, but he kept it covered and out of their view.

"I am all right," he said, pushing Scribble away from him. She didn't stay away for long and persisted in pulling at his hand to get a look at the wound. "It is fine! Take a look at your friend over there. Where did his chains go?"

Scribble turned to Paul, who rubbed at one wrist after dropping the rock. On his chest, the hole remained, but it had shrunk again to the size of a coin and stopped growing. Valerius shooed her closer to him and nodded reassuringly. Eventually, she gave in and took Paul's hands, turning them over and back again. "Where *did* they go?"

Paul looked at her in confusion. "Where did what go?"

"The chains on your wrists. The ones that... weapon of his put on you."

"I didn't see any chains. When I pushed you out of the way, everything went black. I was in that other world. It felt like hours. You... came for me."

"I possessed you. We were in your mind. I think it was trying to make you despair. I've never seen anything like it."

Paul rubbed his head. "I don't know what would have happened if you hadn't come. So, there were chains on my wrists? Like the ones on Dani? Do you think that was the finished version of the weapon he tested out on her?"

Valerius turned towards them. One of his sleeves was now ripped off and tied around his torso, over the wound. His armor lay in pieces on the floor behind him. "It is an Infernal Device, perhaps the most dangerous he has ever created. From what I can tell, it compels the victim to lose hope, shed their wings, and then uses the victim's own life energy to make those chains. He's already used it on so many of my brethren. And it appears he is using a bevy of soulstones to fuel it all." He winced and reached around towards his missing wing. "With all those wings, he can probably go wherever he wants in Heaven."

"Someone has to stop him," Scribble said.

Paul shook his head. "How can anyone possibly stop that thing?" He looked to Valerius cautiously and backed away a little. "You aren't going to try to erase my memory, are you?"

The angel took a long look at Paul before grinning. "You're solid. You're alive! A living human. So, you must be what has Melani—I mean, Scribble— so worked up." He didn't show any hint of pain, despite his massive injury.

"Melani?" Paul asked.

"To answer your previous question, no, I'm not going to erase your memory. Not my department. Besides, I would not do such a thing to Scribble. But where are my manners? I am Valerius, a soldier and old friend of our mutual acquaintance."

Paul cracked a small smile. "She's talked about you."

She blushed and nodded. "Well, I told him a little."

"Wait, he's an angel. You're friends with an angel? But—"

"This was before The Fall of the Angels, when all us Immortals were the same," Valerius said. "We lived together in Limbo until Satan's Rebellion."

Paul put his hand on Scribble's in an almost possessive gesture. "What about other angels? Won't they turn me in?"

"I doubt it. Everything is in chaos right now with Belphegor on the loose. The Order isn't prepared for such a frontal assault and the Lord's Army is spread out and will take time to gather. We have not mobilized in many generations of humans. I am all that's left of my platoon. We're the first line of defense. No one has ever gotten past us, so this is entirely unexpected. Once they see a Demon Prince in Heaven, one human is going to be the last of— aagh!" Valerius had leaned over to pick up his sword's unbroken twin, but ended up gripping his wound in pain instead. Scribble pulled from Paul's arm and helped Valerius stand upright again. When it appeared that the pain had subsided, she handed him the sword. "Thank you," he replied. "A few thousand years late, but what's a little time between friends?" He looked into Scribble's eyes warmly and took the sword, his hand lingering on hers before sheathing the weapon. She glanced self-consciously at Paul, but when Valerius gave another grunt of pain and his holy essence bled red down his side, Paul hurried towards him and ripped at his own shirt sleeve until it tore free. "Is that blood? Angels can bleed? You can't die, can you?" he asked while wrapping the sleeve around the angel to help bind the wound.

"In a sense," the angel said, breathlessly. Despite his objections, Scribble drew his arm over her shoulders so he could lean against her. "We cannot die. But we can get... weak. If left unchecked, we can even falter in our faith. But that isn't going to happen. At least not until I hunt down that demon."

Scribble went pale for a moment. "Why? He already beat you once. Shouldn't you just lay low and heal? I can—"

"It is my duty. My personal safety is not of importance."

"Nothing I can say will convince you, will it?"

"Of course not. Have you forgotten how it is with us Immortals?" Valerius gave her a somewhat bewildered glance.

Scribble clenched her jaw in resolve. "If you're set... then I'm going with you. You're going to need help. Besides, I owe it to you after what I did..."

"But, Dez, how are you going to help?" Paul asked. "What can you do against... *that*?"

She frowned. "I don't know. But it's got to be better than doing nothing!"

"Getting killed isn't going to help!"

Valerius turned his grave expression towards Paul. "She cannot die, Paul Taylor. But you can. Yet you are also the only one I have seen who has recovered from this weapon, and you are the only person in the afterlife who can change his soul weight. I do not believe you are here by coincidence. Will you turn your back on a friend and return home? Will you try to talk her out of a chance to redeem herself? Or will you face this daunting new foe that threatens to harm someone you care about?"

Paul clenched his hands into fists and hung his head. "I don't really have much of a home left to return to. The only good thing in my life wants to help her old friend fight a giant metal scorpion." He fell silent for a long time, then tension left his body as he let out a long-held breath. "I'll come. I'd never forgive myself if something happened to her and I wasn't even there to help."

Valerius smiled broadly and hit Paul's back with enough strength to stagger him. "That is the spirit! Nothing fights despair better than taking action." He then looked back to Scribble. "But what about you, Melani? I have never heard of a demon doing something selfless. Have I been out of touch for so long?"

"Maybe it was the body I borrowed? I don't know. But I want to make up for abandoning you. This is probably the only chance I'll get before I'm punished for disobedience."

Val slowly pulled away from her and looked over his new companions. "Two firsts in one day. A living human in the Afterlife and a demon with a conscience. Well, come on. He cannot have gone far."

"Wait." Paul put his hand on Scribble's shoulder. "Do we even have a plan? I don't know how to fight."

"Leave the fighting up to me," Val said.

Paul frowned. "So, we're just going to walk up to him and, what, insult his mother? I don't think a confused demon or my extensive knowledge of video game cheat codes will impress him much."

They all grew quiet as the reality settled in. Scribble looked down in thought, but when she did, she noticed the broken iBad, its parts scattered among bits of metal and wire that had been chipped off Belphegor. "What about Surli? Maybe she can tell us some weakness."

"Who is that?" Valerius asked.

"She's my assistant," she replied. "And the prototype of Belphegor's despair weapon. I just hope she isn't too broken. Could you get those pieces for me?" Paul nodded and picked up all the pieces and loose wire he could find before handing them to her. Scribble examined them. Though the crack in the screen had grown, it miraculously held together. Each piece snapped easily into place, but the device remained dark. "It's not turning on."

"What about that?" Paul pointed to the black disk as it skittered away from them. He ran to grab it. It tugged at him briefly, but he managed to keep his footing. After a moment of contemplation, he took the stone that held Danielle's soul out of his pocket and compared them. "This is a soul stone." His eyes went wide. "This is my *mother's* soul stone, isn't it?"

"We can't know that," Scribble said.

"I saw her, in my vision. She was attached to this stone."

"That could have been fake. It's probably just a regular soul stone. It's been in the iBad for as long as I've had it." Eager to see if Surli still worked, she tried to take the stone from Paul, but he pulled it out of her reach.

"I can't let you use it," he said.

"But we need it to power the weapon!" Scribble protested.

"If you use it, will it hurt her?" Paul asked. Scribble bit her lip and turned her gaze aside, holding her elbows. "No! Not my mother's soul. I don't care if she *is* in Hell. I won't help you torture my mom!"

"Can any soul power it?" Val asked.

Scribble turned the iBad over and opened the back to reveal where the stone would fit. "I don't know, I guess so." Without hesitation, she took some of the loose wires Paul handed her and tried to work them into the chassis. The wires came to life, digging deeper into the terminals that attached to the stone. Scribble screamed and gripped at her injured shoulder as the other ends of the wires burrowed into her arm. Paul and Val both reached for the iBad to pull it away, but she brought it close to her. "Don't!" After a moment, the pain began to subside. She turned it on, feeling a sharp sting when it pulled power from her. The screen lit up. "It works... now, how do I find Surli?" she said to herself and navigated menus. Without warning, the menus began navigating themselves, moving immediately to a file named, "Surli.tst." A second later and Surli's floating head appeared on the screen.

"Surli! Are you okay? Is anything broken?"

The digital avatar blinked slowly.

"File Surli not found. Please input command."

Scribble looked horrified until Surli cracked a smile.

"You are such a sucker. So, whaddya want?"

Scribble would have pinched Surli in the arm if she had one, but instead, she hugged the iBad to her chest. "Nothing. I just wanted to make sure you were okay."

When Scribble looked back down at the screen, Surli flickered.

"My power source is not stable."

"Oh, I'm powering you myself."

"Well, that's stupid. Why are you doing that?"

Scribble took a deep breath. "Paul knows everything, we're in Purgatory, Belphegor broke loose, and we know the iBad is a weapon. I met with my old friend, Valerius, and Danielle is here, and Paul was shot but I saved him, and we dropped the iBad but we found out the soul stone powering might be his mother's, but we need to power you so we can use the iBad to help fight Belphegor, who is attacking Heaven."

"Ah. Well, then... what are you waiting in Purgatory for? An invitation? Because I'm sure I could print one for you."

Valerius walked proudly but stiffly to the archway. "She is correct. We need to get moving."

The three of them stood in front of Heaven's Gate. It was the first time Scribble had ever bothered to get a good look at it. It had no guards. The gate itself did not seem like anything special. Cut into the rock wall of Purgatory was a gothic archway, pointed at the top. A carved diamond grid decorated the arch in an ascending spiral. Although called a "gate," Scribble saw no actual gate—the only thing beyond the arch was white light that spilled around their ankles.

"It's not like I imagined it would be," Paul said.

"Things rarely are," Valerius responded. With Paul supporting him, he and Paul walked into the light. Scribble took a deep breath, closed her eyes, and stepped forward.

Chapter 31 – Zion

A sense of relief flooded Scribble's mind and soul as if a pressure she had been unaware of suddenly released. The moment the light enveloped her, all the pain she had been feeling ended, replaced with an intense sensation of love—not only of being in love, but of being loved. Sheer joy pushed the breath from her ethereal body. But as quickly as it struck her, it all subsided and the pain in her shoulder and arm once again flowed.

When the light fell from her eyes, she watched in amazement as a scene constructed itself before her. The horizon stretched out. Above it floated shimmering clouds in an azure sky, while below, hills grew into majestic dark peaks with a cloak of pure snow around their shoulders. Scribble had never seen mountains in real life before, but something about the rugged summits drew her to them. At the foothills sprouted a lush forest, which gave way to verdant grasslands. Every color was vibrant, alive. All else Scribble had ever seen was truly a shadow on the wall of a cave.

A city appeared before her, each building as much a part of the landscape as mountains or trees. Some were stout, made of mortar and bricks. Others stood like stretched glass spires that yearned to reach the clouds themselves. Golden streets wove a network of tributaries around them. The city blossomed into a metropolis that followed the foothills to the horizon. Behind them stood the archway they had stepped through, its inside dark. From it wound a path that led down to the city. There were no signs of Belphegor.

"Welcome to Zion," Val said with a proud smile. "The City of God. What do you see?"

Scribble answered without taking her eyes off the landscape. "I see a huge city, and what I think are mountains, and more trees than I knew existed!"

Val nodded sagely. "Everyone sees it differently. Heaven is what you need it to be. I cannot even imagine what a *living* human might see."

"It's... fuzzy," Paul responded. "I can only make out details if I focus on them. When I look away... I don't know, it's like I forget them."

Scribble tightened her grip on the iBad. "It feels like home to me. More like home than anywhere else I've ever been."

"Zion *is* home. Your true home." Val's voice lost some of its melodic nature as he clutched his side. "Of course, not everyone resides here. Many journey to the mountains or over the ocean."

"I don't see an ocean," Scribble said.

"Then it does not call to you, Scribble. If you need—"

A loud crash drew their attention to one of the taller spires. A large, dark figure shaped like a hornet clung to the side, sending a spray of glass cascading to the city beneath. It had a long, curled body with spindly limbs and a set of black wings that blurred into action periodically. The hornet clawed its way up to the top of the spire so Belphegor could look out over Zion from its head.

"That thing changes shape?" Paul asked.

"He's searching for something," Val replied. No sooner had the trio stepped on the path that led to the city than a flight of armed and armored angels soared towards the intruder. Belphegor struck the first blow. Where the hornet's stinger should have been was the soulweight weapon. A dark fissure ripped through the air towards the squadron's leader, scattering the angels in all directions. In the confusion, Belphegor flew away from the tower with an ominous, deep thrum.

"Come, we must make haste!" Val said.

*   *   *

It did not take long before the golden streets of Zion were beneath their feet. Humans and angels alike ran past them in the other direction while they followed the sound of Belphegor's machine. Paul kept looking up to try to find the demon, but the buildings blocked any view of him. They were mesmerizing in their unearthly architecture. He slowed down. With buildings made of ice, paper, and even light, it seemed that no medium was off-limits there. Scribble was about to round a corner with Val when she looked back to see Paul staring at an edifice of water. Out of the corner of her eye, she saw a streak of white shoot across the sky towards him.

"Paul!" she cried out.

He had almost no time to react. The white streak crashed through the building in front of him and sent up a thick spray that obscured him from her view. She ran into it and felt around aimlessly, calling his name.

"Help me!" came Paul's voice from beside her. There was a tone of urgency to it, but not injury. As the mist dissipated, she saw Paul dragging one of the armored angels under the shoulders. The angel looked unconscious and was missing his wings. Without hesitation, she joined him, picking up the angel's feet. The iBad refused to leave her hand, so she had to make do with using her forearm. Burning pain seared her shoulder.

"There's a relief station a hundred meters to your right,"

Surli instructed from the device.

"How did you know that?" Scribble asked as they followed her directions.

Surli led them to a square where several members of the Order were stationed, watching the skies. The low thrum of Belphegor's hornet had died away, but the Order remained vigilant. In the middle of the square were open tents where several other angels lay on tables and beds. All bore wounds; most had missing wings. Angelic blood pooled on the ground. Around them crowded angels and humans alike, tending to wounds with expert efficiency.

"Another injury!" a woman called out in a British accent. Within seconds, several workers took the unconscious angel from Paul and Scribble and carried him to a vacant table. The woman was a human, and like all the other humans, she was ethereal, a partially transparent soul. Her long, flaxen hair fell in curls around her shoulders, framing a slightly weathered face. Paul stood out among the humans as the only person with a truly solid body, while Scribble stood out as the only one with horns. Despite this, no one paid any attention to them.

"Raphael is on Earth. She hasn't been told about the attack," one of the healers muttered.

"Then get Gabriel. He can fetch her," said another.

"Michael must know of this. Send for him first," a third said.

The woman who had called out to them first suddenly pulled Scribble away from Paul. Despite being middle-aged, she somehow kept all the vitality of her youth, which struck Scribble as odd and kept her distracted. The woman examined Scribble's shoulder, but looked confused when she noticed the black wires writhing under her skin, leading to the iBad.

"What is all of this? How did you get up here?" she asked, noticing the horns for the first time. "Are you an accomplice?"

"It's a long story. I'm trying to stop him. Please don't send me away!"

The woman laughed. "Now, why would I do that?"

"Because I'm a demon," Scribble replied, perplexed.

"My job is simply to heal. As long as you are not harming anyone, you are welcome to stay and be healed."

"But don't you hate me?"

The woman rolled up Scribble's sleeve to expose her shoulder and expertly applied an unguent. "Heaven has no room for hatred. What is your name?"

"Scribble. I thought we were enemies."

She gave Scribble an understanding smile and continued working on her arm and shoulder. "Let me tell you a story, Scribble. You see, I was a healer when I was alive, as well. We were at war. Everyone called it the 'war to end war'. I worked on a hospital ship. There was often turmoil on the ship because we took on both British and German wounded, so we tried our best to keep them separated.

"One day, a young man came on board. He'd been in a grenade blast. It was awful. He had on a British pack, a British tag. But when he woke, he spoke only German. I was asked to translate. When I looked at his tag, I realized that it was my brother's tag. I supposed he'd taken it off my brother's body. I was angry and hurt and confused. I wanted to harm him, to refuse, but instead, I helped him. In time, I got to know him. I found I could not hate him.

"Then, one day, he asked me what happened to the tag he had with him. He said it was urgent, that it was from a British soldier he found dying on the battlefield. The soldier handed him the tag and begged him to find his sister so she wouldn't wonder what had happened to her brother. Of course, I told him who I was. The German never thought he'd actually meet me, let alone marry me. If I had let my hatred and anger blind me, I'd never have fallen in love with him."

She finished her work by tying a bandage around Scribble's shoulder to contain the medicine. Within moments, a welcome numbness eased much of the pain. "Regretfully, that is all I can do for you. What is your name?"

"Um... Scribble. Or Melani. Or Dez. I'm not really sure anymore."

"Well, it seems you're confused about many things. I am Lori."

"Thank you. I need to find my friend, Valerius. We're chasing—"

"Oh, him? That boy is so foolhardy. He's over there." Lori pointed to another tent, where an angel in blue wrapped bandages around Val's torso. Others bustled all around, making it hard at first to see him. His robes sat pooled at his feet along with his armor. He showed no embarrassment or hesitation in his nudity, only appearing eager to get back to the fight. His body was strong, youthful, ideal. Scribble felt her face flush and turned away.

"I-is he going to be alright?"

"He should be. We've dressed his wound, so the rest is up to him. His faith is still strong; he should recover if he doesn't do something brash."

"And what if he does?" she asked with a nervous smile. Suddenly, Scribble realized that she had left Paul behind and began to look around for him. "Oh, where's Paul?" As she searched the throng of ethereal bodies, she found one in the distance that stood out, his body solid. "Paul!" she called over the din.

"I'm over here," Paul said. He came up beside her.

Scribble turned in surprise. "Oh! I thought..." She looked back through the crowd but could not find the other solid human any longer. Her search ended when Valerius approached them donning his armor.

"We need to get back to the hunt."

Scribble frowned and shook her head. "No, *you* need to take it easy."

"Nonsense! I'll be fine! Doubt not the healing power of Heaven."

"You were defeated when you weren't injured. What makes you think you'll do any better when you are?" she asked.

"I have you two and your little assistant this time. I have faith in you both."

"Well, I-I won't let you! You'll get hurt again! Let the other angels take care of Belphegor!"

"This is not about me," Valerius stated. "It has never been about me. I might lose my soul to Belphegor, but if that keeps someone else safe, then so be it." He pushed past her.

"I don't want to lose you again!" she cried out. "I lost you once before. Please, don't let it happen again. There's so much we never got to say…"

Paul drew back at her words. He watched helplessly as Scribble hugged Valerius from behind and buried her face against his back. Something began to tug at Paul, making him stumble backwards. One of the black cuffs around his wrists had reformed and a small chain slowly linked itself together, hanging sideways towards the Pearly Gates they had come through. The hole in his chest pulsed.

"Melani, you may lose me even if we walk away from this unscathed," Valerius said. "Stop looking for happiness outside of yourself and you might find it within. You do not need me. You need to make decisions that you can feel proud of."

Paul made a fist and pushed away from the wall. He had a look of determination as he walked past them. "We aren't going to put that monster back where he belongs just standing here," he said. "I don't know what good I'll be, but I intend to find out."

Scribble blushed and stepped away from Valerius. She was letting her all-too-human emotions get the better of her. Without a word, she followed after Paul into the streets of Zion once again. Valerius quickly caught up and took point, leading them towards the faint sound of the mechanical hornet.

*   *   *

Less than an hour passed before the trio caught up to the meandering Belphegor. They stood on a bridge that spanned a sapphire-blue river when a flight of angels sped overhead towards a dark speck in the distance. The speck moved to intercept them with a familiar thrum. It surprised Scribble at just how easily Belphegor dispatched the angels. One by one, they fell prey to the soulweight weapon and were dragged across Zion by dark chains. The angels came less and less frequently. With each defeat, Scribble felt more and more alone, standing against impossible odds.

"Why do they fall so easily?" Paul asked.

"The Lord's Army stationed here is small. These are our reserves," Val replied. "Or recovering from their own injuries. This is just to slow him down so our forces can muster."

"But *you're* injured," Scribble said. "And neither of us—"

"Sshh!" Val raised his hand to stop them.

"What's wrong?" she whispered.

They all trained their eyes to the sky and realized that Belphegor had vanished from their view. The buzz had disappeared as well. Valerius pulled his sword from its scabbard and held it in both hands. He moved to the edge of the bridge to peer over it. With a deafening splash, Belphegor's machine erupted from the waters and landed on the bridge in front of them. Valerius swung a great arc towards him, but missed and lodged his sword into the stone of the bridge.

"If it isn't the little bug I swatted flat." A cruel sneer twisted Belphegor's lip as the hornet paced along the bridge, hungry for more action. Its sharp legs crumpled the stone beneath.

"Whatever it is you are planning, Belphegor, we will stop you," Valerius announced, keeping his grip firm on his sword. A swell of fear filled Scribble at the sight and she backed up into Paul. As an afterthought, she brought up the iBad and tried to scan the demon, but she couldn't get a clear shot while he constantly paced before them.

Belphegor chuckled. "Is that your plan? To use my own weapon against me? Pitiful. Maybe I should just send the three of you to Hell with all those others."

"That's not going to work this time," Paul said, standing proudly in front of Scribble to shield her. "It didn't work on me the first time."

"Tss!" Belphegor hissed. But the human's words actually gave him pause. "Troublesome creature, troublesome life. I may have to take that from you. But not yet. You three have followed me this far. You're too fun to play with. Scribble, is it? The daydreamer from Purgatory. And you must be Valerius, the one she abandoned. Oh, yes, I know about you. Well, this is no daydream. If you want to stop me, you're going to have to get to the Sanctum Sanctorum before I do." His diseased face wrinkled into a grotesque smile. "Of course, I'm not going to just let you go. Let me show you a trick I've been working on."

The hornet lowered its body and its face split open to reveal more of its pilot. Belphegor grunted with effort as he reached one long, pale arm out and touched the bridge. Dark tendrils spread from the point of contact, twisting the stone. The corruption moved quickly, causing the bridge to shake. Its far end began to warp. Belphegor took flight as Valerius pulled his sword free and struck at him, but again, missed. Soon, he was the least of their worries.

"Off the bridge!" Valerius shouted.

The three of them turned to run, but the corruption caused the bridge to curl and tossed them to the ground. Scribble managed to roll back onto her feet and ran as hard as she could for the end. Cracks raced them. She was easily passed by Valerius, who took long strides with little effort, his one wing flapping to assist. When she looked over her shoulder, however, she saw Paul on all fours, gripping at the masonry. The bridge broke apart beneath him. It trembled. She slid to a stop and bolted back towards him.

"Paul, hold on!" The stones beneath her feet spread apart into long fingers, each as wide as she. Paul held on with all his might, but the finger he held onto separated from the others and shifted upwards. He began to slip. A hundred feet below them ran the fast-flowing river. In a last-ditch effort, he threw himself towards one of the other outcroppings of stone. It let out a *CRUNCH*. He'd hit it with his chest but managed to keep ahold, though his feet now dangled freely. Scribble dove towards him and grabbed for his arms. Her wings pumped frantically. She caught him with both hands as he fell, letting the iBad hang from its wires in her arm, but could not pull him up. A sudden jerk from the bridge almost sent the pair into the swift current, but it was the final throe before the black tendrils ceased and the bridge grew still.

"I won't let you go," Scribble said with her eyes tightly shut.

"You shouldn't have come back for me."

"What? I get... berated for running... and scolded for staying?" she said between breaths. "How can I win? Gosh, you're heavy."

Paul's eyes locked on hers, refusing to stray as if glancing down would seal their fate. "Don't hurt yourself. We can discuss it la—aah!"

"This might not be the best time to have a lover's spat." Valerius easily pulled them both up onto the remaining stable portion of the bridge. The moment he released them, Scribble gave Paul an intense hug.

"I thought I was going to lose you," she whispered. "Oh, your wrist. The chain is back."

Paul leaned against her. "Yeah, but it's not very heavy yet. I think I'll be okay for now."

Valerius rolled his eyes and pulled them along the ground until they were off the bridge entirely. "Come on, you two. At least wait until you are on solid ground before making up." He turned his eyes to the sky and listened intently, but all was silent. "Our quarry is gone."

Paul got to his feet and helped Scribble up. "Didn't he say something about some sanctuary?"

"Yes, he named the Sanctum Sanctorum. If that is where he is headed, perhaps we can still apprehend him."

"Sanctum Sanctorum? What is that?" Scribble asked.

"It is the center of Zion, the Holy of Holies," came Surli's voice. They all looked down at the iBad dangling from her arm. Surli's digital image had changed—her impish ears were shorter and the lines that made up her visage were pale, no longer green. Scribble brought the device back into her grip. "It is where the Trees of Life grow from the waters of the River of Paradise. The Throne is there, as is the Great Scroll. There is no holier place in the city."

"Sounds like he could cause some real damage there," Paul said.

"Indeed," Val said. "I do not know what his plan is, but if he is not checked, he could potentially destroy all of Heaven."

"What happens then?" asked Scribble.

"I do not know. I imagine eternal suffering for everyone, no matter what kind of life they lived. No miracles, no guardian angels, no Dexters. Come. The fastest route is this way."

CHAPTER 32 – SANCTUM

Valerius kept a furious pace. Paul and Scribble had to run to keep up with the tireless angel, and were soon panting for breath. They had no time to appreciate the gorgeous villas and blooming gardens they passed.

"Val... wait. Paul and I can't keep up," Scribble called out.

Valerius looked over his shoulder. "Sure you can! We will rest at that fountain up ahead. The Sanctum is near."

The fountain dazzled as a bright glimmer in the distance sitting at the piedmont of taller, more antiquated buildings. They did not look like the structures in the rest of Zion. They looked like they had both been engineered and grown out of the very firmament of the earth.

The closer they got to the fountain, the more crowded it became. The hurly-burly of conversation soon joined with the sound of music. To Scribble, it seemed like the conversations themselves all contributed to the song. When the trio approached, Scribble tugged on Val's robe to get his attention.

"We need to tell them to evacuate."

Val shook his head. "They likely already know—word spreads fast here. We are not ruled by fear in Heaven. Those who wished to leave would have done so by now. Here, take a moment to rest."

The fountain's waters flowed clear and possessed a light, floral fragrance. The fountain itself was made of pure white marble. Pitchers and large shells sat ready for use by any seeking the water's cool respite. Paul leaned against it, trying to catch his breath while Scribble pressed her back against a nearby wall and gripped at her forearm in pain.

After dipping a large shell into the fountain, Val offered it to Paul. "Take and drink, quickly. It will rejuvenate you—body and mind."

Paul brought the shell to his lips. "It's sweet. It's good! What is it?"

"It is water. That is, water as it was meant to be. And as it will be again. How do you feel?"

"Better. It's like I've been thirsty my whole life until now. Here, Dez, you've got to try it."

Paul handed the shell to Scribble, but Val struck the shell to the ground.

"No! She must not touch it," he commanded. Scribble drew her hand against her chest as the reprimand cut right through her. Val's sharp tone softened. "This water is holy. There is no telling what it will do to a demon. I am sorry, but you must endure a while longer."

Paul looked at Scribble in concern, but she just gave him a tired smile. "It's okay, Paul. I'll be fine."

"We should press on," Val continued after an all-too-short rest. "I'm sure Melani could use a little more exercise," he said with a wink.

Scribble moved slowly, constantly clutching her forearm. She was simply too tired to acknowledge Val's playful jibe. The salve given to her earlier had worn off. Paul walked to her side and took her free hand. She leaned against him with a grateful sigh. "You know, you can always turn back, go to the relief station. You don't need to be here. I'm sure someone will help you get home. The store needs you right now."

"So do you, even if it's just to keep you walking upright," he said with a smile. "Why does he call you Melani?"

Scribble looked up at him, a dull pain in her eyes. "Because it was my name before the Fall. All of us Immortals lived together in Limbo. There was a rebellion. Those of us who fell had our names changed."

"That's why you're named Scribble," Paul realized. "So, what is it you did? Why did you fall?"

She looked at Valerius for a moment before casting her gaze downward. "I was... afraid. I ran away from someone I loved when he needed me."

Paul fell silent, watching the angel's back with a forlorn expression.

"Tell me, Paul, what do you think of Heaven so far?" Valerius asked out of the blue. He kept his attention on the road in front of them while they walked through the crowd.

"It is not what I expected," he answered after a pause. "I thought Heaven was supposed to be perfect. No pain, no sorrow, that sort of thing. But I've seen buildings crumble and angels get injured. I've felt pain and sorrow here."

"That is because Heaven is not yet complete. We are waiting for the Beginning."

"The beginning of what?" Scribble asked wearily.

"When the Seven Seals of the Great Scroll are broken, and the Seven Divine Trumpets sound, and the Seven Bowls of Wrath are poured on the surface of the Earth, that is when Zion will descend and Heaven and Earth shall join. That is when all will be complete. The Beginning."

Paul's eyes widened a little. "Revelation. You're talking about Revelation."

"Yes, it is the Revelation that was given to St. John."

"But what do you mean by the Beginning? Don't you mean the end? Armageddon?"

"The end? I do not believe John ever claimed that his visions were of the end of the world. No, the world will not end, though there will undoubtedly be much suffering and death before all is resolved."

"Wait, didn't you mention a scroll at the Sanctum?" Scribble asked. Surli answered this time.

> "Yes, the Scroll is there. When a Seal is broken, the archangels announce it. They act as a countdown to Armageddon—the final battle between good and evil at Tel Megiddo."

"How do you know all this, Surli? Did Belphegor program you with this information?"

Surli's image flickered a little.

> "I draw from databases. Ever since you started powering me, I have been able to access some of Heaven's databanks."

"Why would that make a difference?"

> "Perhaps my power source is no longer damned."

"But I'm... wait, what?"

> "Your soul weight has changed. No demon can change their soul weight, so you must not be a demon."

"But that's impossible! What am I, if I'm not a demon?"

She got no answer. They continued in silence for a time while Scribble lost herself in deep thought. Paul would glance up now and then but neither saw nor heard any sign of Belphegor.

Eventually, a pair of large trees came into view. Their perfectly smooth bark matched the color of the dirt that they grew out of so well that they looked like part of the ground itself. Each of them bore many different kinds of fruit, none of which Scribble had ever seen on Earth. Between them ran a river that flowed silently, its surface like gently shifting glass. The closer they got to the trees, the greater the sense of serenity they felt.

"Are those the Trees of Life?" Paul asked. Valerius shot him a stern glance and brought his finger to his lips.

"Yes," he whispered. "Do not go near them! They are not ready for the living. Now, stay close, the Sanctum is just beyond."

The buildings beyond the trees took on an ethereal quality—something no human mind would have constructed. They looked like they were made of gold stretched so gossamer-thin that you could see right through it when the light hit it from behind. An edifice of stone and crystal stood directly in the path of the river. All around it, the smooth waters of the river formed a sort of lake of glass, surrounded by marble columns. In fact, the crystal walls that made up the building appeared to be crafted out of the water itself. Other humans, denizens of Zion, walked across the lake as they went about their normal business, showing that its waters were, in fact, solid crystal.

"The Sanctum Sanctorum," Valerius said in a reverent breath. "The Holy of Holies."

"And I couldn't have found it without you." The voice came from all around them, the very crystalline ground vibrating with the tone. Impossibly, Belphegor was below them, his machine chewing upwards through the crystal lake from beneath like a giant, toothed worm. The ground shook when he erupted from the lake, knocking everyone nearby over and sending massive shards flying in all directions. Those who could, left the area quickly. Others, including the trio, were thrown by the force. Within moments, a circle of onlookers had formed, giving a wide berth to the demon, as well as Paul, Scribble, and Valerius. Some tried to aid each other, some talked among themselves, but none of them approached.

Scribble rolled to her side and looked around. Massive fissures and sharp jags of crystal now marred the serene, smooth surface. Next to her, the dark figure of Paul stirred. She looked around for Valerius and found him near Belphegor, having been tossed, apparently violently, over an impassable, toothed ridge. He lay still as Belphegor's machine changed its shape. It kept its worm-like body, which wore the black feathers it had stolen like a skin, but pushed the demon out from the front of it. Directly behind him writhed the mass of soul stones that powered his machine, while all around him, the black metal and wires formed into the diamond-shaped head of a serpent, with massive fangs on display. Immediately, the snake struck at the building with tooth and tail.

"Where is the one made flesh? God's so-called son? Show yourself!" As he spoke, coils wrapped around the stone and crystal structure so tightly that it began to crack. "I will tear your Heaven apart if you do not face me!" A large fissure darted up the wall, followed by another and another, until a web of fractures covered the crystal.

The ground trembled frighteningly under the strain he put on the building. Scribble rose to her knees as the mechanical snake's coils twisted and tightened. The Sanctum split apart with a sickening *snap*. The snake lifted a huge portion free and dropped it to the side. This revealed a large, round room with ornate cathedrae in a circle. In the center sat a massive throne of gnarled wood. All of them were empty. However, sitting at a desk just left of the wooden throne, a fiery figure bent over a fiery quill.

"Metatron!" roared the voice box in Belphegor's chest. The figure looked up. He seemed oblivious to the damage all around him.

"Belphegor! What are you doing here? I have much work yet to do." Metatron returned to his papers, only to have his desk tossed aside by a serpentine tail.

"I demand to see your Lord," Belphegor responded. Heavy, thick coils seized the scribe and shoved him up against a stone wall.

"He is not here. He is serving."

Panic settled in as the scene played out before Scribble. Along with it came a cold, paralyzing fear that shot through her limbs, rooting them firmly in place. As much as she wanted to help, the thought of taking Metatron's place blocked any message she tried to send to her body to act.

"What are you doing?"

Surli asked, her voice muffled slightly under Scribble's palm.

"I-I don't know. I shouldn't even be here." She remained perfectly still, not even bothering to look down at Surli.

"While your impression of a deer facing an oncoming 18-wheeler is uncanny, it isn't going to help anyone. I can't scan him by myself, you know."

"Scan..." she repeated absently. Her mind began to piece itself back together. "Oh, yeah... s-scan." She blinked and looked down at the phone just as the machine threw Metatron to the ground. Navigating the menus came intuitively now. Only a second passed before she aimed the iBad's camera at Belphegor. He didn't notice, too busy using the snake's jaws to try to tear off Metatron's wings. For some reason, he seemed to be struggling to get a grip on the fiery appendages. She tried to scan him. A sharp pang bolted up her arm as it snapped a picture. Nothing happened.

"Why isn't it working?" she asked worriedly. Surli replied,

"You're too far away. You need to get closer."

"Closer? But what if it doesn't work? What if it does? Who do I tell?"

As if in answer to her question, Paul stirred beside her.

"Nnggg... Scribble?" He tried to stand but cried out in pain and stumbled against the wall of crystal that shielded them from Belphegor's attention.

Scribble rushed to him, putting her hand on his shoulder and lowering herself to his crouched level. "Paul, what's wrong? Oh, you're hurt!" she said in hushed tones. A few drops of blood trailed to his left foot. His shoe was torn, with more blood collecting at the gash.

"It's nothing. I'll be all right." He forced himself to stand, clenching his jaw and using the wall against his back for support. "What's happening?"

"But you're bleeding! I should never have let you come."

Paul frowned and pushed from the wall, but kept his hand against it. "Don't *you* start questioning things now. We're both in this and we're both seeing it through to the end, no matter what. Right?"

She hesitated, then nodded.

"So, what did I miss? How long was I out?"

Scribble looked over the wall. "Belphegor broke the Sanctum open and found Metatron. Metatron's a scribe. Kind of like a secretary. Now he's demanding something."

"What about your iBad?" he asked. "Did it work?"

"I'm not close enough."

Paul sighed and looked out at the path they had taken. Most of the people had either run for cover or tried to alert the Order, though a few remained to tend to those who had been injured from collateral damage. One woman poured water over a girl's wounded leg. Paul smiled lightly and turned back to Scribble. "How about I distract him and you shoot him with that thing?"

Scribble shook her head. "No, it's too dangerous. Your foot is hurt. You should get it looked at." Paul looked like he was about to object, but she put her hand on his chest and pressed in close for a swift kiss. "Please. I'll try to get to Valerius. I'm sure he'll be able to help." She turned without another word and ran off through the maze of debris.

The wall of jagged crystal stretched around where Scribble had seen Valerius fall. She didn't try to keep silent or out of sight, but instead, relied on Belphegor's assault on Metatron to keep him preoccupied. When she finally found an opening large enough for her to slip through, Valerius had come to. He dragged the sword across the lake's surface before using it to help him stand. A pool of red essence flowed from him and he trembled as he moved.

The sound the sword made rang through the air like nails on a chalkboard. Standing over the ruins of the Sanctum, Belphegor tossed his hapless victim aside and slithered over the crags towards Valerius.

"It seems I've forgotten about the vermin. If the Son of Man doesn't come for Metatron, I'll just have to destroy everyone here, starting with you. Your tortured screams will be the medium for my art."

Belphegor raised up in position to strike. Scribble watched in horror as it darted its head down with unmatched quickness. Valerius managed to deflect the blow using a desperate swing, but a quick follow-up swipe of the tail sent him skittering along the crystal surface. He landed a few yards from Scribble. Belphegor slithered up to him and the jaws of the snake opened, showing off deadly fangs, each about the size of her arm. He rose to strike again. Scribble ran and threw her body full-force at Valerius. They slid several feet just as Belphegor's machine buried its fangs into the ground where they had been. With a mechanical grunt of disapproval, Belphegor tried to free the snake from the solid lake, but it held fast. The struggling only sent lines of cracks racing out into the crystalline matrix.

"Val!" Scribble cried desperately. "Can you stand?"

She struggled to lifted him to his feet. He shook his head but tried anyway. Even with her help, his feet slipped beneath him and he sank back to a seated position. It took effort for him to simply focus on her.

"Leave me, Melani," he commanded with as much force as he could muster.

"No! He'll kill you!"

Val chuckled and shook his head. "You should know better than that. Besides, you have a job to do." He motioned down to her hand, where she still clutched the iBad.

"I don't think so," Belphegor said as he looked at the pair from his makeshift cockpit in the snake's head. The black metal shifted away from him and he reached out with a pale limb. His claw flexed and grabbed for them, reminding Scribble of how he'd corrupted the bridge. She tried to pull Valerius' sword up, but the demon was already too close.

SMASH!

"Aaaghh!" Belphegor pulled his arm back sharply. Welts bubbled up and a malodorous smoke rose from it. The pale skin turned red, as if burned, and Belphegor nursed it. The remains of a clay pitcher lay scattered about him. The demon shot a wicked look at Paul, who scaled down one of the more stable crystalline walls. He held another pitcher in his left hand and had a water skin hanging from his shoulder and across his body.

"Scribble!" he cried out. "Use it now!" At that, he threw the other pitcher. Belphegor pulled his arm back just in time to avoid the explosion of holy water and pottery. He focused on removing the snake. Its head thrashed around. The cracks in the lake grew longer.

The iBad vibrated in Scribble's hand. When she looked down, Surli had opened the scanner. The words, "Now's your chance!" danced over her head. Scribble quickly aimed it at Belphegor and pressed the big, green "scan" button.

> Name: Belphegor
> Type: Unknown
> Age: Unknown
> Estimated Soul Weight: Unknown
> Notes: Nice try, worm. I knew you'd try something foolish like
> this someday.

Scribble stared at the screen in disbelief. She found no other files on him, no weaknesses, nothing helpful at all.

Valerius leaned in closer. "What is wrong?" he asked in a hushed tone.

"He must have erased everything on himself. I don't know what to do!"

"We fight. It is still a weapon, is it not?"

"…It is." She looked over at Paul and felt a rising swell of emotions—fear, pride, anger, love. Paul grabbed a jagged chunk of the wall and broke it free, cutting part of his hand in the process. He then got it wet with the water skin before throwing it as well. He was fighting, despite the danger, despite the pain, despite the warnings.

Quickly, Scribble looked down at her iBad and started scanning through its menus. "Surli. I need you to become the weapon again, please."

Without a word, Surli's digital head nodded and the screen went blank, all except for a single red button in the center. The top let out a mechanical *click* and then split open. A small black ring around a short spike emerged from it. Scribble tensed and let out a whimper when the ring began to crackle with energy—energy stolen from her. On the screen, a progress bar gradually filled.

Belphegor jerked back harder as several pieces of crystal doused in living water struck him inside the machine. He let out a diseased growl from his own real voice and stared directly at Paul. The snake nearly pulled itself free when the vibrant call of a trumpet echoed all around them.

All eyes turned skyward. In the distance, where the horizon split the sky from the land, Scribble could see four dots against the landscape. She narrowed her gaze and was just able to make out the white flash of wings.

"Accursed Archangels!"

The iBad let out a *ding!* Scribble looked down at it. The bar had filled. "Fire" appeared on the red button. She took aim and pressed it. A dark shot screamed across the sky, just missing her target. Scribble let out a pained cry and doubled over. Her arm clenched and seized, leaving her in agony and defenseless.

CHAPTER 33 – SACRIFICE

Desperation showed in Belphegor's face. The archangels moved fast, already visibly larger from when they'd first appeared. He growled. Instead of pulling up to free his machine's fangs from the crystal lake, Belphegor began to twist its viperous head. With a sharp CRACK that echoed through the ground, the fangs snapped off and remained deeply embedded. Belphegor looked askance at Scribble.

"No more of that," he said. The snake coiled around itself quickly, then the tail whipped out at her. Scribble grimaced, but the expected impact never came. Instead, she heard a sickening crunch several yards away. When she looked up, she saw that Valerius had been the intended victim. His body hung from one of the more jagged crystal spires that stood defiantly out of the ground. A huge blade of it ran through him, cutting cleanly through his heart. He dropped his sword and gripped at the crystal.

"Melani... you must..." he groaned, then his head lifelessly dropped. The hand on the crystal slipped and fell limp to his side. Crimson essence flowed down the spire that held him aloft.

"No. No, Val!" Tears filled Scribble's eyes as she watched the color drain out of her friend's face, leaving him as gray as she was. It felt as if the spike had pierced her own heart as well. She had just been getting to know him again, and now she had to lose him a second time. Too stunned to move, she could only watch his remaining wing shed its feathers in a fluttering cloud of white, leaving the bone beneath exposed.

Scribble broke out of her grief and tried to run to him, to get away from the demon that would surely do the same to her, but he was too fast. A quick strike from his tail sent her spinning. Before she could recover, he struck her arm. She felt a brief moment of searing pain as Belphegor tore the iBad from the wires that remained in her ethereal flesh.

It landed with a plastic clatter and skittered along the surface of the crystalline lake. After several seconds, it came to rest just a few feet from Paul. Scribble saw him pick it up, look it over, then pull the two soul stones from his pocket, one black and one white. The black one immediately flew out of his hand under its own soul weight, dancing its way along the ground back towards Hell. "No!" he yelled, but without its added weight tugging at him, he soon stumbled forward into a clearing and away from the wall.

Belphegor's animated tail wound around Scribble and lifted her aloft.

"You will be my hostage," he said and began to slither away with her.

No amount of struggling could overcome that mechanical grip. "Put me down, you monster!" she demanded through her tears.

He brought her close to the snake's head, using her body to shield him from any other pieces of crystal that might be thrown at him. "Be still, or I will leave you like him."

As if on cue, Valerius screamed. He had two distinct voices, one melodic and familiar, the other sharp and acerbic. Belphegor turned his hostage so she could see. Her friend looked like a walking ruin from a bygone time, his armor and robes torn, his body gray, one skeletal wing hanging loosely behind him. The grace of motion he once possessed was gone. He reached up to the spire and snapped it off with ease, then pulled himself free and floated to the ground, showing no emotions or pain whatsoever.

"Grigori. Unpredictable. Dangerous." Belphegor sneered and slithered away from the scene quickly. "You were there the last time one was born. Remember him? Lucifer? The one he disintegrated was my partner."

Valerius looked around at the crowd, but fixed his rough gaze on Belphegor and began stumbling towards the retreating demon.

The Prince put Scribble between him and the grigori. "Wouldn't it be poetic for your partner to do the same to you? Perhaps it will be the distraction I need." Belphegor chuckled at his own words.

Scribble managed to pull her good arm free and grabbed frantically at the coils wrapped around her. A crystal shard that had lodged itself into the snake's corrupted wings caught her eye, but she couldn't quite reach it. No matter how hard she tried, she could only graze her finger against it.

"And what if the archangels get here first?" she grunted, trying to distract him. "You can't move fast enough while carrying me around."

Belphegor pulled her in close and tightened his grip around her. She tried to scream but couldn't get enough air in her lungs.

A scraping noise brought Belphegor's attention back to Valerius. He approached them faster than before, his ruined wing dragging on the ground. With Belphegor's attention elsewhere, Scribble focused through the pain, reached for the sharp crystal shard once more and yanked it free. In the same motion, she plunged it back into the machine. Wild, swift strikes managed to sever wires and caused the machine's grip to loosen until she tumbled to the ground. Belphegor turned to her, but Valerius drew dangerously close. A quick glance at the sky revealed that the archangels, too, would soon arrive.

"You're a nuisance. I'm ending this now. I think two grigori will be enough to give them second thoughts." He turned back to Scribble and brought himself to her prone form. The metal warped away from him again and he reached a pale claw out for her. Scribble let out an agonized wail as he gripped her shoulder and blackness flowed into her.

Pain can both dull and sharpen the senses. Amidst her screams, she noticed Paul limping towards them in the distance. He fumbled with Danielle's soul stone, trying to put it into the iBad as he went. If he could get off a shot, they could still win.

"That's all you've got?" she moaned and stared into Belphegor's eyes defiantly. "Re-remind me to show you... what a papercut feels like."

Belphegor growled in anger and pulled her off the ground by her injured shoulder. He was far stronger than he appeared. "I'll destroy you."

Scribble gasped and held onto Belphegor's arm as a bone in her shoulder cracked. The pain blinded her. Yet, she still egged him on, even as the cold blackness crept further along her body. "Not if... I destroy you... first."

A second hand closed around her neck. The world began fading, spinning. Her strength was failing her. *Click. Whir.* Belphegor looked up just as a dark tear in reality shot straight for him. He dropped Scribble and ducked down. The shot passed right over his back, missing him by mere inches and hitting the snake just behind where he sat. Paul looked on with a defeated expression.

"Ha. Ha. Ha. You missed, silly human." Belphegor ignored Scribble now, ignored the archangels, and even ignored the danger of the grigori. He moved swiftly to his new threat. "I'm done playing. I will *not* miss."

"I wasn't aiming for you," Paul said, his poker face breaking into a smirk.

Behind Belphegor, chains began to appear from the shifting ball of soul stones that powered the snake, pulling on the very souls trapped within them. One by one, the stones popped out of place and rolled, jumped, and slid along the ground, pulled by the combination of their own weight and the added weight of the chains. Belphegor realized all too late what was happening and grabbed futilely to stop them. But by that time, the snake had slowed to a stop and slumped to the ground. When most of the stones were gone, the pieces of metal disconnected from each other. One large strut, tangled in a mass of wire, chain, and soul stones, caught on the pair of stolen wings in Belphegor's back and ripped them out. What was once a snake was now a long pile of black rubble, corrupted wings, and a single, pale, sickly figure clawing at the crystal ground. Wires and metal that had kept him secure pulled loose from his flesh.

"No! This can't be!" He left long claw marks in his struggle against his own massive weight. It proved an insurmountable task. Belphegor's grip failed. He slid along the ground past Paul, back towards Hell, disappearing behind one of the jagged crystalline walls.

Paul wasted no time. He ran towards Scribble as fast as he could with his injured foot. But before he could make it very far, the archangels descended between them. They landed in a diamond formation. In the front was the figure of Raguel. The wheel that normally spun around her head was instead centered around her hand, ready to be used as a weapon. To her right was Gabriel, whose white hair and wings left a niveous trail behind him. He held a spear in one hand and a clarion in the other. On the left was an angel with six emerald-green wings, which matched her hood and robes. Before her, she held a wooden snake in the shape of a shepherd's crook. And in the center of the group was an angel easily ten feet tall, wearing full plate armor of deep gold, with an ornate filigree the color of a fine red wine. This was set against black chain mail, visible where the joints of the armor met. A long crimson plume descended from his helmet. His wings were a brilliant white on the underside, jet black on the reverse. He wielded a sword nearly as long as he was, with a white blade that abruptly turned dark along the edge.

It was this most impressive figure that spoke first. "Raphael, attend to Brother Metatron," he commanded the angel in green. His voice held every quality of a leader, able to inspire, to awe, and even to create a sense of duty in others. Scribble remembered seeing his face before, plastered on warnings all over the first level of Hell—St. Michael.

The six-winged angel nodded in reply and moved towards the wall of the Sanctum where Metatron lay prone. Meanwhile, Michael walked around the broken machine that Belphegor had once controlled, picking up pieces of it to look closer. The others fanned out.

"Wait! My friend, Valerius, needs help!" Scribble pleaded to them. "He was injured and turned into a grigori!"

Raphael approached her with a welcoming smile. When she saw the injuries on her hands and shoulder and the wires still stuck in her arm, the archangel took Scribble's hand in her own and pressed the head of her crook at each injury in turn. The pain vanished, the wounds closed up, and the wires withered and fell to the ground. "Where is your friend, Brother Valerius?" Raphael's melodic voice sounded soft and soothing, putting Scribble at ease.

"He's over there," she said and pointed to where she'd last seen him.

Valerius was gone.

"If there is a new grigori loose, we must find and contain it," Michael commanded. Without needing further instruction, Raguel and Gabriel took flight and circled over the Sanctum.

"Aren't you going to cure him?" Scribble asked her healer.

"I'm sorry, dear, but it is too late for that. He has already turned into one who is between angel and demon. I cannot cure a grigori. All we can do now is contain him and prevent him from annihilating anyone."

"What?! You won't even try?"

"It's not that we don't want to try," Raphael said. "We cannot. He is simply too dangerous. I'm sorry. Grigori are wanderers by nature. Perhaps he has left to find a new purpose." This didn't make Scribble feel any better.

Raguel landed next to Michael and shook her head. "He is gone. His trail follows the debris, and then we lost it." Gabriel touched down close by.

"And what of you?" Michael asked, turning towards Scribble, who glanced behind him at Paul. "You are clearly neither angel nor human, but my sword, Aletheia, seems to trust you. Who and what are you?"

"Scribble, sir. I am... or I was, a demon. For a long time I was an imp. Then I was his Sinister," she said, nodding to indicate Paul. "But I came to truly love him. I don't know what I am anymore."

Michael pivoted swiftly, his wings acting like a cape behind him. "You, Paul Reese Taylor. You are still living. How have you come to be here?"

Scribble cleared her throat and took a step closer. "That was also because of me," she said with a wistful smile. "I didn't want Raguel to erase his memories, so I brought him here, sir. Well, not here directly. I thought I could hide him... in Purgatory."

Raguel gave a huff in response.

"A demon in love? I must admit, I have never heard that story before," Michael said, his eyes turning on Raguel briefly. "But here you stand, at the heart of Zion. Mayhap these matters deserve more than a fleeting glance. Do you know what happened to the one responsible for this assault?"

"I believe he is on his way back to Hell, thanks to Paul," Scribble replied.

Paul looked hesitant to approach the angels and kept watch of Raguel. She'd moved closer to him but stopped at the debris trail caused by Belphegor. A single black soul stone worked its way from the rubble, pulled by its chain, but she caught it before it got too far.

"There is a soul in here. But something else, too," she said. She walked over to Raphael and presented it.

"Oh, goodness. Such an evil aura," Raphael said as she took it. "It's as if this chain is made of pure sin." She brought the stone to her lips and pressed a kiss against it. The kiss lingered, though Scribble was not quite certain she was not actually speaking softly to the stone. The chain snapped off and, like the wires that fell from Scribble, withered.

"It was this," Paul said, his voice cracking. He held up the iBad in a trembling hand. "It's some sort of weapon... ma'am."

As he held it up, a pale hand grabbed the chain that had grown from the cuff on Paul's wrist and jerked him backwards. He let out a startled yell as he lost his footing and slammed roughly against the edge of the crystal wall Belphegor had disappeared behind. The Demon Prince crawled over the edge and up to Paul before pulling the iBad from Paul's grasp. The arm that wrapped around Paul's chest still possessed great strength.

"This is mine." Black tendrils crept along Paul's skin from the pale arm. The demon gave several sharp tugs to pull his victim with him. Paul resisted.

Michael brandished his sword at them. "Free him, or you will taste my holy fury!" Without having to give an order, Gabriel and Raguel both readied their own weapons. They moved to flank the demon around the random crystalline structures in the way. Scribble ran straight toward them until Raphael managed to catch up and hold her in check.

"Back off," the villain croaked. "He's my hostage... insurance that you won't follow me. And when I'm back in Hell, he'll be rather fun to experiment on. I've never had a living human among my toys before. Just imagine what I could do with a soul that changes weight like his, the weapons I could create." He stopped reaching for the edge and instead took the iBad in his free hand so he could close his claw around Paul's neck. "Tell the others to back off, or I'll snap his neck."

"If you kill him, he'll be useless to you," Scribble said, fighting against Raphael's hold.

"But it'll be *fun*."

"Take me instead! My soul is in transition, too. Check for yourself! And I can't die like he can. You can experiment on me over and over."

"Scribble, what are you doing?" Paul asked.

Belphegor glanced between Paul and Scribble in doubt. He pulled up the iBad and awkwardly pointed its camera at Scribble. "Surli. Scan mode."

"Not until you ask nicely, Belphegor, *sir*."

Surli put as much sarcasm into the last word as any computer program possibly could.

"I don't have time for this. I'll put Rotworm in one of those bodies he likes so much just so I can skin him alive if he tries to write another program like this." He pushed his thumb hard against the screen several times as he continued mumbling curses to himself.

"Ooh! Feeling a girl up without asking her out first? What kind of—"

Surli's voice abruptly shut off, and a moment later, Belphegor pointed the iBad's camera at Scribble again.

"So, you're telling the truth," he said, a disturbing smile cracking the skin on his diseased face. "Unknown soul weight. Yes, you'll do. I can do so much more with a soul like yours. An eternity of experimentation. Come here." He clenched Paul's neck tighter.

Scribble put her hand on Raphael's arm and looked at her with pleading eyes. The archangel nodded and let her go. At first, her movements were slow and hesitant, but when Paul started to lose his grip and Belphegor was able to bring a leg around the edge of the wall, she picked up her pace. Once she got within arm's reach of Paul, she leaned in to give him a farewell kiss. Their lips brushed, but it was not to be—Belphegor hooked his free arm around Scribble and pulled her away, keeping a vice-like grip on the iBad. Then he began dragging them both towards the edge of the wall.

Scribble grabbed the water skin around Paul's shoulder and tore it open. Even though it was mostly empty, it held enough holy water to splash all three of them with a few droplets. Scribble felt it, but it did not hurt like she expected. However, foul smoke rose from Belphegor's flesh wherever it touched. Instinctively, he released Paul to brush the burning water off his face. In the ensuing struggle, Belphegor and Scribble rolled past the edge and rocketed towards the Pearly Gates just over the river.

"Scribble!" she heard Paul cry from a distance and saw him reaching out towards her. He never had a chance.

"Foolish cur!" In order to keep away from the river, Belphegor began to flap his emaciated wings and lift them into the air. "You had nothing to gain. Why make such a useless sacrifice?"

Scribble didn't bother to fight anymore. She stared at him with a tearful gaze. "I did it for him."

A sudden sense of relief and warmth flooded Scribble. Belphegor's diseased face twisted in confusion as her body began to glow. "What is this? What are you doing?"

She felt energy and joy fill her, transform her very being. The light grew brighter and Belphegor winced. His fingers curled tighter around her as he cried out in pain. Every moment that passed, she shone with more splendor and radiance, and he began to yell using his real voice. Although it seemed he would do anything to keep his hold on her, it only took a few seconds of this painful resplendence before he let go. "No! You're mine!" he cried out in rage. But he tore away from her, flailing, and sped into the distance.

* * *

Scribble didn't know how she got back to the Sanctum, but when the light faded and the warmth ebbed, that's where she found herself. She stood in front of Paul, who sobbed on his hands and knees. Her flesh, no longer gray, became pink with a healthy blush. The pair of horns she'd always had were now accompanied by a gray halo. Her hair had turned the rich color of India ink. Even her wings had changed, from leathery demon wings to angelic wings with feathers made of folded parchment, like origami. Only her maelstrom eyes remained constant.

"Scribble?" Paul asked as he looked up.

She didn't have time to answer before he sprang to his feet and threw his arms around her. She laughed with joy and hugged him back. "What… what happened?" she asked after a moment.

For a while, the archangels remained silent. While Raphael tended to him, Metatron eventually spoke up. "Whatever happened, it is unprecedented. Never has a demon been redeemed."

"Redeemed?"

Raphael answered her this time. "Your willingness to surrender yourself for this man was a true act of love. By the Grace of God, you've been given a second chance."

"I have?" She looked down at herself, inspecting her hands, her hair, her body. Everything was different. Zion's true beauty shone all the brighter. The slight pain every denizen of Hell felt was gone. Even her sense of guilt had vanished. In their place she felt joy, a lasting joy that made her heart feel like it would burst. But when she looked at Paul, that joy was joined by love. She put her hand on his cheek and he leaned in and kissed her firmly.

Gabriel appeared in a flurry of snow. Scribble hadn't even been aware he was missing. "The demon is gone. But we still have a problem."

"What is it, Brother Gabriel?" Raphael responded.

"Mr. Taylor. He should not be here, and now he knows of the Hereafter."

Paul leaned back, holding onto Scribble's hands firmly. "Please don't erase her from me," he said. "I… I love her."

Raguel heaved a deep sigh and folded her arms in front of her. Her wheel once again spun around her head. "Given the situation, I now believe it would be wrong. These two have obviously formed a close relationship, somehow."

Michael spoke up. "A *forbidden* relationship. Nothing good can come of such. And yet," he countered himself, "some good already has."

"If we erase his memory, we will be preserving the Mystery as well as saving this young man from unnecessary heartache," Gabriel said. "They cannot be together."

Raguel huffed in indignation.

"And *we* will be standing in the way of love," Raphael responded. The stern archangel coming to her aid was the last thing Scribble expected. "Forbidden or not, there is love here. Take it from him, and she will still feel it, it will hurt her. We've never seen an Immortal like her before—we simply do not know what is possible. Taking their love away now could corrupt our newly redeemed sister all over again, for all we know."

Gabriel nodded to Raphael. "I understand, sister. I simply do not want to see a repeat of the past."

Raguel snapped at him, "My past is none of your business."

Michael stepped between them. "The past aside, the need exists to determine their fate," he said. "But first, please send word to the Virtues and Principalities. We have a Sanctum to repair." Gabriel genuflected to one knee, then launched into the air.

Raguel moved to the unconventional couple and shook her head. "Believe it or not, I know what it is like to be in a situation like this." She sighed and shifted her weight. After a moment of silence, her wheel stopped spinning and pointed its great eye at them. "I may have a solution, if General Michael agrees. Brother Boniface is still in our custody, so there is currently an opening for a Dexter. Do you wish to replace him as this man's guardian angel?" Scribble lit up instantly, but Raguel quickly added, "It will not be easy for you, you understand."

Scribble leaned against Paul's side and nodded. "I do."

"Raguel!" Raphael protested. "We do not know anything about her or if she poses a threat to others."

"I have been observing her for some time. I do not believe she is a threat. I will advise her myself. Tell us, what does your Sword of Truth say?"

Michael looked at Scribble discerningly for a long time. He finally nodded. "I will trust your judgment, Sister Raguel. But if she becomes a threat—"

"I will personally see to it that she is dealt with," Raguel said. Although she didn't move, Scribble could tell that Raguel's attention was back on her. "You are fully aware that you will not be able to possess a body like you did before, yes? Even if we were to allow it, we don't know if your soul is stable."

Scribble nodded with less enthusiasm than before.

Michael interjected. "Mr. Taylor, we cannot allow you to keep all your memories." The others lifted their voices in objection, but a raised hand silenced them. "However, the love between you is unique. It would be wrong to rid you of it. Therefore, only your memories of this place will be... modified. You will remember her and her deeds, but will not recall who she truly is or any part of the Hereafter. Is that an acceptable solution?"

At first, Scribble was terrified of the sentence. She took Paul's hand in trembling grip. But the more she thought about it, the more that terror eased.

Paul, however, shook his head. "Does that mean I won't see her again?"

Raguel shook her head. "My child, Brother Michael's counsel is wise. While you live, you two cannot be united as a loving couple. When you pass on, you may have an eternity together. But until then, you will only be able to see her in your memories. I will ensure they remain fresh. When you wake, you will believe that she has given you her heart before returning to her home to correct the wrongs of her past."

Although Paul began to protest this plan, Scribble stopped him and held him close. "I think this is the best we can have, Paul. You'll remember me fondly with no pain in our parting, and I will watch and guide you. Maybe they'll let me write you a letter every so often," she said with a sad smile.

Paul didn't dare look away from her gaze. "How will I—"

"The arrangement is agreed." Michael said. "As Overseer of all human affairs, you will be in my jurisdiction."

Raguel stepped forward. "I am afraid, Brother Michael, that I must insist she be placed under my authority. The Order will ensure both her safety and the safety of others in the event there is an incident. No one knows what she may be capable of."

Stern glances were exchanged between the two archangels, but in the end, it was Michael who conceded. "Very well, Sister Raguel. She will be placed in your purview. However, she will still report to me for guidance in her new role. Sister Scribble, you were once known by a different name. Melani, I believe. I think it is appropriate to allow you to choose between them."

"Scribble," she answered, still watching Paul. "I want to be Scribble."

"Thus it shall be written." The voice belonged to Metatron, angel of fire and lightning. Raphael assisted him in walking to the others.

"Brother Metatron! It is good to see you on your feet again," Michael said, a touch of warmth in his voice for the first time. "How serious is the wound?"

"It is mild."

"I am sorry to put you to work so soon, but I must ask you to call a council of the seven. We have much to discuss."

The conversation between the two meandered from topic to topic. Scribble heard little of it and kept all her attention on Paul. When Raguel approached, she tensed and held onto his hands all the tighter.

"Not yet..." she whimpered.

The archangel put a hand on her shoulder and gave a rather unexpected smile—one that came from a place of both warmth and sorrow. "You have my sympathy. I only wish I could do more to help. You two can have the rest of the night together. There should be a few hours left. At dawn, you will say your farewells. Now, come, let us return you to Earth."

By the time Scribble was ready to be Paul's Dexter, several days had passed. Even though he wouldn't see her, she felt like every muscle in her spectral body twitched in nervous anticipation. "What if he really doesn't remember me?" she asked Raguel as they approached *Othello's Books*.

"I do not believe I've ever seen an angel as excited or anxious as you are, Scribble," she said. "Don't you trust me?" There was a friendly, almost motherly smile on her lips.

"Yes... you've been so helpful and kind. I'm just eager to see how he's doing." She reached to open the front door, but her hand passed right through its handle. "Oh!" Grinning sheepishly, she stepped through the door.

The front of the store looked almost untouched, as if the fire hadn't happened at all. But it was empty. Scribble peered down every aisle before heading to the back, only to be startled by the front doorbell when it rang out.

"Sorry I'm late, Paul," Ginger said. She wore a long, black coat to keep the late autumn chill at bay. Behind her walked in a young, dark-haired man with close-set eyes and the beginnings of a beard.

"Ginger, is that you?" came Paul's voice from the back room. He came out to the front with a muted smile. "Ginger, Derek! Thanks for coming." The closer they got to each other, the more their fortitude faded away. A few feet in front of Scribble, Ginger broke into tears and threw her arms around Paul. He hugged her tightly for nearly a minute—an extremely awkward minute, it seemed, for Derek. When they broke their embrace, they shared a brief kiss.

Part of Scribble just wanted to curl up and cry when she saw Paul kissing another, but she kept her resolve. *She'll make him happy, I'm sure of it,* she thought, but wasn't entirely certain she believed it herself.

"I didn't even get a chance to tell her goodbye," Ginger whispered. "I didn't get to make it up to her for being so—"

"She knows. And I'm sure she'd have wanted to say goodbye if she had time. But her friend, Val, got badly hurt and she had to rush home to see him."

When Scribble realized Ginger had been talking about *her*, she really did start to cry a little. Raguel had said Paul's memories of that night would be a little different, but she didn't know just what to expect.

"I'm sorry. I know you were close." Ginger slipped out of the embrace, rubbing at her face.

"Yeah. I miss her so much," he whispered before clearing his throat.

"Do you think she'll be back?" she asked.

Paul frowned and shook his head. "I doubt it. She said…"

A small chime sounded from nowhere and everywhere all at once. Scribble looked around in confusion, and by the time she looked back, time had frozen.

"Oh!" She stepped up to him and put her hand on his shoulder, but she didn't change size. A rush of flame announced the arrival of Paul's new—or rather, old—Sinister. A miniature Grimtooth sat on his left shoulder, looking more like a large, square-jawed human than the beast she'd first met.

"What happened to the annoying one?" he asked gruffly.

"I believe he's in recovery," she said. When Grimtooth eyed her with slow disapproval, she wondered if he even recognized her.

Why can't I remember what Dez said? Paul's thoughts sounded clearly in the frozen time. *Am I such a terrible person I can't even remember that?*

This time, it was Grimtooth who looked flustered. "Who? Uh, of course you are. Who could forget Dez?" he said with little confidence.

Scribble pressed close to his ear to whisper. "It was a long, difficult night. Don't blame yourself for forgetting. Remember, if Jean Valjean hadn't forgiven himself, he'd never have moved on and helped all those people." Being this close to him brought with it a flurry of conflicting emotions. She kissed his temple before time started back up. Raguel rubbed at her cheek as she watched the scene play out.

"Funny, I can't remember. It was such a long night," Paul finally said.

"How bad was the damage?" Derek chimed in, breaking up the mood.

"Luckily, the fire suppression only came on in the back and stopped the fire from getting out of hand. Most of the books that got destroyed were my mom's, not part of inventory. But there's a lot of clean-up left to do."

The bell at the door rang again and everyone turned to stare at Frank. "Hey, I heard you needed help." When he realized the looks they gave him were less-than-friendly, the life left his face and he grew deathly pale.

"Desdemona's gone, Frank," Paul said. "She asked me to forgive you, and that's the only reason you and your wife and your father-in-law aren't in jail."

Scribble could feel the rage bubbling inside Paul like an angry volcano.

"Oh," Frank said and fell silent for a moment. "Look, I can explain."

"You can? You can explain framing me for stealing?" Ginger growled.

"The boiler? The fire? You could have killed Dez!" Paul sounded livid.

But Scribble felt strangely calm. She remembered how good a friend Frank had been to her, the sage advice given at times of need, the way he broke up monotony with little games.

"He deserves a chance to explain himself," she whispered.

Frank took a step back. "I had nothing to do with those. I'll admit I took the money. Tony wouldn't accept me as part of the family if I didn't. I'm sorry for the part I played in this, but I never wanted anyone to get hurt."

"You were here all day when the boiler blew. You had the key."

"It went missing. I found it in Addison's purse later. And I swear I didn't know about the arson!"

Paul scowled. "You're fired, Frank. Tell your father-in-law that if I ever see any of you on *my* property again, I'll k—" Scribble put her hand in his and squeezed it. It made him pause, and she thought she felt him squeeze back. "Tell him that this building will be the least of his worries. And tell him he only delayed the reopening by a couple of weeks at best."

Being able to physically affect him, however light the touch was, brought joy and hope to Scribble's heart. When Frank left, Paul put his arm around Ginger and walked with her towards the back room, Derek trailing behind. She stood still and longingly watched them.

"Are you sure being his Dexter is what you want to do, Sister? I would understand if the heartache is too much." Raguel did not look the sort to have such a tender side, but Scribble was grateful for it.

"Yes. It is a far better thing I'm doing now than ever before," she said. "I wouldn't want to be anywhere else." Raguel nodded and stepped out of the building, but not before Scribble added, "I just wish I had Surli to help me."

*   *   *

Small bits of metal and stone crunched underfoot. Belphegor's eyes opened at the sound. After he had fallen back into Hell, he'd come to rest just outside his old prison. There was nothing around him except for a few wires and metal scraps. The crunching footsteps grew closer.

"Who is it?" he asked. "Who's there?!"

There was no answer. He pushed frantically with his emaciated limbs to get back to the safety of his cell. Around the corner came a tall silhouette. Its wings flapped once, stirring up more debris as it walked closer.

"Michael? Raguel? I'll return to my cell. Don't, don't hurt me! Aagh!"

The figure loomed over him. Belphegor tried to crawl away on his back, but he didn't get far. A foot pressed down heavily on his wrist and caused him to cry out.

"Ha! You think *I'm* Michael? Pff. Don't tell me you've forgotten me already, Bellpig."

"Worm? What are you doing? I demand that you help me."

"Demand, BilgePicker? I don't think you're in any kind of position to

236

demand anything. Come to think of it, you're not in much of a position at all."
He leaned down and violently ripped the voice box out of Belphegor's chest,
tossing it aside and leaving an open wound behind. Then he wrested the
remains of the iBad out of his former master's grip with the same bloody hand.
Rotworm looked it over and turned it around. "Now that that is out of the way,
I suppose I should thank you, Belldandy." Rotworm brought up a stump
where his other hand once had been and tried to figure out how to open the
back of the device, but such delicate work proved to be quite a challenge.
"After all, you did get me what my true master has been after this whole time."

Belphegor watched intently as Rotworm bit the iBad and popped off the
back with his teeth, revealing the white soul stone inside.

"Ah, there it is," he said, tilting the device back and forth so he could
examine the stone in the dim tunnel. It created a light of its own. "A holy soul
stone. Such a pretty bauble, isn't it? One of a kind." He squatted in front of
Belphegor, dangling the device inches from his face. "And now it's mine. Well,
my master's anyway. And it only cost me an arm."

He stood up and walked away. "I better get going before the Order shows
up. Or the real Michael." He shuddered at the thought. "Good-for-nothing do-
gooders. Ta-ta, Belphy. Oh, and if anyone asks, don't say a word." He kicked
the damaged voice box away as he walked off, his laughter echoing down the
hallways long after he left.

Afterword

A Sinister Love has been a passion project of mine for more years than I care to admit. While writing this book, I had 2 kids, became a stay-at-home dad, moved to a new state, and went through a heap of family drama (which I hope to harness for another book in the near future). For years I read my manuscript to my critiquing group, edited, and sent it off to agents. It was runner-up more than once, but I knew this story deserved more than, "always the bridesmaid, never the bride." That all changed starting in the summer of 2022, while the COVID pandemic was still keeping many people cooped up with a good book inside. The first thing I did was hire a personal trainer—having a strong body promotes a strong mind. I also found myself a good therapist and started taking measures to get my ADHD and depression under control. These changes made a world of difference.

In the summer of 2023, I was sent to a couple of board game conventions—Origins (in Ohio) and Gen Con (in Indiana)—as a host of *Board Game Rundown*, a YouTube channel some friends and I put together. There, I ran into a number of authors (such as Virginia McClain, Christopher Schmitz, Richard Fierce, and Cat Rambo—there were many more and I apologize if I left you out) who let me pick their minds about what happens *after* you've written your novel. The advice they gave me could not be overvalued. Between them and my own research, I learned two important facts for anyone wishing to become a published author: 1) You will sell more books and make more money if you don't use an agent or big publisher, and 2) if you don't step up and just get started, it will never happen.

I contacted a good friend of mine that I've known since we were in Boy Scouts together, Jason Smith. Jason had founded a small press, Wootton Major Publishing, and was nearly as excited about publishing my novel as I was. Then I found my editor, Lauren Wilkinson, and artist, Graziel Joanna Tallongon, through online freelance sites other authors recommended.

And so, we started.

*   *   *

Many things inspired and influenced *A Sinister Love*. The first spark came when I was reading a webcomic (and I do apologize, but I cannot recall its name). It had a minor character, a succubus, who would sometimes look at the protagonist with true longing. That got the wheels turning. The idea of a demon having to learn the trade came from C.S. Lewis' *The Screwtape Letters*. Many of the demonic names I came up with were inspired from it as well. Years of parochial school gave me a good understanding of much of the Judeo-Christian lore I used, but I still had to round out my education with further research (as well as a close reading of *The Book of Enoch*).

I have always been a huge fan of the works of both Terry Pratchett and Neil Gaiman, so I couldn't help but adopt some of the vibes of *Good Omens*. Peter S. Beagle's *The Last Unicorn* played a huge role in my childhood. My sister introduced me to Ursula K. Le Guin, J.R.R. Tolkien, Mercedes Lackey, and so many more. It is impossible to list everything that influenced—and continues to influence—my writing.

One of the things I enjoy playing with is the meaning behind names and words. *Paul* is not only the name of the most prolific writer of the New Testament, but it means "humble," which I felt fit my character. *Scribble* came to me early on and I just fell in love with it as the name for a confused, bookish demoness. But her pre-Fall name, *Melani*, came from a Koine Greek word, μέλαν, meaning "ink," which describes her hair color but also is the source from which scribbles come. And, honestly, *Surli* was a no-brainer. *Sinister* is the Latin word for "left," while *dexter* came from the Latin word for "right" (thus someone who is ambidextrous is "both right"). Because left-handed people were rare and often demonized, in the 14th century the word *sinister* began taking on, shall we say, a more sinister definition.

I have plans for Scribble and the gang, though my next book will be focusing on a different group of beings. There are many trends I'm noticing in my writing, some of which I will try to break. One of them, though, is that they all seem to feature some sort of mental disability or condition. In *A Sinister Love*, it is Paul's depression. Having lived with depression most of my life, I felt I had a good grasp of it, but I did my due diligence and researched further anyway. The result, I hope, is an insider's view into depression backed by facts. I wanted to make sure my readers knew that, although the right person can have a huge, positive impact on someone's depression, proper medication and therapy may still be needed to handle it. If you live here in the United States and you or a loved one has been having thoughts of self-harm, the FCC has set up a suicide prevention hotline (dial 988) that is available 24/7.

I hope you will stay with me as I continue on this journey as an author. May we have many meetings to come.

About the Author

Spencer Hixon was born in Pasadena, CA, but has lived all over the United States. He currently lives in Mishawaka, IN with his wife, two kids, and a small menagerie. He co-hosts the YouTube channel *Board Game Rundown* with his good friends and plays guitar every Sunday for church. It is quite likely that his Sinister is sleeping on the job.

Visit him online at:

www.spencerhixon.com